THE HISTORY OF
THE LIFE AND ADVENTURES
OF MR. ANDERSON

broadview editions
series editor: L.W. Conolly

THE HISTORY OF
THE LIFE AND ADVENTURES
OF MR. ANDERSON

Edward Kimber

edited by Matthew Mason and Nicholas Mason

broadview editions

Library and Archives Canada Cataloguing in Publication

Kimber, Edward, 1719-1769
  The history of the life and adventures of Mr. Anderson / Edward Kimber ; edited by Matthew Mason and Nicholas Mason.

(Broadview editions)
Includes bibliographical references.
ISBN 978-1-55111-703-4

  I. Mason, Matthew.   II. Mason, Nicholas, 1970-   III. Title.   IV. Series.

PR3539.K57H58 2008   823'.6   C2008-905434-2

Broadview Editions
The Broadview Editions series represents the ever-changing canon of literature in English by bringing together texts long regarded as classics with valuable lesser-known works.

Advisory editor for this volume: Martin R. Boyne

Broadview Press is an independent, international publishing house, incorporated in 1985. Broadview believes in shared ownership, both with its employees and with the general public; since the year 2000 Broadview shares have traded publicly on the Toronto Venture Exchange under the symbol BDP.

We welcome comments and suggestions regarding any aspect of our publications—please feel free to contact us at the addresses below or at broadview@broadviewpress.com.

North America
Post Office Box 1243, Peterborough, Ontario, Canada K9J 7H5
2215 Kenmore Avenue, Buffalo, NY, USA 14207
Tel: (705) 743-8990; Fax: (705) 743-8353;
email: customerservice@broadviewpress.com

UK, Ireland, and continental Europe
NBN International, Estover Road, Plymouth PL6 7PY UK
Tel: 44 (0) 1752 202300   Fax: 44 (0) 1752 202330
email: enquiries@nbninternational.com

Australia and New Zealand
UNIREPS, University of New South Wales
Sydney, NSW, Australia 2052
Tel: 61 2 9664 0999; Fax: 61 2 9664 5420
email: info.press@unsw.edu.au

www.broadviewpress.com

This book is printed on paper containing 100% post-consumer fibre.

Typesetting and assembly: True to Type Inc., Claremont, Canada.

PRINTED IN CANADA

Contents

Acknowledgements

The collaborative nature of producing this volume began but hardly ended with our partnership as editors. We have many people and institutions to thank for making this edition both possible and better than it would have been with only our efforts. We assume, however, that no one will think for a moment of charging them with whatever errors or infelicities are here.

Brigham Young University offered invaluable support for us both with this project. The English Department and the College of Humanities provided funds for the maps and a graduate assistant, Joshua Bullough, whose research skills and eye for detail helped move the project along, particularly in its early stages. Funding from the College of Family, Home, and Social Sciences also helped pay for the maps, which faculty and staff in the Department of Geography produced.

In addition to this institutional support, we have also benefited from generous and thoughtful feedback from many students and colleagues. The students in Nicholas's fall 2004 course on eighteenth-century British literature offered several valuable insights on how this edition could prove most helpful to students. Jenny Hale Pulsipher, Brett Rushforth, Matthew Wickman, and participants in the Tenth Anniversary Conference of the Harvard Atlantic Seminar provided useful comments on various drafts of the introduction. Eric Slauter and Neil L. York offered not only perceptive critiques but also references to vitally important source material. Brett Rushforth helped enormously with the identification of various places and names in the colonial borderlands and French sections of the novel, Donald J. Harreld referred us to the websites that helped us do the monetary conversions, and Anthony Jarrells helped track down bibliographical information on Kimber's *London Magazine* publications. Finally, our gratitude goes out to previous scholars who have studied Kimber and his works, particularly T.H. Breen, whose preface to *Tobacco Culture: The Mentality of the Great Tidewater Planters on the Eve of Revolution* first introduced us to this novel.

This began as a family endeavor, and we owe much to our familial relationships. As always, our spouses, children, and siblings have been a great support. Most particularly, we wish to thank our parents, Mike and LeAnn Mason, who raised us in a home where reading, writing, and thinking reflectively about both the past and present were not only encouraged but modeled. To them we dedicate this volume.

Introduction

In the world of literary taxonomy, where one of the most basic classificatory moves is to divide authors into "major" and "minor" orders, a writer like Edward Kimber poses several challenges. To begin with, Kimber remains so obscure that even dubbing him a "minor eighteenth-century novelist" might seem overly generous. All of Kimber's novels were published anonymously, and no one in his lifetime seems to have been particularly concerned with discovering their authorship. It was not until the 1930s that Frank Gees Black and Sidney Kimber (the novelist's great-great-grandson) would identify Kimber as the author of dozens of mid-eighteenth-century books, pamphlets, and magazine contributions.[1] Their discovery, however, has done little to attract new readers to Kimber's novels, and even specialists in the eighteenth-century novel can still pass an entire career without either hearing of Kimber or reading his works.

Why Kimber has proven so persistently unknown is something of a mystery. In terms of sheer productivity, he was quite remarkable. Between 1750 and 1765, a period during which he worked on dozens of side projects and was responsible (from 1755 onward) for editing the *London Magazine*, he was somehow able to write eight novels, an output few of his peers could match. Far from stillborn products of the press, Kimber's novels tended to circulate for several decades beyond their publication date. By Black's count, some 37 editions of his eight novels appeared between 1750 and 1808, including several translations into German and French.[2] Perhaps most tellingly, in 1783, when James Harrison compiled *The Novelist's Magazine*, a series dedicated to establishing a canon of classic British novels, he included Kimber's first novel, *Joe Thompson* (1750), alongside such land-

---

1   Sidney A. Kimber, "The 'Relation of a Late Expedition to St. Augustine,' With Biographical and Bibliographical Notes on Isaac and Edward Kimber," *Papers of the Bibliographical Society of America* 28 (1934): 81–96; Frank Gees Black, "Edward Kimber: Anonymous Novelist of the Mid-Eighteenth Century," *Harvard Studies and Notes in Philology and Literature* 17 (1935): 27–42.
2   Black, "Edward Kimber," 27–28.

marks of eighteenth-century fiction as Defoe's *Robinson Crusoe*, Richardson's *Pamela*, and Fielding's *Tom Jones*.[1]

While Kimber's second novel, *The History of the Life and Adventures of Mr. Anderson*, never received the "classic" stamp, it too enjoyed both initial popularity and a relatively long shelf-life. First published in London in January 1754, by the end of that year it had gone into a first Dublin edition and a second London edition. Over the remainder of the eighteenth century, three other editions would appear, all of which were likely aimed at the burgeoning class of readers who scoured circulating libraries for "new" titles.[2] Despite—or perhaps because of—its apparent popularity with readers, *Mr. Anderson* garnered little critical attention. The only known eighteenth-century review of the novel tersely dismisses it as "probably the work of a professed *adventure-maker*" and declares that "Like the majority of our modern novels, it has little to recommend it, besides a multiplicity of strange stories."[3]

In producing this edition—the first ever critical edition of *Mr. Anderson* and the first resetting of the novel in over two hundred years[4]—we obviously take exception to this assessment. Admittedly, *Mr. Anderson* fails to conform to modern-day standards for complexity in plotting and character development and emotional and didactic restraint, but no more so than most "classic" eighteenth-century novels. And the portrait it offers of the transatlantic world in the first half of the eighteenth century is quite possibly unparalleled in Anglo-American literature. Here, in a relatively short novel, we get detailed and frequently illuminating portrayals of white indentured servitude, the African slave trade, colonial plantocracy, European relations with Native Americans, Franco-British battles for North American supremacy, piracy in the Caribbean, and high-society life in Paris, London, the Chesapeake, and French Quebec. While action and adventure take precedence throughout the novel, Kimber finds several opportu-

---

1 Richard C. Taylor, "James Harrison, *The Novelist's Magazine*, and the Early Canonizing of the English Novel," *Studies in English Literature* 33 (1993): 629, 639–40.

2 For complete publication details on early editions of *Mr. Anderson*, see the "Note on the Text" that follows this introduction.

3 *Monthly Review* 10 (Feb. 1754): 147.

4 In 1975 Garland Publishing printed a facsimile of the first (1754) edition of *Mr. Anderson* as part of its "Garland Library of Narratives of North American Indian Captivities."

nities to broach his culture's most sensitive subjects, including sexual abuse, arranged marriage, the human bond whites share with Indians and Africans, and, perhaps most controversially, the ethics of slavery and the right of slaves to rise up against tyrannical masters. In short, *Mr. Anderson* offers a highly readable, still entertaining primer on transatlantic history and culture, one we expect will prove enlightening for students of literature and history alike.

The Life and Adventures of Edward Kimber

Edward Kimber was born in London on 17 September 1719, the second son of Anna and Isaac Kimber.[1] At the time of Edward's birth, his father had just completed his training for the General Baptist ministry at London's Moorfields Academy, a newly opened school for the children of religious Dissenters,[2] and in 1722 Isaac secured his first appointment as assistant minister at the Paul's Alley Baptist chapel in the city's Barbican district. Over the next five years, Isaac held a series of ministerial posts in London and Cheshire, but, reportedly due to his dullness at the pulpit, he never found a stable position. Sometime in the late 1720s he seems to have given up on the ministry, turning instead to career opportunities in the book trade. This proved wise, as in

---

1 According to the genealogical databases at ancestry.com, Isaac and Anna Kimber had five sons. The eldest, Isaac, lived from 1717 until 1753; the second son, born two years later, was Edward; and the three youngest (John, Richard, and Robert) died in infancy. Further biographical details on Isaac and Edward Kimber are available in the *Dictionary of National Biography*, the *Oxford Dictionary of National Biography*, Kevin J. Hayes's introduction to *Itinerant Observations in America* (Newark: U of Delaware P, 1998), Sidney Kimber's "Relation of a Late Expedition," and Edward Kimber's "Memoirs of the Life and Writings of the Reverend Mr. Isaac Kimber" (in *Sermons on the Most Interesting Religious, Moral, and Practical Subjects. By the Late Reverend and Learned Mr. Isaac Kimber* [London: C. and J. Ackers, 1756]).

2 The terms "Dissenter" and "Nonconformist" were generally used interchangeably during this era to describe individuals and congregations who had broken away from the Church of England or who criticized it from within. For a concise overview of the religious terrain of eighteenth-century Britain and the treatment of religion in the age's literature, see Isabel Rivers, "Religion and Literature," *The Cambridge History of English Literature, 1660–1780*, ed. John Richetti (Cambridge: Cambridge UP, 2005), 445–70.

1732 he received his big break, being offered the editorship of the newly founded *London Magazine*. Conceived of as a rival to the age's pioneering literary periodical, the *Gentleman's Magazine*, the *London* quickly developed a substantial readership. Isaac Kimber would remain the only editor the magazine had known until his death in 1755.

By Edward Kimber's own account, his early childhood was idyllic. Although the family's finances apparently precluded the Kimber children from receiving extensive formal education, their father was trained in the classics and imparted much of his knowledge to his children. Given Isaac's connections in the literary world, books were in ready supply, and Edward seems to have read widely in both ancient and modern literature. A major blow to the family's peace, however, came during Edward's early teens, when his mother began displaying signs of extreme mental illness. "This malady had two several stages," Edward would later record. "For some years it displayed itself in ravings and fury, by which [my father] was often endangered, and then sunk into an indolent kind of frenzy, which continued all the rest of her life."[1] Led by the long-suffering Isaac, the family banded together to care for Anna, but the financial and emotional toll was extreme. When not worrying over his wife, Isaac Kimber had a magazine to keep afloat, and, given limited funds to pay for contributors, he was left to produce much of the material for each month's issue himself. Not surprisingly, then, when Edward began to show a literary bent, he was quickly enlisted into the family business of writing copy for the *London Magazine*. According to Edward's own detailed notebooks, his first publication, an eight-line poem entitled "The Departure," appeared in the *London* when he was only fourteen, and soon thereafter he was regularly contributing poems and essays.[2]

After eight years of assisting his father, wanderlust evidently set in, and in September 1742 Edward boarded a ship bound for America. Following a twelve-day stopover in New York, he was off again, sailing south to Maryland's eastern shore, traveling overland through the eastern counties of Maryland and Virginia, crossing the Chesapeake Bay, and finally arriving at Yorktown,

---

1 Edward Kimber, "Memoirs of ... Isaac Kimber," xiii.
2 Kimber's notebook record of his publications is reprinted in Sidney Kimber, "The Relation," 90–94. Here Kimber gives the publication date for "The Departure" as March 1734, but it actually appeared in April of that year (see *London Magazine* 3 [April 1734]: 213).

Virginia, in late November 1742. For the next month, Kimber toured Virginia's Tidewater region, learning local customs and developing a sense of colonial mannerisms. While there, he apparently met up with military recruiters from Georgia, and—perhaps out of financial need, perhaps out of a desire for further adventure—he soon enlisted. By February 1743, Kimber had sailed to Georgia, pledged his loyalty to James Oglethorpe, the colony's founder, governor, and general, and set out with Oglethorpe's troops on a raid against the Spanish settlement at St. Augustine, Florida. For the most part, this mission proved anticlimactic, involving a series of tactical maneuvers but no significant fighting, and the militia returned to Georgia in late March.[1] Over the next, largely uneventful, year, Kimber remained in Oglethorpe's service, traveling extensively throughout Georgia but never being called into major combat. By March 1744, the young Englishman had apparently seen enough of America, and he set sail from Charleston, South Carolina, back to Britain, arriving home that summer.

Kimber would never return to America, but his eighteen-month sojourn there provided a storehouse of material he would frequently return to over the rest of his literary career. The first major fruits of his journey came in an essay series he published in the *London Magazine* between August 1745 and December 1746. Entitled "Itinerant Observations in America," these essays provide an invaluable record of mid-eighteenth-century American culture and telling glimpses into Kimber's attitudes on a variety of subjects.[2] While Kimber generally avoids the condescension and outright bigotry of conventional British travelogues, he nevertheless portrays America as a brave new world, where most of the trappings of European civilization are in short supply and the barbarity of slavery corrodes the souls of master and slave alike. When Kimber began writing novels in the 1750s, he would

---

1 For extracts from Kimber's account of this mission, see Appendix A1. For a complete facsimile of this document, see John Jay Tepaske, ed., *A Relation, or Journal, Of a Late Expedition to the Gates of St. Augustine, on Florida: Conducted by the Hon. General James Oglethorpe, with a Detachment of his Regiment, &c. from Georgia* (Gainesville: U of Florida P, 1976).

2 Several excerpts from the "Itinerant Observations" appear in Appendix A3–4. For an excellent modern edition of this essay series, see Kevin J. Hayes, ed., *Itinerant Observations in America* (Newark: U of Delaware P, 1998).

regularly draw upon his experiences in America, most notably, as we shall see, in *Mr. Anderson*.

Between his return from America and his becoming a novelist, Kimber made the transition fully into the world of adulthood. Within a few months of his arrival, he married Susanna Lunn of East Keal, Lincolnshire, and soon thereafter the couple began having children.[1] To support his growing family, Kimber cobbled together an income through occasional stints in the British military and literary piecework for the *London* and various other periodicals. In short, his life during this period was very much that of the "Grub Street hack," that legendary figure of eighteenth-century London who, while awaiting his big break, stayed solvent by scribbling out anything that paid. In addition to a number of indexing jobs, Kimber's publications from the late 1740s and early 1750s include articles touching on politics, literature, religion, and even "the sagacity of dogs and other animals."

One of the most revealing publications from Kimber's Grub Street years is a 1750 pamphlet entitled *A Letter from a Citizen of London to his Fellow Citizens, and Through Them, to the People of England in General, Occasioned by the late Earthquakes*.[2] Published, as the title suggests, in the wake of two minor earthquakes that rattled London on 8 February and 8 March 1750, Kimber's pamphlet interprets these quakes as unmistakable signs of God's displeasure with the city's inhabitants. If London doesn't immediately rid itself of theatrical and literary lewdness, Catholic priestcraft, and French-inspired manners and fashions, Kimber warns, it will share the fate of Sodom, Gomorrah, and other biblical cities the Lord has wiped from the Earth. While Kimber was hardly alone in attributing the London earthquakes to heavenly wrath—the Methodist leader John Wesley, for one, argued much the same thing—his Letter from a Citizen of London is remarkable for the insight it affords into just how thoroughly his worldview had been colored by his Baptist heritage. Elsewhere in his writings, including in *Mr. Anderson*,

---

1 Details about Kimber's marriage are scarce, but he and his wife are known to have settled in London and had at least four children: Susanna (born 1748, died 1749), Richard (1750–1829), Isaac (1753–1754), and John (dates unknown). Source: Ancestry World Tree Project (ancestry.com).

2 This pamphlet, published in London by John Hinton, is anonymous, but in his notebooks Kimber identifies himself as its author (see Sidney A. Kimber, "The Relation," 91).

Kimber comes across as a dedicated but moderate Christian, rarely showing any signs of religious zealotry. Here, however, with his apocalyptic visions, pronounced anti-Catholicism, and lamentations over the moral decay of society, he participates wholeheartedly in the rhetorical and theological traditions of English Dissent.[1]

It is at first glance rather surprising, then, to note that in the very year in which Kimber published this jeremiad on the London earthquakes he also published his first novel, *Joe Thompson*. While there was some precedent for English Nonconformists turning novelists—Daniel Defoe, for one, readily comes to mind—generally speaking, devout churchgoers of the mid-eighteenth century, especially those in the Dissenting tradition, were more inclined to see the novel as a principal *cause* of moral corruption than as a *solution* for it. Still a relatively new and evolving form, the novel held approximately the same cultural status during Kimber's lifetime as television does today: widely popular, but just as widely dismissed as a waste of time and as morally dangerous, especially for impressionable youth.[2] The enormous success of Samuel Richardson's overtly moralistic epistolary novels, *Pamela* (1740–41) and *Clarissa* (1747–48), helped ease hostility toward the genre; but, as a general rule, the more evangelical segments of the populace had little patience for novel reading, let alone novel writing. Tellingly, to escape the negative connotations attached to novels, eighteenth-century fiction writers routinely presented their works as "histories" (Kimber's preferred label), "authentic narratives," or "autobiographies." In more creative instances, they went so far as to dub their books "comic epic poems in prose" (as in Henry Fielding's *Joseph Andrews*) or "translations" of long-lost manuscripts (in Horace Walpole's *The Castle of Otranto*).

Given these stigmas surrounding fiction, Kimber's decision to take up novel writing had to have involved a fair amount of anxious reflection. Yet, all things considered, it was the ideal medium for a man of his background, talents, and interests. As

---

1   For useful overviews of Baptist beliefs and traditions in Kimber's England, see A.C. Underwood's *A History of the English Baptists* (London: Kingsgate Press, 1947) and Raymond Brown's *The English Baptists of the Eighteenth Century* (London: Baptist Historical Society, 1986).

2   Appendix D in this edition provides a sampling of mid-eighteenth-century documents reflecting these views.

seen in his voyage to America and his keenness to enlist in Oglethorpe's militia once there, Kimber had a passion for adventure, and the novel had from its beginnings—think *Robinson Crusoe* (1719), *Moll Flanders* (1722), and *Gulliver's Travels* (1726)—established itself as the premier modern form for tales of adventure. Another major attraction of the novel, especially for a young man like Kimber who hoped to make his living by writing, would have been the rapidly proliferating audience for this new genre. Conceivably, writing religious tracts like his pamphlet on the London earthquakes might have proven more spiritually rewarding for Kimber, but if Fielding's *Joseph Andrews* (1742) is to be trusted, "the age was so wicked, that nobody read sermons." By Fielding's report, there were "five thousand volumes at least" of unwanted, unsaleable religious treatises clogging the backrooms of bookshops, and well-meaning theologians like his character Parson Adams couldn't give away the copyrights to their sermons.[1]

In contrast to the sermon, then, the novel offered Kimber a powerful vehicle for delivering his moral messages to a large audience of impressionable readers. As noted above, during the 1740s Richardson had opened up new vistas for the genre, especially with his first novel, *Pamela*. Subtitled *Virtue Rewarded*, Richardson's novel received the ultimate endorsement for its times when several clergymen preached from the pulpit that they knew of no other book, save the Bible, as capable of inspiring chastity, benevolence, and piety in youthful readers. The *Pamela* "media event," as William Warner has dubbed it, almost single-handedly shifted the landscape of English fiction, creating a new vogue for sentimentality and didacticism.[2] Emblematic of the new tenor of the age was the career of Eliza Haywood. During the 1720s and 1730s, Haywood published dozens of scandalous (and highly successful) amatory novels, establishing a reputation, in John Richetti's words, as "the Barbara Cartland or Danielle Steele of her day."[3] In the wake of *Pamela*, however, Haywood refashioned herself as a

---

1 Henry Fielding, *Joseph Andrews and Shamela* (London: J.M. Dent, 1993), 112.

2 William B. Warner, *Licensing Entertainment: The Elevation of Novel Reading in Britain, 1684–1750* (Berkeley: U of California P, 1998), ch. 5. For an illustration of Richardson's style, see the excerpts from *Sir Charles Grandison* in Appendix D3.

3 John Richetti, *The English Novel in History 1700–1780* (London: Routledge, 1999), 38.

reformed coquette, first penning a series of moralistic essays (*The Female Spectator*, 1744–46) and then advocating chastity and refined moral sensibility in such novels as *The History of Betsy Thoughtless* (1751) and *The History of Jemmy and Jenny Jessamy* (1753). Together with widely read contemporaries like Penelope Aubin and Sarah Fielding, Haywood would help establish the sentimental novel as a more virtuous alternative to the bodice-rippers that had dominated the century's first four decades.[1]

It was this burgeoning movement toward didactic fiction that Kimber joined when he took up as a novelist in the mid-eighteenth century. His first novel, *Joe Thompson* (1750), blends the transatlantic action sequences of a *Robinson Crusoe* with the moral sensibility of a *Pamela*. With some variations, Kimber would maintain this style over his next four novels—*Mr. Anderson* (1754), *James Ramble* (1754), *David Ranger* (1756), and *Neville Frowde* (1758)—all of which belong to the "Life and Adventures" genre. Beginning, however, with *The Happy Orphans* (1759) and continuing in his last two novels, *Maria* (1764) and *The Generous Briton* (1765), Kimber shifted into a sort of hybrid between the courtly romance and the novel of manners, creating tales in which English youth are forced to navigate a society filled with would-be destroyers of their virtue.[2]

Rather unusually, for his eight novels Kimber had eight separate publishers. This was likely not, however, owing to his inability to attract readers, as, in fact, all of his novels seem to have sold relatively well. Ever the professional writer, Kimber carefully recorded the sums he made from his various publications, noting that he received between £20 and £31 for most of his novels. By mid-eighteenth-century standards, this was fair, but certainly not lavish, compensation.[3] As Kimber would have known all too well,

---

1   For useful overviews of sentimental novels by these and other writers, see Jerry C. Beasley, *Novels of the 1740s* (Athens: U of Georgia P, 1982), esp. ch. 6; John Mullan, "Sentimental Novels," *The Cambridge Companion to the Eighteenth-Century Novel*, ed. John Richetti (Cambridge: Cambridge UP, 1996), pp. 236–54; and Richetti, *The English Novel in History 1700–1780*, esp. ch. 8.

2   The best analysis to date of Kimber's place in the sentimental tradition comes in Gary L. Ebersole, *Captured by Texts: Puritan to Postmodern Images of Indian Captivity* (Charlottesville and London: UP of Virginia, 1995), 109–16.

3   The amounts Kimber earned for his novels are reprinted in Black, "Edward Kimber," 35. In 1754, £20 had roughly the same purchasing power as £2,600 (or $5,200) had in 2007 (see A Note on Eighteenth-Century Currency, p. 42).

novel writing couldn't be relied upon to provide his sole income, and thus he took on a number of other publishing projects, including writing a history of England and compiling and updating lists of aristocratic families in the British Isles. His most stable income during his later years came from the editorship of the *London Magazine*, a position he inherited upon his father's death in 1755. Kimber would outlive his father by just fourteen years, dying in 1769. Fittingly, he was buried near the two paragons of Dissenting fiction, John Bunyan and Daniel Defoe, in the Nonconformists' cemetery at Bunhill Fields, just north of London.

Rounding off its portrait of Kimber as the prototypical Grub Street hack, the original *Dictionary of National Biography* alleges, "He gained a scanty subsistence by compiling for booksellers, and died, worn out with such drudgery, in 1769." Besides the obvious misstep here of basing a medical autopsy wholly upon the subject's professional status, this account also does Kimber the disservice of dramatically underestimating his literary accomplishment. Certainly, no one would mistake an author essentially unknown in his day as a rival to Richardson, Fielding, or Samuel Johnson. But, whether they knew it or not, most English readers of the 1750s and 1760s would have been familiar with Kimber's writing, whether it was through his novels, his histories and indexes, or the essays and poems he published over 35 years in the widely circulated *London Magazine*. In this sense, at least, Kimber qualifies as a "major" English writer of the mid-eighteenth century.

Mr. Anderson and Traditional Representations of Colonial America

In "Itinerant Observations," the essay series Kimber published soon after returning from America, he records the extraordinary life story of a 70-year-old gentleman he met while traveling on Maryland's eastern shore. By this man's report, at the age of six he was accompanying his father through a seedy London neighborhood when they somehow became separated. Frantically crying out, the lost boy attracted the notice of the captain of a slave-trading vessel, who coaxed the child into believing his father had entrusted him to his care. Soon the credulous boy found himself imprisoned aboard the captain's ship and headed for America, where he was sold into a fourteen-year term of indentured servitude. In the end, however, good prevailed, as not only did his benevolent American master free him upon hearing his story, but he also awarded him his daughter's hand in marriage and bequeathed to him his entire estate.[1]

Given the clear resemblances between this tale and the plot of *Mr. Anderson*, scholars have understandably taken it to be the primary inspiration behind Kimber's novel.[2] It would be a mistake, though, to read the novel in its entirety as a straightforward fictionalization of this particular man's life story, as *Mr. Anderson* draws upon a wide range of source material. In addition to his previously noted borrowings from novelists like Defoe and Richardson, Kimber samples freely from numerous ancient and modern writers. In places, he explicitly models Tom Anderson after Joseph of Egypt from the Bible; elsewhere, the hero's story parallels that of James Annesley, a young gentleman whose sensational tale of being sold into American servitude in an attempt to cheat him of his inheritance captivated British readers in the 1740s.[3]

Another class of literature Kimber's novel both borrows from and contributes to is the highly popular genre of British commentaries upon life in the North American colonies. As Melissa J. Homestead has detailed, *Mr. Anderson* belongs to a large body of novels and memoirs from this period featuring a "there-and-back" plot trajectory, in which a character leaves England in a state of duress, experiences spiritual or financial renewal in North America, and returns home a paragon of virtue and industry.[4] Yet, while the long-term consequences of the protagonist's American sojourn in such narratives are generally positive, this is quite often in spite of rather than because of the norms of colonial society. In fact, most accounts of the New World published in mid-eighteenth-century Britain tilted decidedly toward the

---

1 This excerpt from "Itinerant Observations" is included in Appendix A4.
2 See, for instance, W. Gordon Milne, "A Glimpse of Colonial America as Seen in an English Novel of 1754," *Maryland Historical Magazine* 42 (1947): 241; and Hayes, ed., *Itinerant Observations*, 17.
3 Appendix C4 includes an excerpt from Annesley's fictionalized account of his travails.
4 Melissa J. Homestead, "The Beginnings of the American Novel," *The Oxford Handbook of Early American Literature*, ed. Kevin J. Hayes (Oxford: Oxford UP, 2008), 530–33. Homestead takes the idea of the "there-and-back" narrative from Julie Ellison's essay "There and Back: Transatlantic Novels and Anglo-American Careers," *The Past as Prologue: Essays to Celebrate the Twenty-fifth Anniversary of ASECS*, ed. Carla H. Hay and Syndy M. Conger (New York: AMS, 1995), 303–24.

negative. British literature of all kinds tended to depict the colonies as a place to which only scoundrels or the desperate would willingly go.

This had not, however, always been the dominant British view. In the sixteenth and early seventeenth centuries, writers generally portrayed the colonies in glowing terms, hoping to induce England's growing population of "sturdy beggars" to emigrate to the New World. This view comported with Europeans' long-running view of the New World as an earthly paradise in which humankind might start anew. During this era, for every Briton pushed by desperation to the American colonies, there were many pulled by the dreams of opportunity there.[1] But by the late seventeenth century America's disparagers outnumbered and outweighed her boosters. After the 1660s, a declining birth rate, the plague, and new labor needs ended worries about any surplus population in Britain. Many leading Britons were loath to see their country's population—which they now saw as a vital national resource—drained to the colonies, and they took a dimmer view of emigration. As Britain's elite felt challenged by men of newer mercantile wealth in the eighteenth century, they placed on colonial upstarts much of their defensive snobbery.[2] Those who demeaned the New World tapped into their own

---

1 For a good discussion and summary of early promotional literature, see Howard Mumford Jones, *O Strange New World; American Culture: The Formative Years* (New York: Viking, 1964), 179–92. For the attractions of North America for many late colonial emigrants, see Bernard Bailyn, *Voyagers to the West: A Passage in the Peopling of America on the Eve of the Revolution* (New York: Alfred A. Knopf, 1986), esp. chs. 1–2, 5, 11–16.

2 See Michal J. Rozbicki, *The Complete Colonial Gentleman: Cultural Legitimacy in Plantation America* (Charlottesville and London: UP of Virginia, 1998), esp. chs. 1, 3; Abbot Emerson Smith, *Colonists in Bondage: White Servitude and Convict Labor in America, 1607–1776* (New York: W.W. Norton, 1947), 6, 45–46, 54–55; Drohr Wahrman, "The English Problem of Identity in the American Revolution," *American Historical Review* 106 (Oct. 2001): 1236–62; James G. Basker, ed., *Amazing Grace: An Anthology of Poems About Slavery, 1660–1810* (New Haven and London: Yale UP, 2002), 1–81; Stephen Conway, "From Fellow-Nationals to Foreigners: British Perceptions of the Americans, circa 1739–1783," *William and Mary Quarterly*, 3rd Ser., 59.1 (Jan. 2002): 65–100; Anthony S. Parent, Jr., *Foul Means: The Formation of a Slave Society in Virginia, 1660–1740* (Chapel Hill and London: U of North Carolina P for the Omohundro Institute of Early American History and Culture, 2003), 58–59.

long-running European tradition, what historian Howard Mumford Jones called the "anti-image" to the "Edenic image" of America. In this view the New World was a frightening place, where the terrors and extremes of nature found their consequent companion in the greed and cruelty of native and newcomer alike.[1] When even Virginia's governor William Berkeley wrote that "none but those of the meanest quality and corruptest lives" arrived in his colony, one can hardly expect many Britons to have painted a rosy picture.[2]

Travel and adventure accounts both factual and fictional were enormously popular in the late seventeenth and early eighteenth centuries in Britain, and as various writers plied this trade they drew on the burgeoning "anti-image" of the colonies for stories set there. In 1680, for instance, Londoners read the story and confession of one Thomas Hellier, an English servant recently executed in Virginia for murdering his master and mistress. To put it mildly, this account was not calculated to improve the English public's impressions of Virginia. In an early nonfictional version of what would soon become the typical tale, Hellier's prodigal youth in England rendered him vulnerable to the misfortune of sailing for America. When a scoundrel posing as a ship captain proposed to take him to Virginia, Hellier replied, "I had heard so bad a character of that Country, that I dreaded going thither." But with "fair promises" the supposed captain persuaded the desperate lad to go. Upon arrival he was sold to a tyrannical master and mistress, proprietors of the almost incredibly aptly named plantation "Hard Labour." By "ill-usage," they made his life a "Hell on Earth," provoking him to murder them.[3] The anonymous Virginian who published this pamphlet and offered his own pious reflections on Hellier's life and death insisted that Virginia was a good place, if only for those who were willing to work hard. However, he presented Hellier's being duped to sail for the Chesapeake as "Celestial Vengeance" for his wicked ways.[4]

Prominent fiction writers such as Aphra Behn and Daniel Defoe also followed this pattern. Behn's best-known representa-

---

1 Jones, *O Strange New World*, chs. 1–2.

2 Quoted in Jenny Hale Pulsipher, "*The Widow Ranter* and Royalist Culture in Colonial Virginia," *Early American Literature* 39.1 (2004): 41.

3 *The Vain Prodigal Life and Tragical Penitential Death of Thomas Hellier* (London: Sam Crouch, 1680), 5–15; quotations on 10, 11, 12.

4 *The Vain Prodigal Life*, 23–36; quotation on 36.

tion of the New World comes in *Oroonoko* (1688), a semi-fictional account of an African prince being lured aboard an English slave ship and sold into bondage in the South American colony of Surinam. In a lesser-known work written at about the same time as *Oroonoko*, her comedy *The Widow Ranter* (first staged in 1689), she turned her focus to Britain's North American colonies, specifically Virginia. Behn peoples her play's imagined Virginia with perpetually drunken judges, a parson who is familiar at the whorehouse, and a nouveau-riche "aristocracy" whose members all have sordid pasts in England. Virginia needed "well-born" inhabitants and rulers if it were to prosper, Behn concludes.[1] On its face this was a hopeful conclusion; the colonies might achieve their paradisiacal potential if people of quality would go there. But that people of such rank would cast their lot in such a place seemed an unlikely prospect, especially after such a description. A generation after Behn's colonial tales first appeared, the characters in Defoe's popular novel *Moll Flanders* (1722) still considered emigrating to the American colonies to be a calamity.[2] In *Colonel Jack*, a less widely read novel published in the same year as *Moll Flanders*, Defoe has the main character sail to Virginia with a group of other unfortunates only because they have been hoodwinked. Jack reconciles himself to this fate, thinking of how servitude in the New World will give him the opportunity to break the criminal habits of his youth in England. But upon attaining freedom and prosperity, he realizes just how provincial and isolated the Chesapeake is. So far from Europe, the center of civilized life, he sees that even his plantation's wealth cannot provide for him "the life of a gentleman," and he soon thereafter returns to England.[3]

This storyline also echoed in several nonfictional tales, including one of an indentured servant written in Kimber's day, William Moraley's *The Infortunate* (1743). Much like Colonel Jack and Moll Flanders, Moraley endured a childhood in England marked by both misfortune and squandered opportunities. At his lowest

---

1   Aphra Behn, *Oroonoko, The Rover and Other Works*, ed. Janet Todd (London: Penguin, 1992), 256.

2   See, for instance, the excerpt from this novel included in Appendix B3.

3   Daniel Defoe, *The History and Remarkable Life of the Truly Honourable Colonel Jack* (1722; London: The Folio Society, 1967), 122–28, 163–84; quotation on 182. Later he has Colonel Jack refer to Virginia as "home," and retire there, but only after many years in Europe; see 214 (quotation), 259–60.

ebb, "not caring what became of me, it entered into my Head to ... sell myself for a Term of Years into the *American* Plantations." After years of hard labor on a Pennsylvania estate, however, Moraley emerged to find no real prospects for prosperity awaiting an ex-servant like him in America. Resigned to the fact that the New World was even more miserable than the Old, he eagerly sailed back to England.[1] Moraley's narrative was certainly not as widely read as the works of Behn and Defoe, but it demonstrated that British writers, from the most popular to the most obscure, pursued common themes and even plots when they wrote about America. Conventionally, a voyage to America came as a result of a misspent or misfortunate youth in England. Characters often redeemed themselves there, but only a reverse emigration would complete their rehabilitation.

That so many authors followed this line probably flowed in large part from the fact that very few of them ever visited the colonies. They thus relied on travel accounts and fictional treatments, in which the pejorative was orthodox, for their image of the New World. In contrast, Kimber had personally traveled extensively along America's eastern seaboard and was thus able to offer a much more nuanced perspective. Admittedly, in some respects the America of *Mr. Anderson* closely resembles that found in traditional accounts. The novel's most prominent planters, for instance, seem straight out of anti-American propaganda, manifesting ill-breeding, coarseness, and inhumanity at every turn. One of the novel's most prosperous planters, Mr. Barlow, is introduced as "base," "wicked," and drunken, and we later learn that he "had little notion of the necessity of knowledge himself, as he could but just write his name mechanically" (58). Even more monstrous are the Carters, the enormously wealthy clan of planters who function in the novel as the region's first family. The family patriarch, Colonel Carter, is thoroughly malevolent, having no respect for religion, law, or basic humanity. His son is even worse, as this "lad of bad principles, unlettered, and of coarse manners" (67) unites his father's misanthropy with his own ineptitude. In the novel's lone moment of

---

1   William Moraley, *The Infortunate: The Voyage and Adventures of William Moraley, an Indentured Servant*, ed. Susan E. Klepp and Billy G. Smith (1743; University Park: Penn State UP, 1992), esp. 49–54, 110–11; quotation on 49–50. For a sampling of similar accounts from Kimber's era, see *The Adventures of a Kidnapped Orphan* (London, 1747) as well as Appendix B.

comic relief, young Carter's oafish marriage proposal to Fanny, Kimber satirizes both the cocksure buffoon and the society that considers him its most eligible bachelor. With families like the Carters at the head of Maryland society, it is little surprise that, rather than setting up as a Maryland planter, Tom chooses to take his beloved Fanny and her mother to the more civilized world of England.

In such passages, Kimber's novel encapsulates the treatment planters received in much of the mother country's literature about the colonies. This literature manifestly helped frame generations of Englishmen's views across the Atlantic, which took on a particular significance on the eve of the American Revolution. In 1759 Adam Smith lamented that "Fortune" saw fit to subject Africans "to the refuse of the jails of Europe, to wretches ... whose levity, brutality and baseness, so justly expose them to the contempt of the vanquished" slaves.[1] In the next decade, when the colonists protested the imperial government's taxes, there was no shortage of Britons eager to pour out their contempt in return. One defender of the Stamp Act, for instance, wrote that Americans "are as sober, temperate, upright, humane, and virtuous, as the posterity of ... convicts and felons, savages and negro-whippers, can be." Another asked what the home government owed to the motley crew of immigrants from other nations, mixed with "a multitude of felons from this country," who inhabited the turbulent colonies.[2] Such replies directly echoed the longstanding literary image of American colonists nurtured by the likes of Kimber.

And educated colonists were all too aware of the way they were being represented. Even before the Revolution, Chesapeake planters, such as the Old Dominion luminary Robert Carter, chafed under such condescension.[3] There is no evidence that anyone in North America read *Mr. Anderson* or any other of Kimber's novels, unlike other British writers whose novels were set in the colonies.[4] But in a tantalizing irony, Carter's library

---

1 Adam Smith, *Theory of Moral Sentiments* (London: A. Millar, 1759), 402.

2 Qtd. in Christopher Leslie Brown, *Moral Capital: Foundations of British Abolitionism* (Chapel Hill: U of North Carolina P for the Omohundro Institute of Early American History and Culture, 2006), 124–25.

3 Rozbicki, *Complete Colonial Gentleman*, ch. 3.

4 Contemporary novels, especially of the travel-adventure variety, were far from absent from the offerings of colonial booksellers. But contempo-

contained two works from Kimber: his lists of Scottish and English Peerages.[1] Both planter and writer, it appears, admired Britain's ancient aristocracy, yet Kimber disdained Carter and his kind as vulgar and vicious. This treatment of the colonial grandee at the hands of an obscure middle-class English writer was like a miniature version of the general snubbing the colonial gentry experienced at the hands of the mother country.[2]

Yet, however much his portraits of Barlow and the Carters conform to existing stereotypes, elsewhere Kimber transcends conventional anti-American bigotry by drawing a number of American characters who exemplify learning, refinement, and virtue. In stark contrast to the tyrannical Mr. Barlow, for instance,

---

rary fiction paled as a category compared to others in the colonial book trade from England. See Stephen Botein, "The Anglo-American Book Trade before 1776: Personnel and Strategies," *Printing and Society in Early America*, ed. William L. Joyce *et al.* (Worcester, MA: American Antiquarian Society, 1983), 48–82; Elizabeth Carroll Reilly, "The Wages of Piety: The Boston Book Trade of Jeremy Condy," in Joyce *et al.*, eds., esp. 126–31; Cynthia Z. Stiverson and Gregory A. Stiverson, "The Colonial Retail Book Trade: Availability and Affordability of Reading Material in Mid-Eighteenth-Century Virginia," in Joyce *et al.*, eds., 132–73. The speculation that neither the *Itinerant Observations* nor *Mr. Anderson* crossed the Atlantic is also based on colonial booksellers' notices from Kimber's time: see *Imported in the last Ships from London, and to be sold by David Hall* ... (Philadelphia: B. Franklin and D. Hall, 1754); *Catalogue of BOOKS sold by Garrat Noel, at the Bible in Dock-street* (New York: Garrat Noel, 1754 or 1755); *BOOKS Just Imported from LONDON, and to be Sold by William Bradford* ... (Philadelphia: William Bradford, 1755); *A Catalogue of Books in History, Divinity, Law, Arts and Sciences, and the several Parts of Polite Literature; To be Sold by Garrat Noel, Bookseller in Dock-street, New-York* (New York: H. Gaine, 1755); *A Catalogue of Books ... To be Sold, By Garrat Noel* ... (New York: H. Gaine, 1759); *BOOKS Imported in the last Vessel from LONDON, and to be sold by David Hall* ... (Philadelphia: B. Franklin and D. Hall, 1760?); *Books and Stationary, Just Imported from LONDON, And to be Sold by W. Dunlap* ... (Philadelphia: William Dunlap, 1760). Both Defoe and Behn were staples in these advertisements.

1 See "A Catalogue of Books: In the Library of 'Councillor' Robert Carter, at Nomini Hall, Westmoreland County, Virginia," *William and Mary College Quarterly Historical Magazine* 11 (July 1902): 21.

2 For a suggestive discussion of this dialectic, see the new Preface to the Second Paperback Edition in T.H. Breen, *Tobacco Culture: The Mentality of the Great Tidewater Planters on the Eve of Revolution* (1975; Princeton and Oxford: Princeton UP, 2001), xvi–xxiv.

Kimber gives us Mrs. Barlow, whose nurturing and inner goodness sustain young Tom through his early hardships. Even more
direct foils to Barlow and the Carters come in the novel's model
planters, Ferguson and Matthewson. Like Mrs. Barlow, these ide-
alized men function as surrogate parents to Tom, teaching him
that compassion, godliness, and integrity are the surest paths to
personal peace and financial prosperity. With mentors and loved
ones like these, Tom comes to associate the New World not only
with barbarism and hardship, but also with noble industry and
simple, unpretentious goodness. On the one hand, with great
planters like Barlow and the Carters comprising the ruling elite in
Maryland, people like Ferguson and Matthewson do not get their
due; with such boorish, brutal planters in charge, as Tom puts it,
"good sense, learning, and politeness seem not to be in so much
request as I understand they are in *Europe*" (59). But, on the other
hand, he comes to consider the colony "his native country" and at
multiple points pines for "his innocent *Senepuxon*" and "*Maryland*, his ever beloved *Maryland*" (123). All told, then, *Mr. Anderson* offers a cross between the Edenic image of early American
travel narratives and the "anti-image" of colonial backwardness
increasingly prevalent during Kimber's lifetime.

Slavery, Servitude, and Depictions of Non-British
Peoples

Significantly, Kimber's tolerance does not end with his representations of the American colonies, as in fact his entire novel dis-
plays a remarkably broadminded attitude toward non-British
peoples and cultures. In an era when British authors and politi-
cians routinely defined their own national identity as the antithe-
sis of all things French,[1] *Mr. Anderson* offers a refreshingly progressive model of Franco-British understanding. This is not to
say that Kimber was completely above French-bashing. As we
have already seen, his tract on the London earthquakes decried
the influence of French papists on British culture, and several
scenes in the early chapters of *Mr. Anderson* depict Frenchmen as
oily and double-crossing. Tom Anderson himself bluntly declares
after visiting Paris that he cannot trust a French servant and that
the English "were more to his genius and liking than the *French*"

---

1 Linda Colley, *Britons: Forging the Nation 1707–1837* (New Haven: Yale
UP, 1992), 1–54.

(129). Yet, just as he does with his depictions of Chesapeake planters, Kimber offsets these stereotyping passages with instances of Frenchmen who exemplify goodness, loyalty, and Christian charity. In the Québécois marquis du Cayle, Kimber's hero finds a soul mate; in Captain D'Aville he finds an honorable leader for whom he is willing to risk his life; and in Paris he finds a culture of unmatched genius and sophistication. In one of the novel's more noteworthy turns, Tom even joins the brotherhood of French naval officers, helping them overtake a pirate ship manned primarily by Englishmen.

This balancing act between bigotry and broadmindedness carries over into Kimber's representation of Native Americans. In one of the novel's most heavily typecast passages, a bloodthirsty band of French-allied Indians ambushes Tom and a group of friends while they are exploring the countryside. Tom "found himself in an instant surrounded by enemy *Indians*, who butchered his surviving companions, scalped them before his face, and then stripping him to the skin, made him march before them at a great rate…; and then setting him in the midst, they made a ring, and danced the war-dance" (112). Just when things look bleakest for our hero, he has the presence of mind to play a militaristic march on his flute. "Never was more amazement shewn than now," Kimber's narrator reports, as the Indians "made the most ridiculous gestures of astonishment, then snatch'd the tuneful instrument, surveyed it on all sides, [and] attempted to blow ineffectually" (113). If, however, in scenes such as these Kimber perpetuates a popular caricature of Native Americans as mindless primitives, elsewhere he draws upon a markedly more sympathetic, but no less exaggerated, character type: the noble savage. The most extreme representative of this type in *Mr. Anderson* is Calcathouy, the legendary Indian warrior who, when not on the battlefield, proves himself a man of deep sensibility. In courting his wife-to-be, Taloufa, Calcathouy rejects tribal customs of arranged marriage, instead spending two years "sigh[ing] his passion at her feet" (99) in order to prove his love. This Indian "man of feeling" even argues for women's rights, pledging to Taloufa "that he meant to make her his companion and the friend of his heart, and not to destine her to that drudgery and servile submission, which he abominated, but which was universally practised by the *Indian* women" (99). Not surprisingly, Calcathouy and Taloufa go on to enjoy an idyllic marriage until her tragic death, which throws the tender-hearted warrior into such a swoon that since that time he "has never been seen once to smile" (105).

Taken alongside his portrayals of benevolent Frenchmen and Americans, Kimber's sketch of Calcathouy helps establish *Mr. Anderson* as one of the most culturally inclusive novels of its time. As Joe Snader has suggested, "Within this novel, neither tyranny nor liberty nor subjugation seems attached to any particular culture, but rather all cultures seem capable of despotism in colonial America, while only the exceptional gentleman, of whatever cultural origin, can remain free of taint."[1] However broadminded *Mr. Anderson* may be in some respects, though, its attitudes toward the institution of slavery and the proper treatment of Africans are likely to unsettle many modern readers. Not that the novel ever expresses enthusiasm for slavery: in fact, it becomes quite clear that for Kimber, as for his predecessors and contemporaries, a basic reason the colonies were ultimately less civilized than Europe was the exploitative labor system that prevailed there. Kimber communicates this rather pointedly near the end of *Mr. Anderson* in placing Tom, Fanny, and Mrs. Barlow in a coach drawn to London by six *horses*—this in explicit contrast to young Carter's perverse vision a few pages earlier of a coach drawn by *slaves*. The point here is simple: England stands for normalcy, the colonies for barbaric aberration.

British authors frequently underscored the centrality of slavery and servitude in their vision of America by setting their tales in the Chesapeake. To begin with, given that a high percentage of white servants and the vast majority of transported convicts from the British Isles ended up in Maryland and Virginia, the Chesapeake formed the natural stage for tales like *Moll Flanders* and *Mr. Anderson*.[2] Moreover, this region was home to several of the largest slave plantations in North America. While Kimber's description of America contains its share of factual mistakes,[3] one area where he proves a deft historian is in his decision

---

1 Snader, *Caught Between Worlds: British Captivity Narratives in Fact and Fiction* (Lexington: U of Kentucky P, 2000), 193.

2 Smith, *Colonists in Bondage*, 116–17, 124.

3 At times in *Mr. Anderson*, Kimber shows a tendency to conflate all of the American colonies into one. His Maryland, for instance, abounds in palmettos, a species of tree found only in the southeast; and his fictional Carters of Maryland appear to be based, at least in part, on the real-life Carters of Virginia, one of the southern colony's most prosperous clans. In this lack of particularity, Kimber follows the lead of Defoe, who in *Colonel Jack* remarks that "Maryland is Virginia, speaking to them at a distance" (162).

to locate his slavery scenes in Maryland.[1] In the early eighteenth century, Maryland was the ideal setting for drawing planters as despots, as the colony's laws gave servants far fewer rights and protections than those of Virginia and other neighboring provinces. In examining this difference, the historian Abbot Emerson Smith could account for it in no other way than to speculate that "the planters of Maryland were a harsher breed than those of Virginia and Pennsylvania."[2] These laws may have contributed to an even more negative profile for Maryland than for Virginia among those who cared to differentiate between the two, which would only have heightened Kimber's readers' sense of horror at Tom's debasement.

Having the young Tom sold as a slave for life also intensifies the drama of his sufferings, but accords less neatly with the realities of colonial life. Smith, still unsurpassed as a scholar of white servitude in colonial America, concludes that "there was never any such thing as perpetual slavery for any white man in any English colony."[3] To be sure, colonial labor recruiters abducted hundreds of white Britons. Several cases of kidnapping grabbed headlines throughout the British Isles and led to legal prohibitions on the recruiting agents (known as "spirits" for their dubious practices).[4] Defoe wrote of a regular trade in kidnapped children from England to Virginia.[5] To have young Tommy kidnapped off the streets of London, then, was no grand distortion on Kimber's part. But having him sold for life in Maryland did not square with the racial divide in America: white colonists truly enslaved only people of African or Native American descent.

Kimber, however, was not alone in failing to draw a line between the period of servitude white colonists completed and the lifetime bondage of black slaves. In his poetic autobiography, the one-time indentured servant James Revel reviles planters who treat white servants and black slaves much the same.[6] Likewise,

---

1   For a stimulating discussion of the importance of setting in fiction, see Franco Moretti, *Atlas of the European Novel, 1800–1900* (London and New York: Verso, 1998).

2   Smith, *Colonists in Bondage*, 276–77; quotation on 277.

3   Smith, *Colonists in Bondage*, 171; see also 158, 362 (n.4). See also George Boulukos, *The Grateful Slave: The Emergence of Race in Eighteenth-Century British and American Culture* (Cambridge: Cambridge UP, 2008), 119.

4   Smith, *Colonists in Bondage*, 61–62, 67–86.

5   Defoe, *Colonel Jack*, 23.

6   See Appendix C1.

the preacher who published Hellier's account urges masters in his audience to refrain from "Tyrannizing over Christians, as *Turks* do over Galley-slaves." And in Hellier's own confession, he pleads with masters to stop treating servants like "Dogs," for they "are professed Christians, and bear God's Image."[1] Ironically, these sermons to masters only reinforced the very image of white "slaves" the preachers would have them reverse. Moraley, for instance, describes himself and his fellow shipmates as "Voluntary Slaves" who were "sold of[f]" much like black slaves. After sale, the status and condition of "the Negroes" might have been slightly worse than that of the "bought Servants," but these are small matters of degree rather than of kind in Moraley's narrative.[2] Defoe also uses the terms "slave" and "servant" interchangeably. In *Moll Flanders* the heroine laments being "bound to Virginia, in the despicable quality of transported convicts destined to be sold for slaves."[3] Elsewhere, Defoe has Colonel Jack sold and put in the field alongside slaves in Virginia, where he "worked hard, lodged hard, and fared hard" in the "miserable condition of a slave."[4]

Nor were these writers alone, for Britons in general spoke of the spirits' victims as "slaves."[5] *The Register Office*, Joseph Reed's popular play produced in London in 1761, features a colonial agent attempting to kidnap an Irishman, who protests against being sent "into the other world to be turn'd into a black negro." And an English newspaper of this time complained that indentured servants were sold in America "for slaves at public sale....They might as well fall into the hands of the Turks, [for] they are subject nearly to the same laws as the Negroes and have the same coarse food and clothing."[6] Such widely disseminated accounts created a distorted view in England of both the number of Britons indentured to American masters and the length and nature of their service.[7] Placing Tom Anderson in lifetime bond-

---

1 *The Vain Prodigal Life*, 23–32, 36; quotations on 23, 31, 36.

2 Moraley, *The Infortunate*, 64, 71, 82, 96–97; quotations on 64, 71.

3 Defoe, *Moll Flanders*, 235.

4 Defoe, *Colonel Jack*, 126–30.

5 Smith, *Colonists in Bondage*, 70, 72.

6 Bailyn, *Voyagers to the West*, chs. 9–10; quotations on 299, 324.

7 For data and reflections on the share of bound laborers in the overall emigrant population, see Bailyn, *Voyagers to the West*, esp. 355. For a further example of this literature from Kimber's day (in addition to the material in Appendix A in this edition), see *The Adventures of a Kid-*

age, then, was misleading, but it was merely an exaggeration of the negative aura surrounding emigration and emigration agents in Kimber's England. Hardly anyone in his audience would have protested his failure to draw a line between colonial servitude and slavery; it was a fine distinction that an unsuspicious public was not disposed to make.

While Kimber uses colonial slavery and tyrannical slave drivers to dramatic effect, it would be hard to brand *Mr. Anderson* as abolitionist or even strongly antislavery. Given its 1754 publication date, it is unreasonable to expect that it would be. No sustained antislavery movement, outside of the crusades of marginal Quaker activists, appeared in the Western world before the era of the American Revolution beginning in the 1760s. Whether in Britain, its colonies, or anywhere else in the world, it was not until the concept of liberty was on every tongue that large numbers of people adjudged slavery an abomination and organized to eradicate it. As historian Christopher Brown has aptly phrased it, "the history of antislavery sentiment before the 1760s is the history of isolated moralists."[1]

Earlier works that may on the surface seem antislavery, therefore, must be read with care. Behn's *Oroonoko*, for instance, is remarkable in part because its hero and heroine are slaves, but no outrage with the institution of slavery per se moves her plot. She is matter-of-fact in her brief allusions to slavery in Africa and the slave trade to West Indian sugar islands.[2] She does present the sale of the heroine as a slave to a distant country as a "cruel sentence, worse than death"; but what makes it so is for a woman of her quality to be sold "like a common slave." The noble hero himself, Oroonoko, can "by no means endure slavery," but has no compunctions about selling his own war captives to an English slave trader or offering to buy his freedom once enslaved either by "gold, or a vast quantity of slaves." Throughout her tale, Behn is careful to distinguish between the "noble slaves"—people "of

---

napped *Orphan* (London, 1747). For another good discussion of Britons' general discomfort with colonial slavery and servitude, see Susan Dwyer Amussen, *Caribbean Exchanges: Slavery and the Transformation of English Society, 1640–1700* (Chapel Hill: U of North Carolina P, 2007).

1   Brown, *Moral Capital*, 37–55; quotation on 40. On this point see also the two masterworks of David Brion Davis: *The Problem of Slavery in Western Culture* (Ithaca, NY: Cornell UP, 1966), and *The Problem of Slavery in the Age of Revolution, 1770–1823* (Ithaca, NY: Cornell UP, 1974).

2   Behn, *Oroonoko*, 78, 82.

quality"—and the common bondsmen, who are "by nature slaves." Oroonoko instigates a slave revolt at the plot's climax, calling his fellow bondsmen's attention to "the miseries, and ignominies of slavery." But he declares their bondage ignominious because they had not been fairly captured in battle.[1] Her sympathy with slave rebels and some of their utterances, taken alone, might hint at an antislavery spirit in Behn's story. However, they are juxtaposed with the notion that most bondspeople are slaves by nature, with the hero's own slave-trading, and with the implication in his oration to fellow slaves that some forms of slavery are perfectly legitimate. In short, the tale's pervading message is that the great injustice was that Oroonoko, and some of his noble associates, were slaves. Her message emphasizes inner nobility wronged more than any notion that slavery itself is wrong.

Similarly, *Mr. Anderson* features some noteworthy passages on slavery which should be read carefully and in context. When Tom and Fanny read Locke during their childhood, for instance, they connect to the natural rights tradition, which enables Tom to conclude that all men are naturally free, and which in later decades nourished abolitionism. Later in the plot Tom plays the liberator when he frees all the servants and slaves of his benefactor Matthewson. Fanny's speech upon seeing a slave brutally whipped places slaves on her own level as fully human. Then there is the role the slave rebellion plays in the climactic scene, which is surely one of the most extraordinary passages in the novel. Having the reader cheer for slave insurgents was potentially subversive (although two *white* men become Fanny's *direct* rescuers, and the uprising does not overthrow slavery). It also demonstrates how alien Kimber's sensibilities were from those of the planters he depicts in such negative terms.[2]

Nevertheless, despite these features, *Mr. Anderson* is no abolitionist tract. As with two of the age's most influential tales of New World slavery, Behn's *Oroonoko* and Richard Steele's "Story of Inkle and Yarico,"[3] the real moral of the story is that slavery is wrong in the specific instance of the hero and/or heroine, but cer-

---

1 Behn, *Oroonoko*, 96–97, 101–3, 105–8, 113, 125–26, 130.

2 Amazing for 1754, this plot device would be remarkable in about any age. Certainly it forms the opposite of such modern tales as the influential 1913 movie *The Birth of a Nation*, in which the Ku Klux Klan saves the damsel in distress.

3 For Steele's story, see Appendix B2.

tainly not in every case. Young Tom's high-flying speech against slavery in Chapter III, as applied in that passage, is a complaint against his own, and his Scottish tutor's former, servitude. Elsewhere, Tom is "overjoyed" when Barlow deems an African slave, rather than himself, the "proper person" to perform so menial a chore as pulling off the master's boots (68). In the world of *Mr. Anderson*, like that of *Oroonoko*, the crying evil is when people of quality enter the degradation of slavery. Even the slave-revolt scene serves the major narrative purpose of freeing Fanny—after which the insurgents are put down by a group of colonists that includes many admirable characters. In sum, slavery in the specific, not the abstract, was what concerned the likes of Kimber and Behn. In the generations following Kimber, abolitionists would use the negative reputation of colonial planters to great effect. The image of the American colonies as a scene of degeneracy helped mobilize Britons in the center of the Empire to oppose the slavery that nurtured such moral conditions.[1] Only in this indirect way did Kimber and his kind contribute to antislavery sentiment in eighteenth-century Britain, a commitment they neither shared nor anticipated.

If *Mr. Anderson* makes any plea in reference to slavery, it is for remedying its abuses. When Tom gains the management of slaves, he exemplifies humane treatment. The slaves respond with love, loyalty, and better work. In Fanny's speech after the brutal whipping of a slave, she calls for slaveholders to give "indulgent kindness," not freedom, to their human property (157). When Barlow sees the light at the end, he does not free his slaves as part of settling his affairs. Indeed, the happy ending for Tom's friend Duncan Murray is to buy "a pretty plantation" and to "stock it," presumably with slave laborers (180). Kind treatment within the system, not the removal of the system itself, is what Kimber preaches. In his ameliorationist attitudes, he followed other British writers, including Defoe, whose Colonel Jack also rises from servitude to mastery and shows the superiority of humanity over brutality in slave management.[2]

Furthermore, Kimber's attitude contains much more distaste for the planters than love for the slaves. The excerpts from his

---

1 Srividhya Swaminathan, "Developing the West Indian Proslavery Position after the Somerset Decision," *Slavery and Abolition* 24 (Dec. 2003): 49–50.

2 Defoe, *Colonel Jack*, 129–58. For an insightful analysis of ameliorationism in *Mr. Anderson*, see Boulukos, *The Grateful Slave*, 120–27.

"Itinerant Observations in America" in Appendix A provide ample evidence of his disdain for colonial planters. They also make clear that he did not relish the presence or even particularly value the lives of the actual black people he encountered in his travels (with the tantalizing exception of the African girl he met in Maryland and lusts after in his poem "Fidenia").[1] In *Mr. Anderson*, Kimber has Tom call Carter's slaves "loathsome" (73). The novel does feature the positive black figure Squanto, but most slaves are more like extras in a movie than fully drawn characters.

All told, then, Kimber's depiction of African slaves in *Mr. Anderson* is essentially consistent with the viewpoints he develops toward other non-British peoples elsewhere in the novel. For his time, he is remarkably progressive; yet he is still very much of his time, maintaining a frequently condescending attitude toward America, a suspicion of the French, a stereotypical view of Native Americans, and an implied belief that Europeans occupy a higher rung on the chain of being than those of African descent. Pinning down Kimber's attitudes, amid all his seeming inconsistencies, is just one of the many things that makes reading *Mr. Anderson* so fascinating an interpretive experience. From this novel, we can also gain new insights into British attitudes toward frontier life in North America and the dynamics of transatlantic exchange during the first half of the eighteenth century. From a literary perspective, in *Mr. Anderson* we can almost witness the English novel evolving before our eyes, striving as this story does to incorporate elements of the seventeenth-century courtly romance, the Defovian tale of global adventure, and the Richardsonian novel of moral sensibility. In an era when general readers and scholars alike are increasingly interested in the roots of modern racial identity, the dynamics of transatlantic exchange, and the heterogeneity of the early novel, the time is right for a serious, interdisciplinary re-engagement with *The History of the Life and Adventures of Mr. Anderson*. We hope, then, that this edition not only does this fascinating novel justice but also enables a new generation of students and scholars to benefit from Kimber's wide-ranging mid-eighteenth-century portrait of the Atlantic world.

---

1 For Kimber's "Fidenia," see Appendix A2.

Edward Kimber: A Brief Chronology

1719 Sept. 17: Born in London to Isaac and Anna Kimber.

1722–27 Isaac Kimber holds a series of appointments as a Baptist minister in London and Nantwich, Cheshire.

1732 Isaac Kimber named editor of the newly founded *London Magazine*. Both Isaac and Edward Kimber would be involved with the magazine for the remainder of their lives.

·1734 Edward publishes his first poem in the *London Magazine*. Other Kimber poems and essays would regularly appear in the magazine in ensuing years.

1742 Sept. 11–Nov. 1: Sails from Gravesend, England, to New York.

    Nov. 13–20: Sails from New York to Maryland's Eastern Shore.

    Nov. 20–25: Travels to Yorktown, Virginia.

    Dec. 23, 1742–Jan. 7, 1743: Sails from Yorktown to St. Simon's Island, Georgia.

1743 Feb.: Joins General James Oglethorpe's Georgia militia.

    Late Feb.–March: Participates in Oglethorpe's raid on the Spanish colony at St. Augustine, Florida.

1744 March: Leaves Oglethorpe's militia.

    April–July: Sails from South Carolina to Scotland and then on to London.

    Late summer: Marries Susanna Anne Lunn of East Keal, Lincolnshire; publishes *A Relation, or Journal, of a Late Expedition to the Gates of St. Augustine, on Florida*.

1744–48 Serves intermittently in the British military.

1745–46 Publishes the essay series "Itinerant Observations in America" in the *London Magazine*.

1748 Feb. 6: First child, Susanna, born (died March 31, 1749).

1750 May 20: Second child, Richard, born (died in 1829); publishes *A Letter from a Citizen of London to his Fellow Citizens…Occasioned by the Late Earthquakes*; publishes his first novel, *The Life and Adventures of Joe Thompson*.

1752   Kimber's mother dies after two decades of severe mental illness.

1752–55   Works part-time as assistant editor at the *Gentleman's Magazine*.

1753   Oct. 2: Third child, Isaac Benjamin, born (died Jan. 15, 1754). The Kimbers apparently had a fourth child, John, for whom no birth or death dates have been located.

1754   Jan.: Publishes *The History of the Life and Adventures of Mr. Anderson*.
Dec.: Publishes *The Life and Adventures of James Ramble*.

1755   Isaac Kimber dies. Edward replaces him as editor of the *London Magazine*.

1756   Publishes *The Juvenile Adventures of David Ranger*.

1758   Publishes *The Life, Extraordinary Adventures, Voyages, and Surprizing Escapes of Capt. Neville Frowde, of Cork*.

1759   Publishes *The Happy Orphans*, a translation of a popular French novel.

1764   Publishes *Maria: The Genuine Memoirs of an Admired Lady of Rank and Fortune*.

1765   Publishes his last novel, *The Generous Briton; or, The Authentic Memoirs of William Goldsmith*.

1769   May 20: Dies in London; buried in the Bunhill Fields burial ground, a London cemetery for religious Nonconformists where John Bunyan, Daniel Defoe, and William Blake are also interred.

Maps

[These maps identify almost all of the places mentioned in the novel and appendices. Those not identified are clarified in notes.]

1. Northwest Europe

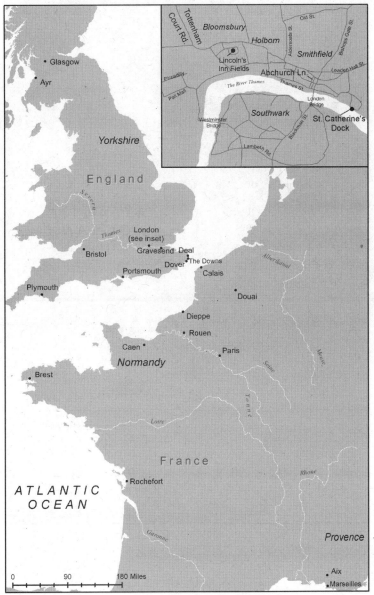

2. Colonial America

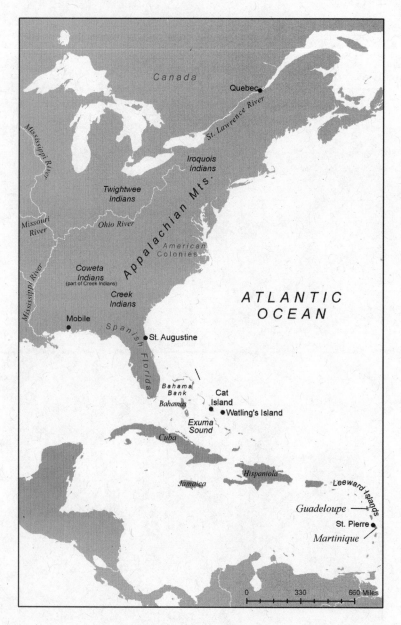

Canada

Quebec

St. Lawrence River

Mississippi River

Iroquois
Indians

Twightwee
Indians

Missouri
River

Ohio River

Appalachian Mts.

American
Colonies

Mississippi River

Coweta
Indians
(part of Creek Indians)

Creek
Indians

ATLANTIC
OCEAN

Mobile

Spanish Florida

St. Augustine

Bahama
Bank

Cat
Island

Bahamas

Watling's Island

Exuma
Sound

Cuba

Hispaniola

Jamaica

Leeward Islands

Guadeloupe

St. Pierre

Martinique

0   330   660 Miles

3. The Chesapeake Region

New Jersey

Maryland

• Annapolis

• Piscataway

Delaware

Worcester County • Senepuxon

• Snow Hill

Accomoco County

Virginia

Chesapeake Bay

• Pungoteague

Rappahannock County

Northampton County

Williamsburg • *Wicomico*

• Jamestown • Yorktown

Magidi Bay

Bay of Kickotan

ATLANTIC OCEAN

North Carolina

0   20   40 Miles

A Note on Eighteenth-Century Currency

When reading past texts with as many monetary references as *Mr. Anderson* has, one question is probably unavoidable: "How much is that worth in 'real' (that is, today's) money?" Attempting equivalencies involves several difficulties, but the naturalness of this question makes it worth exploring.

First, however, a general caveat about what makes this a tricky business. For starters, how much weight a given sum carries in the aggregate can be misleading. Given that the gross national products of Britain, France, Canada, and the United States are so much greater in the early twenty-first century than they were in the eighteenth, unless we appreciate the size of various economic "slices" relative to the entire "pie" we might be inclined to underestimate the value of such large sums. With smaller sums, the best way to measure their relative value is to track the purchasing power of each sum, or how much of various goods it will buy based on economic historians' best estimates of the changing price of, say, a loaf of bread over the centuries.

The conversions that follow come from a few key sources, all of which estimate purchasing power. For conversions of past amounts into current British pounds, we have relied upon the Economic History Association's purchasing power index calculator (available at eh.net). We have based our French conversions on John J. McCusker's *Money and Exchange in Europe and America, 1600–1775* (Chapel Hill: U of North Carolina P, 1978, p. 97), as well as the currency calculator mentioned above.

The charts below offer conversions for all significant monetary amounts mentioned in the text of *Mr. Anderson*. All figures are rounded, so as not to convey an idea that they are absolutely precise. Part of the difficulty with the French conversions is the necessary (but possibly debatable) assumption that Kimber used French rather than Canadian money in his account. These conversions also proceed on the assumption that Kimber used 1754 values even for stories set decades earlier so that his audience could relate to the figures. Given these difficulties, these charts aim only at offering a general sense of how much is involved.

1754 British £	2007 British £	2007 U.S. $
5 pounds, 5 shillings (5 guineas)	£685	$1,370
20	£2,600	$5,200
100	£13,000	$26,000
500	£65,000	$130,000
1,000	£130,000	$260,000
5,000	£650,500	$1,310,000
20,000	£2,600,000	$5,200,000

1754 French livres	2007 British £	2007 U.S. $
100	£570	$1,140
500	£2,850	$5,700
1,000	£5,700	$11,400
60,000	£340,000	$680,000
150,000	£850,000	$1,700,000
800,000	£4,560,000	$9,120,000

A Note on the Text

Between its original 1754 publication and the end of the eighteenth century, Kimber's *The History of the Life and Adventures of Mr. Anderson* appeared in at least six editions.[1] Other than minor variations in style (e.g., "dress'd" becomes "dressed") and formatting, all these editions essentially reprint the first edition faithfully. Given this lack of authorial revisions or significant textual variants, we have used the first printed edition (London: W. Owen, 1754) as our copy-text.

Overall, this Broadview edition strives to reproduce Kimber's text exactly, preserving the sometimes creative spelling and punctuation of the original.[2] For the most part, the first edition of *Mr. Anderson* is quite clean, but in places where obvious spelling or punctuation mistakes occur in the original, we have silently corrected them. The largest editorial liberties we have taken with the text are structural, as we have divided it into chapters (the original runs from beginning to end without interruption) and added most of the paragraph breaks. On this first point, it is useful to remember that when Kimber was writing, the organization of novels into chapters was not nearly as conventional as it is today. Fortunately, *Mr. Anderson* is episodic enough that it lends itself quite readily to chapter divisions, an addition we hope will make the text more accessible for both readers and instructors. As for paragraph breaks, the paragraphing in the original is seemingly haphazard, with breaks gradually becoming less common as the novel progresses. At times in the latter half of the novel especially, single paragraphs often stretch to over five pages. Anticipating that this might quickly prove tiresome for today's readers, we have taken the liberty of regularizing the paragraph breaks. For readers interested in seeing the novel in its pristine original form, a 1975 facsimile of the first edition, published by Garland as part of its "Library of Narratives of North American Indian Captivities" series, is available in many university libraries.

---

1   London: W. Owen, 1754 (1st ed.); London: W. Owen, 1754 (2nd ed.); Dublin: Richard James, 1754; Berwick: W. Phorson and London: B. Law, 1782; London: W. and T. Bailey, ca. 1780–1800; and Glasgow: William Neilson and R. Scott, 1799.

2   This, of course, is hardly particular to Kimber, as prior to the spread of dictionaries in the late eighteenth century, spelling varied widely from book to book.

THE
HISTORY

OF THE
LIFE and ADVENTURES

OF

Mr. *ANDERSON*.

CONTAINING

His ſtrange Varieties of Fortune

I N

EUROPE and AMERICA.

———————————

Compiled from his Own Papers.

———————————

———If there is a Power above us,
And that there is, all Nature cries aloud,
Thro' all her Works, he muſt delight in Virtue,
And that which he delights in muſt be happy. [1]
ADDISON.

———————————

LONDON:
Printed for W. OWEN, at *Homer's-Head*, near
Temple-Bar, 1754.

---

1 Joseph Addison, *Cato, A Tragedy* (1713), V.i.15–18.

CHAPTER I

THOUGH it is the usual custom of the biographer to set forth to his subject by a detail of the family and parentage of his hero; yet my readers will at once perceive that an attempt of that kind, would be unnatural, if not impossible in me; as Mr. *Anderson* plunged into the deepest calamities of life, from being accidentally deprived of that knowledge himself; and, from that fatal cause, experienced a series of misfortunes equally capable of affecting the head and improving the heart. If the narrative I am about to present to the public, insensibly, under the guise of a rational entertainment, steals instruction upon the peruser, and produces benefit to the mind; if it should draw the hard bound tear from the eye of inhumanity; if whilst the souls *that bleed for others' woes, that feel for suffering merit's deep distress*, lend an attentive ear, or eye, to this strange story; it serves to mollify unfeeling, obdurate cruelty, I shall have my wish, and the trouble I have been at to fashion my friend's memoirs, will be well repayed; for I am of the poet's opinion, that

> *One moral, or a mere well natur'd deed,*
> *Does all desert in sciences exceed.*[1]

In a most delightful evening of the month of *May* 1697, a well dress'd man coming from an house in *Portugal-Row* in *Lincoln's Inn Fields*,[2] with an amiably featur'd child in his hand to appearance about seven years of age, made a sudden stop, as if he had forgot somewhat in the house he came from, and saying, *Tommy stay at the door a minute, I'll be back directly*, left him at the gate and returned in doors. This whole action was perceived by a man in a seafaring dress, who had sauntered down the row and who passing the child, and being witness to the circumstance of leaving him, ey'd him with great pleasure, and, chucking[3] him

---

1 John Sheffield, 1st Duke of Buckingham, "On Mr. Pope and His Poems" (1740), ll. 21–22. "Desert" here means excellence or worth.

2 Lincoln's Inn is one of London's four Inns of Court, where aspiring barristers have traditionally gone to be admitted to the bar. The adjacent square, Lincoln's Inn Fields, was widely associated with vagrancy and crime during the late seventeenth and early eighteenth centuries. For this and other specific locations mentioned in the novel, see the maps on pp. 37-39.

3 Gently nudging.

under the chin, asked him if that was his pappa, who was just gone in, to which the innocent pratler[1] answered yes, and, unused to so rough a voice, fell a crying.

The enquirer then left him and walked to some distance, but finding the father did not return so suddenly as he expected, and that no servant came out to him, he again walked towards the child, and told him he would carry him to his pappa, who was gone out another way, upon which he very willingly gave him his hand. For some minutes he walked slowly, still looking for the father's appearance; but, perceiving, when he got to the end of the row, that the coast continued clear, he took him up in his arms, and hasted out of the fields as expeditiously as his legs would carry him. The few people that were passing and repassing, it may be supposed were either too intent upon their own affairs to take notice of these incidents, or else imagined the seaman had some acquaintance with the child, or his parents; or if otherwise, might be of that class of mortals who would not turn out of their ways or busy their heads to do a humane or charitable action, where the least trouble or difficulty attended it; contenting themselves with this merciless adage, *People must take care of their own — I have enough to do to mind one*; for such wretches really exist in human shape.

The fellow hasted through the city, soothing the infant with tarts, apples and other trash,[2] which he bought as he went along, and with the repeated assurances of bringing him to his pappa, for whom he often enquired with a whimpering tone; by which devices he kept him pretty quiet till he came to his rendesvouz in St. *Catharine*'s,[3] where he pretended that it was a child of a relation, that was going with him to *Bristol*,[4] for which place he was to set off the very next morning; but notwithstanding all the arts he made use of, and the assistant sollicitude of his land-lady and her people, the poor innocent cry'd most piercingly till weariness closed his eyes, and left him in the quiet custody of ruder hands than ever before he seemed to have experienced the touch of. As soon as the morning dawned, he was carried on board a small

---

1 Youngster.
2 Cheap treats.
3 The St. Katharine Docks on the banks of the Thames near the Tower of London were widely associated with overcrowding, poverty, and crime.
4 This city in southwestern England was a thriving hub of Great Britain's involvement in both the African slave trade and the trade in colonial servants.

coasting vessel, in which his present possessor was a passenger, which quickly unmoored and stood seaward.

The floating, volatile ideas of children, soon shift and change from one object to another; their loves and aversions arrive to no degree of steadiness, before reason begins to dawn upon their minds, and, consequently, as all the contrivances were made use of to keep him in good humour, during the passage of only three days, he was brought to the intended port pleased and contented, and still buoy'd up with the promise of seeing his pappa, whom he now and then faintly enquired after, and his mamma, whom he three or four times mentioned, during the voyage.

Dreadful, no doubt, was the situation of the unfortunate parents of the unhappy boy. Can paternal or maternal tenderness receive a greater pain than such an uncertain privation, perhaps of an only, fondly beloved pledge of mutual affection? would not an assurance of death — the following him to the grave, have been infinitely more tolerable, than the thousand heart-breaking, anxious fears, that tortured their souls in the perplexing doubts of the hands their child had fallen into, the usage he had or was likely to meet with? but we must leave them to their killing anguish, and to prayers to the protector of innocence, and return to our young adventurer.

The man who had thus kidnapp'd this little cherub was the master of a vessel belonging to *Bristol*, then lying in *Kingroad*[1] bound to the coast of *Guinea*,[2] upon the slave trade, and had taken a sudden trip to *London*, to consult with one of his owners[3] there, upon some matters relating to his voyage; he was a single man, and having no house or lodgings on shore, repaired, upon his arrival, on board his own vessel, with poor *Tommy*, whom he destined for his companion and bedfellow, in the long and unhealthy voyage which he was going. He had all the roughness and brutality usual to his profession, mingled, however, with an insinuating air, that was the process of an abominable vice, that I must too soon be obliged to hint at. As to his principles, I shall not need to describe them; the facts, that will follow will afford

---

1 A sheltered place in the River Severn near Bristol where ships could anchor. It was one of two main places of this sort where ships anchored while waiting to fill up with bound laborers headed for the colonies.

2 A generic term for the West African coast from which Europeans drew most of their African slaves.

3 That is, one of the owners of the ship who employed this man as its captain.

sufficient portrait of them to my readers. Still he continued highly to caress and fondle his little messmate, by which means he in a manner obliterated all the remaining traces of his parents, and soon brought him to call him by the endearing appellation of his pappa; so that, bating[1] the little sickness of his former voyage, after having proper necessaries and linnen provided for him as a child of the captain's relation, he felt no other uneasiness, and the ship set sail, whilst he diverted himself in the round house with the toys that had been given him for that purpose.

Hitherto, the reader will be apt to imagine that the captain had conceived a sudden fondness for this child at first sight, from a view of his enchanting countenance which was continu'd by farther knowledge of his pretty society; a desire solely to breed him up as his own, and to supply the defect of offspring, without the cares or turmoils of matrimony, at the expence only of making a family miserable; contenting himself with the salvo[2] of supplying the tenderness of the parents, by his own. Such instances perhaps may be produced; but this alas! was far from being one of them. *Tom* was, though small of stature for his age, and backward in his speech, of a most exact proportion of body, and a charming symmetry of features, and by his dress and behaviour, evidenced his being born of parents above the common rank, his eyes were black, and already, his hair of the same hue, hung in tresses curling in his neck, his skin was fair as alabaster, and his little plump lips and cheeks were like roses: a painter could not have had a finer original to have copied a *Cupid* from, or a statuary to form one of those cherubs that are seen hovering over the monuments of the departed great and good.

When some few days had passed, and the distance from any superior authority left this wretch tyrant of his wooden world, without appeal or controul, and *Tom* had, in some measure, conquered the sickness of this unusual element, he began to treat him in the villainous manner, for which he had reserved him; to make him the subject of the worst, most shocking and most unnatural lust. The poor child much injured, much abused, soon lost his colour and complexion; but innocent and ignorant of any ill, but the pain he suffered, upon the least complaint was severely whipp'd, under the notion of illness none of the ship's crew were permitted to see him, and he was kept closely confined in

---

1 Except.
2 A saving clause, or justification.

Williamson's state room,[1] for that was his tormentor's name, which ever will be remembered with the infamy it deserves.

CHAPTER II

We must not expect that all seeing Providence should, according to our expectations, always punish even the most degrading and abominable crimes:

> *The ways of heaven are dark and intricate,*
> *Puzzled with mazes, and perplex'd with errors:*
> *Our understanding traces them in vain,*
> *Lost and bewilder'd in the fruitless Search;*
> *Nor sees with how much art the windings run,*
> *Nor where the regular confusion ends.*[2]

The success of a voyage that one would imagine would have been disappointed by thunder from heaven, of a ship that seemed marked for the blast of avenging lightning, from the divine displeasure, was so extraordinary, that they completed their lading[3] of slaves in less than six weeks, and safely arrived at *Sene-puxon* inlet in *Maryland*,[4] where *Williamson* disposed of his cargo to advantage, and had almost completed his returns for *Europe*, before he determined the fate of the hapless boy.

By this time, he had completed his eighth year, and though so cruelly treated, so wickedly robbed of the instructions and cares of his parents, discovered a promising genius, and a softness and good nature of disposition, that would have melted any heart, but that of the villain who had him in his power; but he was grown pale, thin and emaciated, and his condition threatened no great number of additional days to his existence. To this state of his health he owed his deliverance; the brute, who was actuated by avarice as well as worse passions, apprehending he would die at sea, determined to make money of this innocent venture, before his departure, and accordingly agreed with an eminent planter to dispose of his future liberty for the sum of 10 *l*. ster-

---

1   The captain's chambers on a ship.
2   Joseph Addison, *Cato, A Tragedy* (1713), I.i.49–54.
3   Loading the ship.
4   The town of Senepuxon (or, more commonly, "Sinepuxent") was destroyed in a hurricane in 1818 and never rebuilt.

ling,[1] which the planter was the more ready to pay, as he had an only daughter of near the same age, on whom his pride and vanity told him, he would be a very ornamental attendant.

Williamson did shew so much humanity and shew of conscience as to persuade him to be kind to him, telling him he was the son of an unfortunate relation, that he had bred as his own, and with whom he would not have parted, could he have dealt as well by him on shipboard, or had he a settlement at home to fix him at. By these means poor *Tommy* shifted masters, and was delivered to Mr. *Barlow*, for that was his present patron's name, who was a man of large possessions, the lord of many thousand acres and of several hundred slaves;[2] but as to his disposition, full as base and wicked as *Williamson*. *Tommy* was had to his house, and received by Mrs. *Barlow* and her little daughter *Fanny*, with delight and tenderness, and in a few days discovered his perfect recovery, the benefit he received from the air, and his distance from the wretch who had near destroyed him, and from whom, so sensible the little fellow was grown, he parted without the semblance of a tear.

Barlow who was concerned in *Williamson*'s cargo did not accompany his purchase to his house, which was near twenty miles from the sea; but stay'd tipling[3] on board, and at the neighbouring plantations with the captain, till he was ready to proceed

---

1 For approximations of how much the various monetary references in *Mr. Anderson* are worth in today's currency, see the Note on Eighteenth-Century Money on p. 41. Here and below "l." is an abbreviation for pounds, the principal unit of British currency.

2 This level of land and slave holdings was very unlikely in the colonial Chesapeake. On average even the very elite, known as "great planters," held 3,000 acres and 80 slaves (140 counting "back plantations" [see n. 1 on p. 79]). Only a dozen individuals held 300 or more slaves, and none held more than a thousand. The largest slave-owner in eighteenth-century Chesapeake, however, with 785 slaves, was Charles Carter, and the extended Carter clan held "the wealthiest family estate." These numbers come from the 1780s, and the size of property holdings had declined somewhat from earlier in the century. But it is still true for the entire eighteenth century that, as Jackson T. Main explains, it is "not accurate to speak even of these wealthiest Virginians [or Marylanders] as owning 'hundreds' of slaves" ("The One Hundred," *William and Mary Quarterly* 3 [1954]: 354–84). Given that the Carters' wealth far outpaces that of the Barlows, the Barlows may still be "great planters" but they were obviously not meant by Kimber to be at the top of that category.

3 Drinking liquor.

on his voyage. In one of these drunken bouts, as is often the case, both rogues alike and birds of a feather, they began to crack[1] of the many arts they had practiced to defraud in traffick, and, from thence, to brag of the various enormities they had been guilty of, in the gratification of their passions, with impunity. *Williamson* scorned to be outdone, and layed him a wager that he had got money that voyage, by a method the cunningest *Marylander* had never thought of, and, in fine, betrayed the whole secret of poor *Tommy*'s capture, defying *Barlow* to match it with a stroke of so much *éclat*.[2] *Barlow* at first was somewhat shock'd, and damn'd his companion for a miscreant and a villain; but soon join'd him in his laugh upon the occasion, and agreed to applaud it as a masterpiece, concluding — well d—n me, perhaps he'll make as good a man under me as he would at home. As soon as *Williamson* sailed, the righteous planter returned home; but before we enter the house with him, let us take a survey of the treatment *Tommy* received before his arrival.

Mrs. *Barlow* was a woman of sense and humanity, of many extraordinary endowments, and a mother; she was surprized that there could be persons so hard hearted to sell innocent and helpless infancy, to perpetual servitude; when perhaps, as ills are common to all alike, and the most affluent may meet with a reverse of fortune, their own children might be exposed to the merciless hands of strangers. This was the reflexion she made at the first sight of the helpless boy; but, when his spirits were a little revived, he appeared so lively and of so amiable a temper, that, before the return of her husband, he had made such a quick progress in her affections, she began to look upon him, even with the tenderness of a mother, which was sensibly encreased by her *Fanny*'s fondness for her new playmate, who could not bear him out of her sight, and for whom he seemed to have contracted an equal affection.

Indeed, bating the difference of sex, they were so alike, now *Tommy* had recovered from his usage and fatigues, that every body were surprized at it, and pronounced, if they had not been certain of the contrary, they should have believed them twins from the same womb. *Fanny*, as to temper, had all her mother, but nothing of her father about her, and, as the plantations lie pretty wide from each other, and the prudence of her mother had

---

1 Boast.
2 Daring.

kept her from any intercourse with the children of their *Negroes*, she had seen few white children, and consequently was still the more pleased with *Tommy*'s company.

For a fortnight, thus all was happiness with him, at the expiration of which time, *Barlow* arrived, and his spouse and daughter ran to the door to meet him; but I must assure my reader, that it was in token of respect, not of affection; for he had ever behaved to this amiable wife and child with a moroseness very near bordering upon ill usage and brutality; so that they looked upon him with a kind of fear and trembling, whenever he was at home, and yet *Fanny* could not help crying, Pappa, see, here's *Tommy* — my pretty *Tommy* at play with me! for this was the only name he went by, and immediately took him by the hand to bring him forward; upon which her father exclaimed, G—d d—n me, madam, I sent this brat as a servant for your girl, not as a companion — let loose his hand you little b—h — fine work truly — get you gone sirrah[1] into the kitchen.

Fanny and her partner looked earnestly upon Mrs. *Barlow*, and fell a crying; and poor *Tommy* remembering the old discipline of the whip, innocently fell upon his knees, and with his little hands uplifted, begged pardon, and said he would do so no more — Pray don't whip me! — Mrs. *Barlow*, quite melted at this sight, took them both in her arms, with the tears standing in her eyes, saying, for God sake, Mr. *Barlow*, don't frighten the children so — don't speak so roughly to 'em — can't you soften those ungracious features for once? You may be damn'd, and they too — my will shall be obey'd — and so surlily passed 'em, and walked into the parlour, where the taking off his boots gave time to the good woman to sooth *Tommy*, and carry him into the kitchen, to the care of a female servant, from whence she could hardly get her daughter away without him, to go with her to attend this piece of wedded inhumanity.

The servant's name was *Molly Beedle*, a native of *Bristol*, and remarkably fond of children; and, indeed, in everything else of a disposition that merited a better fate, than to have been indented[2] to such a master; so that she took great care of *Tommy*, and dried up his tears, but could not prevent his looking often anxiously towards the house, and asking for his mamma and

---

1 "A term of address used to men or boys, expressing contempt, reprimand, or assumption of authority on the part of the speaker" (*OED*).
2 Indentured.

sister; for so the good Mrs. *Barlow* had instructed him to call them, and praying her not to let that great angry man carry him away and whip him. Mean time, *Barlow*, having a little recovered from his ill temper, began, all at once, to tell his wife the story he had learned from *Williamson* of *Tommy* — concluding with— D—n me he'll be better done by here than at home, perhaps — some beggar's brat I suppose — but, by G—d, never was so bare-faced, so impudent an affair executed before — D—n me, he beats me all to pieces — d—n me if he don't. —

The poor woman was so overcome with this execrable narra-tion, that she was ready to faint; and, as soon as her tears would permit utterance, she cried, Good God! is it possible that you can treat so ludicrously, so base, so criminal an action? Oh Mr. *Barlow*, you have a child of your own — if please God, our head were laid,[1] what miseries may she not be subject to — gracious heaven! what must be the sufferings of his poor parents! — dear infant! — how ill has he been treated — Lord avert from me and mine, the judgments this husband has called upon us, by being privy to this damnable deed, and not stopping the rascal who committed it, for punishment; but I am resolved to make him amends — I'll consider him as my own — he shall however feel the tenderness of a mother. D—n your preaching, the brute returned — he's my slave for life, and a good bargain he'll be — where's *Fanny*! —

Fanny indeed was gone slily out of the room, and Mrs. *Barlow* suspecting where, ran into the kitchen (which in *America* is gen-erally distant from the house) where she found her daughter with her arms round *Tom*'s neck, and his round her's, kissing each other, and heard her say at her entrance, Pappa shan't beat you, *Tommy!* — he shall beat me — and him reply — no not beat you — beat me before! Charm'd as she was at the sight, she was obliged to give him a sudden kiss, and tearing *Fanny* from him, returned with her to her father, who shaking her rudely by the arm, said, Hussy, how dare you go away the minute I came in — I'll knock your brains out if you do so again! Pappa, she inno-cently reply'd, I only went to see my *Tommy* brother — shall I go and fetch him here too? —

This pretty speech quite irritated her father, who getting up, cried, Oh, by G—d, I'll soon see your *Tommy*, and snatching a cow-skin up (a twisted thong with which they usually discipline

---

1 If God wills we should die.

their *Negroes*) stalk'd away to look for the innocent victim of his fury; but *Molly* perceiving him coming, clap'd him into a cupboard, bidding him not speak, by which his search was eluded, and he returned, cursing and swearing, into the house, that he had given so much money for him — adding, D—n me, if I wanted children, I can get 'em myself fast enough — but I'll work his buff,[1] I warrant him — he shall learn to hoe very soon — I'll punish you and your daughter for your fondness, I say I will!

He continued raving thus for the remainder of the evening, till weariness closed his eyes, and removed him to bed before his usual time, on occasion of his coming off a journey and hard drinking; and, as soon as he was fast, Mrs. *Barlow* went into the kitchen with *Fanny* to see the little prisoner, who soon forgot his frights in their embraces: she told *Molly* the story, and consulted with her how to dispose of him the next day, till she should have time to bring her husband into a better temper in regard to him; and they agreed, the best method was to send him to one *Ferguson*'s, who had formerly been their servant; but at the expiration of his time, had set up for himself in a small neighbouring plantation, where he also practiced the business of a surgeon[2] and schoolmaster, and had lately been talked of by *Barlow* to instruct his daughter in reading and writing. This was immediately put in execution, after many tears shed by *Fanny* and *Tommy* at their separation. The honest *Scotchman* received him with great readiness and good nature, saying, at first sight, he was a lovely boy: and here we must leave him for the present, to see how his absence worked upon his patron, and what steps were taken to soften his severity.

The first thing he enquired after in the morning was *Tom*, which gave occasion to Mrs. *Barlow* to remonstrate against his unreasonable severity and antipathy towards the poor child, who had never offended him; and to beseech, in the most winning manner, that he would consider his misfortune, and the misfortune of his parents, and be rather a father to him than a tyrant. Little *Fanny*, who was present, and lent an attentive ear to every word, inforced what her mother said, by falling upon her knees, and praying her father to let him live with her, for indeed she loved him better than herself. This action, so enchantingly pretty in the lovely maid, had, for some moments, an effect upon his mind, and he surlily replied, that he might play with her; but she

---

1 Bare skin.
2 In this usage, a general practitioner of medicine.

must look upon him as her servant more than her companion, and promised he would neither threaten nor beat him, if they did not spoil him; upon which promise, whilst he rid out to view his grounds, *Tommy* was sent for home by *Molly Beedle*, who found *Ferguson* very loth to part with him, he had gained already such an hold in his affection. Mrs. *Barlow* taught the little cunning folks how they should behave to each other; and they obeyed her lessons so well, that whenever the husband appeared, miss shewed an haughty distance, and *Tom* a lowly reverence and respect; but never were happier than when he was out of their way, and they could indulge their innocent familiarities with each other.

Three years passed on thus, without any sinister accident to this young adventurer; in which time the good Mrs. *Barlow* had learnt her daughter, and, by stealth, poor *Tom* to read, very prettily. The vanity of the planter had imposed a livery[1] upon him, and, as well as his young mistress, he daily improved in wit and beauty, and was the admiration of all that saw him; and so tenderly fond he grew of *Fanny* and her mamma, as to change countenance upon the least complaint they either of them made; nay, so respectfully humble was he to *Barlow* himself, that he frequently, surlily, bestowed the epithet of good boy upon him, which was equal to any commendatory phrase he ever used to his daughter herself.

Mrs. *Barlow* had forbidden every body to mention to him, for it had been whispered about, the story of *Williamson*'s treachery, fearing it might make too deep an impression upon the softness of his temper; and as she was a woman of the best descent in *Maryland*, and had been well educated; she also had a pretty female collection of the politest authors, in whom *Fanny* and *Tom* amused themselves so much, that their ideas of men and things began to open surprisingly; and after having exhausted all this stock of knowledge, they thirsted for more, which a very fortunate accident soon supplied them with.

Mr. *Gordon*, a *Scotch* clergyman, and missionary for some years at a neighbouring town, happened to pay Mr. *Barlow* a visit; and being mighty fond of children, having none of his own, took a prodigious liking to miss and her pretty attendant, who had now both reached their ninth year.[2] One evening Mrs. *Barlow*

---

1 A suit of servant's clothing.

2 Clearly an oversight on Kimber's part, as two paragraphs earlier he has told us that three years have passed since the then-eight-year-old Tom arrived in Maryland.

was lamenting her misfortune in not having a better collection of books, and telling her assistant that her children, as she called them, had exhausted her stock: upon this he answered, that he had brought a tolerable library into the country, and had since much enlarged it by orders from *England*, and promised to let them have one by one his whole riches, as their encreasing years fitted them for their perusal; and, knowing *Barlow*'s temper, told her he wished they were to be sent to *Ferguson*, for instruction, by whose means they might be qualified in such sciences as were more immediately necessary to the offices of life, and thro' whose hands they might receive the promised treasure, without suspicion.

In short, he proposed the matter to Mr. *Barlow*, at supper, who readily agreed his daughter should go over every day, to learn to write and cast accompts,[1] the only qualifications he had any notion of the necessity of; but not a word of poor *Tom*, of whose being able to read he was still ignorant. This however was sufficient; and, as *Tom* was to accompany his young mistress, by the liberality of Mrs. *Barlow*, he could not fail of reaping the same advantages. In a few days then, they began their visits to Mr. *Ferguson*'s, twice a day, and very frequently staid there a whole week together, which was rendered still the more pleasing to them, as *Tom*'s old friend *Molly Beedle* had near twelve months before been married to their master at the expiration of her time;[2] so that here they experienced all the tenderness of a father and mother, and all the freedom their innocent affection made desirable.

Mrs. *Barlow* was over and above liberal to the good folks, not only paying extraordinarily for the instructions given to her adopted son, and for their casual board, but also sending daily presents for the care and pleasure they seemed to take of their charge. *Ferguson* and his spouse grew tenderly fond of them, and they returned it by the like affection, and when they staid away for ever so short a time, even shed tears of joy at their arrival. *Barlow* himself never troubled his head about them, contenting himself with the report of his wife, as to his daughter's proficiency; for he had little notion of the necessity of knowledge himself, as he could but just write his name mechanically, and consequently was somewhat excusable in thinking any instruction for *Tom* of no manner of service. Mr. *Gordon* frequently

---

1 Keep accounts.
2 At the end of her term of indentured servitude.

remembered his promise, and by this means *Tom* and his mistress became conversant with, by degrees, and could talk upon most topics with ease and grace; nor did the good clergyman forget to instill into their minds the principles of religion and morality, which took so deep root, as no after misfortune of their lives could ever tempt them to violate.

CHAPTER III

Thus, four years winged their round; in which time, under the notion of only learning to write and cast accompts, *Fanny* became the most accomplished maid in *Maryland*; and poor *Tom*, who was supposed by *Barlow* to still be as ignorant as himself, became a proficient in *Latin* and *French*, in all the useful branches of *mathematics*, spoke and wrote correctly and elegantly, and acquired such additions to his native dignity of soul and sentiment, that Mrs. *Barlow*, and even Mr. *Ferguson* and Mr. *Gordon* stood amazed at him. He had indeed nothing to complain of but the frowns of his master, the concealment he was obliged to make of his perfections, and the degrading dress he wore; in which, however, he appeared as handsome as a *Ganymede*,[1] and said frequently, he thought it the most honorable livery in the world, as it betokened his servitude to his lovely *Fanny*, whose livery he hoped to wear to the end of his life. *Fanny* grew so lovely and charming, that her fame reached far and near, and the sons of many wealthy planters began to speak of her as the most desirable match in the colony.

One day the amiable mistress and her servant, sitting, after supper, with the people to whom *Tom* owed so much; he surprized them with the following address. Dear sir, to whom I have so many obligations, I have often been ruminating within myself, what could oblige persons of so much merit, to forsake their native skies, to partake of the toils of servitude in this country; which, tho' now happily overpast, yet you are far from being in the station of life for which providence seemed to intend you. I love you both, to such a degree as seldom children love their parents, and long to know, and so does this excellent mistress of mine, thro' what disasters you came to *Maryland*, where good sense, learning, and politeness seem not to be in so much request as I understand they are in *Europe*; but what do I ask? perhaps I

---

1   A beautiful Trojan boy whom Zeus made his cupbearer.

am going to call up a number of griefs, that may give you pain to remember, without, alas! the most distant prospect of being of the least future service to you; however, dear Mr. and Mrs. *Ferguson*, here is this charming young lady will, no doubt, one day or other, have it in her power to recompence your worth, and perhaps may remember how much she also owes you on account of her servant; and haply,[1] for I have too much awe before my dear mother to make her such a request, you may be able to inform me how I came to be so nobly and tenderly used by her, to have, thro' her cares, the stores of wisdom opened to me, and to be treated by her, and her lovely daughter with such affection, whilst my master treats me with superior disdain and contempt: for my part, I remember no more of myself before I came to *Maryland*, than that I made a long voyage, in which I was barbarously used by a man, whose looks I shall never forget, and whom I believed to be my father; but who, from the treatment I see other children meet from their parents, I now imagine to have been my worst enemy.

I am sensible I am now in the condition of a slave; but how can that be, for I could never dispose of myself, and you have told me, no man is lord of another's liberty; that we are all naturally born free, and, as *Englishmen*, have an excellent constitution that protects every individual in his freedom.[2] These are matters my young lady and I have been often dwelling upon, and have both agreed that only you can set us right. To her I am proud to be a slave and an attendant; but I have a conscious dignity of principle, that tells me I have an equal right to all the blessings of providence with my neighbours, and, except the offspring of love and gratitude, which I owe only to five persons living, that I know of, am neither naturally nor legally obligated to serve any man on earth, unless he can prove that I voluntarily made myself his property, by contract or indenture.

Never was surprize and astonishment equal to *Ferguson* and his wife's, at the conclusion of this sensible speech, the matter of which these two young folks had been debating between themselves some days before, and had agreed to recur to them for explication. *Fanny* inforced the request with her intreaties, and, in short, they were quite at a loss what to do; however, to give

---

1 Perhaps.
2 A reiteration of the English philosopher John Locke's theory of liberty and slavery in *Two Treatises of Government* (see Appendix C.2). That Tom has been reading Locke is made clear on p. 68 below.

time for recollection, as to the latter and more important affair, Mr. *Ferguson* began to break silence, in this manner, with the tears standing in his eyes. My amiable pupils, I can deny you nothing, and though the relation of the incidents of my life will recall many melancholy ideas to my mind, yet you shall be gratified in the rehearsal of them; and without stop continued, I was born at *Air*[1] in *Scotland*, where my father was minister, from whom, and an endearing mother, myself and a brother received all the instruction that our years required; for, before I had reached my ninth, or he his seventh year, providence thought fit to deprive us of them by death.

An uncle took us under his roof, who behaved with great affection to us, and, having no children of his own, determined to make us equal sharers of his fortune, which was near two thousand pounds sterling, acquired in trade, which now in the decline of life, he had quitted for retirement and rural enjoyments. When I became of proper age, I was sent to the university of *Glasgow*, whilst my brother was put 'prentice to a master of a vessel trading to *Virginia*, the sea being the element he chose to seek his fortune upon. I went thro' my studies with approbation, became a graduate, and, at the usual time, quitted the university, to return to my uncle's, who proposed to me the practice of *physic*,[2] for which indeed I was well qualified, having directed my researches more into that science than any other.

In short, I became a successful practitioner, but soon experienced it was all I had to trust to, for my uncle becoming, though near seventy, enamoured of a young woman in our neighbourhood, of more policy[3] than honesty, he was forced, as the first step to so unnatural an union, to jointure her[4] in the whole of his fortune. I remonstrated against this instance of dotage[5] so warmly, that he was never reconciled to me afterwards, and as to my new aunt, she pursued me with an inveteracy that proved in the end my ruin. Thus I experienced, that to oppose the favourite passions or opinions, even of a man of sense and virtue, in other things, is the most impolitic step a young man can take, at his first entrance into the world. I felt the loss of my uncle's table very much; for the fees of a physician being but small in that part of

---

1 This town's name is also spelled "Ayr," which is the spelling used on the map in this edition.
2 Medicine.
3 Deviousness or shrewdness.
4 To give her joint ownership of his property.
5 Either foolish affection or advancing senility.

the kingdom, I could scarce support myself without his usual assistance; and, as an addition to my chagrin, I soon after received the melancholy news that my brother was drowned in his sixth voyage, homeward, being then first mate of the vessel, and in such credit with the owners, as made it believed he would have the command of a ship the next trip.

A year, however, I weather'd my situation; but at the end of that time, my uncle dying, his rapacious widow sued me for a debt of two hundred pounds, which she found my bond for in her husband's escrutore,[1] and which he had, at the time, taken such security for, only, as he said, to make me diligent in my business, and respectful to him. In litigating this affair, I disturbed my head, neglected my practice, and made away with all I had; and, at last, to avoid a gaol,[2] was obliged to fly to *London*, where, notwithstanding my knowledge and my profession, and a recommendatory letter or two, I was forced to subsist, as long as I could, by the meanest applications, and at length my sordid appearance exposed me to all the distresses and miseries of want and poverty.

I grew desperate — at home my landlady allowed me no repose, and two or three other creditors joined in her perpetual clamour. You'll think it strange, that in a city, such as you have heard *London* is, a man of any talents could be so reduced; but let me tell you, if a man cannot make a respectable appearance, or is not bred to some servile employment, he may rot, starve and die, as well there as in the most wild parts of *America*. Few are the humane and charitable, and those subject to so many impositions as to be rendered very slow and cautious, and, as to the generality, they are employed in raising their own families and friends, and can spare little time, from the bustle and hurry of their affairs, to think of the *mercies* so strongly said by our blessed Saviour to be due to our fellow creatures, in affliction, and which, indeed, he has made one condition of their enjoyment of future happiness.

I had now neither money, friends, food, scarcely raiment, and not a moment's peace; but indeed the want of the first included all the rest — a ship was put up at the exchange for *Maryland*, in which servants of any profession were invited to a passage, upon indenting themselves to the captain or agent for five years. I happened to see the bill in one of my hungry melancholy walks — in

---

1 A type of writing desk often used to safeguard important documents.
2 A variant spelling of "jail."

short, I obeyed the direction, and as I understood both physic and surgery, was soon engaged as a very necessary man, both in the passage and in the country; had a sum advanced me, which sufficed to pay all my little debts, which my principles directed me to do, rather than to indulge myself in any superfluity; and, in short, I embarked, sailed with the first fair wind, and arrived in this part of the colony, whither the ship was bound; and there, by way of bargain and sale, fell into Mr. *Barlow*'s hands.

Excuse me, dear miss, his behaviour was so rough and boisterous, that, for some time, I endured all the miseries of subjection; but after he found me useful in curing diseases that had for some time infected his *Negroes*, he began to use me in a milder sort, and the perpetual goodness of your dear mamma I shall never forget, nor ever be able to repay. By the time my obligation expired, I had so much his good graces, that he put me into a small plantation, which my industry, in raising tobacco, and my exercise of the two professions of physic and surgery, and now and then turning tutor to the neighbouring children, has enabled me to call my own, and to improve, and, since I am happy in the wife I have chosen, here shall I set up my rest, never more think of returning to my native country; but endeavour to do all the kind offices within my sphere of action, and make my future peace with a *Being* that none of us lives a moment without offending.

The adventures of my spouse, in which you also interest yourselves, may be related in fewer words, as I have had them from herself. Her father was a tradesman at *Bristol*; and, tho' a good sort of man, failed in the world, and made his exit in the prison there, through the merciless principles of revenge, of a few creditors, who yet were church goers, and every day repeated, *Forgive us our debts, as we forgive our debtors.*[1] Her unhappy mother broke her heart at the sad catastrophe of her husband, and poor *Molly* was left to the care of their parish; tho' she had some relations that could well have provided for her, had they had either christianity or humanity. In the hopeful seminary, a parish workhouse,[2] of which you can neither of you have any idea; but in

---

1 From the Lord's Prayer in Jesus' Sermon on the Mount (see Matthew 6:12).

2 Parish workhouses were part of the Poor Law, a system of relief for paupers and vagrants which dated back to Elizabethan times. Under the Poor Law in operation in Kimber's day, each parish collected a tax from the better-off to provide for the paupers in that parish. Kimber's view of the Poor Law as a ramshackle, niggardly system run by corrupt officers was common for this time.

short, upon which, the money collected in each parish, would produce happiness and frugal plenty to the miserable, if the guttling[1] of officers and committeemen, the embezzlement of collectors, and the extortion of the keepers, did not make misery more wretched: I say, in this hopeful place, she passed the first years of her life, in which nothing but a good natural understanding, and some innate principles of virtue, could have protected her from vice and debauchery. She was afterwards bound out an apprentice, to houshold drudgery, to a devotee in the same city, who daily humbled herself at church, and returned from thence to ill-use and plague her family.

Her treatment, by this piece of sanctity, was so hard and rigorous, that she could bear it no longer, and took the same course to be relieved from it, that I did to escape starving. She arrived safely here, was also bound to Mr. *Barlow*, and being solely under the direction of your good mother, weathered her term with much less oppression than servants ever feel in this colony. I shall make it the study of my life to recompence all her former sufferings, and at this time — tenderly as I love her — cannot help shedding tears, of anguish, over an innocent creature, who was born in distress — nursed in poverty — educated in slavery — and all without any crime of her own; but merely from the misfortunes of her parents — but all these things prove a future state — where matters will be made even — *where the wicked cease from troubling, and the weary be at rest.*[2]

Had it not been for that sweet, supporting hope, the extremity of despair, in which I have often been involved, would have tempted me to lay violent hands upon myself; for

> —*Who would bear the whips and the scorns of times,*
> *Th' oppressor's wrong, the proud man's contumely,*[3]
> *The insolence of office, and the spurns*
> *That patient merit of the unworthy takes?*
> *When as himself might his* quietus[4] *make,*
> *With a bare bodkin.*[5] *Who would fardels*[6] *bear,*

---

1 Gluttony.
2 A biblical description of heaven from Job 3:17.
3 Scornful abuse.
4 "Discharge or release from life; death, or that which brings death" (*OED*).
5 A mere dagger.
6 Burdens.

To sweat and groan under a weary life;
But, that the dread (as well as hope) *of something after death,*

—————— ————— ————— —————

—— *Puzzles the will;*
And makes us rather bear those ills we have,
Than fly to others (or, forfeit that good) *that we know not of.*[1]

And thus, my dear *Tommy*, you have had our disastrous story; but if I can at all read the destiny of persons, from their ways of acting and thinking, for all others are pretending and fallacious, for you, are reserved, by heaven, happier and smoother hours, and uninterrupted content: 'tis true, you have been hitherto unhappy in the want of knowing your parents; but except that, and the sourness of Mr. *Barlow*, which is his natural disposition, you have met in his wife and daughter, all that can make you amends for these misfortunes, and in me and Mrs. *Ferguson*, and Mr. *Gordon*, friends that love and esteem your opening worth.

As to the story of your being brought to *Maryland*, your good mother has ever enjoined secresy to us both, no doubt for just reasons, and to her we must therefore refer you for it: mean time, I shall not disguise my sentiments; but tell you, that I think you were born free, and are free; but that, in respect to your worthy mother and sister, here, you ought not yet to assert that freedom, as it would produce much disturbance in their family. Here he ceased, and from the tender, sympathizing hearts of his young auditors, redoubled sighs proceeded, and tears trickled from their mournful eyes. In this attitude, Mrs. *Barlow*, who had taken a ride over on purpose to see her friends, as she stiled them, and her little folks, found them at her entrance, and was quite struck at the sight; but Mr. *Ferguson* soon relieved her astonishment, by telling her his pupils had made him relate the disastrous fortune of himself and his wife, their sensibility of which had cast them into such disorder. I'm glad of it, cry'd the excellent woman; shedding tears for others' woes, betokens a goodness and nobleness of nature, that I hope my children will never be deficient in.

At the instant she had uttered these words, *Fanny* and *Tom* both flung themselves on their knees before her, and the latter said, Dear, dear mamma, whom I love better than all the world — and I'm sure I have reason to do so — pray let my sister and

---

1 This slightly misquoted passage comes from Hamlet's famous "To be, or not to be" soliloquy (*Hamlet*, III.i.69–70, 72–77, 79–81).

me know how I first came to your house — how I came to be your slave — who, and what I am? — To be sure I am, and ever shall be, your slave, by inclination, and my sister's slave — but oh! tell me, madam, why my master does not like me, and why I wear this coat, so different from other children — Indeed, I'll never tell my master — but behave dutifully to him as long as I live. Do, mamma, *Fanny* added, do tell us, and let me know if *Tommy* is my relation or my brother, as I have been indulged to call him?

Mrs. *Barlow*, though quite disconcerted at all these close questions, raised them from their suppliant posture with abundance of goodness; and, after some pause, occasioned by her dread lest her husband should ever come to the knowledge of these circumstances, and her fear of confiding a secret of such a nature to so young persons, at last resolved to betray it to them, and leave the issue to providence. She then informed them how *Tom* came first into Mr. *Barlow*'s possession, the declaration of the villain *Williamson*, who had never been at *Senepuxon* since, and so amazed and thunderstruck the poor sensible boy and her daughter, with the narration, that it was a long time before they came to themselves: during this silence of amazement, she had leisure to say, As to my husband's antipathy to you, *Tommy*, it is much harder to account for upon rational principles, or indeed upon any principles at all — you are innocent — you never offended him or any one else — Alas! I fear his aversion springs from want of humanity, and from pride, which cannot brook an intimate connection with the poor and unfortunate.

On this account you must, in return for my tender affection — for all that I have done for you, go on to behave as you have hitherto, and I'll still take care to make you amends privately, for your public mortifications, and with regard to your dress, consider, that virtue and good sense cannot be disgraced by any apparel; and on the contrary, that vice and wickedness receive no lustre from outward ornaments. Perhaps some accident may render my husband more tractable, and more a friend to your merits; and it is our duty to wait the happy moment, without murmuring: as to my part, I must say sincerely, that I felt a tenderness for you the first moment I set eyes on you; you have approved yourself worthy of it, and I now know little difference in my heart between you and your sister.

She concluded her speech with an hundred embraces, dried up their tears, and *Tom* promised that he would in nothing depart from his usual behaviour; but ah! mamma, cry'd the sensible lad — what pain it gives me, and ever will, to think of the grief and

trouble my unknown parents must undergo at the loss of me —
sure it must break their hearts — mine is almost broken at the
reflection — but sure I shall live to punish that execrable villain
for his baseness — then recollecting himself, and turning to his
Fanny and her mamma — but yet I cannot, on my own account,
be angry with him, since he was, tho' a bad one, the instrument
that made me known to you, and without that knowledge, I had
far rather not existed.

Mrs. *Barlow* cast a kind glance at these words, and squeezed
his hand, with a tender pressure; and *Fanny* replied, with a fervency that touched all present — and upon my word and faith,
my dear *Tommy*, I would rather die than ever be forced to lose
you! Soon after the discourse dropp'd; but left strange impressions upon the three grown persons, particularly Mrs. *Barlow*,
who, perceiving *Fanny* and her servant each engaged with a book,
winked to *Ferguson* and his wife to take a turn in the garden,
where she unbosomed herself in the following manner. God
knows, my friends, what I have been doing all this while, I have
nursed up an affection between these young people, that I appre-
hend will soon lose its innocency in love; they are arriving to an
age when that passion generally predominates, and seem to like
nobody but each other; with regard to myself, I should like my
Tom for a son-in-law, better than any one, and think he deserves
my daughter; but Mr. *Barlow*, haughty in his riches, would
commit murder if such a thing were but hinted at; nay, I know he
has thoughts of matching her with Col. *Carter*'s only son, who
you know will be the richest man in the province, though a lad of
bad principles, unlettered, and of coarse manners; and I know
too much the misery she must endure in such a match, by my
own experience.

I was going to ask your advice — but I see you are at a loss
what to say in the matter, as much as I am: in short, this shall be
my resolve, to leave the issue to providence — if heaven approves
and directs their union, no human power can dissolve it; and
therefore, in God's name, let it operate as it will. Perhaps you'll
say that I am very superstitious; but truly, I know of no other way
to make myself easy, and perhaps my desire to be so, increases my
trust in heaven on this occasion. Perhaps poor nameless *Tommy*,
had he not been robbed of his parents, was of a rank to have
claimed a far better match in his own country.

Ferguson and his wife, who had a real affection for *Tom*, were
quite frightened at the beginning of her speech; but did not fail
to applaud the conclusion, and say a hundred things to

strengthen her in her resolution. They returned to the apartment they had left, with great good humour, and found *Tom* explaining a passage in *Locke*[1] to his mistress, with her arm gently reclined upon his shoulder; nor did their innocence tempt them to alter their posture at their entrance. That night they all lay at *Ferguson*'s, and determined to spend a day or two after at Mr. *Gordon*'s, which they had the liberty to do, as Mr. *Barlow* was gone over to the western shore of *Virginia*, from whence his business would not permit him to return for near a month, so that these were like to be halcyon[2] days with the good folks at *Senepuxon*. They were received by Mr. *Gordon* with transport, as persons he most desired to see in the colony; and, after staying there three or four days, Mrs. *Barlow* made him go over to her house with her, and called upon Mr. *Ferguson* and his wife to oblige them to the same visit, and, as the season of the year gave them leisure, insisted they should keep her company till her husband's return.

Tom never had enjoyed so felicitous a time as the present, he saw none but those he loved, and that loved him — he was perpetually with his *Fanny*, and mingling in the sweets of improving conversation; but a period was put to it, by the arrival of *Barlow*, who had such extraordinary success in the business he went about, that he returned with more good humour than ever he was known to put on, and thanked Mrs. *Barlow*'s guests for accompanying her, kissed *Fanny*, and asked for *Tom*, who had skulked into the kitchen at his approach. *Tom*, hearing him call, came in with a modest reverence. Well boy, says his master, How art? see here, Mr. *Gordon*, this grows a proper lad, doesn't he? — I shall make a man of him, I fancy, by and by; but think I should give him a little learning too. *Tom* seeing his boots undone, went readily, and fetched the jack to pull them off. No, no, d—n it — I believe thy hands were made for somewhat better; but mum for that, — call one of the negroes — here — *Pompey!* — *Caesar!* — *Squelch!*[3] — bid some of 'em come here. *Tom* overjoyed at this unusual goodness, soon found a proper person to do the office. Mrs. *Barlow* and the rest stared at each other with astonishment;

---

1 The influential English philosopher John Locke (see p. 60, n. 2 above and Appendix C.2 below).
2 Peaceful, idyllic.
3 Such names were common for eighteenth-century slaves in North America. As historian Ira Berlin has written, they "reflected the contempt in which their owners held" their slaves. Names like "Squelch" here were meant "to emphasize their inferiority," while those derived

but in short it continued the whole evening, and he went to bed with a complacency of temper, particularly towards *Tom*, that they had ever been strangers to before.

It was not much otherwise the next day, nay it continued till something occurred that ruffled his temper, and then he became again the brute, to all about him. In the old situation then, matters went for near three years more, when *Fanny*, according to the custom of the country, was arrived to a marriageable age, and was really a perfect beauty, nor was there ever seen a handsomer youth than *Tom*, and so alike were they, that even the brute *Barlow* mentioned it sometimes with wonder. *Fanny* had had a master from *Annapolis*, to learn her to dance; and *Tom*, by the indulgence of Mrs. *Barlow*, obtained the same accomplishment in the usual way, by stealth; and having a great genius for music, Mr. *Gordon*, who was excellent in that science, had given him such instructions, that he played upon the violin and *German* flute[1] to admiration, and the worthy clergyman had made him a present of the latter instrument, and several compositions of the best masters, with which he often entertained his mother and *Fanny*, and beguiled the tedious hours with softest melody.

The kindness of his behavior to the servants, his humanity and his consideration of the *Negroes*, and their families, gained him all their loves; and, in short, he and his *Fanny* were become blessings not only to their own, but all the surrounding plantations. As no body loved *Barlow*, but every body feared him, he was still quite ignorant of *Tom*'s improvements and importance; and though all that approached the house were used to see him treated as a son, in his absence, yet Mrs. *Barlow*, and her daughter, as well as he, were so much esteemed, and did so much good to all about them, that no body had the temptation either of ill-nature, envy, or malice, hitherto, to betray their secret.

---

from "the name of some ancient deity or great personage" — like "Pompey" and "Caesar" here — were meant "as a kind of cosmic jest: the more insignificant the person in the eyes of the planters, the greater the name" (*Many Thousands Gone: The First Two Centuries of Slavery in North America* [Cambridge, MA: Harvard UP, 1998], 95).

1 Whereas ancient flutes had a mouthpiece at the end, the more modern "German" (or transverse) flute is played by blowing through an orifice on the side.

CHAPTER IV

But this calm was not to last long, and a storm succeeded, that involved them all in the greatest distress. Mr. *Barlow* came home one evening, and, with his usual peremptoriness,[1] told his wife and daughter, that the next day he had appointed young Mr. *Carter* to pay a visit to *Fanny*; and that the colonel, his father, and he, had agreed upon a match between them. They were thunderstruck with this intelligence, and Mrs. *Barlow* recovering herself, replied — agreed upon a match, Sir, before you know whether your daughter likes him or no? — Is that dealing like a father, in an affair whereon all her future weal[2] or woe depends? — Hold your nonsensical prating — Isn't he the richest heir in *Maryland*? — is not *Franck*[3] the best fortune hereabouts? — Aren't they of the same age? and am I not her father, and can do with her as I please? — A fine thing truly! that a puling[4] modest girl must be consulted, if she likes a man or no — no, no, child — marry first, and he'll put love into her afterwards, I warrant him.

In such a strain the brute ran on, and upon his wife's reasoning with him further, flung out of the room, with curses and oaths, that he would be obeyed, without reply in what concerned his own property. *Tom* soon after entered the apartment, and beheld a scene he had never been witness to before, at which he was struck quite speechless; but *Fanny* soon let him know the dreadful sentence, as soon as she could command her voice, which was interrupted by the interjection of sobs and tears. Had lightning transfixed him — had instant death presented itself before his eyes, he could not have expressed more dismay or grief; he sunk down upon the seat of the window, and was at once deprived of sense and motion.

It was well for all three, that *Barlow* was out of hearing; for the minute he left the room, he walked down to the *Negro* quarter near his house, and so was half a mile distant by this time. Mrs. *Barlow* and her daughter gave a great cry, and running to him, the former chafed his temples, whilst the other held a bottle of drops

---

1 Stubborn decisiveness.
2 Prosperity.
3 Given that Barlow later calls Fanny "Frank," this surely refers to her and the fortune she would stand to inherit as his only child – not to mention the dowry she would undoubtedly bring. The different spelling here is likely a printer's error in the original.
4 Feeble or whiny.

to his nose; by the aid of which he soon came to himself, and remembring the danger of his situation, and seeing the fright he had occasioned, to persons he loved so dearly, he, with all the strength he had remaining, humbly begged pardon for his involuntary offence, adding, but oh! to part with my dear sister! — to a brute that can never know her worth, is death, is worse than death! I shall not long survive it!

Poor Mrs. *Barlow*, quite distracted at the condition of her children, did nothing but exhort to patience and consideration; but she might have talked in vain to either, had she not at length made use of these reviving expressions — come, perhaps means may yet be found to break off this dreaded match, which I own I never approved. These words had so sudden an effect, that they both fell on their knees, blessed her for her encouraging expressions, and became somewhat calm; and it was happy they did; for not a quarter of an hour after, the tyrant returned, but said no more that night, contenting himself with casting such looks at his wife and daughter, as made them tremble.

This was the first instant that *Tom* felt he really loved, nor was his love without return; and if he passed the sleepless night under the utmost anguish, his *Fanny* had little more repose. They recalled each other's tenderness to remembrance, the perfections, the every grace they were possessed of, and could not bear even the most distant idea of eternal separation without despair: but, in his situation, what could he oppose to the will of a father? — how could he even dare to hope any thing in his own favour? — a foundling — a wanderer — a wretch — a purchased slave! Ah miserable that I am, he cry'd — no body owns me — I am an alien and a stranger every where; and, except from the excellent mistress of this house, her lovely daughter, and two or three more good people, never could boast the least protection or care — nay, all the learning and knowledge I have acquired — is it not the source of pity — of charity — to an exposed and deserted orphan! To me — *relations dear, and all the charities, of father, son, and brother,*[1] have been, alas! unknown — but I will meet my fate like a man — and though, till this moment, such audacious thoughts never entered this breast — yet will I own to this delightful fair — this charmer of my soul — that I love her — that I shall die — and die for her! — yes, tomorrow's dawn shall see me at her feet — there to vent my passion and my despair! —

---

1   Milton, *Paradise Lost*, IV.756–57.

In this manner he raved, till the early cock proclaimed the day with his shrill note, when he arose, but had hardly strength enough to dress himself, his body had been so weakened by the tumultuous perturbations of his mind. As to poor *Fanny*, the return of light found her in an high fever, with very dangerous symptoms, which filled her mother with severe apprehensions, insomuch that she threw herself at her husband's feet, and begg'd him, if he would not be the murderer of his only child, not to precipitate the marriage, and to postpone the visit for some days, till she could be prepared, by her arguments, to yield to his will. Well, well, he replied surlily, he shan't come to day — I'm going over to the colonel's, and will stop the visit — but, by G—d! will she, or nill she[1] — a very little time shall terminate the business; and therefore I command you to discharge your duty, by endeavouring to bring her to compliance. D—n it, a fine thing truly — the minute a girl is talked to about lying with a lusty young fellow, she must fall ill upon it — well, well, he'll cure her I warrant him.

Much more such stuff proceeded from his ungenerous mouth; and after breakfast, he took horse, and gallop'd away, without bidding his daughter adieu. Mrs. *Barlow* went to *Fanny* with the reprieve she had obtained; but however, she was too weak to quit her chamber all that day, and when poor *Tom* first entered it, he looked like a walking ghost, he was so altered. Tears were shed on both sides, and Mrs. *Barlow* joined them with her's; but told them their extreme sensibility of parting with each other, would render every prudential method she could make use of, in their favour, abortive; conjured them to give truce to their griefs, to endeavour not to be cast down, and said, that she believed the young oaf, who was proposed for her husband, knew nothing yet of the matter, and was so insensible a clod, that he would not pursue the matter, with any vigour, it being merely a scheme of the two fathers; and that therefore they had the greatest reason imaginable to be easy; that she had put off the visit for that day, and doubted not of doing it for a longer time; and that it was proper to dissemble their chagrin the more effectually to counteract the design.

By these and other arguments, which, however, she knew had little foundation, she so far consoled them, that a sudden alteration ensued, *Tom* put on again his chearful looks, miss made shift to get up, and they spent the remainder of the day in her

---

1 Will she not.

apartment. At dinner, the next day, for *Barlow* was not yet returned, they came down into the dining-room, and after that was over, *Tom*, whose mind was bent upon a disclosure of his passion, desired leave to take a walk with *Fanny*, into the neighbouring pine grove, to which Mrs. *Barlow* assenting, they departed, hand in hand, all the way fondly gazing on each other.

After he had led her to the most retired part of the grove, where a seat was erected for the convenience of sitting in a summer's evening, they sat down, and, for some time, looked wishfully at each other, without being able to speak: at length *Tom* flung himself on his knees before her, and clasping her hand in his, whilst the tears trickled down his cheeks, said, Oh! my dear *Fanny*! my adorable sister! pardon my presumption, which the immediate danger of losing you, for ever, has occasioned. Innocently, hitherto, we have loved each other; but ah! I now feel all that the fondest passion can create within this wretched bosom! Forgive a wretch, a forlorn slave, for telling you this — but, before these eyes are closed for ever, as shortly they must be — if you are torn from me — I must let you know all the power of your charms. With humble reverence, I love you as the supreme arbitress[1] of my destiny — to make you happy — to form your bliss, would be ever my end and aim — no sordid view of mine, has the least mixture with my hopes — were you married to a man you loved — that knew your value, and would consult your felicity — I had only inly[2] mourned — nor dared this declaration — but, to see you sacrificed to a wretch, who has barely the image of a man — but whose mind is all low and mean — and so far from being fitted for the refined enjoyments of love and friendship, that he is not even an eligible acquaintance — to see this, to behold all those various beauties, those resplendent graces, in the possession of a wretch, who shall embrace them in common with the loathsome slaves he is master of — is horror and distraction! — And yet, what can I propose — all friendless and destitute as I am — by desiring you to crown my faithful love, with the return of yours — nothing but mutual misery; but ah! lovely charmer of my heart, tell me if you count me worthy of your affection? — if you do, I shall die in peace — for death too sure will terminate my unfortunate, but brief date of life.

Every word that this excellent youth uttered, struck the amiable *Fanny* to the heart — they had lived together from their

---

1 Determiner.
2 Inwardly.

infancy — she had never seen a more accomplished man — or one she could so much esteem — he spoke the language of artless passion; and she, in melodious accents, made him this reply — for neither had learned, in these happy retreats of innocence, to dissemble their loves or their aversions. Why, my *Tommy*, why do you make the least doubt of my affection? — though, till this crisis, I never knew how much, or in what manner I loved you — it seeming, 'till now, only the innocent and simple fondness of a sister to a brother — yet, the thoughts of losing you for ever, have stirred up a thousand nameless longings and desires in my bosom, that I was unacquainted had harboured there. You had no need to describe the worthlessness of the object that is designed for me; for were he one of the most accomplished youths breathing — he could never eclipse your merit. I shall never be able to love but you, and if I am forced from you, death will soon release me from my misery. Tell me not of your condition — of your want of fortune — of your want of friends — you have all the virtue, and all the goodness that I desire — and ah! were it in my power, you should soon find every friend in my breast, and all the goods of life in my disposal. Wretched am I, that this cruel father cannot see with my eyes — but must barter me for sordid expectations of worldly riches, without considering that nothing can ease or cure an uneasy mind; why was he not formed like our excellent mother — ready to promote his children's happiness, and not, from ignorance and caprice, to plunge them into inexpressible woe? Oh *Tommy*, and here she held out her charming hands to raise him, and laid her cheek to his — believe me, I'll be constant to death, and if my hand is forced, I will never live to surrender my person, which I vow before God is yours, and never shall be any other's.

The raptur'd youth at this instant forgot all his griefs, he pressed the sweet creature, blushing like the opening rose, in his arms, and they exchanged the chastest and purest embraces that ever lovers witnessed. Arm in arm they were returning towards the house, *Fanny*'s was circled round *Tom*'s neck, and *Tom*'s enclosed the delicate slender waist of *Fanny*.

When mortals seem arrived to the height of human felicity, when, as in these lovers, all the powers of the heart are easy and at rest, some malign influence often conspires to plunge them into unutterable woe. Indeed we should be too happy, too gaily thoughtless of a better state, if we could for any length of time ascertain a continuance of mortal felicity. As ill fortune would have it, *Barlow*, the tyrant *Barlow*, was returning home that way, and they were so engaged in fond vows and protestations of constancy, that he had leisure to ride close behind them for some moments, without being in the least perceived, and overheard every word they said.

Contrary to his usual impetuous custom, he stifled his rage for some moments, tho' all the devil was uppermost in his heart; but hearing at length the innocent *Fanny* say, Oh *Tommy*, how happy should I be if my father would consent to an union between us, I should not envy — his patience was quite exhausted, and just as his daughter, hearing a rustling of the leaves under his horse's feet, turned her head, and saw his dreadful form, at which she gave a piercing shriek, and fell down senseless before him; he club'd his whip,[1] and aimed so sure a blow at *Tom*'s head, that he fell prostrate by his mistress, weltering in his blood. Here was a sight that one would have imagined might have given pause even to diabolical fury; but the wretch not yet satisfied, nor regarding the condition of his daughter, bestriding the poor youth, repeated his blows, on his back, breast and sides, 'till weariness obliged him to give truce to his fury.

Oh! thou heavenly, thou amiable guest, by what name shall I call thee? Thou, who inspirest us with patience, forbearance, loving-kindness and tenderness, towards one another? *Humanity, compassion*, are epithets that bespeak not enough thy worth, or importance! Of celestial original art thou, of immortal lineage — known by the endearing titles of RELIGION, of CHRISTIANITY. You it is that have refined and ennobled our nature, that have corrected our brutal part, that have taught us *to do as we would be done by*,[2] and cleared away those seeds of wicked implacability, that natively dwell about us! Behold the various savage nations that have yet not known thy inspiring influence! What shocking barbarity attend their wars, what cruel inhumanity even their civil institutions! Let us here pronounce, that the man who is not conscious of you, is unfit, altogether unfit for, and destructive to human society.

When he had a little recovered himself, he mounted his horse, and took up his daughter, still insensible, before him, by mere strength of arm, and gallop'd homewards, cursing and swearing, and still breathing out threats of further vengeance upon poor

---

1 Used the handle of his whip as a club.
2 A paraphrase of the Golden Rule from Jesus' Sermon on the Mount (see Matthew 7:12).

Tom. Well it was for *Fanny*, that she did not see him in that condition; that sight, without further violence, would have been sufficient to have winged her soul to a kinder, better parent. When he arrived home, his entrance was proclaimed by repeated execrations, and poor Mrs. *Barlow* running to see what was the matter, was one of the first that perceived his inflamed countenance, and her daughter before him, by the jolting of the horse now just capable to open her dying eyes. She immediately guessed the rest, and, but for Mr. *Gordon*, who happened providentially to be just come in, had fallen upon the floor, with grief, terror, and apprehension.

The good clergyman having seated her, and advancing, before any of the servants, who seeing the condition of their master, stood aloof full of dread, and fearing to approach him, received the young lady in his arms, and said, for God's sake, Sir, what has so discomposed you? — have you met with any insult? — has any body assaulted you? He vouchsafed no answer to this, but bolting into the parlour, where by this time Mrs. *Barlow* had found strength to crawl, flung himself into a chair, and related his adventure, in the following manner, by way of soliloquy: G—d d—n my blood — what a d—d thick-scull'd rascal am I — not to have imagined the girl flesh and blood, and to let her be followed by a handsome fellow of such years? — Now, by G—d, the secret's out, this was the reason of her d—d tears, and her feigned sickness — but d—n me I have silenced her paramour[1] — I'm sure he'll never rise for one while — I'd rather be hang'd, by G—d, than see my daughter debauched by a scoundrel, of neither here nor there, that I have purchased with my money, and brought up to inveigle[2] that hell-fir'd little b—h to her ruin.

Then turning to his wife, you, madam, must have been acquainted with their intrigue, it could not otherwise have arrived to the height it has. Indeed, Mrs. *Barlow* had just strength enough to reply; I never knew any thing but what was innocent between the children, if you mean my daughter and *Tommy*; and I fear your mistaken jealousy has caused you to do a deed we all may repent of! D—n the deed, he replied, but was really frightened when he thought of the condition in which he had left *Tom*, I have drubb'd him, by G—d — there he lies, in the pine barren, and there he's likely to lie, for I'll be d—d if ever he gets up himself.

---

1 Secret lover.
2 Entice.

God forbid, replied Mr. *Gordon*, and immediately sallied out, followed by several of the weeping servants and negroes, who had overheard what their master said; but who can describe the condition of poor *Fanny* at these words, she fell back into a swoon, attended with such strong convulsions, that her mother could not hold her, but was obliged to call for assistance, whilst she was in little better condition herself; and the cruel obdurate father, cried, D—n her, let her die — it's good enough for her — a disobedient b—h!

Mean time Mr. *Gordon* arrived at the spot, where poor *Tom* lay still quite insensible, and, to all appearance dead, a vast quantity of blood having run from his wounds; but applying his hand to his mouth, and examining his pulse, he found there were still some remains of life in him. Upon this he ordered the servants to get some branches of the neighbouring trees, with which they made a kind of hand-barrow to convey him to the house, every one shedding tears as they bore him, and recounting to one another his good-nature and kind-heartedness, and cursing their master for this detestable action, the reason of which they were totally strangers to.

At the house a new scene of confusion presented itself; upon the arrival of the corpse, for all but the good clergyman imagined him dead. Mrs. *Barlow*, for miss had been put to bed, raving distractedly upon the name of her dear *Tommy*, fainted away; and all the family wept aloud, and *Barlow* himself, now terribly apprehensive of the consequences, ordered Mr. *Ferguson* to be sent for. Happy was it for the unfortunate youth that his kind tutor was then upon the way, and soon after meeting the messenger, alighted, all full of sorrow, at the gate. The inhuman master had withdrawn himself privately, and *Tom* being undressed, and put to bed, his wounds were searched, which proved to be one large fracture on the hind part of the head, and near twenty contusions in various parts of his body.

Every one was amazed at the inveteracy[1] with which he must have been struck, and Mr. *Gordon* solemnly swore, that if he did otherwise than well, he would never leave the country, till he saw his murderer hanged. In some time, however, after proper preparations were used, he came so far to himself as just to open his eyes, for an instant, and close them again with a deep sigh, to the joy of all present. This a little revived poor Mrs. *Barlow*, who flew

---

1 Unabated fury.

to her dear daughter with the tidings of his being alive, (and a little further she went, in policy) likely to do well. This amiable creature soon shewed the effects of such glad tidings, by a return of the colour into her pallid cheeks, and a perfect restoration of her senses, so as to be able to tell her mamma how every thing had happened; at which she appeared inconsolable, as this unlucky accident had defeated every scheme she could possibly invent, to break off or procrastinate the threatened match. She was bled[1] by way of precaution, her spirits being in such agitation as to threaten a violent fever, and *Tom* was left in a fine dose, Mr. *Ferguson*, after dressing him, having assured every body that none of his hurts were mortal, tho' another blow upon the pit of the stomach, where he had received several, would have decided his fate.

The two gentlemen, and the kind lady of the house, now met together, began to consult in what manner to behave; Mr. *Gordon*, who was independent of Mr. *Barlow*, was for immediately getting a warrant to secure him, and told his wife, that in such a case she ought to publish what her husband had said as to *Williamson*'s villainy, that the youth might be set free by due course of law, and no more be subject to such tyranny, nor go constantly in danger of his life. This was indeed a very nice point, it was somewhat like a wife's betraying the secrets of her husband, and perhaps it was making her own life eternally miserable; beside, as *Barlow* was known to be a man who stuck at nothing, it was not doubted, in that case, but he would take some private opportunity to destroy him. Upon the whole then, it was judged most adviseable, that Mr. *Gordon* should search him out, represent *Tom* as in imminent danger of his life; by keeping up his fears, keep him from home till his recovery, and at the same time endeavour to purchase him of his master for the same sum he had given for him; which it was not doubted, his avaritious temper would jump at, as he was likely, if he recovered, to be a cripple all the days of his life; and indeed there was such a danger, which however he was to exaggerate with all the art he could.

This was a very good and feasible scheme; but was accidentally disappointed, for *Barlow* having taken shelter at Colonel *Carter*'s, who was a man of just his own stamp, and not knowing of *Ferguson*'s arrival, dispatched over the colonel's surgeon to

---

1 Letting blood was a common contemporary treatment based on prevailing medical theory.

inspect the wounds, who arriving just at the close of their consultation, insisted upon viewing the patient; to deny his request would have looked oddly, and therefore they were forced to acquiesce, and the creature they had sent, tho' a skillful surgeon, being as great a brute as themselves, turned about with this sentence: Pish — here's no murder — nothing but a slight fracture and two or three contusions — his greatest malady is loss of blood; and with these tidings hasted back to his employers, by which he relieved *Barlow*'s fears, and sent him home full as much a devil as he was when he fled away.

In vain his spouse, Mr. *Gordon*, and Mr. *Ferguson* endeavoured to display to him the enormity of his crime — he swore he had provocation sufficient — that he would do as he pleased with his own daughter and his own slave; and that one should speedily marry to please him, and the other, as soon as he was able, should be sent to one of his back plantations,[1] and kept to drudgery the remainder of his life. The good clergyman, quite astonished at the devilish frame of his mind, took his leave with these expressions. Ungenerous, barbarous man! some dreadful judgment will follow such brutal proceedings! you are an accountable creature, as well as the lowest person in being, and there is a just God that will put a period to your crimes! Of this you may too late be convinced — tho' you now make a jest of it. But remember another thing, and tremble — we have laws — and, thank God, righteous magistrates — I'll be a spy upon all your actions, and if that innocent boy suffers in life or limb, by your cruelty — hear me, Sir, your great riches shall not protect you from condign[2] punishment, if I am forced to sell the gown from off my back. — I declare I'll never again enter the doors of such a miscreant, such a devil in human shape.

So saying, without further ceremony, he bowed to Mrs. *Barlow* and Mr. *Ferguson*, and mounting his horse, rode away, leaving the wretch speechless, with mingled rage and terror, and the two others, charmed with his resolution; but chagrined at the latter part of it, which was a kind of sentence of banishment from Mrs. *Barlow* and the two lovers. *Fanny* at length recovered, and *Tom*, by the care of Mr. *Ferguson*, likewise, got well without the least remain of his hurts, to the joy of every one.

---

1 It was common for the largest planters to own more than one contiguous parcel of land, and to work slaves and servants on more than the parcel their own family lived on. A "back plantation" refers to such an operation in a remote location.
2 Appropriate.

And now the tyrant, who had inly growl'd over his projects, and during all this while, had scarce ever afforded even his wife a word or a good look, began to execute them, and first he introduced young *Carter* to his daughter, charging her to receive him, as her future husband; but she resolved upon a conduct that nothing could make her alter, after trying the force of reason to dissuade him from his attempt, in vain; for it was a creature that no reason could operate upon, she kept an obstinate silence, nor would afford him the least look or answer to any impertinence he uttered; minding her work or her book without being moved, either with his entreaties or his grimaces.

CHAPTER V

As to *Tom*, who was destined to pay for all his mortifications, he forbid him ever to enter the room where she was, and kept so strict watch himself, that it was impossible for him to see the darling of his soul, nor did Mrs. *Barlow* herself dare to parley[1] with him; and, at last, urged thereto by the *Carters*, one morning rising before the rest of the family, they forcibly put him on an horse, and carried him, round-about ways, through the woods, to a plantation at the back of the country, near forty miles distant, where, when they alighted, *Barlow* harangued him in this manner. Now, dog, if you stir from this spot without my orders, I'll chop you into pound pieces, here are twenty negroes, beside women and children, whom I deliver to your care as their overseer; a post you do not, by the way, deserve to be exalted to. But, in consideration that I have once given you your deserts a little too severely, I am thus gracious to you; and, mind what I say, I shall call every fortnight to see the improvements made, and what work is done, and every deficiency shall be had out of your hide with a good cow-skin; mind me, by these hands, which you have already felt the weight of. That fellow, pointing to a white servant, will teach you your duty, and is to be subject to your directions, when you have learned your business. *Tom* was preparing a reply, but, with a laugh of derision from both, they rode away, *Carter* halloing out — I think we have him now — the devil's in't if he has any stomach left for love.

With a generous look of contempt he surveyed their parting steps — and turning to the white man, who, by the way, was principally left there as a spy, he asked him in the sweetest and most

---

1 Converse.

engaging manner, what his name was? My name, sir, he replied, is *Duncan Murray*. Well, Mr. *Murray*, I hope we shall live happily together, and do our duty. He then examined all the little cottages upon the premises, chose one for himself, and in a few days apprehended what he had to do so well, as raised the admiration of his instructor. By his sweet treatment of the *Negroes*, he gained their good-will, and shewed that kindness and clemency to those miserable creatures will make them more serviceable than cruelty and brutality; for, in the first fortnight, he had more tobacco hoed and housed, and more work of every sort completed, than was ever seen upon that plantation before.

In short, when *Barlow* rode over at the appointed time, he was amazed, and seeing *Murray* first, at his entrance into the grounds, and looking round him, said, What, have you had the devil here? — d—n me, you are all clear'd in,[1] I see. *Murray*, who was no bad man at the bottom, replied, Why truly, sir, if you have such an overseer at every plantation as you have here, you'll soon be richer than all the planters in *Maryland*, and yet all is done mildly, nor has a blow been struck since his arrival. Well done, by G—d, then I have brought him into his proper element, I see — Call him to me — *Tom* soon came with an open carriage, and at his order gave him a verbal account of all his transactions; at the close of which he could not help saying, Well, well — by G—d this is not amiss — go on as you've begun, and perhaps I may become your friend. Then, after visiting every place, he rode away on his return.

By this mildness in his carriage, *Tom*'s spirits were raised, for tho' he dared not enquire, and could see no-body to tell him, he gathered thence that his dear mother and his *Fanny* were well: then again he feared she had been forced to marry, which thought racked his bosom with cruel violence, and drew floods of tears from his eyes. Often would he reap encouragement to his labour, by saying to himself, let me not think of this barbarian — let me only tell myself it is the father of my *Fanny*, and that all the pains I take is for the advancement of her fortune.

Thus he would often console himself, and would retire to the shadiest and most private retreats of the woods to vent his love and his grief. His flute, which, by good chance, happened to be in his pocket when he was taken away, was his only companion, and the groves around, ecchoed to softest, saddest melody. *Murray*, instead of being his spy, insensibly conceived a love for him, and became the partaker of his sorrows; and, struck with the

---

1 You have harvested the entire crop.

superiority of his talents and conceptions, even descended to perform for him the servilest offices. His genius being very poetical, he frequently vented his plaints in song; and the following, as a specimen, is preserved to my readers, who must note, that he takes his images from the country where he then mourn'd his absent fair.

The AMERICAN SONG

TUNE. *Sweet are the charms of her I love.*[1]

I.

WHERE is my fair, ah tell me where?
Where does my charming Fanny *stray?*
Oh! were I swift as yonder deer,
At her lov'd feet I'd instant lay;
But absent — wretched fate is mine,
Alas! in anxious grief I pine.

II.

The gay Savannah[2] *chears the eye,*
All blooming, rich with various sweets
Romantic views the woods supply,
Each purling[3] stream the prospect greets
But tasteless all the beauteous scene,
Each tinct[4] that paints the vivid green.

III.

More pleasing far the turtle's note,[5]
That plaintive, wails his absent mate;
Or Philomela's[6] *warbling throat,*
Lamenting her unhappy fate:
Delightful pair! ye sooth my woe,
And aid the tears that constant flow!

---

1 A popular early-eighteenth-century love song by the renowned English actor Barton Booth (1681–1733).
2 [Kimber's note] Open meadow land.
3 Rippling, murmuring.
4 Tint.
5 The song of the turtle-dove.
6 The nightingale.

IV.

Ye Mock birds[1] cease your numerous song,
Nor mimic chaunt amidst the grove;
Tir'd of your lays, the whole day long,
To sadder sounds the wretched rove:
When night has spread its veil around,
I court the Bull-frogs'[2] *croaking sound.*

V.

Abandon'd, hapless, and forlorn,
Oh! heavens behold th' ill fated youth!
Struggling with ills, as soon as born,
A martyr now to love and truth:
But hear, oh! hear a wretch's prayer!
Protect me from that fiend despair!

VI.

But oh! I rave — for Fanny's *chains,*
With gladsome, willing mind I bear,
All o'er my soul — my heart, she reigns,
Search every vein, you'll find her there:
Fanny, *more* sweet *than every flower,*
Reviving more, than cooling shower.

VII.

Oh! could I call the fair one mine!
Around her clasp, these circling arms!
On her dear breast this head recline,
And feast on all her killing charms!
Chas'd far, would be each pain, each care,
From this sad mind, nor torment there.

VIII.

Delightful thought! — but distant far,
Illusive, see my hopes expire,
Twinkling remote like yonder star,
Or glimmering like that cabin fire
E'en faintly now they met my eye,
Now lost — like misty vapours fly.

---

1 [Kimber's note] Birds that imitate the song of all others.
2 [Kimber's note] A frog that haunts the marshes, remarkable for a loud melancholy noise.

IX.

Protect her, oh! ye powers above!
That guard the innocent from wrong.
Protect my joy! my life! my love!
Inspirer — burden of my song!
Alone let me, unhappy youth,
A martyr bleed to love and truth!

Thus poor *Tom* vented his amorous complaints, nor was his *Fanny* more at rest; wild and distracted to know what was become of him, but denied intelligence by her monster of a father, she once more got rid of the odious sollicitations of *Carter*, by the attacks of a fever, so much the more to be dreaded, as it prey'd upon her spirits with dreadful violence. Mrs. *Barlow* could neither get from her husband the secret of his disposal, nor a promise to break off the designed alliance, and, by the intolerable vexation and grief it occasioned her, became like a walking shadow. *Barlow* hugged himself in what he had done — called it a triumph over canting,[1] nonsense, and love; and, tho' the story spread about by Mr. *Gordon*'s means, and he began to be shunned by all his sober neighbours, he yet persisted to carry on his project.

Thus three months rolled away, and tho' *Fanny* again recovered, yet her strength was so visibly impaired, that it was apprehended a consumption[2] would succeed; when one day Mr. *Ferguson*, who, with his wife, took an intimate share in their calamity, making many painful researches after *Tom*'s place of confinement, at length recollected, that *Barlow*, since he left him, had purchased this distant plantation, which he resolved immediately to explore, and accordingly setting out early, one day in the morning, the succeeding one at noon, after much wandering, made a shift to find it, tho' deep in the bosom of a very obscure wood. But before he reached it, his ears became his directors; for *Tom*, it being the heat of the day, was sitting under the shade of a copse,[3] and tuning his flute to the saddest notes he could remember. The good man's heart jumped for joy, when he heard the instrument, knowing it was modulated by his pupil's masterly hand, and soon came near enough to distinguish his person, and,

---

1 Moralistic humbug.
2 A wasting away of the body as the result of disease.
3 A thicket of trees.

in alighting from his beast, made a rustling that reached the ears of our lover, who casting abroad his eyes, perceived it was indeed his worthy tutor.

A ship-wreck'd mariner, with more delightful surprize, after having been thrown on one shore of a desolate island, believing all his crew to be lost, could not have surveyed an old mess-mate advancing towards him, that had escaped by another, than *Tom* expressed at the sight of this good man. The tears filled his eyes, and, running with all the speed he was master of, before he could speak a word, clasped him about the neck, being able only to say oh! my saviour — my mother — *Fanny* — Mrs. *Ferguson*, are they alive! Indeed, his master was so much affected himself, that he could not answer him for a long time; but embraced him strenuously, with more than common affection.

Perhaps at all times the tongue cannot express our sensations — no — words are far too faint on certain occasions — the dumb shews of sincerity have somewhat infinitely more striking and cordial. However, at length their tongues were loose, and *Tom* being the exile, Mr. *Ferguson* first gratified all his enquiries. The generous, grateful youth, wept incessantly at the condition of his *Fanny* and his mother, and even wished he had not been born to be the cause of such disturbance to them; then again, ran out into such raptures on the young lady's constancy and tenderness towards him, and that of Mrs. *Barlow*, that his friend thought him inspired with more than mortal eloquence.

The friendship of Mr. *Gordon*, of Mrs. *Ferguson*, and of his visitor, next employed his tongue, and he went on till he was quite tired and jaded,[1] before *Ferguson* could put in a word. His looks emphatically continued the rest — he surveyed him from head to heel, with ardent love and gratitude, and seemed wildly to doubt if what he viewed was real, or only an illusive shadow: he at last let him know the manner of his being conveyed away, his master's visits and surly approbation of his proceedings, his melancholy and dejected state of life, and the constant anxiety he had been under about his dearest *Fanny* and her friends; but my dear preserver, he continued, my impatience has rendered me forgetful that you must needs want refreshment — come, let me lead you to my homely cot, the seat of so much perpetual misery, and, calling a ready *Negro* to take the horse, conducted him a near way to his quarters, and *Murray* being there, who was

---

1 Worn out.

become his sincere friend, cried, see, mess-mate, providence has sent me a guest to whom I owe every thing — to whom I owe my life! With the same vivacious gratitude, the table covered with their coarse provisions, consisting of the remains of a piece of salt beef, with the leg of a curlieu[1] which *Tom* had shot the day before, and a desert of wild grapes and *parsimons*.[2] As to liquor, a *calabash*[3] of water supplied them, and Mr. *Ferguson* protested he had not eaten a heartier meal for a long time.

He staid with them a whole day longer, and would have continued longer still, but that the time of *Barlow*'s visit was approaching. Within some hours of their parting, *Tom* said, with a melancholy air — I must lose you then, dear sir — and ah! I have neither paper, pens, nor ink, to send my compliments to my protectors, I am destitute of every comfort of that sort. I should long ago, indeed, have ventured to escape from this banishment, but the idea of some time or another hearing from my *Fanny*, and the thought that if I ran away, I should still be at a greater distance from her, deterred me.

No, my dear child, *Ferguson* replied, rely upon providence, and don't leave us, as your only pain now, is want of the sight of your friends; some kind chance may restore you to us, and ease your torments, without recurring to such desperate measures; and now we know where you are, and the times of your master's coming, depend upon it our visits will be frequent, as the distance will permit them. I had, you must know, some forebodings that I should find you, and, as I imagined you quite destitute of entertainment, for I did not think that you had even so much as your flute, I brought you a quire[4] of paper, some pens and some ink, in my bags, and this pocket *Horace*[5] with me, to alleviate and brighten some of your solitary hours; I should also have brought you my pocket *bible*, but really forgot.

Never was joyful gratitude like *Tom*'s at hearing this, he fell upon his knees, and thanked God aloud — he embraced his good friend, and cried, Were I emperor of the *Indies*, I should never be

---

1 Now usually spelled "curlew," this is a species of bird.
2 In the original, Kimber annotates this "Wild medlars." The medlar tree, which bears fruit resembling small brown apples, is native to southeast Europe. The persimmon tree, native to North America, produces yellow or orange plum-like fruit.
3 The hollowed-out shell of a gourd or pumpkin used for carrying water.
4 Twenty-four sheets of writing paper.
5 A small, portable book of poems by the classical Roman poet Horace.

able to return such great, such unmerited goodness; but, if an heart replete with acknowledgment could speak, it would tell more than my tongue can utter; but now, dear, dear sir, will you be so kind to let me commit a few lines to each of my friends, to your hands. To be sure, my child — and whilst you are writing, I'll take a view of the plantation with Mr. *Murray*; for I think it is as beautiful an one as ever I surveyed. Indeed, sir, he returned, 'tis a charming spot; but all its delights are thrown away upon a person that has quite lost a relish for pleasure.

The bags being brought, and the implements delivered to him, he sat down, and wrote a most dutiful and affectionate letter to Mrs. *Barlow*, and others full of acknowledgment to Mr. *Gordon* and Mrs. *Ferguson*, in which he described his situation and his grief and distress of mind, at being so remote from them. Last of all, he wrote a letter to his *Fanny*, which was conceived in the following terms.

"Charmer of my heart,

"Oh what inexpressible joy I experience, in this kind, this longed-for opportunity, now providentially given me, of laying myself at your feet, and displaying all the gratitude with which my breast is replete. Every conscious grove and stream has heard my mournful plaints, and every mimic eccho has resounded my love and my despair. But can I now despair, when I hear such glad tidings of your constancy and affection; that you are still alive, and still mine? Could my arm but obey the dictates of my mind, you should soon be freed from the addresses of my hateful rival; but alas! I am impotent in every thing, but that transcendent flame that warms my soul for you.

"Oh heavens! why was I born to such variety of sorrows, to such unintermitted misfortunes? Why has the most lovely, the most amiable of her sex, deigned to meet my passion, whilst I want power to assert my claim? To be robbed of my parents, to be abused by a villain, to be treated with all the marks of slavery and subjection, are trifles, mere trifles to this consideration; but if there is a Being, as sure there is, whose good providence rules this world, we still shall taste the fruits of that bliss, our fidelity, our pure and holy affection merits.

"Mean time, my sweetest *Fanny*, endeavour, for the sake of your poor exile, to support your courage and preserve your health; some kind influence may perhaps speak reason and moderation to the heart of our persecutor, whom I must love under all the sufferings he has inflicted upon me, because so nearly allied to you. That dear mother! *how shall I repay, the gratitude and duty that I owe her?* May heavens protect my fairest, dearest creature! may we at length — presumptuous thought! — be bless'd with each other, and may all our woes be forgotten. Adieu, delight of my soul. I should write for ever, but Mr. *Ferguson* is in haste to depart!

"*Your most tender and faithful adorer and servant*

Thomas ————

"Would to God I knew another name to add to it — but his will be done!"

Mr. *Ferguson* being now returned from his tour, *Tom* folded up his letters, and presented them to his care, and after a mournful and tender embrace, they bid adieu to each other, the youth with straining eyes pursuing his welcome guest, till the envious woods covered him from his view.

This was, indeed, the last time he was to see the face of any of his dear friends, for during the little space he had been enjoying such bliss, his enemies were contriving a scheme to send him away far from *Maryland*, and all the longings of his breast. *Fanny*'s obstinate silence to young *Carter*, who, if he could not love, began to lust after her possession, prodigiously chagrined both their fathers; and, as bad men are ever mistrustful and suspicious, they not in the least doubted but *Tom* and she had found out some secret method of correspondence, that tended to support her in her resolutions. This thought no sooner entered the colonel's head, but he proposed to *Barlow* to send him out of the country. *Barlow* at first, considering the service he had already been of upon his plantation, the profits whereof were encreased one half, and the further improvements he was likely to make, was loth to lend an ear to this proposal; but having it dinn'd in his ears, day after day, at length, through fear of missing the desired match, gave his consent, upon condition he was reimbursed the money he cost him.

This agreement made, they next cast about for a proper purchaser, and as distant a place as possible, and fortunately, as they thought, one *Matthewson*, an *Indian* trader, who had never been down that way before, came accidentally to purchase some commodities for his traffick at the neighbouring stores, or warehouses; with him, then, unsight unseen, they struck a bargain, and representing *Tom*'s talents and abilities, though they knew of none but his natural ones, to the best advantage, *Barlow* received twenty pounds sterling for him, which was a profit that was very grateful to his sordid soul.

Thus the innocent victim was made over, once more, as a slave, to another master, and all three rode down to the plantation to deliver him up to his purchaser. The poor youth had been industriously busy, most part of the day, and was then retired into his cot, with his *Horace*, and pleasing himself with the fine conceptions of that elegant poet. He rose when he saw his betrayers approach, met them with a sweetness and condescending humility, that at first sight captivated his new master, to such a degree that he could scarcely believe it was his purchase.

Barlow, after praising him highly, told him he had thought fit to make him over to that gentlemen whom he was to serve for the future. This sentence, which seemed to include further banishment from his *Fanny*, called terror to his heart and tears into his eyes; but, recovering himself, he said — Sir, what have I done to deserve so much severity? or how came you by a right to dispose of a man that was born free, that you came by clandestinely, and have kept in involuntary slavery ever since?

These words he uttered in the first anguish of his bosom; but on Mrs. *Barlow*'s account, repented himself immediately afterwards, and wished, silently, that he had not spoken them; but it was too late, and the brute fired at hearing these truths, which he thought him totally unacquainted with, began to vomit forth a thousand curses, and would have struck him, but that the more humane *Matthewson* held his arm. The colonel inforced his abuses with his own, and young *Carter*, coming close to him, gave him two or three cuts with his whip, saying, You dirty dog, how dare you prate so saucily?[1] — d—n me, I'll cut you in two — but we've done for you however!

If ever *Tom* indulged passion and fury, it was now — he struck his odious brutish rival — he could not bear it, and at one spring, catching him fast by the collar with one hand, with the other sent him senseless to measure his length upon the earth, by a blow over his temples. Then turning to *Barlow*, he said, in the same instant — excuse me, sir — if you have an authority to strike me, no body else has I'm sure. The two old ruffians remained some moments, looking at each other, as if astonished at his boldness, and then both together made towards him, with their weapons elevated, swearing they would whip him to death; but his new master stepped in, cried, Hold, hold, gentlemen! two to one are odds! — the young fellow has done as he ought to do; and if you

---

1 Talk so insolently.

offer to strike him — for remember he's mine now — perhaps both of us together, harkee,[1] may be as good as you three, and snatching up an hoe, that laid beside him, prepared to make good his menace, crying at the same time to *Tom*, Hold up your head, my lad — I'm on your side!

These words forced the assailants to make a pause, and relinquish their attempt; for *Matthewson* was a strong man, a rich man, and afraid of neither of them; nor do the planters care to affront the *Indian* traders, who are frequently their good customers, so they contented themselves with casting malign looks at *Tom*, but seemed to court a truce. He, being sensible to whom he owed this reprieve, making an handsome bow, said, Sir, I am glad I am fallen into such considerate hands, and will endeavour to serve you to the utmost. Already you have inspired me with gratitude, which is a principle that cannot fail of making me faithful. — I am content to leave that tyrant, looking fiercely at *Barlow*, who does not understand how to use a fellow-creature: and then turning to young *Carter*, who just got up, quite dismayed, he continued, As to you, sir, have I ever offended you? or is it your superior wealth — join'd to your superior pride and ignorance, that has made you so wantonly free of your blows? If this gentleman will permit me, I'll even now, upon this fair stage, convince you that you struck a better man than yourself, and use you as all such scoundrels ought to be treated.

The coward slunk away at these words, and mounting his horse, gallop'd off full speed, to the great diversion of *Matthewson*, who clapping *Tom* upon the shoulder, told him he was a lad after his own heart! Then ordering him to get what things he had, on which occasion he did not forget his flute, his *Horace*, or his implements of writing, he bid adieu to *Carter* and *Barlow*, who remained very moody, and was going to mount his horse, when *Tom* came to him, and addressed him in this manner: Sir, I should reckon myself still infinitely more oblig'd to you, if you would wait some minutes, 'till I have taken leave of a parcel[2] of poor creatures that love me, and who have been the companions and assistants of my labour, and wish that gentleman, nodding to *Barlow*, may set a person over them that may use them with equal humanity for the future. Do child, Mr. *Matthewson* replied, quite taken with his person and behaviour, your time shall be mine.

---

1 A contraction of "hark ye," meaning "listen to me."
2 Group.

Murray had given notice to the *Negroes*, who, men, women, and children, flocked around their overseer, lamenting, in their uncouth tone and broken language, that he was going to leave them: all pressed forward to shake his hand, and all wept sincerely. And afterwards, advancing to *Murray*, they embraced, and affectionately bid each other farewell, *Tom* leaving it in charge to deliver a few lines he had hastily wrote to Mr. *Ferguson*, when he should call, and they both mutually promising to remember each other.

Matthewson was quite melted at this scene, and *Barlow* and the colonel seemed touched; but strove, thro' pride, to conceal their approbation. And now *Tom*, having mounted upon a spare horse his master brought with him, turning towards his two enemies, said, Gentlemen, I'll leave you a piece of advice that may be of service to you — if you use your servants and dependents with kindness, your work will be done chearfully, and you'll gain as many friends as you purchase; on the contrary, you'll have as many enemies about you as there are men, who having no reason to the contrary, will take all opportunities to spoil and destroy you. And now Mr. *Barlow*, I pray heaven to soften your barbarous disposition, and enable you to amend your life — in which case, may providence, which has hitherto wonderfully protected me against your mean and base designs, and now, when you intended my hurt has directed me, in this gentleman, whom I am proud to call my master, to a friend and a patron, bless you with every blessing in life — but above all, may that excellent lady, who to me has been a mother, and her amiable daughter, be for ever happy here, and bless'd hereafter, as their merits deserve, and their goodness to the miserable and the unfortunate; so saying, with tears in his eyes, he turned his horse's head, and followed his master, who was not sorry to be relieved from the company of two men, to whom he had taken a very great dislike.

CHAPTER VI

They were within a few miles of the borders of *Virginia*, at this plantation, and soon entered *Northampton* county, the first on the eastern neck of that colony, and at passing the line, his master let him know he was leaving *Maryland*, at which he could not help turning back, with the utmost passion in his gesture — crying out, Oh my dearest *Fanny*! — I am going to leave thee for ever! then addressing *Matthewson*, continued, pray sir, excuse me — I'll transgress no more! That gentleman was silent for some moments, and then said — There is somewhat more in your story than I am aware of — otherwise, how could your master think of parting with so good, so sensible a servant! Ah! sir, he replied, my story is a very calamitous one, and will too much affect you, or, as you have now a right to know every thing concerning me, I would give it you as we rode along.

Do, child, he replied, I am all attention — look upon me as your friend. *Tom* then gave him his adventures from the time of his coming into the colony — the account *Williamson* gave *Barlow* — the goodness of Mrs. *Barlow*, and the rest of his friends — the manner of his education — the cruel treatment he received from his master — nor did he conceal his passion for *Fanny*, and the distress he feared that young lady must be involved in, when she should know of his departure.

Matthewson was a man of good sense, and had a very tender heart; he had come young into the country, as a servant, after losing all his friends in *England*, but having had a good master, who had no children, he left him all he had, which he converted into goods, proper for the *Indian* trade, and had been settled in several of the *Indian* nations at the back of *Virginia*, for above twenty years, where his success had been so extraordinary, that, besides the goods in his several stores, and near a hundred horses, and many servants and slaves, he had eight thousand pounds sterling in the hands of the merchants of *Williamsburgh*[1] and *James Town*. He had neither wife nor children, and remembering his own destitute state, when he came first into *America*, he was wonderfully affected with *Tom*'s distress; and, every now and then, whilst he was telling his story, broke out into exclamations against the villains *Williamson* and *Barlow*, and applauses of Mrs. *Barlow*, her daughter and Mr. *Ferguson* and *Gordon*.

In short, the young man told his tale with so much grace — that he insensibly insinuated himself into his affections; and when he had concluded, his master shook him kindly by the hand, and said — Poor creature! — never was a more lamentable story — but, however, set yourself at rest — I'll be your father and your friend — At first, when I purchased you — I intended you for a mere servant — I knew nothing of you — but your talents and your integrity entitle you to the chief post under me — you shall manage all my affairs — without compulsion — from this moment you are free — If you can get the love of the *Indians* as I observe, you have that of the *Negroes*, you'll be the richest man soon in *America* —

---

1 The capital of colonial Virginia.

and perhaps providence may yet make you happy in the possession of that worthy girl — you seem to deserve each other. — I perceive you have no name but *Thomas* — from this time you shall make use of mine — you shall be called *Thomas Matthewson*, and shall be the repository of all my affairs and secrets.

There is a certain somewhat, in certain countenances, that prepossesses us in the favour of the wearers at first sight, an openness, an ingenuity, and an amiableness, that immediately strikes the beholder — such was *Tom*'s, and that and the many noble instances he had given of his sentiments and his fortitude, had quite captivated his master, so that he really began to look upon him as a son. The mingled starts of joy, gratitude and love towards this generous man, which inspired *Tom*'s breast, at the conclusion of this speech, no words can paint — it actuated his whole person, it heaved his bosom — it flushed his face, and deprived him of utterance; but, flinging himself from his horse and kneeling by the side of his master's, holding his stirrup in his hand, at length he brought forth this return! Oh, sir, how happy you make me — can I ever deserve such goodness? — I looked upon you as my father, when you first interposed between me and *Barlow*'s fury — I loved you without knowing why — but here I vow, that if the most respectful duty — the humblest attendance — the exactest fidelity, can at all make me worthy of your favours — it shall be my study night and day to deserve them — your name, sir, — shall never be disgraced — and I am as happy this moment, as if I had recovered my real parents!

Matthewson still more and more delighted with this unexpected action, raised him — endeavoured to calm his overbearing sensations, and began to experience, in the society of this youth, more happiness than ever he had known before. At the house of all his friends, as he passed along, he introduced him as his near relation, made him his bedfellow, had a suit of his own clothes altered for him, trimmed with silver lace; and was pleased to observe that every body entertained the same sentiments of him with himself. He let him into the manners of the several tribes of *Indians*, with whom he trafficked, introduced him to the whole knowledge of his fortune and concerns, and to the merchants and storekeepers with whom he dealt; and his pupil improved so fast upon his hands, that he soon eased him of all trouble and solicitude.

The *French Indians*[1] beginning to be troublesome to our back

---

1 Indian tribes allied with the French in their contest with England for control of the frontier (or "back") settlements west of the Appalachians, a struggle ongoing throughout the eighteenth century.

settlements, before they departed from *Virginia*, Mr. *Matthewson* obtained a commission from the government to raise and command a troop of rangers,[1] which was not only a public service, but a security to his own private property, and, by his desire, young Mr. *Matthewson*, as *Tom* was now called, was made cornet[2] to the troop, and with this honour they set out for their stores in the *Indian* country, where they were going now to act in the double capacity of soldiers and merchants. In their journey, of near three hundred miles, through this beautiful, but wild and uncultivated country, he became quite expert in the methods of traveling, living, camping, and hunting; and, before he arrived at their first station, was as complete a woodsman as *Matthewson* himself, who beheld with delight and pride his ready proficiency.

At their arrival he presented him to the *Indian* head-men and warriors, and taking him to his several stores, initiated him into their management, and let all his servants and dependants know, he was to be obeyed next to himself. The troop they were commissioned to raise, was composed of their own people, by which the captain had the double advantage of their service and the government's pay; and they were soon made compleat enough in their exercise, for the rough duty of that part of the world, consisting of twenty-five white men and fifteen *Negroes*, besides their two officers.

It is amazing with what facility *Tom* learned the *Creek* dialect,[3] which is the general speech for trade, throughout the several nations; and by his firmness, sobriety, punctuality, and honesty towards the natives, he was become in a little time of more importance than even his principal, and equally beloved and confided in, so that the rest of the traders could make little of it in their neighbourhood, but were obliged to shift their quarters to a greater distance. Mean time he was so affectionately obsequious[4]

---

1 White troops operating in frontier areas, often in conjunction with regular imperial troops in wartime. Rangers specialized in woodlands warfare, and many imperial officials hoped they could thus lessen the Empire's reliance on Indian allies.
2 Flag-bearer.
3 While the Creeks were a powerful confederation of tribes, their dialect did not serve as a trade language (something Kimber suggests here). But the lingua franca of the region (known as the "Mobilian jargon") was from the same language family as Creek, so Kimber was not very far off.
4 Dutiful.

to his father, as he stiled him, that he could scarce bear him out of his sight, and a fit of sickness, he was attacked with, and by which he was reduced to death's door, completed so thoroughly the conquest this young man had made of his affections, by his tender assiduity,[1] his sensible grief, and his easing his mind of the burden of his affairs, that he made no secret after his recovery of his design to make him the heir of all his fortune.

Thus this abandoned, persecuted boy was now as happy as his utmost wishes could reach; but still a worm within destroyed his peace: To the woods and wilds, he oft ecchoed his *Fanny*'s name, and with all this success and good fortune, would have sunk under the burden of absence and despair, if that cordial, reviving guest, hope, of returning to throw himself at her feet, crowned with laurels, and loaded with riches, had not insinuated its soft balm into his troubled soul. Thus four years wore away, and they had yet exercised their military capacity very little; but as to their trade and riches, they were improved at least a third, and *Matthewson*'s fondness had so increased for *Tom*, that he had made a will in his favour to bar all accidents, by which he became his sole heir and executor, and lodged one copy, properly witnessed, with a merchant at *Williamsburgh*, and the other he preserved in his own custody.

Notwithstanding the peace of *Utrecht* of the year 1713,[2] the designing *French* underhandedly kept up the animosity between their *Indians*, and those attached to the *English*; and the former had made dreadful inroads into the territories of the allies of the latter. As they had begun to settle all the country at the back of us, they were willing, if possible, to engross the whole trade to themselves, and to drive us, by degrees, intirely out of that profitable branch. If ever they appeared themselves, it was under the notion of auxiliaries; but they gave free leave to their traders to accompany and support the *Indians* they dwelt amongst, to supply them with fire arms at the expence of their government,

---

1 Constant attentions.
2 The treaty which ended the War of the Spanish Succession (1701–13). Kimber gives the right gist of the situation from the English point of view, for while this treaty decreed peace between England and France, the English accused the French of using attacks on English settlements by their allies among the Indians to undermine the peace. The French, of course, accused the English of doing the same thing. The Ohio River Valley was the heart of these struggles for colonial supremacy for much of the eighteenth century.

and drive us out of all the neutral part of the country. The *British American* governors, particularly those of *Virginia* and *Carolina*,[1] ordered our people, on their side, to repel force by force, so that though there was peace between the two crowns, a hot *Indian* war was carried on in that part of the world. But as a provision against making the quarrel national, the governments, on both sides, withdrew their commissions, leaving every thing to private decision, but supplying them secretly with arms and ammunition.

A store, that captain *Matthewson* had in the *Twightwee*[2] nation, was broke open by a party of *French Indians*, two of his servants carried away captive to *Fort Moville*,[3] and the inhabitants most of them killed, valiantly fighting, and disputing every inch of ground. Upon this news he dispatched *Tom* to the tribes nearest in our alliance, who gave them the *long-talk*,[4] and engaged them to take arms to revenge so notorious a treachery. By his insinuating eloquence, he brought down seventy gun-men to his patron's residence, who joining them with twenty *Whites* and *Negroes*, they marched into the enemy's territories, for upwards of one hundred and fifty miles, burning and destroying all before them.

This news was no sooner brought to *Moville*, than the governor, who was a marquis, and knight of the order of *St. Louis*,[5] went with one hundred *Indians*, and forty *French* to oppose them, and, after a laborious rout,[6] came up within two days march of them on one of the branches of the *Ohio*. *Matthewson*'s scouts soon brought an account of their superiority in numbers, which a little intimidated his *Indians*, but he and the young warrior represented so well the shame of turning their backs, that they

---

1 Present-day South Carolina and North Carolina were chartered as a single colony, Carolina, in 1663. They split into two colonies in 1729.

2 Miami Indians whose settlements lay southwest of Lake Michigan. While nominally allied with the French, they sometimes traded with the English colonists from Pennsylvania, Virginia, and the Carolinas.

3 Named after the Mauville Indians, Fort Moville was the first French settlement in colonial Louisiana. It was located in what is now Mobile, Alabama. As unlikely as it may seem given the distances involved, it was not impossible to find a northern tribe like the Miamis visiting Fort Moville.

4 [Kimber's note] So they call their solemn debates on peace and war.

5 The Ordre Royal et Militaire de Saint-Louis, established by Louis XIV in 1693 to honor officials who had rendered long and distinguished service (and who were also staunch Catholics). It was named after his namesake, the thirteenth-century Crusader King Louis IX (1214–70).

6 March.

agreed at length to stand battle. They took them in this humour, for the *Indians* are very fickle, and waited in a convenient situation, with a steady countenance, for the arrival of the enemy.

Tom, who, upon this occasion, shewed all the conduct of intrepidity of an old warrior, formed the right wing with 14 *Whites* and *Negroes*, and captain *Matthewson* with 6 *Whites* and 15 *Indian* warriors, took post on the left; both parties, being entrenched up to the teeth, by a ditch they had cast up, and secured from view or aim by palmettos.[1] The main body of *Indians* formed the center, and were secured by a fortification of pine trees, felled on purpose, and intermixed with palmettos, and at their head were posted the *Mico*[2] *Calcathouy* and his son *Talapache*, both redoubted warriors.

It was, however, near three days before they came in sight, and during that space, they finished completely the disposition of their little army, which was so secured, that it would be a difficult and dangerous attempt to force their posts; and one of those evenings the worthy *Matthewson* and his adopted son, discoursing of their *Indian* auxiliaries, and particularly of the great qualities of *Calcathouy*, the former said, that *Indian* had endured many sorrows from the *French*, to whom he had behaved in former years with the humanity and generosity even of a Christian, for which he had been ungratefully rewarded; and proceeded to oblige *Tom*'s earnest enquiries, with the following relation of some adventures that happened, just after he entered the country, and in which he had had a considerable share.

CHAPTER VII

The Story of CALCATHOUY and TALOUFA.

OF all the war captains of the upper *Creeks*,[3] none has so much deserved reputation as the redoubted *Calcathouy*: he was the son of a *Mico*, whose prowess the *French* had often mourned; who had

---

1 A note Kimber included in the original explains that the palmetto is "a shrub with large, fanlike, leaf, with which in *America*, huts and cabins are cover'd, or thatch'd." This seems to demonstrate some geographical confusion on Kimber's part, for this plant grew *south* of the Chesapeake, not *within* that region, let alone *west* of it. Thus in botany, as with some human details such as plantation size, Kimber seems to have conflated all of "America" together.

2 The Creek title for a ruler or chief.

3 Most Upper Creek settlements were in present-day Alabama. The Lower Creek resided in present-day Georgia.

scalped some hundreds of them and their *Indians*, at their first settling in the country; and, untameably free, had resisted all their flattering arts to draw him to their interest; his tomohawk never returning without being dyed in their blood. His son became early a follower of his steps; and, at a greener age than ever was before known, forsaking the society of the women and the boys, was admitted to all the consultations of their *beloved men*, and partook in the military achievements of his nation. He performed the war dance with grace and propriety, he knew all the retreats of the woods, for some hundred miles round, was nimble as his fellow natives the deer, was the most expert marksman with his gun, would transfix the smallest of the feathered race with his arrows, was practised in all their stratagems of war, in which he had uncommon success, and, before he was twenty-five, was looked upon by the enemy as the most formidable bar to their encroachments in this part of the world.

Nor did he less excel in the milder offices of life; he was a huntsman that no prey could escape; the swift-footed buck, and the heavy buffaloe became his ready prey, and the fish of every lake seemed to croud to his suspending hook; and, in debates, either relating to the improvements of peace, or the meditated ravages of war, outstripped the wisdom of the greyest old man. But what more than any thing made him loved and dreaded by the *Indians* and *French*, was that greatness of soul which he displayed either in prosperity or adversity, the justice and honesty of his actions, the inflexible disposition he displayed to preserve that jewel liberty, and the strong attachment he had to the *English*, which no offers or advantages from the other side could induce him to forsake.

With these great and good qualities, it was not surprising that he should be elected, upon the death of his father, to succeed him in the supreme magistracy, in civil concerns, and command, in war, with the unanimous voice of his countrymen; nor that he should lead them to conquest and victory, or inspire them with a contempt of death and danger in the common cause; so that they became the most happy and envied people, in few years, of all the numerous nations of *North America*.

'Twould have been unhappy if the other sex had not afforded an object worthy the addresses of so excellent a youth; but he beheld in the amiable *Taloufa*, who was the daughter of a *bead-man*[1] of great account, all that could appear charming to the eyes of an

---

1 Holy man.

Indian, nay, of an *European*; her temper was mild and gentle, her heart soft, and susceptible of the noblest passions, her person beautiful, and her features quite transporting. Two years peace allowed him to sigh his passion at her feet; for he scorned the ways of the *Indians*, who marry as they are bid by their parents, and would accept of *Taloufa*, upon no other condition, than that of convincing her he sought her happiness in his own, and that he meant to make her his companion and the friend of his heart, and not to destine her to that drudgery and servile submission, which he abominated, but which was universally practised by the *Indian* women. Her cabin shone with the richest spoils of the chace, was adorned with the finest shells culled from the sandy beaches of many distant coasts and rivers, and her neck and lovely bosom, as well as her delicate arms, were adorned with bracelets of gold and pearl, which he had purchased of the *English* traders. Tender assiduities like these, such nobleness of sentiment, such generosity of soul, did not fail to incline the ear of the delightful *Taloufa* to his suit; and, at length, they were married, to the universal liking of their subjects, and the brave *Talapache*, now with us, and another youth, were, in due time, the issue of a mutual affection, which never could admit of inconstancy or alienation. So fond was this charming spouse, that she even attended him in many of his warlike expeditions; at home soothed his cares and anxieties, and, in short, no story can tell of a more inseparable more happy pair.

In an expedition against the *French*, in the year 1695,[1] fortune declared, for the first time, against *Calcathouy*; he was defeated, near fifty of his followers slain, himself made prisoner, and carried away towards *Quebec* in triumph. A young *French* nobleman, named *De Courcy*, who commanded against him, struck with his noble and majestic air, the dignity of his behaviour, and the undauntedness of his countenance; and at the same time knowing the importance of such an ally, if he could be gained over, refused to give him up to the rage of their *Indians*, who insisted to burn him, and when he was brought before him, said, *Indian!* you are a slave to my fortune! — you are my prisoner! — I have granted you life, against the voice of all my people, *French* and *Indians*, who burn to revenge the many mischiefs you have done them: I shall carry you to *Quebec*, from whence, if you can

---

1 If Kimber meant to reference a real battle here, it would have been an engagement in the War of the League of Augsburg (1689–97), which, like the other wars of the era, pitted New France against the English colonies as an adjunct to the more central European struggles.

perswade your nation to an alliance with us, and become our friend yourself, Count *Frontiniac*,[1] who represents our great emperor *Lewis*,[2] will, no doubt, spare your life, and return you, loaded with presents, to your nation; otherwise you will be forced to expiate all your cruelties with your blood.

This was spoke in *French*, and interpreted by one of their traders; but, as soon as *Calcathouy* heard the import of it, stung with a generous disdain and contempt, he returned the following answer. — *Frenchman!* that I have been a formidable enemy, is all you know of *Calcathouy*; you have heard, no doubt, that far as the eagle flies around these nations, so far my conquests, and, high as he soars, my fame, have extended; but *Calcathouy* is also to be known, as a man not to be cast down by a reverse of fortune, which the wisest conduct cannot always prevent — as a man who has looked death too often in the face to be scared at his approach, tho' armed with torments severe, as the most fell[3] wretch can invent; — nor can the view of any personal danger tempt me to break my engagements with a valued ally — the *English* — who fight, like me, in the common cause of mankind, against their enslavers. No — I value not your emperor or his substitute, and will sooner submit to all you can inflict, than purchase life at the price of losing my honour. Long as our lofty pines extend their branches into the air — long as our lakes supply us with the scaly prey, or our spreading woods afford us retreat and food — our nation will be your enemy; — and were I once again free — I would pour desolation upon your fields, and destruction upon your heads. Know *Frenchman*, that an *Indian*, who in prosperity could refuse your offers, scorns to be biassed or directed by the severest stroke adversity can inflict.

At this conclusion, of a speech that made all the hearers tremble, *De Courcy* turned pale, and without reply, ordered him to be bound, and immediately set forward on his return to *Quebec*, committing him to the custody of a chosen guard of *French*, who marched in the front, as well to secure so important a prisoner, as to prevent the *Indians* of his party from killing him in the rout. *Calcathouy* suffered every indignity with patience, kept silence with a surly sullenness, employing all his thoughts, however improbable, upon the means of an escape, and now and

---

1 Louis Bouade, Comte de Frontenac (1620–98), governor general of New France during this war.
2 Louis XIV, who reigned over France, and was the most powerful single monarch in Europe, between 1643 and 1715.
3 Ruthless.

then sent a deep sigh after his beloved *Taloufa*, and his family. The person who commanded this party, was a young gentleman of the name of *Marsillac*, and a knight of the *Holy Ghost*;[1] he appeared charmed with *Calcathouy*, and behaved so assiduously, to gain his good opinion, that the gloomy chief was softened, and they became friends, by the *Indian* ceremony of exchanging a present; and the chevalier[2] even loosened him from the bands that fastened his arms, and he was so far at liberty.

It happened, that after ten days march, a party of the *Iroquese*,[3] who hearing of the *French* designs against their distant allies, were out to way-lay them, luckily came up and attacked them. *De Courcy* made the best dispositions he could; but it was all in vain — he was vanquished, and forced to retreat with great precipitation, with a handful of his *French* and *Indians*, leaving the rest of his party stretched upon the earth. *Calcathouy*, at the beginning of the skirmish, seized a gun from a *Frenchman*, with which, after having knocked out his brains, he broke away to the *Iroquese*, and did prodigious execution upon his late conquerors.

His friends, overjoyed at having redeemed him, sent him home, and he returned to his nation to the inexpressible consolation of his mourning *Taloufa*, and his faithful subjects, who were gathering together with their allies and the *English*, to revenge his death, which they had looked upon as certain. He did not suffer this ardour to cool, but, full of his late usage, marched at the head of the three hundred gun men, assisted by fifty *English*, to join the *Iroquese*, and, with unbated diligence, spread fire and sword to the very gates of *Quebec*: the governor did all he could to oppose this insult, but it was so sudden, that he had not time to call in the assistance of his *Indians*, and *Calcathouy* returned, after having laid many plantations in ruins, within the sight of the town, and carried home forty *Frenchmen*, whom he had made prisoners, with whom he entered the *Creek* towns, with songs and shouts of triumph, after an absence of only fourteen weeks.

In the first fury of his people, he had much ado to prevent their burning all the *French* prisoners, without exception; and at last was forced to agree to the sentence of the *beloved men*,[4] that

---

1 The Ordre du Saint-Esprit, a military order begun in 1578 to uphold Catholicism in the wars of the Reformation.
2 A general title usually reserved for members of the French knighthood.
3 The Iroquois were a powerful confederation of tribes along the north-western borderlands of Britain's North American colonies.
4 The tribal elders.

ten should be chosen, by casting lots amongst themselves, for execution; and that the rest should be made slaves. Accordingly the forlorn number were prepared for their horrid fate. — Already the posts were erected, in the principal town, the bands prepared — the light-wood placed around — the trembling victims were bound to the stake; matches tied in all parts of their bodies, and the women and children were eager to begin their torments; when, one of them looking wistfully towards the place where *Calcathouy* and the *bead-men* were seated, cry'd out, in the *Indian* tongue, with a trembling voice, Ah! *Mico* — will you burn your friend, will you see him expire in torments, who loosened your chains? No sooner were the words out of his mouth, than *Calcathouy* recollected the voice and person of *Marsillac*, who had till that instant no opportunity to make himself known — struck thereat, he gave orders to stop the lighting of the dreadful fire, and, having represented his behaviour to the *bead-men*, he, with tears and prayers, besought his exemption from punishment, which, with some difficulty he obtained, and immediately flew to him, and, with his own hands, having unbound him, sent him to the care of his *Taloufa*, at his cabin; nay, he did more, he, with so much success, intreated for the other prisoners, that only one suffered the fiery trial; for he was resolved to spare all he could to the merit of his *French* friend.

When he arrived at his hut, he embraced him, told his wife of his obligations to him, and, with her, endeavoured, by every kind and hospitable treatment, to render his captivity easy. *Marsillac* was a thorough *Frenchman*, was supple, fawning, and obsequious, and soon so gained upon the hearts of his patron and patroness, that they made him a party in all their pleasures — he fished, hunted, and feasted with them, and partook of the innocent delights of those rural retreats, that were sacred to the love and friendship of the happy pair and their family. Perhaps *Marsillac* was sincere in his first attachment to his deliverer, and might have persisted in it; but frequent views of the graces of *Taloufa*, soon made an impression upon his heart, and he burnt, slave and dejected as he was, with an impure passion, which however he had not the temerity to declare. He grew melancholy, spoke little, and had so lost his gaiety of temper, that it was soon perceived, and his kind host and hostess ascribing it to his absence from *Quebec*, and his condition of a captive, at length prevailed for his liberty, with two of his fellow prisoners, and had them conducted safe into their own territories.

Three years passed away, at the end of which *Marsillac* was sent to garrison a new fort, then erecting, since called *Moville*, and which was not quite defensible; and the being so much nearer to *Taloufa*, recalled his old desires, and he resolved to hazard the breach of gratitude, virtue, and honour, nay his own ruin, rather than not enjoy the tempting bait. For this purpose, having selected a chosen few, he privately marched, for several days, on good horses, till he arrived at one of the well-known retreats of that excellent woman, and her fond husband; found them there, overpowered them, and their two or three attendants, all unprepared and unarmed, and having bound them, returned with his prey to the fort, before any alarm could be given in the towns, which had been used to these absences of their king sometimes for several days.

No words can paint the mingled fury, horror, and detestation, that *Calcathouy* expressed, when this wretch discovered himself, and barefacedly owned his baseness, and had the audacity even to threaten him with death to his face, unless *Taloufa* complied with his lust. *Frenchman*, he cry'd, all enflamed — thou convincest me there is neither justice nor gratitude in thy nation! — well it is for thee — that I am bound and unarmed, and that thou art surrounded with thy men — otherwise, words like these, should have cost thee thy life — well am I repaid for trusting to any of thy faithless tribe; but know this, thou wretch, that *Taloufa* can die before she can suffer such disgrace, and that *Calcathouy* dares the completion of thy abominable and black treachery. *Marsillac* ordered him away to a dungeon, loaded with irons, not being able to face him longer, or to reply, and *Taloufa* was conducted full of rage and despair, to an apartment next his own, with two men, to see that she took no desperate methods against her life.

His overbearing lust did not permit him to stay long from her, and, entering her chamber some hours after, he ordered the attendants away, and began to sooth her to his purposes; but was answered with the contempt and disdain that the virtue of that amiable woman inspired. At length he proceeded to force, and bearing her to the bed, would have triumphed over the chastity of so many years of purity, when *Taloufa* espied a sword upon it, lying behind her, which one of her guard had uncautiously left behind him, which, seizing hastily, she plunged into his bosom, and he vomited out his black soul in a torrent of blood. By the threats and menaces he had used towards her *Calcathouy*, she imagined, ere now, he had been made a sacrifice, and, knowing she was in the power of wretches who would not fail to revenge the death of their chief, she, without hesitation, bravely run herself through the heart, and fell upon the floor, an example of consummate virtue and heroic fortitude.

For some hours this dreadful catastrophe remained undiscovered; but at length *Marsillac* beginning to be missed, by his servants, they broke into the room, and were witnesses to a scene of horror, that chilled their blood; and the story was soon spread thro' the garrison. The officer that hereupon succeeded in the command, being apprehensive of the ill effects of such an action, and the odium it would bring upon his nation, amongst all the *Indians*, friends and enemies, was at his wit's end how to act; he knew the prowess of *Calcathouy*, and that, after he was informed of the death of *Taloufa*, he would, if set at liberty, breath nothing but implacable revenge, and soon overturn their new-erected works; and tho' he detested the baseness of *Marsillac*, and resolved not to take his life; yet he determined to send him to *Quebec*, with a letter of the affair, to *Frontiniac*, and his advice to keep him a secret and perpetual prisoner.

Whilst these events happened at *Moville*, *Calcathouy's* attendants, who had escaped when he was taken, for *Marsillac*, blinded to every thing but his passion, had suffered them to go unhurt, came home with the news of his capture by the *French*, which caused the utmost consternation. Tho' I[1] was young in the trade, I had received so many favours from this great man, that I was really afflicted with his loss, and determined to acquiesce in every measure for revenging his fall; and a body of *Indians*, to the number of eight hundred, being assembled, I joined them with near sixty other *Englishmen*, traders and their servants, and immediately marched towards *Moville*, to which place we imagined, truly, that he and his *Taloufa* were conveyed: before we set down to the siege, however, a *French* deserter joined us from thence, informed us of the fate of *Marsillac* and *Taloufa*, and that *Calcathouy* had two days before been conveyed from the fort, and was gone towards *Quebec*.

Upon this intelligence, myself, with ten *Whites*, and fifty *Indians*, immediately set off in pursuit of the party that had him in custody, and, it being a rainy season, and the waters much swelled, after three days journey, we came up with them, on the banks of the *Misouri*,[2] and finding them only forty men, we

---

1 Matthewson.

2 Here, as elsewhere in the novel, Kimber dramatically underestimates the time it would take to journey between far-flung points in North America. As the crow flies, Moville (or Mobile, Alabama) is over 550 miles (or 900 km) from St Louis, the southernmost point on the Missouri River (see Map 2 on p. 38).

attacked them, killed every soul, after a very brave resistance, and once more set the unfortunate chief at liberty. The most informed and polite *European* could not have, in more lively terms, expressed his gratitude, and, when he heard we were before *Moville*, me-thought his figure and attitude resembled that of the fabled god of war; but alas! when, in a prepared and prudent way, I let him into the catastrophe of his wife; all the fierceness of the warrior, and the firmness of the man was lost for some days, the *Indian* stoicism was not proof against so home a stroke[1] — he fainted, and, when recovered, made the saddest and most moving complaints, till rage and fury broke in upon his soul, and the thoughts of vengeance, occupied, in its turn, his breast.

In short, we arrived at the camp before *Moville*, and, after three weeks lying before it, in which actions of bravery were performed on both sides, worthy of eternal remembrance, the commanding officer proposed a capitulation, by the articles of which all concerned with *Marsillac* in his baseness, were delivered up to us and burnt; one thousand pounds were given in presents to our *Indians*, and the fortress was dismantled; after which the rest of the garrison, now reduced to a very small number, were conducted safe into the territories of *Quebec*, and we returned in triumph to our nations. Poor *Calcathouy*, though happy in his children, has never been seen once to smile since the loss of the amiable *Taloufa*, and though alive, but half lives without her inspiring presence. Mean time he has perpetually harassed and plagued the enemy, and, had his counsels been followed by our neighbouring governments, *Moville* would not now be a thorn in our sides, but we should ourselves have had a fort there, which would have bridled the *French* incroachments, and given us a larger extent of country to trade in.

CHAPTER VIII

Here the captain ceased, and *Tom* began to conceive the highest regard for this worthy *Indian*, and wished the *French* would approach, that he might have a fresh opportunity of chastising that base and perfidious people. At length the *French* appeared, and either for want of intelligence, or from a confidence of their numbers, suffered their *Indians* to move forward, promiscuously,[2] without order or command. As soon as they came within gun-

---

1 Such a direct blow.
2 Carelessly.

shot, *Tom* ordered half his men to give fire, and *Matthewson* doing the like on the other flank, they dropped great numbers, and the whole body made a sudden halt of the greatest astonishment; at which time, as they were all huddling together, the reserve let fly, and plainly could perceive upwards of twenty more fall to the earth.

The *French*, meantime, who were at a considerable distance, seeing their friends engaged, marched briskly up to their assistance; but it was too late, for the *Indians*, quite scared, fell back upon them, and put them into such disorder, that *Matthewson* gave the signal for the main body of his *Indians* to move up, and attack them to the very teeth. This they did, with such courage; that, after two or three discharges, by which they killed more of their own *Indians* than ours, they began to retreat, in as good order as possible; but *Matthewson* and *Tom* having march'd about, unperceived, thro' certain defiles,[1] attacked them in the rear, so that, finding no possibility of escape, they performed wonders of bravery, and disputed every inch of ground with the utmost obstinacy.

Both parties were now at close quarters, with pieces clubbed, matchets, hangers,[2] and *Tomohawks*, making wretched butchery of each other, till, of the enemy *Indians*, very few were left alive, and most of those prisoners to ours, and the *French* had lost half their number. *Matthewson* and *Tom* fought like heroes, and dealt death at every stroke; but the former encountring the *French* commander, hand to hand, unfortunately received a pistol ball thro' his heart, which at once robbed the generous man of life.

Tom, who was within view, seeing him fall, gave a loud cry, and pressing to the spot, shot his adversary thro' the head; and now, full of revenge and resentment, spread such destruction around him, that the miserable remains of the forty *French*, being only twelve in number, flung down their arms, and cried for quarter.[3] In the first sallies of his grief and rage, he was going to refuse it, and cut them all to pieces; but humanity and reason soon resumed their empire over him, and he ordered his men to protect them from our *Indians*.

So obstinate an engagement was never known in that part of the world, nor the *Indians* to stand their ground so firmly: it lasted full six hours, and was perfect butchery all the while. Of

---

1 "A narrow way or passage along which troops can march only by files or with a narrow front" (*OED*).

2 "Matchet" is a variant of "machete." A "hanger" is a short sword.

3 Pled that their lives be spared.

the forty *French*, only twelve remained alive, and most of those desperately wounded. Of their hundred *Indians* forty-seven lay dead on the field, near twenty were knocked down in the pursuit, ten were made prisoners, and the rest got off by swimming across the stream. On the side of the *English*, poor captain *Matthewson* and *Talapache* were killed, four negroes and three white men; and *Tom*, now commander in chief, and eight more, slightly wounded — of the seventy *Indians*, besides *Talapache*, twenty-five were slain, and an inconsiderable[1] number wounded.

After having disposed the prisoners under proper guard, they interred, first, *Talapache* and their own dead, and the *French* marquis, with military ceremony, and then the rest of the *French*, and their *Indians*, in one deep pit, firing three rounds over their graves. This care of the dead got *Tom* great reputation with both parties; and now having wept sincere tears over the body of his dear friend and patron, whose loss lay heavy upon his grateful mind, he had thoughts of carrying it back to be interred on friendly ground; but as they were near eighty miles from his nearest store, he found it impracticable, and therefore prepared to give him the best funeral his circumstances would afford. They hollowed a tree for a coffin, in which they placed him, after cleansing him from the blood that had soiled his visage, and, digging a deep grave, they let him down into that peaceful habitation, his adopted, mournful son, shedding floods of tears over him, and speaking an oration to his praise in the *English* and *Indian* tongues; then firing three vollies over him, they covered him with his parent earth, and neatly sodded the grave with green turf.

But *Tom* was not yet satisfied, and knowing he had an *English* servant of the captain's left alive, who had served his time to a carver,[2] he ordered a proper tree to be sought, and encamped upon the spot till it could be fashioned for a monument, and the following inscription, cut upon it, which he drew up on the occasion.

Whilst humanity and virtue exist in the world,
To all those, who knew
Capt. JOHN MATTHEWSON,
His memory will be ever dear.
He was a man,

---

1 Incalculable.
2 He had been an apprentice or indentured servant to a sculptor.

Of wisdom and knowledge,
Of such integrity,
So just, so merciful, so charitable, so frugal, so temperate,
That his death
Is a public loss.
Valiantly fighting,
Against the *French* and their *Indians*,
Tho' superior in number,
He received a wound, which robbed him of life,
After he had secured victory to his party,
On *Sept.* 17. *Anno*[1] 1719.
Friend or enemy!
Oh! spare this remembrance
Of so excellent a person,
Erected,
A poor testimony of affection, by his mourning son
THOMAS MATTHEWSON.

This pious work took him four days, and having finished it, they began to march homeward, where they arrived in six days more, with all their prisoners.

The *Indians* being dismissed with the accustomed presents, and carrying their prisoners with them, whom they afterwards burnt, as is their practice; *Tom* retired into one of his houses, and would see no company: he sincerely regretted the loss of a man to whom he had been so much obliged, nor did the splendid fortune to which he succeeded, at all alleviate his sorrows: for some time, even that perpetual guest, his dear *Fanny*, was banished from his thoughts. At length he resolved to go to *Virginia*, to take possession of his patron's effects, and to carry his *French* prisoners with him, whom he had treated with the utmost humanity; from thence to return, dispose of his goods, and break up his stores, for he could no longer endure the country, and thence to travel to *Maryland*, to make his dear friends partakers of his fortune, and see the jewel of his soul, the uncertainty of whose situation was worse than death.

This resolution formed, he began to prepare for its execution, and, in the time that took up, frequently dined with his prisoners, one of whom, the others treated with great deference and respect, which made him curious to know his quality, which they as stu-

---

1 Latin for "year."

diously concealed, imagining he would demand a ransom for him. He was about his own age, and, through an overwhelming sorrow and a sordid dress, shone forth such traits of dignity and beauty, as visibly testified his superiority to the rest of his companions.

When they heard he intended to carry them to *Virginia*, they were greatly terrified, particularly this youth, who, one morning, desiring a private audience of the captain, addressed him thus: Your amiable behaviour, ever since the fatal day I fell into your hands, tells me, you have a soul superior to any thing mean and sordid; your compassionate disposition convinces me you are a friend to mankind, and particularly under the pressure, the anguish of misfortune. You killed my father, but you killed him honourably, and I am obliged not to hate you: you saw him destroy the dearest friend you had. I am the son of the marquis *du Cayle*, governor of *Moville*, and commander of the party you vanquished. I had a tender passion for a lady of my own age, at *Quebec*, whom I left, forced by my duty, some months ago, ready to be forced to a match that would undo her, and make me eternally miserable. If you carry me to *Virginia*, you rob us both of life, for in that case it will be impossible to fly to her succour in time — and perhaps, even now, the news of my death has broke her heart, or rendered her an easier prey to the designs of our enemies. Ah, sir, if you ever loved, you'll pity me! name my ransom, I'll give you my parole[1] of honour to remit it to you, and let me, alone and unarmed as I am, return to *Canada*, and your generosity will call down the blessings of heaven upon your head.

Circumstances so similar to his own, moved the young captain extremely; it brought his dear *Fanny*'s sufferings at once into his mind, nor could he refrain tears; and after some minutes pause, folding his arms about him, he replied, Chevalier, I sympathize in your distress! I myself, at this instant, feel all the weight of your calamity, by sad and woeful experience; if we entered the territories of your *Indians*, it was in return for the like insult, and for very unwarrantable depredations and excesses — you lost a father — I lost a father and a friend. Let us remember these things no more — The two governments are not concerned in this affair — go — I give you your liberty, and that of your companions, without ransom, and will furnish you with arms to defend, and provisions to subsist yourselves in your tedious march. — Go — and may you reap all your wishes — Let my gen-

---

1 Oath.

erosity make you a friend to any *English* subject, you may see a captive with your nation.

Never was seen a more sudden transition from grief to joy, than that of this young *Frenchman*. He, over and over, embraced his deliverer and friend, as he called him, promised to hold his kindness in everlasting remembrance, and to relieve and comfort every *Englishman* he ever saw in distress. It was two days before he departed with his fellow prisoners, plentifully furnished with arms, ammunition, and provisions, and attended by a friendly *Indian*, to see them safe to *Moville*, and in that time they contracted an intimate friendship with each other, and parted with promises of mutual remembrance.

And now our young hero, having left all his concerns in the *Indian* country in the hands of his remaining faithful servants, till his return, set out with two attendants for *Williamsburgh*, and made such expedition, that he arrived there in less than fifteen days, and immediately repaired to the merchant's, where one of the copies of his patron's will was deposited. Already the joyful news of the late victory had reached them, and the melancholy death of the captain, so that he was condoled with on his arrival by the governor and all the principal inhabitants, who vyed which should shew him the greatest honour and respect.

Having administered to the will, he found himself, after paying all the debts upon the estate, and the few legacies specified in the will, master of nine thousand pounds sterling in ready money, and by computation near one thousand pounds worth of goods, besides book debts to a considerable amount. The merchant who was his patron's principal banker and cashier, now received every thing in the name of *Thomas Matthewson*, and gave security for the monies in his hand. *Tom* gave mourning to all the deceased's friends, with rings in token of remembrance,[1] and put himself into the same livery,[2] and what opened every body's mouth in his

---

1 In eighteenth-century British and American society, it was customary for friends and families of the deceased to memorialize them by wearing "mourning rings" for an unspecified period after their death. As Matthewson's adopted son and heir, Tom would have been responsible for issuing these rings.

2 I.e., Tom is following the model of the friends and family of the deceased by also wearing a mourning ring. "Livery" can denote clothing or provisions given to servants, but it can also mean, among other things, a suit of clothes or a badge or token (*OED*). Here we assume Kimber intends something close to the latter meaning.

praise was, his clearing the prison of unfortunate debtors, and bestowing benefactions upon many poor families; and, as his friend the merchant was upon marrying his daughter, he, in the politest manner, made the bride a present of five hundred pounds.

Every tongue spoke his praises, and he was caressed by all ranks of people, and, as he declared his intention of quitting the trade, many of the best matches were offered him, which he courteously declined by letting them know he had determined first to visit his native country, for so he called *Maryland*. Before he set out on his return to the *Indian* nations, he wrote to Mrs. *Barlow*, his dear *Fanny* and all his friends, acquainting them with his adventures and good fortune, and promising speedily to visit them, enclosing the letters in a packet to the good Mr. *Ferguson*; he also sent some rich presents to them all, by the same sloop,[1] and particularly a gold repeating watch[2] to his *Fanny*; but still remained in the utmost terror and apprehension at the alteration so many years absence might have occasioned, by death, or what was worse, the odious match with *Carter*.

These affairs transacted, he bid adieu to all friends, and set out, on his return to a last view of the dusky race amongst whom he had conversed. He arrived safely after a month's journey, for it was now winter, and the rivers were much swelled, at his stores, and found every thing in good and thriving condition; but terrible apprehensions of a visit from the *French*. After taking a survey of his whole stock, he called to him the three men who had been in the principal trust under his late patron, and the rest of the servants, and spoke to them as follows: My friends and companions, you have lost an excellent master as well as myself, and I think you ought to lose nothing by his death — I have sufficient without following trade, and shall therefore resign all my interest in it to you three, whom I know he intended, had he lived, to provide for. I have therefore brought this instrument, by which I give you, in equal proportions, all my right and title to the stores, horses, storehouses, and every thing that belongs to me, by his devise,[3] in this country, which upon an exact computation I think will amount to near three hundred and fifty pounds a-piece; I

---

1 A relatively small, single-masted ship.
2 A watch with an internal bell that sounded each quarter-hour or hour. Invented in the 1680s, such a timepiece would have remained something of a curiosity and luxury in the early eighteenth century.
3 By the terms of his will.

would have you, with this beginning, which is superior to your late master's, trade in joint stock, and I have secured you such credit in *Virginia*, that you may have one thousand pounds worth of goods at any warning. God bless you with it, and prosper you! As to you gentlemen, turning to the others, you have most of you some years to come of the time you were indented for — this I discharge you from, and set you free, and to every man will give twenty pounds to engage his remembrance of our good departed benefactor. The *Negroes* also I set at liberty, and desire you three, gentlemen, will take them into your service at proper wages.

To attempt to describe the expressive gratitude these worthy creatures shewed in word and gesture, upon this generosity of their master, would surpass the power of language. All were transported — every one was happy! And now having disposed of all his concerns, he went round to take leave of his *Indian* friends, and particularly took a tour of near one hundred miles to see his old and brave companion in war *Calcathouy*.

Here he diverted himself for some few days, in hunting deer and buffaloes, in the manner of the people, with whose customs he was as familiar as our own. One day, being out with a very small party of only six *Indians*, besides himself and the chief, they laid them down to take some refreshment under the shade of a cypress grove, which on one side was obscured from view by a rising hillock, and on the other, by the surrounding woods; and whilst they were regaling, upon cold venison which they had brought with them, on a sudden, from behind, a volley of small shot was fired amongst them, by which three of the *Indians*, and the great *Calcathouy* were shot dead, and the other three desperately wounded, and *Tom* had one corner of his hat shot away; he was going to take up his piece to defend himself, but it was too late; for he found himself in an instant surrounded by enemy *Indians*, who butchered his surviving companions, scalped them before his face, and then stripping him to the skin, made him march before them at a great rate, till they imagined themselves out of danger of pursuit; and then setting him in the midst, they made a ring, and danced the war-dance.

Tom was always endowed with an extraordinary presence of mind, and was pleased to discover that, by their dialect, these were not of the same nation with those he had used so roughly, in the late engagement; but a party of the *Ocuni*,[1] in the alliance of the *French*, who he understood meant only to convey him to *Moville*,

---

1 It is unclear which tribe Kimber has in mind here, as no tribe is known to have gone by this name.

to get the usual present. Had it been the other, he knew he must be a dead man. Thus behold a reverse of fortune — he, who but a small space of time before, was happy, and employed in making others so, is now strip'd naked, bound with thongs, and a spectacle of triumph and reproach to a barbarous gang of savages! He lamented his imprudence and the death of his friends; but the false step they had taken was not now to be remedied.

After they had danced and sung till they were tired, they began to search the pockets of the prisoner, and to divide his garments; in one of his coat pockets happened to be his old favourite flute. This caused a good deal of wonder amongst them, and at last they applied to the owner, by signs, to make it speak, or let them know the use of it; upon which, in the *Creek* tongue, he told them, if they'd unbind him, he would divert them with it. They shewed a pleased surprize to hear him talk a language they understood, and complied with his request.

As soon as he was unbound, he played Prince *Eugene's* march,[1] which he thought would best please these warlike people. Never was more amazement shewn than now; they made the most ridiculous gestures of astonishment, then snatch'd the tuneful instrument, surveyed it on all sides, attempted to blow ineffectually, and then applied to him to tell them how, particularly their chief. He shewed him how to place his lips and his tongue, and when he made it sound, he danced about in the utmost triumph. Seeing him so fond of it, he took an effectual method for his preservation and good treatment, by presenting it to him with these words — you are my friend — yes, the other returned, putting his hand upon his head, and you shall be mine, making him at the same time, a present of a painted *Tomohawk* (or small *Indian* battle-axe). This is so sacred a compact amongst the *Indians*, that it is never broken, and they think themselves obliged to protect their friend in any evil and danger. He then enquired in the *French* tongue, if he understood him, and found he talked that language very intelligibly.

Hearing all this, they began to like him extremely, and let him march with them without being bound; and in this naked manner, after nine days travel, they arrived within a mile of the fort, he not having suffered the least ill usage, and eating and drinking in common with his masters. One of their number was

---

1 This popular march by the English composer Jeremiah Clarke (1674–1707) was first published in 1705.

dispatched before, to give notice of their arrival, upon which the gates of the fort were thrown open, the garrison went under arms, and they entered it with their scalps displayed, and their prisoner in the center, chanting the dreadful notes of the war-hoop, whilst the cannon on the ravelin[1] were fired, and the garrison made three discharges to do them the more honour.

The governor was seated ready to receive them, and, after thanking them for their services, and applauding their bravery, the usual presents were brought out and distributed, and then they presented their prisoner; the chief telling him, he talked his own language as well as theirs. This *Frenchman* was a man of humanity, and ordered one of his domesticks to fetch a coat, which after *Tom* had put on, he began to question him, as to his profession, and how he came amongst the *Indians*. My lord, he replied, I am an *Englishman*, and curiosity brought me from *Virginia*, to see the customs of our *Indians*; we had been innocently hunting upon our own territories, when these savages treacherously fired upon us, destroyed my companions, and brought me here, to experience the polite usage of your generous nation, with whom I think our crown is in perfect peace and amity.

Sir, he returned, I pity your condition — you may depend upon good treatment whilst you are here — but I have orders to send all prisoners, taken by the *Indians*, to *Quebec*, to which place you will depart in a few days, with an escort of my garrison; and if no more appearance of ill is visible, you will be returned to *Virginia* in safety. He then rose up, and taking *Tom* by the hand, led him to his apartment — ordered wine, and some cold provisions, desired him to eat and forget his mishap, thank God he was got so well out of their hands, and told him he seemed so much of a gentleman, that he should lodge and table with him, during his stay, and had liberty to walk about the fort upon his parole.

The worthy creature made all the acknowledgements he was capable of, in words, for this goodness, and making a virtue of necessity, assumed a pleasing air, conversed with freedom, and so as to gain intirely the good will of his host, the baron *Detonville*;[2] but as to the going abroad, he did not embrace that offer, fearing to be known by some of the *Indians*, and betrayed to be the conqueror of M. *du Cayle*.

---

1 A triangular fortification placed in front of a castle or fort.
2 If Kimber meant to reference a real person here, it most likely was the Marquis de Denonville (1637–1710), who held (among other posts) the position of governor general of New France between 1685 and 1689.

CHAPTER IX

The next day his benefactor supplied him with a complete suit of rich cloaths, with all appurtenances[1] of dress; and when the escort was ready, he set out, after they had exchanged mutual promises of friendship. They were three weeks in the journey to *Canada*,[2] partly by land, and partly upon the navigable lakes, which the enterprising *French* had every where made to communicate with each other, and, considering the country, he endured as few hardships as could be expected; but the encreasing distance between him and his lovely *Fanny*, caused him cruel inquietudes, and had he not had the comfort of knowing, that before this time she must have heard from him, would have produced all the funest[3] consequences of despair. With wonder and astonishment he frequently ran over the occurrences of his past life, and in humble and pious ejaculations adored and praised that almighty Being, who had protected him thro' so many dangers and difficulties, and still continued to watch over his steps.

He was perfectly astonished when he entered *Quebec*, to see so populous and sumptuous a city, far surpassing any thing he had seen before in *America*, and silently said to himself — Ah! this settlement will be a perpetual and terrible thorn in our sides in this part of the world. The governor received him with a great deal of distinction, as well on account of his easy and polite behaviour, and from a letter he had received recommending him to his favour from *Detonville*, as the report his conductors made of his carriage in the late tour from *Moville*. He answered his interrogatories with all the prudence he was able; but being pressed very close, could not be so disingenuous as to deny that he had been concern'd in the *Indian* trade for some years, saying his name was *Barlow*: For he had the mortification to hear, on every hand, the consternation the late defeat and death of *Cayle* had occasioned, and threats of vengeance against the young *Matthewson*, whenever they got him in their power.

After his examination was finished, the governor said — I am extremely sorry, sir, for you really have gained my good opinion, that I cannot set you liberty; but so many insults have been committed by the gentlemen in the trade, on your side, that upon the

---

1 Accessories.
2 Another instance where Kimber underestimates North American distances. As the crow flies, Mobile is 1430 miles (2300 km) from Quebec, and hence this overland party would need to have averaged a superhuman 70 miles per day to complete the journey in 3 weeks.
3 Fatal, disastrous.

report thereof, the king my master has ordered all prisoners taken on his territories, for the *Indians* have made it appear you were without the *English* limits, should be sent to *France*. The *Flora* man of war[1] is now ready to sail — I will recommend you to the captain, and, tho' a prisoner, I'm sure you'll be considered merely as a passenger, and enjoy liberty all the voyage — and thus much farther I will do — you may have any money advanced you, upon drawing bills on your agent in *Virginia*, and what letters you think proper to confide with me, I assure you, upon my honour, shall go there by the first conveyance, unopened.

Tho' the thoughts of so tedious an absence from *Maryland* gave him inexpressible pangs, he was obliged to dissemble, and thank his excellency for his goodness, and acquiesce with a good grace, and he desired the advancement of a hundred livres to fit himself for the passage, and bills for a thousand more on *France*, which was immediately complied with, and thereupon he drew upon his agent in *Virginia* for the like sum sterling, and as much more as to defray his charges of drawing,[2] signing his bills *Thomas Barlow*; but in the letter he wrote, he, after giving a long account of his misfortune and treatment, and the sending him to *France*, explained the reason of his alteration of name, and desired due honour might be paid to his bills notwithstanding; and also gave orders to him to remit to his correspondent at *London* a thousand pounds, with orders to him to lodge a letter of credit[3] with M. *Alexander*, banker at *Paris*, for the like sum on his arrival, to whom he was recommended by the governor.

As the governor had given his honour, he without any scruple wrote all that his mind dictated, and indeed found that he was really the man he pretended to be. He was so caressed by the principal people in *Quebec*, that he was obliged, though under great terror, to be more public than at *Moville*, but never enquired after the chevalier *Cayle*, whom he had used so generously, for fear of making a discovery that would be fatal to him. In three weeks he was out of all his pain, however, by going on board the Man of War, after waiting upon the Governor and his Friends to pay his compliments of departure; and the next day she sailed down the river of St. *Laurence* to proceed on her voyage.

The Governor strictly just to his promises, had so recommended him, that the Chevalier *D'Aville*, Commander of the

---

1 A ship commissioned for naval warfare.
2 The bank fees associated with transferring his money.
3 A letter from one bank to another authorizing the withdrawal of funds.

Ship, and all his Officers treated him with the utmost respect and distinction, and in a few days began to bless themselves at having so agreeable a companion; for, tho' sadly uneasy in his mind, he put on the gayest and most placid air and mien in the world, in return for the kind usage he met with. The *Flora* had orders to touch at *Martinico*,[1] on which account she shap'd her course for the *West Indies*, and after three weeks blustering voyage, came into the lat. 35, and long. 80.2' being abreast of the great *Bahama bank*[2] where the commander had instructions to look into the neighbouring keys, after an *English* sloop and a *French* brig[3] who had lately turn'd pyrates, and infested the trade in the gulph of *Florida* and to *Cuba, Hispaniola*[4] and *Jamaica*, and had been also very troublesome to the *Leeward* islands.

But the time was arriv'd when the villains should pay for all their mischiefs and cruelties; for as they were standing under a very easy sail,[5] the long boat[6] which had been detached to *Cat* and *Watling*'s islands,[7] and the adjacent coves, was seen rowing towards the ship with the utmost expedition, upon which the captain order'd the sails to be back'd,[8] and in less than an hour she got on board, with intelligence that the ships, they were in search of, lay in *Exuma* sound, and that one of them was upon the career.[9] The whole ship's crew gave a great shout at this intelligence, but as the *Flora* which was a frigate of thirty-five guns,[10] could not venture in, a consultation was held, at the conclusion of which, the long boat, yawl and pinnace,[11] were order'd to be well mann'd, and the former had two 3 pounders clapp'd into her

---

1 The French colonial sugar island of Martinique.
2 Up until the late eighteenth century, navigation was notoriously imprecise. Not altogether surprisingly, then, the coordinates given here are rather off target, placing the action not in the Bahamas, but in central North Carolina.
3 Both relatively small ships, a sloop having one mast and a brig two.
4 The island on which the present-day nations of Haiti and the Dominican Republic are located.
5 Moving slowly under gentle winds.
6 A long rowboat, usually seating eight or ten rowers, kept aboard sailing ships for trips ashore.
7 Islands in the Bahamas. Watling's Island is also known as San Salvador.
8 To lay the sails back in order to slow the ship down.
9 Tipped over on its side for repairs.
10 A fairly large naval ship, presumably too deep and wide to navigate the sound.
11 Rowboats of three different sizes.

bow,[1] and their crews being furnish'd with small arms and ten rounds of powder and ball each man, they were thought capable of taking the pyrates.

Our young adventurer was present at all these consultations, and two of the lieutenants being ill, and the vessel coming out without either ensigns or cadets, a person properly qualified seemed wanting to command the yawl. After a modest introduction, in which he mention'd his being a prisoner, he wish'd he might be permitted to shew his gratitude, by accompanying them, as the punishing such pests of society was the common business of every nation upon earth. My dear friend, the captain reply'd, I'll venture to trust you with the vacant command — 'tis true you are under a kind of restraint; but your offence is not known, and I fancy you are only sent to *France* by way of form, and merely in obedience to the letter of the governor's instructions, tho' had the spirit of them been consider'd, I believe we should not have been honour'd with your company.

Tom made his acknowledgements and immediately enter'd upon his command, and all three stood away[2] for the sound under an easy sail. The first lieutenant commanded the long boat as commodore, and the master the pinnace. It had been agreed, as it was imagin'd, and as it prov'd, the pyrates had not seen the long boat, that that and the yawl should lay the sloop on board her quarters, and enter her at once, and that the pinnace should attack the brig which was upon the careen, by landing her men and taking possession of all the men and arms ashore, and then righting the ship to get her off. They fortunately, it being very hazy weather and the dusk of the evening, and as they did not row but sail, got up within two boats length before they were discover'd, and the strange confusion it put the wretches in, was evidenc'd by the oaths, execrations and curses that resounded on every side; and as they suspected no danger their guns were unshotted,[3] their sails unbent, and they had nothing to oppose with but small arms and desperation.

The lieutenant and *Tom* soon got on board after exchanging a few shot, by which they receiv'd no damage, and whilst the former secur'd all upon the main deck, which, seeing themselves

---

1 The sturdiest of the rowboats, propelled by both oars and a sail, the pinnace could carry small cannons designed to fire three-pound balls.
2 Sailed away.
3 Unloaded.

over-power'd, they suffer'd without much resistance, tho' most of them drunk; the latter made his way, pistol in hand, to the round house,[1] which he found barricaded suddenly against him, and several random shots were fired thro' the loop holes; but being now join'd by the lieutenant with such of his party as were not on guard, they pointed the three pounders against the barricado, which had such success, that, in less than twenty minutes, those within call'd for quarters. The two commanders enter'd sword in hand and pistols cock'd, and found the pyrate captain, mate, quarter master and eight more, who surrendered prisoners of war, and were conducted to their fellows who were ty'd, and under guard in the forecastle[2] and the captain's cabin.

Mean time a gun was fir'd from the other ship, which was the signal agreed upon, when she was taken, at which the men on board the sloop gave a loud huzza and were answer'd by those on board the brig, who could plainly hear each other. But the master had had pretty warm work of it, having three men kill'd and four wounded before he got possession, and ten of the *French* pyrates were slain. On board the sloop only two of the *Flora*'s crew were wounded, and two of the pyrates, and one killed. Thus, by the drunkenness, want of order and confusion of the villains, a cheap and easy conquest was gain'd and prisoners made of thirty seven *English* and eighteen *French*, besides the two captains.

By the time the whole was atchiev'd the next morning dawn'd, and the *Flora* came to an anchor close upon the north breakers[3] at the mouth of the sound, and *Tom* had the honour to carry to the captain the first news of their victory, as a token of his satisfaction with which, he presented him with the gold hilted sword from his side, and tenderly embrac'd him. Three days were taken up in classing and examining the prisoners, who were then brought on board the *Flora* and put in irons, to receive their due deserts at *Martinico*. The sloop mounted ten 6 pounders, and the brig six 4 pounders besides swivels,[4] and had been in concert many months.[5] A great quantity of money and goods was found on board, to the joy of the captors, who were like to be well paid for the service they had done to mankind.[6]

---

1 A cabin on the upper deck.
2 The deck at the fore of the ship.
3 The rocky coast.
4 Pivots for the guns.
5 The ships had been pirating together for many months.
6 According to naval law, sailors were entitled to a share of the money and goods seized aboard captured vessels.

Tom was an interpreter for the *English* prisoners, who were last examined, and the third man that came into the cabin, namely the pyrate quarter master,[1] he was at once struck with the sight of, and was inly sure he had seen him somewhere before, but, judge his situation, when upon asking him his name he said *John Williamson*. At that well known name and well remember'd, and once dreaded, voice — he fell some paces back, to the admiration of all present, and falling on his knees, cry'd, Oh God! ever just and good, I thank thee, that I behold and am render'd an instrument in punishing the greatest villain breathing! The prisoner, without knowing why, trembled every joint at these words, whilst *Tom* begging the captain's patience for some moments, tho' he could scarce hold himself still — made shift to put the following questions to him — Was you ever at *Bristol?* Yes sir. Did you not command a vessel call'd the *Anne* of that port, in the year 1697 or thereabout, and after slaving on the coast of *Guinea*, dispose of your cargo at *Sene-puxon* in *Maryland?* Yes, he answer'd, without the least hesitation, tho' much startled at being so well known. Pray sir, did you know one *Barlow* a planter there, and did you not sell an innocent child to him, that you stole from his parents in *London?*

At this question the blood forsook his cheeks, and had the guard not supported him, he would have fell upon the cabin floor — he made no reply, but hanging down his head continued silent. But the question being repeated, again and again, he at length answer'd surlily — you have taken me — I know I'm a dead man[2] — I'll answer no more questions; nor would break his obstinate silence, but was oblig'd to be carry'd to his confinement untractable.[3] After the whole were examin'd, and the captain, first lieutenant, and *Tom* alone, he told them so much of his own adventures as related to this villain, but prudently stop'd there, not at all accounting for his present condition, so that they imagin'd he had again found his parents.

Their resentment at so base, so wicked an action, carry'd them out into exclamations against the villain, and the captain added — how just is providence — who has permitted you to see the miserable death of your persecutor! I am convinced that, in

---

1 A low-ranking officer primarily in charge of steering the ship. That Williamson has been demoted from a captain to a quarter-master signals the extent of his ruin.
2 Captured pirates were generally executed for their crimes.
3 Against his will.

crimes of an enormous nature, heaven most commonly punishes the criminal even in this life. And now having properly mann'd the two pyrate vessels, they stood on their course, and without any other interruption safely arriv'd in fourteen days more at port *St. Pierre* in *Martinico*, where the prisoners were put on shore, and in ten days after, all but fourteen who appear'd to be forc'd, were condemn'd at a court of admiralty.[1]

Only two days intervening between the passing sentence and the execution of it; *Tom* visited once more the villain *Williamson*, to see if haply[2] he knew any thing of his parents. He now found him lamenting the errors of his life — resign'd to his fate, but full of terror and apprehension of futurity. The minute he enter'd the dungeon where he was chain'd — he cry'd, thank God, sir, you are come — I acknowledge I am the wretch you suspected me to be — that helpless innocent has weighted my guilty soul down to hell, ever since, and I have never had a moment's rest — Oh! the tears standing in his eyes, all over convuls'd, — how can I expect pardon of God that had no mercy upon an infant!

If it is in the power of that infant to speak peace to you in your departing moments, *Tom* reply'd, I freely forgive you — tho' you made me miserable — I am that child — preserv'd thro' all the evils you expos'd me to — and to merit pardon of Heaven, you ought to disclose what you know farther of my parents or my name, or any thing you know relating to me. — For some minutes he kept wildly gazing at him, without reply — at length, his very irons rattling with the convulsive starts of his body — he roar'd out, oh! I feel the pains of hell already! I am damn'd for ever! — Oh! would to God the minute I first saw you had been my last — that face of thine will hurl me to destruction! Then recovering himself a little, oh! I never knew nor heard of your parents — I took you from *Lincoln's-inn* fields — as to be sure *Barlow* has told you, and when I had sold you I was too wicked to trouble my head about you again — but the righteous God has curs'd me ever since — twice I was shipwreck'd — totally ruin'd — at last turned pyrate, and you'll have the pleasure to see me hang'd — damnation! do you want more satisfaction — then know I shall be damn'd eternally — I feel hell flames already.

Thus the wretch went on, and tho' the good youth endeavour'd to calm his mind and bring him again back to the good dis-

---

1 A court dealing with maritime crimes.
2 Perhaps.

position he seemed to shew at his entrance, it was all in vain, he continu'd to curse, swear and blaspheme, and even to wish he could finish all his crimes by dashing his brains out, and was so outrageous that he concluded the sight of him and the sense of his complicated crimes had turn'd his brains. At the gallows he would say nothing, but dy'd with execrations in his mouth — a just example of the righteous vengeance of heaven!

These things made *Tom* very melancholy; he lamented that a fellow-creature should launch so desperately into eternity, and now concluded the recovery of his parents quite impossible and impracticable. However, he would often say to himself, wheresoever you are, ye authors of my being, if grief for my loss did not instantly destroy you, may heaven calm your sorrows, and help you to forget your son — a son that will continue to behave so in this life — as to entitle him to the knowledge of you — if souls hereafter know each other — in a better and happier state! These thoughts, together with his distance from his charming *Fanny*, and his uncertainty with regard to her and his friends in *Maryland*, insensibly threw him into a deep melancholy, and it required all his art to support the weight of conversation, which now was more than ever courted, as his strange story had spread about the island, where the ship staid near two months, in which time he received the greatest honours and civilities from the governor, and all the principal inhabitants.

CHAPTER X

At last they set sail, and arrived safely at *Brest*, on *December* the 11th, in the year 1721, and he again set foot upon *European* ground, after an absence of twenty-four years. The chevalier *d' Aville* immediately sent the governor of *Canada*'s packet to court, together with an account of his prisoner's noble behaviour on board, and requested orders in what manner to act to him, and advised *Tom* to employ a sollicitor there, who might, for an handsome present, sollicit in his favour with his majesty, and nam'd to him, for that purpose, a certain *Abbe*[1] who had much the ear of the minister. He told this good friend he would be rul'd in all things by him, and accordingly having chang'd his bill of a thousand livres, *D'Aville* dispatch'd a trusty agent to the

---

1 French for "abbot," the head of a monastery. Such men often wielded both great political and religious influence.

Abbe with a state of the case, and a present of a bill for three hundred livres.

In short this was the right way of going to work, for, in a fortnight's time, a letter arriv'd to the captain from the intendant of the marine,[1] to let his prisoner have his freedom, and this favour, without further trouble, was owing as well to the report of the governor of *Canada* and captain *D'Aville*'s as to the intercession of the *Abbe*. And now being once more his own master, he was prevailed upon to take a tour with *D'Aville* to *Paris,* charm'd at every step with this new appearance of things, fine churches, stately palaces, populous towns and cities, splendid equipages,[2] and the hurry and bustle of commerce, to all which he had hitherto been a stranger; but he soon became acquainted with men and things, and as he had never seen *England* since his infancy, and spoke *French* so perfectly, and had been so long us'd to their manners, he appear'd in every thing like a native of the country, and was generally taken for one.

He waited upon *Alexander* the banker, the day after his arrival, and, to his great joy, found a letter from his agent in *Virginia,* another from the agent's correspondent in *London,* inviting him to *England,* and the bill of credit he had order'd, which had lain near six weeks at *Paris.* His friend's letter gave him an account of his having paid his draughts[3] from *Quebec,* and receiving his long letter safe and unopened, the contents of which he hop'd he had comply'd with to his satisfaction. He lamented his misfortunes, but advis'd him to comfort himself under them, and promis'd to be a faithful steward in his absence, wishing him all the pleasures that *Europe* could afford; but what interested him above all was, that he acquainted him, soon after the receipt of his letter one Mr. *Ferguson,* from *Sene-puxon,* had been to enquire after his welfare, and that when he heard he was a prisoner with the *French,* he was greatly affected; but rejoic'd to hear he was in health, and that he left a letter with him, which he sent by another vessel with a duplicate of his own.

This advice call'd all his tenderness up into his eyes, and he resolv'd very soon to go to *England* and take passage for *Maryland,* his ever beloved *Maryland.* His chagrin at not receiving this letter of his kind tutor's, which would have eas'd all his uncer-

---

1 The French administrative office governing the colonies.
2 Carriages and horses.
3 Bank drafts, or withdrawals.

tainties, was inexpressible — but it could not be, for in a letter from the merchant in *London*, he understood afterwards, that the ship it was sent by was burnt accidentally at sea, few of the men escaping with their lives. Tho' the situation of his mind dispos'd him more to retirement than company, he could not decline attending the generous captain of the *Flora*, who led him to court, to all the public places and curiosities about *Paris*, and was never tir'd of doing him good offices; but he being at length oblig'd to attend his duty at *Brest*, *Tom* once again was left to himself, to brood over his melancholy ideas. He would have fasten'd a very genteel present upon him, in return for his noble treatment in the passage and since; but he would not hear of it, saying, you gave up your share of the prizes to us and that was enough, you ought to have had a thousand livres, and they parted promising to preserve each other in memory.

And now as *D'Aville* was gone, and with him the servant that us'd to attend them both, he retir'd to the house of a widow gentlewoman in the *quartier du Louvre*,[1] there to board, for he had a natural antipathy to entertaining a *French* servant. Here he employ'd himself in acquiring a knowledge of the *French* literati, and in making a collection of the best books in that tongue, with the pompous *Dauphin* editions of the classics,[2] all which he sent to the merchant in *London*, from whence he propos'd to carry his whole purchases of that sort as a library for himself and his friends in *Maryland*, where no such treasure had ever before been seen.

One day as he was curiously viewing the labours of the great *Blondel* over the gate of St. *Anthony*,[3] a coach with a gentleman and two ladies pass'd him, and on a sudden he heard the gentleman order the driver to stop, of which he took little notice, still continuing to look at the devices over the middle postern[4] of the

---

1   An area of Paris just west of the medieval wall of the city and just north of the Seine River.

2   François Pomey's bestselling handbook to classical literature and mythology, *Pantheum mythicum, seu fabulosa deorum historia* (1659), which was originally written for the education of "the Grand Dauphin," the eldest son of Louis XIV.

3   Prior to its destruction in 1789, la Porte Saint-Antoine, or the Gate of St. Anthony, stood next to the Bastille, France's most notorious prison. The renowned architect François Blondel (1617–86) had overseen a reconstruction of the gate between 1660 and 1672.

4   Archway.

gate; but he was soon awaken'd from his reverie by a strenuous embrace, and these words — I were the most ungenerous wretch breathing could I forget my dear deliverer captain *Matthewson*! The sound of this name, which he had so long studiously conceal'd, made him tremble; but when he had look'd at the person who pronounc'd it, the joy of his heart was visible in his eyes, and, returning his embrace, he reply'd, — and I should be very unhappy had I not endeavour'd to deserve the friendship and remembrance of my dear chevalier *Du Cayle*, for that young nobleman it really was.

So unusual a sight in that quarter of the town, where the people are naturally curious,[1] drew a great many gazers about them, seeing which *Du Cayle* taking him by the hand, and leading him to the coach said, Come sir, let me entreat you to accompany me to my *Hotel*; in this coach is a lady that has the greatest obligations to you, as well as myself. It was no time to refuse this favour, and therefore saluting the ladies with his usual grace, and begging pardon for crowding them, he got in, and in a little time alighted with them at a superb house in the *place du Dauphine*.[2] As soon as they had enter'd a magnificent apartment, the chevalier turning round to the eldest of the ladies, who seem'd to be about twenty five, said, See, madam, the author of all our happiness in the generous, the brave, the humane captain *Matthewson*; upon which he advanc'd to salute her, and afterwards the other lady, who both, particularly, express'd their pleasure in seeing him, and the eldest said, turning to *du Cayle*, Well, my lord, this indeed is a happy moment — I have now my wish, which was, once at least in my life, to see a man to whom I am so much indebted.

To these compliments he reply'd with his usual complacency and politeness, and in short they all seem'd charm'd with their guest. After they had repos'd themselves, *Du Cayle* ask'd him what fortunate adventure brought him to *Paris*, upon which he gave them a detail of his misfortunes and transactions since, in a manner so engaging as finish'd the conquest of the ladies' hearts in his favour. *Du Cayle* sympathiz'd with him in his late distresses, congratulated him on his safe arrival, and concluded with insisting upon his taking up his residence with him, during the rest of

---

1 Presumably because of its proximity to the Bastille.
2 An exclusive, triangle-shaped commercial and housing development on the Île de la Cité (an island in the Seine River in central Paris).

his stay at *Paris*. This request was back'd by the two ladies, one the wife and the youngest her sister, and that very night, bidding adieu to the widow lady's, he remov'd to his new apartment, which was one of the most superb in the house, and where he was treated with the distinction of a prince.

The next morning, after breakfast, *Du Cayle* carried him into his closet whilst the ladies were dressing, and afresh embracing him, told him he retir'd on purpose to acquaint him with his adventures, from the time he so generously set him at liberty till now, and without staying[1] for an answer pursued his discourse as follows.

Full of gratitude, sir, at your noble treatment of me and my companions, we got safely to *Moville* and from thence I hastened to *Quebec*, and had I staid a day longer from thence I had been undone. You must know, the lady who is now my wife, and the other, her sister, were the daughters of the late governor of *Canada*, who at his decease left them sixty thousand livres each, in the hands of his brother, who is superintendant of the customs in that province. This uncle had form'd a design of marrying them both, to his two sons, their first cousins, men every way disagreeable, and both of them much superior in age; but before the death of her father, my addresses prov'd acceptable, and my family and expectations render'd me a very powerful rival. In short, we had agreed to steal a marriage,[2] as we were both at age, when unfortunately orders came for me to join the detachment of the regiment, in which I was an officer, instantly, at *Moville*, where my father, as you know, commanded, which orders cruel honour oblig'd me instantly to obey, and we parted after shedding a flood of tears on both sides; before I got to *Moville* I was overtaken by a trusty servant, who conjur'd me to be speedy in my return, for that their uncle was using some very unwarrantable means to force his nieces to marry in my absence.

I was distracted at this intelligence; but what could I do? Love, tho' all powerful, was no excuse for deserting my post with infamy, and disobeying the orders of a father. Therefore I sent a letter by him, wherein I promis'd to be at *Quebec* the minute our expedition was over, and in the mean time prescrib'd some rules to her, that I imagin'd would delay matters till my arrival. The rest, till the time of my return again to *Quebec* you know already.

---

1 Waiting.
2 Elope.

When I arrived in town with my trusty companions, to lose no time I sent privately to know how matters stood at the superintendant's, and was soon inform'd that by repeated acts of tyranny and cruelty, and, at length, by the news of the death of me and my father, which he industriously propagated, he had prevail'd upon them to give their hands to his sons.

I knew he had no other coercive power over them than what he had obtain'd by his relation-ship and his terrors; and that with regard to the article of marriage when at age, as my wife was, he had no manner of right to controul their inclinations, their father's will leaving them free in their choice. I therefore immediately waited on the governor, pleaded my services and the misfortunes of my family, made him my friend, and he immediately sent for the young ladies and their guardian, who were all differently affected at the sight of me, and my wife fainted away with joy and surprize. His excellency then ask'd them if they approv'd of marrying their cousins, to which, embolden'd by my presence, they both answer'd no; he then ask'd my wife if she chose for an husband the marquis *Du Cayle*, to which she reply'd with remarkable spirit — yes my lord, and no one else. Upon this he sent for his chaplain and we were marry'd in his presence, the uncle flinging away in anger and disgust. The governor then permitted the youngest to choose another guardian, and she nominated me and in a week afterward both their fortunes were paid into my hands.

The death of my father made my return to *France* necessary to take care of our paternal estate: This was the reason of my so suddenly quitting *Canada*, with my spouse and sister, and the large possessions of an uncle having devolv'd upon me since, I have no further temptation to rambling, but intend in my native country to enjoy the sweets of ease, love and friendship. If any thing could add to the relish of my present enjoyments, it is the wish'd for, unexpected sight of a gentleman, who is the author of all my felicity; we talk'd of you almost every day, with grateful remembrance, and my spouse ever long'd to see you, and providence at length, in this unexpected manner, has granted our desires. And now, my dear friend, I shall have it in my power to repay your invaluable favours in the manner my heart dictates, and, but that I remember you inform'd me your affections were engag'd, would court you to a nearer alliance with me by a marriage with my sister, who you may perceive has wit and beauty, and whose fortune is not contemptible.

At this conclusion, they again embrac'd each other, and captain *Matthewson* made the warmest return for his kind and unmerited offer; but let him so much into his story as to convince him he could not accept of it. He said however the handsomest things imaginable of the young lady, and they vow'd an eternal friendship for each other. It was very opportunely that the marquis came to this explanation; for his sister's repose began to receive some disturbance from the soft impressions, the merit and beauty of *Matthewson* had made upon her heart; but when her brother let her into his engagements, she strove betimes to overcome a passion that could not possibly meet with any return from the object of it.

Whilst he staid with *du Cayle*, who with his wife and sister did every thing to make his abode agreeable, he was inform'd that a ship was ready to sail from *Marseilles* to *Quebec*; this intelligence brought to his remembrance the favours he had received from the baron *Detonville* at *Moville*, and the good governor at *Quebec*, and he besought his friend and his lady to assist him in preparing magnificent presents for the former, and a token of his gratitude to the latter, of such things as would prove agreeable and useful from *Europe*, which he put on board the vessel with a letter to each, expressing his acknowledgements for their favours, and begging to have advice of their health and welfare, directed to his agent in *Virginia*. And now he thought it high time to think of visiting his native country, of which tho' he had no remembrance, and to which tho' he thought he had no tye, yet a longing that is not to be express'd dwelt upon him, to set his foot on *English* ground — a longing not dictated so much by curiosity, as by a certain stimulus that he could not account for, so true is what is said by *Ovid*,

> *Nescio qua natale solum dulcedine cunctos*
> *Ducit, & immemores non sinit esse sui.*[1]

And having taken leave of all his friends, for that purpose, and parted with *du Cayle*, his wife and sister, who accompanied him to *Calais*, and shed tears at his departure, and forced upon him some presents of great price as tokens of remembrance, he embark'd in the packet, and after a smooth passage landed safely at *Dover*.

---

1 "Our native country attracts us with some mysterious charm, and never lets us forget we belong to it" (Ovid, *Epistulae ex Ponto*, I.iii.35–36).

CHAPTER XI

The minute he got to a private apartment at his inn, he prostrated himself and returned thanks to God, that had so miraculously preserv'd him hitherto, for all his mercies, and once more besought him, if it was his blessed will, that he might find out his parents. When all his baggage, which was now grown very considerable, was landed, he order'd it to be sent to *London*, directing it to his friend's agent, whom he advis'd of his arrival, by the waggons which set out that very day, keeping only one change of linen and a riding frock richly lac'd for his present use; and after he had seen all that was worth beholding in *Dover*, *Deal* and their neighbourhood, set out himself, with hir'd horses and a guide, for that famous metropolis.

He found himself quite reviv'd with the sight and enjoyment of *England*, charm'd to the highest degree with her verdant plains, fruitful fields, rising hills, and all the beauteous prospects they afforded him. The people too were more to his genius and liking than the *French*, so that had his *Fanny* been with him, he would have tasted the highest satisfaction; but her distance, and the pain he was under about her, lay too heavy upon his mind to permit any untainted enjoyment. He was now thirty one years of age, and perhaps as handsome a man as ever was seen, and his countenance had natively such a mingled dignity and sweet humanity, that it was impossible to look without loving him at first sight.

As he visited every remarkable place, and often made excursions out of the road, for twenty or thirty miles, to gratify his curiosity, his guide being a very intelligent clever fellow, it was near ten days before he got to *London*, where he put up at the *Talbot* inn in west *Smithfield* for the first night, and the next morning having discharg'd his horses and his guide, with suitable acknowledgements beside his hire, he took a hackney coach,[1] and ordered it to drive to *Abchurch lane*, where the merchant resided to whose care he had been so much oblig'd, and who had been so punctual and diligent in his affairs, whilst he remain'd in *France*.

The house was a very grand one, to which you enter'd a large pair of gates, and went thro' a court yard, surrounded on every side with warehouses. His fine person and gay appearance, soon brought out a clerk from the compting house,[2] without his giving

---

1   A coach, with seating for six passengers, hired out like a modern taxi.
2   A building or room where accounts were kept.

farther notice of his arrival, whom he ask'd if the gentleman was within, and bid him tell him one *Matthewson* would be glad to speak with him. At the mention of his name the clerk bow'd low, and said he was, and conducted him into a back parlour whilst he dispatched a footman to his master with intelligence of his guest. Ten minutes brought down stairs a fine looking man, seemingly about fifty, who approach'd him, welcom'd him to town, and to every thing his house afforded, and seem'd so taken with the young gentleman, that he could hardly remove his eyes from him. *Matthewson* on his side also felt a wonderful inclination to his host — nay even some tender emotions of pleasure that were near shewing themselves at his eyes.

After the first questions were over, he besought him to walk up into the dining room, where sat his lady, who seem'd nearly of his own age, and who was as much struck with the sight of our adventurer as her husband, and as to *Tom*, he approach'd her with more reverential awe than ever he had a woman before. Breakfast was serv'd up, and the lady, who as well as her husband was of a very melancholy cast of temper and seldom smil'd, seeming as tho' they labour'd under some distress of mind, told him, she hop'd he would oblige them by accepting an apartment in their house, where he should receive all the attendance of the nearest relation, and that, tho' herself and her spouse did not take much pleasure in any thing this life could afford, they had relations and friends that were nearly of his own age, and would be proud of attending him to view the curiosities of the town. *Tom* return'd her his thanks, was pleas'd with their conversation, which he enjoy'd for the remainder of the day, and in the evening was shewn to an apartment that declar'd the opulence of its master, where he found all his baggage safe, and retir'd to rest with a mind full of the various and uncommon adventures of his life, and dwelling upon the idea of his lovely long lost *Fanny*.

The next day his kind host and hostess introduc'd their chief clerk to his acquaintance, who was a near relation, of a genteel carriage and person, and a generous and obliging turn of mind, and, in little time, they conceiv'd a perfect friendship for each other. Under his guidance he visited every part of the city and suburbs, with its curiosities and entertainments of so many various kinds, and the adjacent country and villages, which for their pleasing situation surpass any thing in *Europe*, so near a great and opulent city. In this manner several weeks pass'd away, and tho' *Tom*'s disposition was very melancholy, yet he could not omit to gratify his researches into every thing remarkable, and, as the theatres furnish'd him with the most rational amusement, he frequently spent his evenings there.

Mean time he daily more and more ingratiated himself with the family, and conceiv'd such an affection for the merchant and his lady, that he whil'd away his hours of retirement in their company, and they, who had no children, began to love him with the fondness even of parents. In the neighbourhood he never heard of any distress but he was ready to relieve it, contributed to the public charities with munificence, and bestow'd his alms largely on the poor confin'd debtors in our prisons, a race of men, he would often say, much more to be pitied than the sordid mendicants[1] that so croud our streets and avenues.

One night, as his friend and he were coming thro' *Lincoln's inn Fields*,[2] a place he always took in his way when he went to the other end of the town, and in passing thro' which he often vented many a mournful sigh, just beneath *Lincoln's inn* wall they heard the clashing of swords, and three or four repeated blows, and at the same time the cry of murder! — murder! — from a man's voice. The brave *Matthewson* and his friend, without hesitation, drew their swords, and hastening to the spot, found a gentleman-like man upon the ground, and heard the ruffians, who had attack'd him, running away at their seasonable[3] approach. His sword hilt was in his hand, which, insensible as he was, he grasp'd with great force, and the blade lay shatter'd in several pieces beside him, his hat and wig was gone; but as they could discover no blood they apprehended he was only stunn'd and not wounded. So indeed it fortunately prov'd, for, having rais'd him up between them, and endeavouring to convey him to some tavern in *Holborn*, he came so far to himself as by several indications to discover that he was about recovering his senses.

With some difficulty at length they got him into the nearest tavern, and sending for a surgeon he took some blood from his arm, which soon brought him to the perfect use of his reason. He then inform'd the company, in broken *English*, that he was a *French* gentleman, but a week before arriv'd in *England*, and that returning to his lodging in *Bloomsbury*, he had been attacked by four ruffians, who he believ'd intended to take his life as well as

---

1 Beggars.
2 The same high-crime district where Tom was kidnapped at the beginning of the novel.
3 Well timed.

his purse; that he had defended himself till they had broken his sword by their bludgeons, and was knock'd down, and suppos'd, to the two worthy gentlemen that brought him there, he was oblig'd for his life; and then return'd them his thanks in the most grateful and polite manner.

Whilst he was talking thus, *Tom* ey'd him with a very visible surprize and amazement, he ran him over from head to heel, and, at length advancing suddenly to him, and flinging his arms about his neck, he cry'd in *French*, — thank God! that has made me thus an instrument in preserving the life of a dear and valued friend! Ah captain *D'Aville* is it you, to whom I have so many obligations? 'Twas indeed that gentleman himself, who raising himself, with the utmost astonishment in his countenance, said — I am indeed *D'Aville* — that happy *D'Aville* who has thought of nothing but his excellent *Matthewson* since he has been in this town! — Happy! happy event! — the blessing of life is endear'd by the hand that bestow'd it. Their behaviour was so tenderly moving that it drew tears from the eyes of the spectators, — they went into a private room, Mr. *Perkins*, the name of *Tom*'s new friend, was introduc'd to the captain, who again and again repeated his acknowledgments, and he yielded to their entreaties of going home with them to *Abchurch lane*, where he was receiv'd by the family with the sincerest testimonies of respect, on account of their esteem'd guest.

CHAPTER XII

When they retir'd to rest, *Matthewson* once more express'd to *D'Aville* the joy he felt in beholding him, and having seemed to wonder at his being in *England*, the generous *Frenchman* gratified his curiosity by the following relation.

The Adventures of Jaques Augustin d'Aville.

You will, no doubt, be surprized, when I acquaint you that necessity, and not curiosity, my dear friend, brought me into this country; but to make the matter plainer to you, I will begin my story from my very birth.

I was the son of the sieur *d'Aville*, intendant of *Normandy*,[1] and was born at *Rouen*, in the year 1684. My father was rich, in

---

1 The province's top civil official.

great authority, and my mother was of one of the best families in *France*, and, as I was an only child, I was bred up in all the splendor and elegance that high birth and great fortune could bestow. At a proper age I was sent to the university of *Aix* in *Provence*, went through my studies with applause, which were directed, by my father's order, to the civil law, and I complied with his injunctions in that particular, though mathematics was my favourite science, and a desire of wandering at sea, the longing of my soul.

At twenty-two I became an advocate of parliament[1] in my native city, but still the wrangling of the bar was my utter aversion, and what encreased it, was the arguments of my uncle, the famous count *Forbin*,[2] whose merit and success at sea has been applauded all over the maritime world. In short, I ventured to tell my father and mother, that I resolved to quit the law for arms, and besought him to use his interest to get me promotion in his majesty's marine. Long they combated my inclination, with all the arguments in their power, but finding it ineffectual, at length they permitted me to go a voluntier; and, during the late war,[3] I acted with such success, that I, in a few years, was promoted to the command of a ship of the first rate, and have ever since dedicated myself to the service of my king and country in various parts of the globe.

My mother died in two years after I went first to sea, and though by her death I came to the immediate possession of an estate of five hundred livres *per annum*; yet I found myself involved in numberless difficulties by her loss, which I mourned with sincere grief. My father, whose birth was not very elevated, was naturally of a sordid, covetous temper; but his love and esteem for my mother had kept it within tolerable bounds hitherto; it now soon began, after her decease, to flame out, and one of the first instances I perceived of it, was as odd an one as ever I believe was heard of.

When the funeral was over, and matters a little settled, he called me one day into his office, and said — *Jaques!* this little thing you possess, by your mother's death, I fear will make you

---

1 Public prosecutor.
2 Count Claude de Forbin (1656–1733), a French naval commander under Louis XIV who earned international fame with his victories at sea.
3 Based on the dates here, this most likely references the War of the Spanish Succession (1701–13), one of two large-scale conflicts that kept all of Europe in almost constant conflict between 1689 and 1713.

extravagant — Come, come, I know the management of money better than you —Your pay, and my house and table are sufficient for the subsistence of a young man — Here, I'll buy it of you — here's one thousand livres for your immediate use — it's time enough at my death for you to be burdened with the charge of money. — I was quite astonished at his mean proposal; but I loved him, and imagined I should never want whilst he lived; and that I should enjoy his whole immense fortune at his death, and therefore, without hesitation, took the money, signed the instruments, which depending upon my compliance, he had got ready, to make my right over to him, and he received it with as much avidity[1] as if it had been saved from the fire, and the next day borrowed five hundred of my thousand livres, which I could never get again from that time to the hour of his death.

Thus my father cunningly choused[2] his child, laughing in his sleeve at my folly, and yet he loved me — I was his only son and heir — had been guilty of few extravagancies or follies, and was esteemed by all that knew me. Can there be a meaner or more degrading vice than avarice, which deadens and destroys all the tender ties of nature, and deforms the best and most valuable properties? My father was no bad man; but his passion after money — his desire of beholding heaps of gold that he had not the heart to touch, obliterated his good qualities, made him unnatural, brutish, and cruel, and commit follies that he did not live to atone for.

Madame *Humieres* was the widow of the president[3] of that name, and was possessed, by his death, of one hundred and fifty thousand livres; and tho' she was only forty, and my father near seventy, he resolved to make himself miserable for the few remaining days of his life, by marrying her; in order to which he tempted her with a jointure of more than double what she could have expected from any match in the province. Here he caught a *Tartar*,[4] however — the lady was as cunning as he was, and full as covetous, and contracted the obligation with him, in hopes of being the longest liver, which was the very motive he went upon himself, and explained to me, to make me easy under the match.

---

1 Eagerness.
2 Defrauded.
3 In this context, this most likely means the president of a private company.
4 A colloquialism meaning "to tackle one who unexpectedly proves to be too formidable" (*OED*).

I was cut to the quick at this instance of dotage, and saw, with a grief equal to despair, that I was likely to lose all my father's possessions, which, except a thousand livres a year of paternal estate, was all subject to his arbitrary devise. But I was afraid to remonstrate — I was wholly in his power, and therefore assisted at the wedding with a tolerable good grace. As my father had an only son, so this second wife had an only daughter, who was some years younger than me, of a charming temper and beautiful as an angel. Her the old gentleman formed a scheme for me to marry, and so become a joint possessor of both their fortunes. This indeed would have been a real happiness, if it could have been brought about, and the lovely *Jannette*, which was her name, soon made a deep impression upon my heart, and felt for me a sincere and mutual passion.

In short, in a few weeks, I began to bless a match which was likely to make me the happiest man in the universe, when a baleful[1] cloud overshadowed my reviving prospects, and plunged me into many subsequent misfortunes, which yet I have not been able to weather. The first blow we received was a separation; for my mother had entertained such thoughts as made her look upon our growing love with dislike, and therefore, poor *Jannette* was sent as a pensioner to a nunnery,[2] to which I was obliged to accompany her, by the orders of our mother and our father, who was become the dupe and the slave of his wife, and fearful to oppose her will, and we took leave of each other, shedding unfeigned tears on both sides.

At first I imagined this was solely intended for her further improvement in her education; but I soon was convinced that my mother-in-law[3] had looked upon me with amorous eyes, and she tempted me, by the most lucrative offers and the most inticing arts, to satisfy her incestuous passion. I must own I was quite astonished at her behaviour and her declarations, and at first endeavoured to recall her to reason by the mildest and most forcibly prevailing arguments; but it was all in vain, and, in short, I was so pestered with her continued sollicitations and entreaties, that I made her several rough returns, and at length determined intirely to quit the house; for which purpose I applied for a ship at court, and obtained the command of the *Argonaute*, bound to

---

1 Pernicious.
2 A paying lodger at a convent.
3 Step-mother.

her station at *Guardaloupe*,[1] after having lived on shore near two years.

My father, who did not love to see me out of the way of getting money, applauded my resolution; but his wife was filled with rage and fury; and, after upbraiding me in the coarsest terms, for my insensibility,[2] as she stiled it, she told me I should repent of my usage of her all the days of my life, adding, as to your favourite, your *Jannette*, you shall never see her more — had you complied with my desires, perhaps it would have been the best step you could take to her possession. I was so stunned with this wicked speech, that I remained unable to reply, and quitted the house, after taking leave of my poor deluded father, with horror and detestation; but I found one part of her menace immediately fulfilled, for going to the nunnery to take leave of my fair, I found strict orders were given, that we should not see each other, nor could I any way get a letter conveyed to her, so that I departed to *Rochefort*, where my ship lay, like one unblessed, and sailed in a few days for my station, under the greatest torture of mind imaginable.

Three years I remained in *America*, and though there I had several advantageous proposals of marriage made me, I could by no means obliterate the remembrance of the lovely cause of all my pains and sollicitudes, nor did my father, in the two or three letters I received from him, during my absence, ever condescend to answer any enquiries I made after her, which I suppose was owing to the instructions of his precious wife. No wonder then, that I long'd to return to *Europe*, and that I received the orders for that purpose, as a mandate sent from heaven for my relief.

We arrived safe at *Brest*, and as soon as my ship was got into the dock to receive the necessary repairs, I procur'd a leave of absence from court, to return to my native province. My father who was alive, but very feeble, I found still the same avaricious man; and he receiv'd me so coldly, that I soon discover'd his weakness had been impos'd upon to my prejudice. I was at no manner of loss for the source of it, and in the first motions of my resentment was going to declare all that had pass'd between my mother in law and me, to him, but recollecting how much it might hasten the few remaining sands of his life, my piety towards him oblig'd me to desist. It was not long before an old servant, that lov'd the memory of my mother, let me still further into the

---

1 The French colony of Guadeloupe.
2 Lack of proper feeling.

cause of his unusual strangeness, by convincing me that his new mistress had plaid her cards so well, as to cajole him to cut me off entirely of his personal estate, and to make her his sole executrix[1] and residuary legatee.[2]

As to her, she us'd me hardly with common civility, and whenever she met me, which she seldom did, it was with the eyes of a fury. The unhappy *Jannette* I found had been remov'd from the nunnery and was convey'd, no body could tell me how or where, by her mother's orders, who still gave me some speaking hints, that she would be reconcil'd to me upon the same abominable conditions, I had so many years ago refus'd and shudder'd at. With regard then to the affairs of my family and my love, I found myself very miserable, and imagining a woman of so lascivious a constitution, that could tempt a son to commit incest with her, was hardly likely to confine herself to the arms of an old man, I set all my wits to work to find out some of her secret intrigues, in order to undeceive him in his opinion of her virtue; nor was it long before that all powerful solicitor, gold, prevail'd with one of her maids to betray to me an amour she had with a lieutenant of one of the *Irish* regiments quarter'd in our city,[3] who, at a certain hour in the night repair'd to the garden gate, where he was let in by his mistress, and, in an adjoining summer house, gratified her libidinous inclination; to two or three of these meetings I was an eye witness, conceal'd from their view by a grove of trees at some small distance, and in the first sallies of my fury, was going precipitately to discover myself and to make him pay for the dishonour he did my father; but cooler thoughts came to my aid, and I now no longer wonder'd at the cruelty she was guilty of to her daughter; for where such passions reign in a woman's soul, such inordinate desires, all natural affection flies before them.

I now, one morning, desir'd the old gentleman to take a turn in the garden, before madam was up, laid open what she had so long ago propos'd to me, the injury he had done me thro' her means, in its proper colours, and promis'd to make him an eye witness to his adultress's infidelity. He was ready to drop at this recital, and told me, sternly, if I did not satisfy him that very night, that my suspicions were true, he would not only disinherit

---

1 Executor of his will.
2 Inheritor of what remains of his estate at his death.
3 Irish troops regularly fought alongside the French in the conflicts of this era. Given religion's central role in these wars and the fact that both Ireland and France were heavily Catholic, this was a natural alliance.

me, but never suffer me again to set foot in his house. Well, sir, I reply'd, I accept your condition with all my heart.

The night came, but, as ill fortune would have it, neither of them appear'd, which I was afterwards inform'd was owing to the double dealing of the aforesaid maid, to whom, having imparted my design, she sold the secret again to her mistress, at a larger price than I had given her for her's, without bringing herself at all into the scrape, saying, I had found the matter out accidentally, and that she overheard me and my father talking of the design. My confusion was extreme, after keeping the old gentleman up, most part of the night, to find myself disappointed, and the consequence was, that he look'd upon it as a villainous scheme of mine, to set him at variance with his wife, for my own purposes; and, in short, forbid me ever again entering his doors.

I immediately left the house, with sorrow and indignation, and became so sick of my native country that I exchanged commands with the captain of the *Flora*, in order to banish myself at as great a distance as possible from it, and had been four years out when you arriv'd with me at *Brest* from *Canada*. I had determin'd not to go to *Normandy* again, and when I left you at *Paris*, to repair to my ship, resolv'd to accept the first command, of again leaving the nation, but an accident prevented me, providentially, from the execution of it.

As I was again order'd for *Canada* I had directions to take on board some families that were going there to settle, with their servants, and as they came upon deck, surveying them, one by one, who should I discover amongst them, to her great confusion, but the quondam[1] maid, that after betraying her mistress, had also betray'd my design upon her, and disappointed my revenge. I had prudence enough to conceal my knowledge of her in public, and at night sending for her to my cabin, she fell on her knees, own'd her baseness, and full of fear and trembling told me if I would pardon her, she could do me infinite service. I did not suffer her to go on, but, with precipitancy, ask'd if my father was alive. No, Sir, she reply'd, he has been dead a year and more, and your mother in law is not only in possession of all his personal estate; but, for want of your appearance, of the real one that belongs to you.

I could not help shedding tears at the news of my father's decease, notwithstanding his unkindness, and, after some pause,

---

1 One-time, former.

ask'd her what service she propos'd to do me, to attone for her faults. Sir, she reply'd again, I can help you to news of madam *Jannette*, to the possession of your father's whole fortune, and to the punishment of his murderers, for he dy'd, indeed, by poison. I shudder'd at this last expression — it was not strange I had never heard of my father's death, as in a moody melancholy manner, I studiously avoided all enquiry, and as I presume the letters my relations in *Normandy* sent me, on the occasion, miscarry'd, thro' my so often shifting my cruizes from one part of *America* to the other, which was my enducement for exchanging into the *Flora*.

Never was astonishment greater than mine, when this creature told me he was poison'd by his wife, at the instigation of her *Irish* paramour, who was now in garrison at *Douay*, where my mother intended to follow him soon, and get him to throw up his commission, and return with her to *Normandy*. That having been her accessary in the fact, with a man servant that was now her husband; she had given them two thousand livres, on condition they went and settled at *Canada*, where he had some relations. She added, that she had never been at rest since the fatal deed, and believ'd, with her spouse, that their coming on board my ship, was by the direction of Heaven, in order to discover the murder: that they were ready to become evidences against my mother in law, if I would pardon them, and that *Jannette* was confin'd in an *Ursuline*[1] nunnery, at *Caen*, where she was us'd with great severity to make her take the veil.

You need not doubt my taking her at her word — I burn'd to revenge my father's death, and, sending for the man, promis'd them both my pardon, and to intercede for the king's, and, over and above, a great reward. They then inform'd me, that they had, by her order, put *Arsenick* into his wine, for two nights successively; but it was not in sufficient quantity to take effect; and that, thereupon, their mistress had trebled the dose, and at the same time, in the night, run a bodkin[2] thro' his ear, whilst he slept, which at once dispatch'd him, and that he was bury'd privately the next day, under the notion of having dy'd of an apoplectic fit, which the good character she had maintain'd, and her known

---

1 "A religious order of nuns, established under the rule of St. Augustine in 1572 from a company founded at Brescia in 1537, for the teaching of girls, nursing of the sick, and the sanctification of the lives of its members" (*OED*).

2 Dagger.

fondness for my father, with the grief she shew'd at his death render'd not at all suspected.

Good God! how just thou art! The inórdinate desire of wealth, caus'd my father to marry this devil in human shape, and the crime he committed was his punishment! I immediately wrote to the intendant of the marine to resign my command, which being easily granted to my long and faithful services, with my evidences, who were really penitent for their misdeeds, I set out for *Rouen*, and being arriv'd, repair'd to a friend's house whom I could trust, who had been my fellow student at the university, and was then first counselor of the *Chatelet*;[1] by his advice the next day, I appear'd and claim'd my patrimony, which the widow immediately surrender'd, and then we had her secur'd upon a *criminal process*. When she was given to understand her crime was known, she shew'd the utmost dismay; but when the evidences against her were nam'd, she fainted away and soon prevented a public execution by poisoning herself in prison.

Such was the exit of this unfortunate wretch; but as she had been my father's wife, and was the mother of my *Jannette*, I gave her a funeral suitable to her rank, had she trod the paths of virtue. By a sentence of the great chamber, myself and *Jannette* were declar'd joint heirs to near eight hundred thousand livres, and the lovely maid being absent, I took upon me the management of both our concerns, till I could go to *Caen*, which I did, in a few days, and found her true, constant, and still mourning, like myself, our forc'd absence of such a number of years from each other. We both deplor'd the fate of our parents, but could not help acknowledging the hand of divine justice in their fall.

We were marry'd, and began to live in the utmost happiness, when *O'Shean*, the *Irish* lieutenant, came to *Rouen*, not knowing of the fate of my mother in law. It had not been thought proper to bring him to the bar of justice, as no overt act could possibly be prov'd against him; but as I knew him to be one cause of the calamities of our family, and every body else thought the same, I sought him out, and, in a private rencounter, kill'd him. The edict against duelling[2] being very severe, I was oblig'd to fly, and being

---

1 The chief attorney at the local court of justice.
2 For centuries, various monarchs in France had issued edicts against dueling, but, despite what Kimber says here, they were very rarely enforced with any stringency and thus did not lead to the abolition of dueling in France.

a distant relation to our ambassador in *England*, chose this for my place of residence, 'till I can obtain leave to return again into *France*, which will not I hope be long, as my two evidences, whom I procur'd pardon for, are ready to testify the occasion, the just occasion of our quarrel, which will be included in a memorial[1] to the king; but happy beyond expression I am, here to have met with so dear a friend, who has seldom been out of my thoughts, since I parted with him.

CHAPTER XIII

Here the captain ceas'd his melancholy relation, and was sympathiz'd with by *Tom* in the most cordial and engaging manner, and, to repay the good natur'd and friendly freedom he display'd in relating his story, he, in his turn, let him into the knowledge of all the accidents of his life, at which he expressed an amazement beyond bounds, and sincerely congratulated him upon his present situation, and hop'd he would find his *Fanny* alive, and ready to reward his matchless fidelity. And now the captain, Mr. *Perkins* and *Tom* became inseparable, the former, at their desire, removing to lodge with them at the merchant's, where he was treated agreeably to his worth and fortune, and, they once more to oblige him, went over all the public and private places of resort, curiosity and entertainment.

In a month however, they were forced to separate, for *D'Aville* at the instances of his great relations, and upon a true state of the case, having obtain'd his king's pardon, took a tender adieu of his new friends, and after bestowing very extraordinary marks of his bounty upon the servants, embark'd on board a vessel, in the port of *London*, bound for *Dieppe*, and once more return'd to enjoy uninterrupted delight with his faithful *Jannette*, and soon after was created a marquiss,[2] in consideration of his great riches, and extraordinary merit, and had the cross of the order of St. *Lewis*[3] bestow'd upon him, by his sovereign.

This late intercourse with *D'Aville* had made *Tom* very conversant at the *French* ambassador's, where he and Mr. *Perkins* continu'd to be highly caress'd; that nobleman being quite taken with their society; and you may judge of *Tom*'s agreeable astonishment, when one day, entering his apartment, he beheld his old friend M. *du Cayle*, his wife and lovely sister, who had just arriv'd

---

1 Petition, remonstrance.
2 An elite rank in the French peerage, below a duke and above a count.
3 See p. 96, n. 5 above for this order.

from *France*, to take a tour through *England*. *Cayle* express'd his joy in the most lively terms, and the ladies cry'd the little sickness of their late voyage was all forgot, in the sight of captain *Matthewson*. He introduc'd Mr. *Perkins* to them, as his valu'd friend, and they receiv'd him with their usual politeness, and promis'd, the next day, to take a dinner with them, at the merchant's, where now *Tom* took all the liberties of a son, and they began really to love him as if he stood in that tender relation to them; so that the next day a very superb entertainment was provided, and the invited guests, together with the *French* ambassador and his lady, were treated with the magnificence of a prince. *Perkins*, who was not much unlike *Matthewson*, at this second sight of madame *du Cayle*'s sister, receiv'd impressions that disturb'd his repose, and that young lady, struck with his personal perfections and his merit, after a few weeks courtship, with the entire consent of her brother in law and sister, became, to the greatest delight of *Tom* and all parties, the wife of the young merchant.

A fortnight after the marquiss and his lady again embark'd for *France*, having been to most of the principal cities and towns in *England*, and, at their arrival, remitted their sister's fortune to Mr. *Perkins*, who, being taken up in the delightful enjoyment of his new situation, once more left his friend some leisure, to indulge the melancholy of his soul, and to ruminate over his distance from his charming *Fanny*: Often would he sigh and say to himself, oh! my beloved creature! how ignorant I am of what passes at this awful distance; perhaps, ere now, the austerity of a father has broke thy heart! — perhaps, alas! an unwilling victim, thou art sacrificed to the loathsome embraces of the odious *Carter*, in either of which cases misery is included, and certain death to me. Often he would with longing heart think of his beloved *Maryland*, his innocent *Senepuxon*,

> *Where jocund damsels, with their well pleas'd mates,*
> *Pass the delicious moments, void of care,*
> *And only study how to laugh and love,*
> *Contented, happy, under* Calvert's[1] *sway.*[2]

---

1 The Calvert family were the founders and proprietors (or owners and overlords) of Maryland.
2 Kimber here quotes ll. 147–50 of his own poem "A Letter from a Son, in a Distant Part of the World, March 2, 1743," which first appeared in the *London Magazine* for July 1744. As the title suggests, Kimber wrote these lines during his travels in America.

and say, why do I loiter? — why have new friendships and new connexions delay'd me from the sight of all that can constitute my happiness, that to me is valuable in this world? Ah! I'll fly to your arms, my dear mother! my excellent *Fanny*! my esteem'd and valu'd friends! and no more be separated from your embraces! oh! how many years absence have I endur'd!

These thoughts inspir'd him with an immediate desire to take his leave of his *English* friends. The merchant and his wife were now his only society, and the melancholy that seem'd to cloud all their enjoyments flattered his own disposition. As yet, they had never ventured to ask him, even what countryman he was, nor any of the events of his life, and he, with equal gentility and distance, refrain'd enquiring into the misfortune that seemed to hang so heavy on their minds; but one evening, as they were sitting together, and the discourse roll'd upon their Friends in *Virginia*; she ask'd him, after begging his pardon for her freedom, if he was born there. No, madam, he reply'd — I was born in *London*; but left it very young. In *Maryland* I was brought up, and since that my life has been that of a wanderer, exposed to various and great misfortunes! Perhaps greater than any other person ever experienced! Somewhat, he could not tell what, prompted him to this freedom, in short, he had such a likeing and esteem for the persons he was talking to, that he thought they had a sort of right to his secrets!

Ah, sir, the lady return'd, the tears standing in her eyes — no condition is exempt from troubles — I have had my share of them too — Ay, but the husband put in — That so young a man should be exposed to the ills of life — is my wonder, especially bless'd as Captain *Matthewson* is, with the goods of fortune. If the goods of fortune, sir, she return'd to her husband, could exempt us from misery, you and I had never had occasion to mourn — here the gentleman put in, with forc'd smile, saying, come my dear, we must endeavour to forget our griefs — it's rude to entertain a gentleman in this manner — mirth and jollity and the gratification of his curiosity, are what he should always be treated with, who has come so far to revisit *England*.

Oh, sir, *Tom* return'd, — to a man like me, who soon after birth struggled with adversity, and has continu'd to do so almost ever since, and who has two dreadful worms gnawing at his heart, every moment he lives, mirth and jollity have ever been disagreeable — 'tis true I seek the gratification of my curiosity and the improvement of my mind thereby, in my travels, because I think it becomes a rational creature so to do, that he may be of more extensive service to that part of mankind, amongst whom at last he takes up his abode. Otherwise constant gloom and melancholy — best befits a man (here the tears perforce fill'd his eyes) a wretch who is even now ignorant of his parents — was robb'd — cruelly separated from them, and all their tenderness, before he could ever know them! —

At these words, which he could not help uttering with unaffected passion — the lady, starting wildly in her chair, cry'd out — the tears trickling down her cheeks, and almost devouring him with her eyes — Robb'd of your parents, sir, did you say — oh where — can you tell where they dwelt — gracious Heavens! — what do I hear! — Oh, madam, he returned — whilst they both look'd like pictures of wonder — all that I know is from the report of a villain, who since has met his punishment — he vauntingly in his cups,[1] told another — and confirmed it to me since, before his death, that he took me from *Lincoln's Inn-fields* — at this word the lady fell back in her chair, and fainted away, with a deep sigh, but he had not time to run to her assistance, for the merchant springing to him and flinging his arms about him — cry'd oh! my son! my son! and fell senseless upon the floor.

Poor *Tom* could scarce support himself — in the present whirl of his ideas — joy, astonishment, tenderness, grief, at the condition of these two persons, whom yet he hardly dar'd to think were ally'd to him — caus'd nameless emotions in his bosom, and at last, unable to support sense any longer, he fell into the same state, and with his fall gave so loud a stroke to the wainscot,[2] that the servants came running up to see what was the matter. Their amazement may easily be guessed when they saw their master, mistress and their visitor in this condition — but they were soon acquainted with the occasion, for the merchant coming first to himself — tenderly endeavoured to recover his wife, and then ran to *Tom*, using the endearing epithet of son, so often, that, as they knew the misfortune of the family, they were sensible of the happy alteration of things.

The lady at length open'd her eyes, when both ran wildly and eagerly to *Tom*, who was now seated and surrounded by the domestics, endeavouring to recal him to life; but when they saw the blood trickle down his comely face, caus'd by the blow in his fall, they were near giving up the ghost in earnest. The affection-

---

1 Boastfully while drunk.
2 The room's hard oak paneling.

ate youth was long before he open'd his eyes, and his bosom being unbutton'd to give him air, the distracted mother — cry'd — oh! I forgot — one more thing, and I am happy — and bareing his breast, discovered the plain mark of a grape upon his left collar bone[1] — at which she afresh exclaim'd — oh merciful heaven! — 'tis he — 'tis my dear long lost *Tommy*. The overjoy'd father — was mean time so oppressed with the goodness of providence, that he was fallen upon his knees at the other end of the room and striving to calm his tumultuous joy by prayer and thanksgiving.

At length the young gentleman reviv'd, and throwing his eyes around cry'd faintly — Oh — where — where are they? Here, the raptur'd lady reply'd — here, thou cause of all our sorrows — thou dearest sufferer — but we'll make thee amends for all thy distress! At these words he disengaged himself from the hands of those who had supported him, and running to her fell on his knees, crying oh happiness! — I feel — madam, you are — you are my mother! — Never was joy so complete, she raised him up with a world of tenderness, and the father now coming forward, they almost devour'd him with alternate embraces, which he return'd with eagerness, but humble reverence.

In short, for some time — it was all a fond extravagance of passion — a madness of delight on all sides. The servants soon spread the news thro'out the house, business was at an end and they divided themselves into parties, to discourse of this wonderful event. Joy and rapture fill'd every heart — for the good superiors were intimately belov'd by all about them. 'Twas the next day before they could be calm and temperate enough to ask one another many questions; but at length they desir'd their recover'd son, the only one they ever had, to recapitulate his adventures in the presence of Mr. *Perkins*, who was his first cousin, and his lady, which as he did, their hearts and eyes accompany'd the mournful tale; now they are lavish in their praises and protestations of friendship and eternal esteem, for Mrs. *Barlow*, *Fanny*, Mr. and Mrs. *Ferguson*, Mr. *Gordon*, and the memory of Captain *Matthewson*, and anon[2] raving against the villains *Williamson* and *Barlow*, the fate of the former of which they heard even without the least compassion.

---

1 Kimber here borrows a convention from courtly romance, where the true identities of orphaned, kidnapped, or otherwise lost heroes are established via a distinguishing birth-mark.
2 Unanimously.

When he had done, they, in their turn, related the sorrow, terror and fear Mr. *Anderson*, for that was the name of his father, was under after he return'd to the gate and found his son lost; he rov'd about in search of him all night, like a madman; and when Mrs. *Anderson* came to know of the accident she fell ill and continued so a long time: They had been at some hundred pounds expence in advertising and sending to all parts of the three kingdoms, to no purpose; but for some years they had resign'd themselves to the disposal of providence, still worn away with inward grief, which had at last work'd this miracle in their favour. They further inform'd him that his father had for some time resolv'd to quit business, and for that purpose had lately purchas'd an estate in *Yorkshire*, their native county, of 700 pounds a year, to which and near 20,000 pounds in the funds, he was sole and universal heir. That having few relations and those rich, if they had never been so happy to recover him, they had intended, after the decease of the longest liver, to have left their fortune towards a provision for exposed and deserted young children.

They mutually join'd in returning thanks to God for his wonderful loving kindness towards them, the father saying, he had met with even a greater mercy than *Jacob* did, in having his son *Joseph* restored to him.[1] All their relations, friends and acquaintance crowded to congratulate them, upon such an unexpected event, and all admir'd the person, behaviour and abilities of young Mr. *Anderson*, whose parents every hour survey'd him with an encrease of tenderness, and could scarce bear him out of their sight, and he, for some weeks, thought of nothing but how to render himself agreeable to them.

His dear *Fanny*, absence from whom was now the only care or concern he had, at length again resum'd her empire in his heart, and he found he must see her or dye. One morning then being retir'd with these indulgent parents, he bespoke them thus. Dear sir, dear madam, I have one only favour to beg of you — I am supremely happy in you, in every thing, providence has left me no wish to make with regard to fortune; but with regard to my mental enjoyment it can never be perfect unless I go to *Maryland* and fetch my adorable *Fanny* to your arms. Oh! do not deny your consent — the lovely mourner is wretched — if alas! she lives, till my arrival. I shall then settle all my affairs there and in *Virginia*, and never leave you more.

---

1 A reference to the biblical story recorded in Genesis 37–50.

Ah son, his father reply'd — must we again lose you then — yes — we must consent — your happiness is ours — we long to embrace this amiable maid, and to call her daughter — and may that God — who has been so kind to us in every circumstance — protect and send you back to our arms, with your *Fanny*, and as many of your friends as choose to live in *England*! — One of my own vessels is now ready to sail — of her you shall have the disposal — and in *Virginia* you may finish my affairs as well as your own with Mr. *McKensie* (for that was the name of the young gentleman's faithful agent who had dealt with his father many years.)

He was all gratitude at the ready compliance, and was soon ready to embark, with a large quantity of the richest presents *London* could furnish for his *Fanny* and his friends, and the library of books he had purchas'd in *France* and *England*, which he intended as a present for Mr. *Gordon* and Mr. *Ferguson*. His father sent a diamond ring of great value to his intended daughter in law, and Mrs. *Anderson* a fine snuff box of mother of pearl set in gold and adorn'd with jewels, and some of the richest silks to her and Mrs. *Barlow* and Mrs. *Ferguson*. And now after a tender adieu, the father and mother, having quite quitted business, to Mr. *Perkins* who was their nephew, and was charm'd with this event, retir'd into *Yorkshire* to their estate, and favourable winds and smooth seas brought their son in safety within sight of the well known shores of *Maryland*.

CHAPTER XIV

As *Senepuxon* inlet was but shallow, he advis'd the Captain to stand into the great bay of *Chesapeak*, and cast anchor close to the *Eastern* shore in *Magidi* bay, which they did accordingly, and they both, procuring horses, set out, richly dress'd and attended by two servants in livery, for *Senepuxon*. They made such expedition that in less than two days they travers'd the two *Virginian* counties of *Northampton* and *Acomoco*, and enter'd *Worcester* county in *Tom*'s beloved *Maryland*: And now being less than forty miles from the spot, where he was either going to complete his felicity or to be render'd eternally miserable, a gloomy melancholy overwhelm'd him — he long'd, yet fear'd to approach his *Senepuxon* lest he should hear some fatal tidings of his *Fanny* that might destroy his peace; but he was soon put out of his pain, for seeing a man riding towards them, as he came nearer and nearer, he recollected somewhat in his features that he thought he had seen before; but how overjoy'd was he, when coming close to him he knew it to be the identical *Duncan Murray*, who had been his fellow servant at *Barlow*'s remote plantation.

That honest fellow was some time before he could be convinc'd it was *Tom* himself; but when he was thoroughly assur'd of it, he broke out into rapture — which however the other would not suffer him to indulge — he put at once so many questions to him. A faithful lover may guess his situation when he was answer'd that his dear *Fanny* was alive, and single, as also Mrs. *Barlow*, but that *Barlow* was dead, and his wife had dispos'd of all his possessions, and liv'd retiredly with her daughter at Mr. *Gordon*'s; that *Ferguson* and his wife were also alive, and that they had been in daily expectation a long time of his return to *Maryland*.

My friend, says Mr. *Anderson*, we'll waste time no longer; but you have made me so happy, that it would be the height of ingratitude not to repay you, and so saying he put five guineas into his hand, and order'd him to call at Mr. *Ferguson*'s the first opportunity — Sir, says he — I live with that gentleman now, and am going upon his business. I am glad of it, the other returned — then I shall see you again without difficulty, and so saying they parted.

The tone of Mr. *Anderson*'s voice, the turn of his countenance seemed elevated upon this intelligence, and, clapping the Captain on the shoulder, he said, Now sir, you'll have a better companion of me — I shall trouble you with sighs and tears and melancholy no more — the lovely *Fanny*'s mine! Wings now seem'd added to their speed, and in less than four hours they came within sight of Mr. *Ferguson*'s; for there *Tom* first propos'd to alight, for fear of too much surprizing the two ladies. But his precaution was render'd abortive, for they happen'd to be that day there, and were at supper in a kind of alcove at the upper end of a long walk, on one side of the house, from whence they could see whoever enter'd it without being perceiv'd themselves, and were then expressing their wishes for his speedy and safe arrival.

Just at that moment the two gentlemen and their servants enter'd the walk, alighted and left their horses to go round to the house by another way, whilst they went up this well known shady grove. The appearance of two such fine folks attracted all their regards — but *Fanny* could not be long ignorant who one of them was — no, that constant fair, as he approach'd nearer, perceiv'd the air, gait and features of a man she had ever before her eyes, and the surprize at so unexpected a sight, threw her into such an extacy of joy, that she fell senseless into her mother's arms, who then cry'd out — oh! it is my dear son!

Just at that instant the two gentlemen got sight of the company, all of whom were known to one of them, upon which springing forwards, with an eager pace, he was in a minute in the alcove, and soon seeing the reason of the disorder they were in, cry'd oh! my dear friends let me warm her into life, — look up my queen! — my lovely *Fanny*! — my wife! — by what tender name shall your faithful slave conjure you to hear him? — and, taking her in his arms, by his warm pressure soon restor'd her to herself. Simple language is quite too low and faint to describe the mutual raptures and delight of all present. In short, nothing was to be heard for some time, but exclamations of excellent mother! — best of friends! — charming *Fanny*! — Dear son! — worthiest youth! and such expressions as sudden joy dictated to them all.

Fanny's eyes ran over her accomplish'd lover with an eager and wild transport — *Tom* gaz'd upon the beauties of his *Fanny* with a soul full of love and desire. At length he was composed enough to present his friend to them, whom they received with the utmost politeness, and all being seated, and supper over, of which the new comers partook, Mr. *Anderson*, at their earnest request, immediately related his adventures to that moment, from the time he left them. They were seized with awe at the exemplary punishment of *Williamson*; but when he came to the discovery of his parents, there was not a dry eye in the company, and every one congratulated his good fortune.

Fanny wept during the whole narration, at the conclusion of which her lover thus addressed her. At length, my love, you see at your feet (kneeling) the man that heaven intends to bless you; no more the sordid, despis'd, persecuted slave, but the heir to a splendid fortune and the possessor of sufficient wealth of his own to make you happy. — Nothing remains but your hand, to make me the most easy, contented creature breathing — say, my lovely fair! — are you still as well inclined as ever in my favour! I see, both looking at Mrs. *Barlow*, our mother yields her consent, and intends to recompence me for all my pains and sufferings.

The adorable creature, blushing like the morn, held out her hand, — saying — yes — my dear *Tommy* — suffer me still to call you by that endearing name, my whole soul — my heart and every thing is yours, if my mother consents to our mutual desires. Yes, my love, that excellent woman reply'd — and may heaven bless and prosper you together, and on the day of your marriage, according to the will of your poor unhappy father, I will pay my son 8000 *l.* Ah, madam, he return'd, you are ever good and beneficent — my late master I feared to mention — for I heard he was dead before I arrived — because it might revive your sorrows — but I long ago forgave him all that he acted against me. Mr. *Ferguson* and his wife and the good Mr. *Gordon* join'd the conversation, and the next day se'n night[1] was appointed for the latter to perform the matrimonial ceremony that should unite the amiable pair for ever.

CHAPTER XV

When the twilight grey had embrown'd the dusky shades, Mr. *Anderson* taking his *Fanny* by the hand, (after the tenderest endearments,) walk'd for some time in a neighbouring grove, and, being impatient to hear it, whilst the nightingale was pouring out her mournful notes, besought her to acquaint him with all that had happened for the many years of his absence, which she did in the following terms.

After we received your letters by our good Mr. *Ferguson*, from the plantation, I began to be somewhat easier in my mind, for my fears and cares about the welfare of my dear *Tommy*, had just reduced me to death's door, and brought myself to wait with patience the dispensations of providence. Whilst we were forming schemes and pleasing ourselves with the thought of paying you frequent visits, that excellent friend calling a second time at the plantation brought us the first tidings of your being sent from thence, which again involved us in the most grievous distress; but the little note you left with *Murray*, assuring us that you imagined you had fallen into good and kind hands, I endeavoured, once more, to wait the mercies of heaven in my favour.

My father after his return from the plantation with the two *Carters*, staid for some days at their house, and there was laid a scheme, in consequence of your being sent out of the way, that tended, had not providence interpos'd, to complete our mutual unhappiness. The Colonel, who had observ'd, at his several visits to our house, the coldness of my dear mother towards

---

1 A week from tomorrow.

him, and had been inform'd by my father of her aversion to the match between his son and me; began to think, that if, by any means, I could be got out of her hands, and at a distance from her, my youth and inexperience would bend to his son's assiduities, sollicitations and presents, and accordingly inveigled my father into his design, of getting me to visit a niece he had, of near the same age with myself, and, when there, to keep me from returning again to my own house, till the marriage was perform'd.

At first he seem'd, hard-hearted as he was, somewhat shock'd at such a proposal; but at length, the arguments of my enemy prevail'd, and it was agreed to put it in execution the very next week. You may remember, that I had latterly entertained a fondness for a servant maid we had, nam'd *Martha*, who was indented to my father, and, after you was carry'd away from us, that good creature shew'd such concern for your loss, such a tender care and regard of me and my mother, that she entirely engag'd my love and friendship, and became the repository of all my secrets; of my passion for my *Tommy*, and my griefs and despair.

My mother, who had observ'd somewhat mightily taking in the girl, encourag'd me in my liking, and got my father to consent to her constantly attending upon me, and doing no other business; which he did, after having, with a volley of oaths and execrations, wish'd I had never had any communication with servants of the other sex. To this confident I daily and nightly vented my complaints, and sigh'd forth all the pains that tortur'd my bosom; to her I ever was talking of my dear wanderer's merit and perfections of body and mind, and reiteratedly renew'd every oath and vow, to be true and constant to him, even under all the cruelties my tormentors could possibly inflict; leaning pensively on her arm, I us'd to traverse every well-known-walk, and visit every grove of shady retreat, where, innocently, we had enjoy'd each other's society; particularly, that fatal *Pine barren*, where my cruel father laid the foundation of all our succeeding misfortunes, by his fell barbarity to my dearest youth and me.

This companion of mine was thought an obstruction to their project; but my father would, however, by no means hear of any attempts to separate her from me, nor to take me away, without my mother's knowledge, which they had also gone so far as to hint the expediency of doing: No, that he thought was going too far; nor could he think, brute as he appear'd, that now you was remov'd, my mother was so dreaded an obstacle as they wanted to make her appear; but as to my visiting miss *Betsey Oulton*, for that was the name of the Colonel's niece, for a few days, and even being detain'd by his own commands, and a strict watch, he had no objection: His weakness and bad principles had not been work'd upon so far, as to permit them to mention half the villainy they intended, to poor forlorn *Fanny*.

However, one day after we had din'd, he address'd my mother in this manner. See madam, that *Frank*[1] has her things ready to-morrow, to accompany me to the Colonel's, and *Martha* shall go with her for a few days, to visit *Bet Oulton*; she's a girl, against whom your d—'d squeamishness can have no objection I suppose, and I have been hunted a long time, to bring her over to see her; and, observing my mother turn pale and look very grave at these words, he added in his usual ill-natur'd manner, What, d—n it — I suppose now you think some d—'d mischief, or mar-riage is intended; but I tell you only a simple visit is meant, and she shall go, by G—d, that I am resolv'd upon.

My mother reply'd, Well Mr. *Barlow*, your will must be obey'd I think then; but she is quite a stranger to Miss *Betsey*, and besides I have heard some things of her, that make me think her no very elegible companion, for a young creature of prudence and virtue, as I am sure your daughter is: I shall however say no more — I know your positive temper[2] — but if any harm is intended to my child, God, who sees all things, will I hope grant her his protection, and turn the machinations of our enemies upon their own heads. Alas! you have made me miserable enough already — you need not encrease my woes!

At this conclusion, the tears stood in her eyes, and my fore-boding fears had almost overcome me; but he deign'd her no answer,[3] and flung out of the room, cursing and swearing; and stung to the quick with her keen reproach, which he knew glanc'd at you.[4] She then endeavour'd to chase away my appre-hensions, saying, she could not imagine any ill was meant me, as *Martha* was suffer'd to accompany me, and gave her a strict charge never to be absent from the room where I was, upon any account.

The night was spent by my mother and me, in conjectures of the reason of this command, and the morning found me still

---

1 A nickname for Fanny, or, more properly, Frances (see p. 70, n. 3 above).
2 Stubborn, or dictatorial, manner.
3 He thought it beneath himself to answer her.
4 That is, she was alluding to Barlow's villainous treatment of Tom.

awake, and ruminating over all the gloomy prospects that my busy fancy set before me. At ten, after breakfast, at which my father put on a forc'd good humour, as it plainly appear'd, he commanded us to mount the horses he had prepar'd for us, which, after taking a tender farewell of my mother, and tears shed on both sides, we did, and set forward on our journey; for the Colonel's was some hours ride from our house.

For a long time we rode in silence, not a word issuing from my father's mouth, and as to my part, I was too full of dismay and fear, at being oblig'd to enter the house of my odious enemies, which I also thought was in some small degree forfeiting my obligations to you, and breaking thro' the conduct I had prescrib'd myself; but oh! what would have avail'd all my reluctance, all my tears and prayers, with this tyrannical father? who at length broke out into praises of young *Carter*, principally deduc'd from his wealth and the possessions he would enjoy, and finally told me, that if I would oblige him by giving my consent to marry him, he would not only forgive me all that was past, but I should have every penny of his fortune at his death; which, if I continu'd deaf to his entreaties, he would sooner leave to a mere stranger, than to one who had given him so much vexation.

I had never before assum'd courage enough to expostulate[1] with him; but, upon this fair opening, I was resolv'd, let the consequence be ever so dreadful, that he should know my real sentiments and my ultimate resolutions. My dear father, I reply'd, what have I done that you want to send me for ever from the arms of my mother, and from your cares! I have ever, to the best of my remembrance, behav'd with duty and reverence to you, and cannot yet bear the thought of parting with my parents. Let me Sir, oh! let me still live with you, watch your desires, and obey your commands, with ready attendance, and let me not be forc'd to give my hand, where I can never surrender my heart. Mr. *Carter*, no doubt, has some good qualities; but neither his manners or behaviour suit with me, and it is utterly impossible I should ever love him, with the affection of a wife. Why will you make me miserable, my dear Sir, and why must all my future repose be sacrific'd to a darling whim of other people? Believe me, Sir, so far as reason and religion obliges me, I'll ever shew you a ready obedience; but will either inform me, that I must sac-

---

1 Argue.

rifice my present and eternal peace and happiness to gratify the vanity of one person, or the pride and way-ward inclination of another? No, my father, you are too good, and I'm sure love me too well, to insist upon this condition — I will behave with becoming decency where you have oblig'd me to go — but I must declare, that rather than marry Mr. *Carter*, I'll go a virgin to the grave, curs'd with your frowns and displeasure, and depriv'd of every farthing[1] that is in your power to bestow upon me; and yet, dear Sir, oh! hear me, before you answer — here I protest and vow, that without your consent and liking, I will marry no other man breathing.

The courage with which I was enabled to utter these words, the determin'd air I display'd, and the reasonableness of my desires and arguments, for some moments spread his face over with a paleness, that I could perceive proceeded from the passionate motions of his mind; but he soon return'd me an hundred curses, and the most bitter oaths that I should marry whether I would or no, if he was sure of my death the minute after, and that I should never look upon my mother or home again, till he had seen it perform'd. In short, I never saw him in such a fury before; he abus'd you, absent as you was, my mother, every body that he imagin'd took my part, and, if I had not been on horseback, I believe I should have felt, as well as heard his anger; to which I made no other answer, than a torrent of tears, and reiterated sighs, which declar'd my terrors and apprehensions.

Still I was collected within myself, and resolv'd firmly to abide death, nay the most excruciating tortures, rather than be in the least tittle false to you, whose image was ever before my eyes, and whose virtues and softly amiable qualities, were never out of my mind; and I silently put up my petitions to heaven, to strengthen me under the ills I now found I was destin'd to endure, and a calmness succeeded that I knew not how to account for, otherwise than thus: When misfortunes rise as high as they possibly can, and we have few worse consequences to expect, the soul, as it were, is tortur'd to such a degree, as, admitting of no encrease of pain, resigns it to all that is to ensue.

In this mood we alighted at the Colonel's, who, with his son and niece, were ready to help us to dismount, and receiv'd us with the greatest civility; the niece, to whom I had no quarrel, and

---

1 A farthing is a quarter penny, and hence this is the idiomatic equivalent of today's "every last penny."

whom I did not know, seem'd very fond of my company, and we spent the remainder of the day with expressive satisfaction to every person but me, being entertain'd with every dainty that great affluence and a plentiful table could afford; nor had I the mortification of exchanging one word with young *Carter*, who now thinking himself sure of his prey, only view'd me, from time to time, with a look rather of insulting pride than of tenderness. At night, my father, with a forc'd smile, said to me, well *Fanny*, I'll leave you for a day or two, and don't doubt but Miss *Bet* will agreeably entertain you, to which I made no other reply, than a courtsey; and by sending my duty to my dear mother, whilst the tears stood in my eyes.

And thus I was now left in the custody of my deadliest foes, with no other guard but virtue and innocence, and poor *Martha*, which had all prov'd too weak for my protection, if Heaven itself had not rescu'd me from their detested hands. When the two *Carters* were retir'd, the young lady made me an offer of part of her bed, which I handsomely declin'd, by saying that *Martha* always laid with me, which excuse she as handsomely accepted, and I retir'd to rest in a very splendid apartment, in a situation of temper that you may easily guess, and then gave vent to my grief, in which I was accompany'd, and at the same time had comfort administer'd me, by *Martha*; who yet had spoke in vain, if she had not represented the feasibleness of an escape, if matters should be driven to an extremity.

I think you never saw the Colonel's late plantation, and therefore in a few words, I'll describe the situation of it. The house, which was very large, was handsomely built of brick, and far superior to ours; the apartments were spacious, and set off with very grand and gay furniture; on three sides extended the clear'd land, of near 500 acres, skirted by the surrounding woods, which, at such a distance, had a pleasing romantic appearance; and, behind the house, instead of clearing, they had caus'd the wood to be cut into an hundred mazey walks, and meandring alleys, which run back near a mile, and afforded a most charming rural retreat; diversify'd with groves, shades and thickets, and water'd by a branch of the neighbouring river, which art had taught to murmur thro' every glade. At the extremity of these walks was a fine level *Savannah*, where the lowing kine[1] and the bleating sheep, cropp'd the flowery herbage, and the sportive steed frisk'd

---

1 Cattle.

and gambol'd o'er the plain; and on the farther side of it were the huts, a little town in extent, of near 300 *Negroes* and their families, who thence, every morning, issu'd to labour and tyrannic usage, in the plantations which were overlook'd by the house.

I was so taken up with my sorrows, that it was late before I clos'd my eyes, and then, fancy presented a scene that I shall never forget, to my waking soul. Forgive me, my dear *Tommy*, for laying any stress upon dreams, an opinion you have often combated with me, but it made such an impression upon me, and tended so much to support my spirits, under my following trials, that I must impart it to you. Methought I was transported into a wide, howling, savage desert, that extended farther than my aching eyes could reach; the soil was adust and sandy, and nothing green or chearing appear'd about me, save here and there a weed or thistle that intruded its sun burnt head thro' the scorch'd plain. The lamp of the day shone intensely hot over my head, and render'd my situation still more wretched, as I press'd forward to a rising hill, at a distance, which seem'd crown'd with lofty trees, and bespread with reviving verdure; and down whose sides flow'd a thousand wanton rills,[1] that seem'd murmuringly to sport with each other, and to guggle[2] over the shining pebbles, which appear'd as radiant as the richest treasures of the *Indian* mines.[3]

Methought on the summit of this delightful mount, was a gaily decorated alcove, spread with carpets of the richest workmanship; I us'd the utmost toil to reach its base, which at length with incredible labour I effected; but oh! the terror I was seiz'd with, when I perceiv'd two tremendous fierce lions, issuing from their dens at the foot of the hill, and with glaring eyes, hideous roar and eager pace, pressing forward to devour me! I turn'd back again towards the desart to endeavour an escape! but lo! the whole sandy waste was moving like the waves of the ocean, by the impetuous wind, and the dreadful sea rolling to overwhelm me.

Thus beset, and unknowing where to fly, I turn'd me again to the mountain, when I perceiv'd my *Tommy*'s form, his face adorn'd with his usual placid smile, and found he had destroy'd the two wild beasts, and was approaching to meet me. A serene satisfaction overspread my soul; he embrac'd me, saying, come

---

1 Brooks.
2 Gurgle.
3 The mines in Spain's New World empire, which were worked by Native American laborers.

my lovely mourner, all your ills are now o'er-past, come and enjoy, in yonder bower, all the charms of love and friendship! Methought he then took me in his arms, and we ascended in a minute to the alcove, where my joy was so overbearing that it caus'd me to awake; but 'tis impossible to describe to you the salutary effect my dream had upon me, and, having imparted it to *Martha*, we both agreed that it was a heavenly notice of relief from all my pains, and of future happiness in your arms.

Miss *Oulton* came to my apartment before I was quite dress'd, enquir'd complaisantly how I spent the night, and said I look'd better than at my arrival. I thank'd her politely for her complement, and follow'd her down to breakfast, where the first scene that presented itself, a piece of gallantry to me I suppose, was a negroe ty'd up to a tree before the window, and the redoubted[1] *Carter*, the younger, belabouring his sides with the *Cowskin*, whilst his father stood by, encouraging him to lay the strokes on home, tho' the poor creature's blood follow'd every one that was struck. This was a discipline I never in my life had seen before, for, tho' my father perhaps us'd his slaves with little less cruelty, you know his executions of that sort were never perform'd near our house, or in our hearing; a piece of respect he had just goodness enough to pay to the humanity and sensibility of my mother and me.

I own the sight, for I could not help seeing it, made me almost faint; but my tenderness was laugh'd at by Miss *Betsey*, who treated the matter as a joke, which gave me a high distaste to her, for I ever consider'd the poor wretches as a part of my own species and not upon the level of the brute creation, which was what she insisted upon, and therefore entitled to all the regard and indulgent kindness that their forlorn and unhappy condition call'd for. At length weariness caus'd a truce to this diabolical exercise, occasion'd, as I understood afterwards, only by the fellow's having knock'd down a favourite dog with his hoe, that run at him and made a wound in his arm with his teeth.

At breakfast, both father and son avoided any thing that could give me dislike as to myself; but contented themselves with laughing and joking at their late exploit, numbering up the poor fellow's groans and piercing cries, with a kind of triumph, and fondling and pitying the dog that had been the cause of all this barbarity. But this was only the first essay[2] I beheld of their skill,

---

1 Either "dreadful" or, ironically, "distinguished."
2 Demonstration.

in such usage, and every day afterwards, that I staid, exhibited such acts of unfeeling, obdurate inhumanity to their wretched negroes, that I wonder not the judgment of heaven overtook, at length, the perpetrators of such enormous crimes. In fine, all the tortures that we have read are practis'd in *Barbary*[1] to *Christian* slaves, all that the cruel inquisitions of *Spain* or *Portugal*, act in their prisons and dungeons, were outdone by these two monsters, which at the same time it render'd them fear'd, nurs'd up a spirit of hatred and revenge, in the breasts of the slaves, which had hitherto only wanted opportunity to be brought fatally to light.

After breakfast was over, as by design, the son was left alone with me and *Martha*, who remembering my mother's injunction was blind to all the hints given her by Miss *Oulton* to leave the room; hints which we both plainly perceiv'd, and which gave me to know what I had to expect from her friendship and acquaintance. *Martha* took up a book that lay in the window, and, seeming engag'd with that, *Carter* drew his chair towards me, and harangu'd me in the following manner; but with an aukwardness of gesture, and folly of face, that had I not been concern'd so nearly, would have excited laughter and derision. —

Miss, he drawl'd out at last, after several coughs, hums and has, — how do you do to day? — pretty well, I hope — well I hope you like our place — it's fine and pleasant isn't it — ha? I hope soon to call you mistress of just such a one — what d'ye say? — will you at last consent to have me! — 'pon my faith — and I'll be d—d if it ant true, I love you better than the eyes in my head — better, by G—d than any creature alive — better than father a great deal — what d'ye say? — I see you won't speak — as soon as we are tack'd together, d'ye see, father says we shall keep coach,[2] and I'm sure it will be the first kept in *Worcester* county, 'pon my soul will it — then who but we — ha? what a figure you'll make at church, and I at the *Court-house*; for you must know I'm commission'd for the peace[3] as well as father, and am a lieutenant of the militia too, — no, there's not another on

---

1 A reference to the slavery of white sailors captured by pirates along the coast of Northern Africa. For a specimen of English awareness of and response to this phenomenon, see Mary Barber's poem in Appendix C3.
2 Keeping a coach was a conspicuous sign of wealth.
3 Designated a justice of the peace. Kimber here perpetuates the British stereotype of American courts being ruled over by illiterates and buffoons.

this side *Anne Arundel*[1] I'm quite tir'd of going like the petty planters on horseback[2] — Then I shall soon be chosen a *sembly man*[3] and may hap, be before I dye, one of the governor's *council keepers*[4] too, and then we shall go to town and live as gay as the best of 'em — and you shall have all the finery that can be brought from *England*, and wear nothing but silks and sattins, and jewels and gold and silver — egad, we'll out do all the country, and buy out all the little folks about us — here's father has 700 negroes, besides women and children, and is worth above 40000 pounds — all which will come to me, my girl, when he's dead, and I believe he won't live long any more than old *Barlow*, — for, by the bye, they are d—ble drinkers — that I can tell you — and he has offer'd me 8000 *l.* down, with you, and the rest when he dyes — except a small pittance for your mother — and, mind me, when they are all dead and rotten, we shall be the richest people in all the colony — Come — don't stand shill I, shall I;[5] but to bed, at once, let's go — I don't understand a great deal of palaver,[6] of this, and that, and t'other — you are handsome and have a good fortune — I'm a stout young fellow — sound wind and limb[7] — and have a good estate — burn me, if you'll say the word — your coach shall be drawn by *Negroes* instead of horses. What d'ye say to it? —

At this conclusion my raptur'd swain,[8] with open mouth, star'd and gap'd for an answer. I protest, notwithstanding my unhappiness, I could scarce refrain laughing in his face, at his extraordinary address; and *Martha*, I perceiv'd, was forc'd to bite her lip almost till it bled, to contain herself: at length however I assum'd so much composure as to return the following answer. Mr. *Carter*, I have heard all you have said, you see, with patience, and wonder you should address me again, upon a subject on

---

1 [Kimber's note] Annapolis.
2 [Kimber's note] In *Maryland* and *Virginia* they are such great horsemen that a planter will go or send 5 miles to fetch his horse up, in order to ride one mile to church.
3 A member of the colonial legislature.
4 A member of the governor's council, an advisory board in the colonial executive branch.
5 Don't be so indecisive.
6 Idle talk.
7 A common colloquialism for good health.
8 An ironic comparison of the bumbling Carter with the amorous, eloquent shepherds of pastoral poetry.

which my words and actions had so well explain'd my sentiments before; beside, Sir, methinks it is unlike a man of honour, to attack me in this manner, a visitor and under your own roof, where I lye expos'd to all your assaults, unable to help myself; but, however, I am now resolv'd to give you a full answer, Sir, such an one as will shew you my fix'd and determin'd resolution, take it how you will. How, Sir, could you pretend to address a daughter, in such a manner, and, in order to ingratiate yourself with her, found your hopes of wealth encreas'd, and future joy upon the death of her parents? Let me tell you, Mr. *Carter*, if you have been brought up in such irreverence to those that begot you, it has been far otherwise with me, who think it the greatest of crimes to despise or wish harm to those dear persons, to whom I am indebted for my being; and if my poor father, who indeed you have taught to see only with your eyes, has some foibles, it does not authorise me to notice them, or retort upon him the injuries he consents shall fall to my share. By these few hints of our difference in opinion, you'll conjecture what a wretched pair you and I should make, — your notions of things are all taken from outward objects — your education has been amongst your slaves, and this very morning you gave me a specimen of such brutality, that I shudder when I think what my fate would be, with such an unfeeling, unpitying husband.[1] — My mind, Sir, aims rather at intellectual happiness, than at the vain gewgaws[2] that riches afford, — to dwell, even in an obscure cot,[3] with a man of my

---

1   This is an interesting, if half-formed, anticipation of Thomas Jefferson's famous writings three decades later depicting the influence of slaveholding on "the Customs and Manners" of Virginia. "The whole commerce between master and slave," Jefferson observed from experience,
    "is a perpetual exercise of the most boisterous passions, the most unremitting despotism on the one part, and degrading submissions on the other. Our children see this, and learn to imitate it....The parent storms, the child looks on, catches the lineaments of wrath, puts on the same airs in the circle of smaller slaves, gives a loose to his worst of passions, and thus nursed, educated, and daily exercised in tyranny, cannot but be stamped by it with odious peculiarities. The man must be a prodigy who can retain his manners and morals undepraved by such circumstances"
    (*Notes on the State of Virginia, by Thomas Jefferson, with Related Documents*, ed. David Waldstreicher [1785; Boston and New York: Bedford/St. Martin's, 2002], p. 195).
2   Trifles, meaningless luxuries.
3   Cottage.

own sentiments — a man adorn'd with knowledge, good sense, good nature, virtue and humanity, I should prefer before all the ridiculous and idle parade, you have laid before me, with such elegance of diction. No, Sir, but don't be affronted, I must assure you, if I am to make my choice either of death or you — I shall think the first most eligible: — I never will consent to such an unnatural union, — The coarseness of your language, is of a piece with the grossness of your sentiments, and equally an affront to delicacy and good manners; and, now Sir, I hope, I shall be pester'd with your addresses no more; at least in this sojourn with your cousin, to whom I was brought on a visit, and, on my side, you shall discover nothing but good temper and civility, whilst I stay under your protection.

I had no sooner finished these words, than the great oaf seem'd turn'd into stone, and remain'd, in a kind of inanimate silence, with mouth stretch'd open — eyes straining and staring me full in the face, and every other mark of stupid amazement; and thus he would longer have continu'd, if his father and cousin had not enter'd the room, which they no sooner did, than he got up and left it, with an action that betoken'd him humbled and mortified, and at the same time brim full of malice and spite. At dinner my spark[1] did not appear; but at supper was drunk, and affected to be very good temper'd, and the next and several succeeding days, I heard no more from any party upon this hated subject.

All this while my father had never appear'd, and I was in great pain to know how my dear mother did; but expecting soon an end of my banishment, I put on as easy an air as possible, and frequently, with Miss *Oulton*, took an evening turn in the walks which I have describ'd, at the back of the house, and sometimes obtain'd the pleasure of being alone there, with my *Martha*, to whom, whilst the whispering zephyrs wanton'd[2] amongst the leaves, I oft vented my passion, and my grief for the absence of my dearest *Tommy*. You know, dear Sir, that you flatter'd me formerly with having somewhat of an agreeable voice, and, by your tuneful example, I became a poetess, and my situation having soften'd and melted my soul into harmony, I dress'd my complaints in verse, which often, in these retirements, this faithful girl teaz'd me to sing. I have but a mean opinion of the lines; but as

1 Young fop, or would-be lover.
2 Winds played.

they were a testimony of my affection you shall have them; and then the amiable Miss *Barlow* sung the following stanzas to her raptur'd *Anderson*.

SONG.

Tune, *All in the Downs the fleet lay moor'd.*[1]

I.

THE *silver* moon, from *clouded state*,
  Diffus'd abroad her *peerless light*;
The radiant stars around her wait,
  Chearing the *rugged brow of night:*[2]
When mourning *Fanny*, hapless, wretched fair,
  Thus to the silent grove reveal'd her care.

II.

And whilst she sung, sad *Philomel*[3]
  Instant, her plaintive note forbore;
Superior griefs, she heard her tell,
  The wailing virgin's bosom tore;
Each *zephyr* ceas'd, at once, his wanton play,
  And hush was every leaf and sportive spray.[4]

III.

Ah! me, she cry'd, what fate is mine!
  To pride and avarice a prey!
And absent he, for whom I pine,
  An exile, wandering far away!
What tearful sorrows may attack my swain,
  Before these eyes behold him once again?

IV.

Nature disclaims in me her share,
  A father acts the direful part;
Pleas'd witness of my sad despair,
  He plants the dagger in my heart:

---

1 A popular early-eighteenth-century folk song, the words of which were composed by the renowned poet John Gay.
2 Fanny here borrows a series of images from Milton's *Paradise Lost* (IV.606–09) and *Il Penseroso* (l. 58).
3 Common poetic name for the nightingale.
4 Playfully moving limb or branch.

Celestial powers! in pity, change his mind,
  Make him more just, more generous and more kind.

V.

Can wealth impart, or health, or ease
  And calmness, to the tortur'd breast?
Can gaily sliding moments please,
  A maiden sorely so distrest?
For me, nor morn awakes the joyous song,
  Nor e'en provides the friendly, mirthful throng.

VI.

Thus the poor trembling hare, pursu'd
  By ruthless man and barb'rous hounds,
With one last scream alarms the wood;
  Each hill and dale the cry resounds;
As I, all frantic, yet by hope beguil'd,
  Breath my complaints, in notes uncouth and wild.

VII.

But Heaven, perhaps, has bliss in store,
  For constancy and faultless truth;
These arms, may then embrace, once more,
  My *Tommy*, virtuous, lovely youth;
Yes, yes, some angel whispers in my ear
  "Rewards await a passion so sincere."

CHAPTER XVI

Mr. *Anderson*, charm'd to the highest degree, eagerly press'd the fair songstress in his arms; call'd her his *Sapho*,[1] and told her her verses were like herself, all sweetness and softness, and complemented her upon the agreeable use she had made of *Milton*'s epithets, in the first stanza; and then she again resum'd her story.

One evening, when I, with *Martha*, had travers'd the longest of these alleys, which brought us into the *Savannah*, a negroe, with great submission, accosted me, somewhat in whose face, methought, I recollected; and was soon eas'd of my doubt by the honest fellow's saying — Oh! mistress, you not know poor *Squanto*? — you goodee mistress — you lovee poor negroe, no

---

1 The most famous woman poet of classical Greece.

beatee them — no whippee! Ah! *Squanto*, I cry'd, we have miss'd you at home a long time — how came you here? —

You may remember *Squanto*, no doubt, who was one of the most docible[1] negroes about our house, and who had a particular respect for you, and made such lamentations when you was thought kill'd by my father, in the *pine barren*, that he never afterwards forgave him: Some trifling fault having heighten'd this distaste, my father, under the pretence of sending him to another plantation, had exchanged him with Colonel *Carter*, where he knew pretty well he would meet with more labour and punishment, than, even he thought proper to trouble himself with the infliction of; and, to the many enquiries my mother and I made after him, he only reply'd that he was at a plantation he had at *Pongoteacq*.

I was really glad to see *Squanto*, and so was *Martha*, nor could I help placing him in the light of a fellow sufferer, from the same barbarous and inhuman people; so bow'd my spirits were with the idea of being in such hands. *Squanto* then, shaking his head, and the tears standing in his eyes, from the sense of his condition, return'd, oh! mistress, you no livee here — here is de Hell — de Devils — torture poor negroes! — and then proceeded to give me a detail of such unheard of, wanton cruelty, from his two masters, nay from Miss *Oulton*, that nothing but his back, sides, arms and legs, furrow'd with stripes, and mark'd with wounds, could have induc'd me to believe.

I gave the poor fellow some shilling bills[2] I had in my pocket, and assur'd him, if possibly I could, or if you return'd to *Maryland* we would redeem him from his slavery, the very thought of which made him jump and skip about, like one bewitch'd with joy. As I knew a negroe would be question'd how he came by money, a commodity they seldom see, I mark'd upon every one of the bills (the gift of *Frances Barlow* to *Squanto*,) to prevent his being expos'd to any punishment under suspicion of theft, and then we parted, *Squanto* returning to his hovel, and we, with weeping eyes and sighing hearts towards the house; reflecting upon the forlorn condition I was in — my *Tommy* absent — perhaps dead! my mother dying with grief at my loss — and yet unable to help me or herself; — my father my enemy, and bent

---

1 Teachable, submissive.
2 Although generally considered a unit of British currency (worth one-twentieth of a pound), the shilling was occasionally used in colonial America.

on my destruction, and myself in the custody of creatures totally destitute of goodness or humanity, and ignorant of all the principles of virtue. Could any state be more wretched? — no — and my eyes rain'd incessant tears, as with melancholy soul I ruminated over it.

When we came in doors Colonel *Carter*, with an air of good humour, banter'd me upon my solitary turn of mind, and took occasion to tell me, that my father was just gone, and that he would not stay to see me, for fear I should want to go home, which he would not permit me to do till I had been marry'd to his son. To all this I made no answer, but a forc'd smile and a courtsey, not willing to exasperate the old man; for I had a scheme brewing in my mind, which seem'd to promise fair, in its execution, to extricate me from my present distress.

This sight of *Squanto*, had put it into my head, that, with his assistance, an escape might be made from my prison to Mr. *Gordon*'s, under whose protection I resolv'd to put myself, and to hazard the loss of fortune and every thing else, rather than forfeit my faith to you, or make myself *splendidly* wretched, as my tormentors proposed: And, as to *Squanto*, I knew that gentleman would either protect him, or buy him from his master, and relieve him from his barbarous usage. In bed I imparted the affair to *Martha*, who seem'd entirely of my opinion, and we both resolv'd to set about it the very next evening, by first sounding the spirit and abilities of *Squanto*.

That faithful slave was at his old station, expecting me to walk that way, and I, after some other discourse, by which I found his courage and resolution of a proper cast, told him my situation and intention, and ask'd him if he would risk the hazard of helping me out of durance.[1] In short *Squanto* was overjoy'd at the proposal, and the thoughts of living with Mr. *Gordon* and serving me; and we agreed, that two nights afterward, we would walk down the same alley, and that *Squanto*, after his work was ended, should secure 3 horses in the wood on the other side of the *Savannah*, and that if we came alone and the coast was clear, a signal should be given him, and then we were immediately to mount, and, thro' private ways, which were well known to *Squanto*, go to *Snow-hill*, the town in the neighbourhood of which Mr. *Gordon* resided.

I put on, for the intermediate space of time a more than ordinary chearfulness; nay even said a complaisant thing or two to

---

1 Forced confinement.

your hated rival; so that they began to bless themselves at so sudden an alteration of behaviour, which they already attributed to the impressions, a sight of their riches, splendor and large possessions had made upon my mind. As to our cloaths and linen, we could convey none of them with us, except those upon our backs, and contented ourselves with leaving them at the mercy of the enemy.

The day arriv'd, and with it a thousand difficulties and fears that had escap'd my reflection before; the evening began to approach, and to encourage us the more, young *Carter* rode over to my father's, about some business; and, I took an opportunity when Miss *Oulton* was busy in her household affairs, to saunter with *Martha* towards the place of rendezvous, and got out, quite unsuspected of any other design than to take the refreshment of the cool breeze, that sported thro' the groves. *Martha* was also so provident as to commit to her pocket a pint bottle of brandy and 2 or 3 biscuits, which she found in a cupboard in our apartment, and had been left there and forgotten.

Well, at the *Savannah* we arriv'd, scar'd at every tree and rustling noise, and making the signal agreed upon, which was 3 loud hems, *Squanto* readily appear'd; in an instant we cross'd the *Savannah*, and mounting upon the wretched furniture[1] the poor creature had affectionately provided, we set out on our journey, following our guide, thro' the gloomy retreats of the wood, incommoded, at every step, by the *Palmetto* roots, which gall'd our horses feet, and by the vines, *China* briars[2] and brambles that continually cross'd our way, and threaten'd to pull us from off our horses. Silently, I put up prayers to the Divine Being, for his assistance and protection, and the success of our enterprize; and then, by chearfulness and proper incentive expressions, enliven'd and encourag'd my companions; particularly poor *Martha*, who was a little scar'd at our midnight adventure.

Thus we travell'd incessantly, fear keeping us from any inclination to sleep, till the morning twilight began to appear thro' the trees; nor had we fail'd to dole out frequent sips of the brandy to

---

1 Saddles.
2 It is difficult to discern what Kimber is referring to here, as this plant is not associated with the flora of Maryland. It could be that, as with the palmetto earlier, Kimber is imagining a plant from elsewhere growing in the Chesapeake. Or he could be referring to an indigenous plant by some other name more familiar to Englishmen.

Squanto, however, with a caution to take care of his head, which he observ'd very punctually; and then he told us, we were within 5 miles of *Snow-hill*, and had only private ways to go thro', except about half a mile of the high road, which we were now entering, and must use the utmost expedition to pass. My heart went pit a pat at the danger we were in, for it was not above a mile and half also from my father's, and a strange foreboding melancholy, over-spread my mind, apprehensive of some accident that might retard my flight, and, too true were my presaging fears, for we had not got a stone's cast upon the road, when we heard the feet of horses, and two voices which were, alas! too well known, to put our misfortune into any doubt; for indeed it was my father and young *Carter*.

I trembled like an aspin leaf; but my soul was still firm and prepar'd for the worst, all my concern being for *Martha* and *Squanto*, the latter of whom I advis'd, in as few words as possible, to make the best of his way to Mr. *Gordon*'s, tell him the story and claim his protection; but the poor wretch was so scar'd, that he with difficulty sat his horse, and, before he could recollect himself, the two gentleman had caught us with their eyes, and, I heard my father say, d—n it, there's *Frank!* — *Squanto* and *Martha!* — I'll be d—'d if they are not running away — and *Carter* reply ay, by G—d — to be sure; but I'll take care of one, and immediately clapping spurs to his horse, sprung upon *Squanto*, and with one blow from his whip fell'd him to the ground, and, alighting, beat him over the head, face and every part, in the most unmerciful manner, whilst I, quite frighten'd at the scene, in vain beg'd and pray'd him to desist, for he had done nothing but at my sollicitation and by my orders.

Who doubts it, return'd my father, all in rage — and I've a great mind here to make a sacrifice of you for it — you d—'d, dissem-bling, disobedient little b—h — but your comrades shall pay for it, however — I'll see that! Tears choak'd my voice; I could not reply, and poor *Martha* look'd like the picture of anguish and despair. They then put *Squanto*, quite senseless and bruis'd all over, across his horse, and, ordering me and *Martha* to ride before, follow'd us, hallowing and hooping like two savages, at the good luck, as they stil'd it, of meeting us, my father saying, in a most provokingly scoffing manner, — by G—d, *Carter*, you must marry her out of hand, or the cunning w—e[1] will be too hard for us all.

---

1 Whore.

By this time I had regain'd some courage, and now, thinking the worst had happen'd that could possibly befal me, resolv'd to prepare for the most dreadful event that was threatened, and, oh! God forgive me! but despair what soul can withstand! began to meditate upon the means of destroying myself, to get out of such merciless hands, and to escape a fate that I dreaded much more than death. *Martha* was loaded with curses and threats, to which she made no reply, and poor *Squanto* groan'd incessantly; but was answer'd only by denounciations of the most tormenting and bitter cruelties, my father and his comrade vowing, they would see his ribs bare, with the *Cow-skin*, before they went to rest.

In this mood we came once more to the Colonel's, and there found every thing in an uproar, the old man fuming and swearing, and Miss *Oulton* raving at our escape; but, at the sight of us, it was all converted into triumph, accompany'd with such a turn of expression from both, as convinc'd me their souls were of the meanest and basest cast, and I bore their laughter, insult and derision, without a change of countenance, or uttering a word. Soon after we alighted, my father lock'd me into a room by myself, and *Martha* into another, saying to me, d—n it, as you don't understand the use of liberty — and abuse it so — you shall enjoy it no more, by G—d. At that instant, but I soon check'd myself, I forgot he was my father, and exclaim'd, monster in nature! I shall soon be out of your power! Then too late you may repent having sacrific'd your daughter to a villain!

It was however, tho' not intended, exercising mercy to us to confine us, for *Squanto*, weak and bruis'd as he was, underwent a series of punishments, meantime, that would terrify the hardest heart to conceive. All three of them assisted, after tiring 5 overseers in the devilish office, to send his soul from its suffering mortal habitation, and, when let down from the tree, he spoke or breath'd no more. Oh! Heaven! when I was told that direful tale, my breast was wounded too deeply to support the thought — wild and distracted. I rav'd — call'd them butchers! — fiends! — Devils! — I fainted, and, for two days, was in such strong convulsions that even my cruel father began to relent, and talk'd of sending me home. But the Almighty Ruler of the universe, thought fit to raise me once more, and restor'd my strength; yet my mind, fill'd with nothing but gloomy despair, impress'd most dismal traits upon my countenance, and I observ'd an obstinate silence to all about me, resolving never more to open my lips, unless it pleas'd my kind Creator to rescue me from the hands I was in, and once more, restore me to my dear mother's arms.

As to *Martha*, she was convey'd away I knew not where, for I never saw her afterwards, and I was now in a more forlorn state than ever maid was before; forc'd to bear the insulting taunts of the ungenerous *Oulton*, the gibes and lewd jests of the Colonel and his son, the rage of a father, and my own agitated imaginations, which now were become of the most dark and deadly complexion.

CHAPTER XVII

In this temper my father, the next morning, left me, after having endeavour'd afresh to sooth me to his purpose, which finding in vain, he bid me prepare for marriage or d——n,[1] when I next saw him, which should be in 2 days time, for then he was resolv'd I should have *Carter*; and all this was spoken by the inconsiderate man in the hearing of my three enemies.

I must own, at this time, all my affection for my father was extinct, I look'd upon him as my deadly foe, as a murderer, and was even pleas'd when he was gone from my sight, as if I had one tormentor the less to encounter with; but these last expressions of his, and his stedfastness in the match, encourag'd the others to a brutal attempt, which had well nigh been executed; but for the watchful protection of providence, whose goodness I adore every moment I live! In short, this vile father and wicked son had contriv'd, with the abandon'd *Oulton*, that the very next night, for I was now forc'd to be her bedfellow, by my father's command, she should let the young one into my apartment, not doubting but when he had triumph'd over that silly pride of mine, as they call'd it, my chastity, I should be ready enough to marry him, and sue for a favour which I now with so much obstinacy refus'd; but before you hear the dreadful tale, I must make a small digression from my own affairs to another subject, which you'll soon find will have an intimate and miraculous connexion with them.

The various and unprecedented barbarities exercis'd by these men upon their unhappy slaves, for a number of years, having met with no manner of opposition, from wretches bow'd to the yoke by the continu'd hard hand of oppression, and who even began to think they were born to the usage they receiv'd; was consider'd by the Colonel as a matter of the highest satisfaction, and he us'd to boast that he had the tamest and most orderly *black*

---

1 Damnation.

flock in the whole colony. But this tameness proceeded from yet a more generous temper in the negroes; for the policy of their master, as well as his profit, having induc'd him to provide them wives, or however the greatest number,[1] of their own complexion, the soft tye intimidated them from any revolt or rising, terrify'd with the idea of losing the objects of their care, and the numerous progeny, which alas! were born to misery and sordid slavery, and to enrich the worthless *Carters*.

About a year before my captivity, the Colonel had purchas'd an additional stock of *Negroes*, all brought from the *gold coast*,[2] who are more remarkably bold, cunning and revengeful, than any other natives of *Guinea*, and, as a natural spirit of freedom taught them to disdain the servile labours they were destin'd to, they obstinately, often, refus'd to be instructed, and, when instructed, to practise the lessons they receiv'd, or practis'd them so aukwardly, as to engage punishment, which they bore hardly and were bent upon a thorough revenge, which they were egg'd on to the more, as they saw the slaves of no other plantation suffer'd such cruelties as they did.

These *new Negroes* then, had absolutely refus'd the wives that had been offer'd them, and drew in all the unmarry'd old ones to the same sense of the injuries they endur'd, and the same schemes of revenge. *Squanto*'s catastrophe, who was likewise a *gold coast negroe*, and had embark'd in their designs, work'd them up, almost to madness, and, at this time of my dismallest distress, they were contriving to make speedy and effectual examples of our common persecutors; having fix'd upon the very night, which was destin'd for my undoing, to execute their project.

The day preceding it, being *Sunday*, when the *Negroes* are suffer'd (the only pleasure they enjoy) to be with their families, and to work in the little spots that yield them vegetable food, they had more abundant opportunity for their machinations, and 11 at night was pitch'd upon for them to rise, surround the house, burn it, with all the out-houses, and to massacre the *Carters*, father and son, with *Oulton*, who had frequently been the cause of, and promoted many of the cruelties acted towards them; but if they met with no opposition from the white servants and overseers, determin'd to shed no more blood, but to seize what provisions and arms they thought requisite, and then escape, or fight their way

---

1   Or at least most of them.
2   Part of the West African coast, near the Bight of Benin.

thro', towards the *Apalachian* mountains, where they propos'd to maintain their liberty against all opposers.[1]

Thus, my dearest *Tommy*, you see how Heaven order'd things in our favour, which frequently reminds me of those excellent lines of our favourite poet,

> *So dear to Heaven is saintlike chastity,*
> *That, when a soul is found sincerely so,*
> *A thousand livery'd angels lacquey[2] her,*
> *Driving far off each thing of sin or guilt.*[3]

As to my part, little imagining either the danger or deliverance that awaited me, I pass'd the day in my usual perturbations of mind; and, in short, preparing for the exit, which I had resolv'd upon, if my hand was forc'd in wedlock's band with your contemptible rival; nor did the then situation of my labouring, anxious bosom, suffer me to reflect that God *had plac'd his canon 'gainst self murder*;[4] but I have heard you say, that many such instances of suicide arise from frenzy, induc'd by misfortunes or weak nerves, and that you could never imagine any persons of reason or reflection, could cooly and deliberately make away with himself; that the *Greek* word signifying madness, imply'd almost as much, and that the suicide, like other madmen, dwells too constantly and intently upon some fix'd gloomy thought, which causes his lunacy. To be sure I was, and reason I had, quite delirious with my griefs, or so vile a method of escaping my pains had not found harbour in my brain.

---

1   This is a realistic description of the tactics and aims of a slave rebellion. Arson of plantation buildings was not only a common form of resistance among slaves, but was also a typical signal that an uprising had begun. The goals expressed here – setting up an independent community in which the escaped insurgents could maintain their freedom – were typical of what were called maroon communities throughout the New World. The fact that these rebels were out to gain their own freedom but not the freedom of all slaves is also an accurate portrayal of slave rebels throughout the New World before the American, French, and Haitian revolutions.

2   In Milton's metaphor, the angels operate as footmen to Lady Chastity, wearing her livery (or servant's uniform) and doing her bidding (or "lacqueying" for her).

3   Milton, *Comus* (1637), ll. 459–63.

4   Loosely quoted from Shakespeare, *Hamlet*, I.ii.132.

As to the *Carters* and Miss *Oulton*, they put on a more reserv'd air than ordinary, all the day; but towards evening, I observ'd so much whispering, backwards and forwards, such queer and quaint looks at me, so many sly winks and nods, that I began to be alarm'd, and, Heaven to be sure inspiring me, resolv'd to sit up late in our chamber that night to finish the reading a book, which happen'd by some accident to be in the house, which was not worthy of such a treasure; namely *Lucas* of happiness.[1] When the soul is overspread with gloom and melancholy, we become superstitious, and the lightest circumstances administer to our disorder; my nose accidentally drop'd 2 or 3 drops of blood; this you may be sure I also constru'd into a warning of some intended evil, which still confirm'd me in my resolution.

Thus, differently affected, we separated at our usual hour, which was 9, and Miss *Oulton* and I went up to our chamber, where observing me take the book and seat myself down, she us'd great persuasions for me to come to bed, and insisted upon it with a warmth, that still more and more surprized me, and, seeing me resolv'd to the contrary, sat down at the table by me, and seem'd to fall into a dose, which continu'd for near half an hour: she then appear'd to wake, for it was all grimace,[2] and again pester'd me to go to bed, which I excus'd myself from doing to finish the book; by this time the clock had struck ten, and madam, with a mortified air, told me she would not go to rest before me, and, in about a minute after, fell asleep, to all appearance again, for another half hour, at least; when, seeming to wake, she cry'd, it is a fine night, I'll go and take a walk before the door, since you won't go to bed, till you have done, and, so saying, bolted out of the room and down stairs; she had not been gone above a quarter of an hour, before I heard her, as I thought, come softly up again; but, good God! what was my surprize, to survey the young *Carter*, in his night-gown, enter my door, and, the minute he had got into the room, fasten it on the inside.

At first my tongue was ty'd by the strange sight, and I trembled from head to foot, no longer doubting but some bad usage awaited me; but resuming myself, after these moments of sudden amazement, I cry'd, in an elevated tone of voice, and with a countenance all inflam'd, What is your meaning, Mr. *Carter*, that,

---

1 Authored by the Anglican clergyman Richard Lucas, *Enquiry After Happiness* (1685) was a decidedly optimistic devotional text that still enjoyed tremendous popularity in the early eighteenth century.
2 Affectation.

without any ceremony, you enter my apartment at this late hour, and that you have secur'd the door? pray retire, Sir, and learn to act more becomingly to a visitor and a person of my sex. Whilst I spoke these words, I look'd stedfastly in his face, and perceiv'd him turn pale, and it was with a faultering voice, that, after 2 or 3 minutes pause, he drawl'd out — why, you won't have me by fair means — and you must by foul, I think, then — you can have no help — father knows of my coming, and so does Miss *Bet*, by G—d! and proceeded to utter such a heap of balderdash nonsense, that never sure intruded upon a virgin's ears before.

In short, I was so astonish'd that I could make no reply, and the brute at once seizing me in his arms, endeavour'd to bear me towards the bed, which, crying and screaming, I endeavour'd to prevent with all the little strength I had. Oh! my *Tommy*, what were my thoughts at this dire moment! — words are too insufficient to paint all the horror and terror of my mind! however, my efforts were so powerful, that my antagonist began to tire, and, seeing he could carry me no further, let me fall on the middle of the floor, with dishevel'd hair and torn attire, and would have proceeded to liberties that are shocking to me, even in idea.

Just at this instant, when I was quite weaken'd and jaded, rather dead than alive, and almost incapable longer to support the cruel conflict, I heard *Oulton*'s voice at the door, and continu'd knocking, attended with these words, Mr. *Carter!* Mr. *Carter!* Lord help us! the *Negroes* are all in arms, and have set fire to the stores and out-houses! — for God sake! make haste! — we shall all be murder'd! — your father is getting up! and, indeed, turning my weeping eyes towards the window, I perceiv'd an extraordinary light, as of fire, and resum'd spirits enough to cry — Blessed powers! — this is your goodness! — Oh! fire! — murder! any thing let me meet, rather than stay in this cursed house!

Upon such alarming tidings, the wretch, at once, disengag'd me, and, running to the door, open'd it and went down stairs, with his cousin, whilst I got up and flung myself into a chair, a torrent of tears streaming from my eyes, and, Heaven forgive me! wish'd the *Negroes* might prevail and punish my unworthy foes; but in less than half an hour I was rais'd from my state of insensibility by the report of guns, the shouts of slaves, and now and then repeated groans, and I thought that I heard Miss *Oulton* scream and cry for mercy, in her turn: The horrid confusion of sounds soon drown'd her voice, and, looking thro' the window, I perceiv'd the house surrounded by the sable mutineers, and in a few minutes after the flames ascending up to my apartment.

'Twas in vain now I thought, to think of living more, and bating some tender thoughts of my dear mother and you, which still dwelt in my suffering mind and turn'd my views to life, I was resign'd to the fate that awaited me — had known too many sorrows to quit this mortal stage with reluctance, and, falling on my knees, in that posture, expected the devouring element to surround me; fervently thanking God for all his mercies; particularly for the last, my escape from violation, — praying for my parents — you — my enemies — and recommending my soul to his gracious care.

A calm accompany'd this holy exercise that was surprizing, and a dying Martyr could not have felt more inward peace and consolation: Providence, however, thought fit to relieve me from my condition, and, hearing a noise at the door, I turn'd my eyes towards it, and perceiv'd a white man enter, who, approaching me with great respect — seem'd struck with my posture; — but, all in a hurry, cry'd — Miss! for God sake let me save your life! — if you stay a minute you are lost! and taking me by the hand, led, or rather pull'd me down stairs, whilst I heard the wainscots of the adjacent rooms crackling with the flames which had even caught the ballustres,[1] and was almost scorch'd in descending them.

My guide hurry'd me to the back of the house, and, thro' a door that open'd into the garden, we made our escape, and then, holding by his arm, fear adding wings to our speed, we travers'd, unobserv'd, the back walks to the *Savannah*, where another white man waited with three horses, on one of which being plac'd, and my assistants mounting the others, the silence all along observ'd was broken by my deliverer's saying, Miss, pray ride as fast as possible — an hour will bring us out of danger. With eyes lifted up, in humble acknowledgement to the Divine Being, I follow'd him — nor could utter one word, my heart was so full, and in this condition, in about the time mention'd, we stop'd at a large house, the inhabitants of which were alarm'd by my companions acquainting them of the mischief doing at *Carter*'s.

I did not recollect that I had ever seen the face of any person about me; but a well looking matron-like woman eying me with tenderness, said to one of the men, is this young gentlewoman a relation of your master's? No, madam, he reply'd, 'tis Miss *Barlow*, whom I rescu'd at the hazard of my life. At these words

---

1   Stair banisters.

she welcom'd me to her house — told me she was sorry for my fright, and said she knew my mother very well. Hearing that dear name, I now thought myself in a place of security, and soon learn'd that it was the house and plantation of one Mr. *McDougal*, and that it was near 6 miles further from our house, than Colonel *Carter's*.

After these good men had withdrawn, for they soon went to raise the country, I understood by my kind hostess, that one was the clerk and the other an overseer of *Carter's*; but as to their thinking of me and inducement to run the hazard of saving me, that I was to learn from their own mouths. The family was in such a consternation, that no one offer'd again to go to bed, and, as to my part, tho' advis'd to that refreshment, I was in no condition to take it. In an hour after, the house was full of planters, all arm'd, for Mr. *McDougal* was a major of the militia, who soon march'd off, headed by that gentleman, towards *Carter's* plantation, and my two rescuers a little while after returning, inform'd us that they had alarm'd the whole country about us, and that above 200 men were marching from all parts to quell the rebellious *Negroes*.

It was now broad day, and the same persons then acquainted us of every thing relating to the *Negroe* conspiracy, which I have told you before, and further inform'd us that old *Carter*, his son and Miss *Oulton*, with 7 or 8 white men, were murder'd; the whole plantation destroy'd, and nothing spar'd but the *Negroe quarter* at the further side of the *Savannah*: That the father and son were shot, and *Oulton*, flying away, was overtaken at the wood side and stabb'd: That the persons who rescu'd me, coming from a plantation at some distance drawn by the fire and report of guns at their master's, found her alone, expiring, and that she utter'd these words, Oh! I have deserv'd all this! — for God sake, if possible fly to my room! — save poor *Fanny Barlow*! — let me be the instrument of doing some good to that young creature! — whom I have so much abus'd! and with a hideous groan she immediately surrender'd her breath: That they then, perceiving all lost, and the slaves employ'd in loading themselves with plunder from the stores, for they took nothing from the house, burning it with all in it, one of them hasted to provide horses, and the other, at the utmost risque, generously obey'd the orders of his dying mistress, as I have related.

I express'd my sincere gratitude to my preservers for my life, and promis'd to procure them a suitable reward from my parents, to whom Mrs. *McDougal* promis'd to convey me the next day, and soon after they departed with another party, in pursuit of the rebels, promising to come to my father's, when they had contributed all in their power to revenge their master's death. The next morning, major *McDougal* return'd home, and inform'd us that the *Negroes* had retreated towards *Virginia*, having lost 20 of their number, and that the whites had already had 11 kill'd: he was wounded, which was the reason of his leaving his duty.

And now the good gentlewoman perform'd her promise, and, after taking leave of the worthy family in a manner suitable to my obligations to it, attended by two servants, I set out for my father's house, to which I had now been so long a stranger, full of eager expectation to embrace my dearest mother. My thoughts, during the journey, were taken up in reflecting, with a thankful mind, on the wonders wrought in my favour and my happy deliverance, and I sincerely pray'd for forgiveness and mercy to all my late enemies, who now were gone to give account of their misdeeds, before a *Being* whose anger they had so much provok'd.

It was evening before we came to our house, having met with no interruption in our journey, but from the number of arm'd parties that question'd us as we past them. My father, scar'd out of his wits, was upon the same expedition, so that I found only my mother at home, who receiv'd me as one from the grave; we mutually shed tears of unaffected joy, and were never tir'd of embracing one another; she had been impos'd upon all this while and told that I was well and easy, and desir'd her, from time to time, to permit me to prolong my stay at *Carter*'s; but when she understood all I had underwent and the cruel usage of my father, I thought she would have dy'd with anguish. She was so much irritated against the unfortunate family, that she should not help even shewing some satisfaction at their punishment; but soon check'd herself by a more Christian spirit of thinking.

Ten days after, my father return'd with the news that the *Negroes* had, at last, gain'd the fastnesses[1] of the mountains, to the number of 60 or thereabout, the rest being kill'd by their pursuers, where they still hold out against all the force of the two colonies.[2] He farther inform'd us, that he had receiv'd an account from the men who sav'd me, of all that miraculous affair; but added, to my great and sincere grief, that the generous worthy creatures had both lost their lives by the enemy's fire, about 5 days before; by which, continu'd he, I have lost the opportunity of rewarding so much merit.

---

1 Fortresses.
2 Maryland and Virginia.

He then, with a tenderness that amaz'd me, embrac'd my mother, and, advancing to me, folded his arms about me, and cry'd — the tears standing in his eyes — my *Fanny*! — my dear *Fanny*! — can you forgive me? — I have us'd you sadly indeed: I now suffer more than I can speak! — Oh! that I should wrong so much virtue! I was so affected with his expressions, that I fell on my knees, and said, dear Sir, — I shall never remember any thing that has pass'd — my future life will be too short to repay this goodness — now indeed I know what it is to have a father! — all that I have endur'd is fully repay'd!

My mother's eyes ran over with tears of joy, she bless'd this happy unexpected change, hung about his neck, and said, this was the most blissful hour of her life. In short my father had been so truly affected with the fatal catastrophe of *Carter*'s, that it made a total change in his disposition and temper, and a day or two afterwards, which was the first time he mentioned you, except in passion, since he sent you away, or that we dar'd to mention you before him; he surprized my mother and me by the following words. Oh! my dear daughter — I have wrong'd you — Heaven has declared against us — would to God, my dear, turning to my mother, — I had taken your advice with regard to poor *Tom* — he generously told us the consequences of using our *Negroes* with cruelty, and read the destiny of his enemies the two *Carters*, at whose instigation I sold him — I wish he was here — I would ask his pardon — Nay, I think I could give him my daughter!

No surprize was ever greater than ours; but, poor man, tho' his repentance was late, it was sincere — he from that day always spoke of you with affection — hop'd he should live to hear from you, and us'd his servants and *Negroes*, as well as my mother and me, so tenderly, that our usual dread of him was turn'd into sincere love and reverence. He reconcil'd himself with Mr. *Gordon*, and, but for your absence, we had been entirely happy.

Indeed one thing very much troubled me, for enquiring after my poor faithful *Martha*, my father, with great contrition, told us that he had us'd her with great severity, had then sold her to another planter, who having behav'd inhumanly to her, she fell ill and dy'd the 2d day of her illness, of a violent fever. Thus I was disappointed in that earnest desire I had, to display my gratitude to those who had been my fast friends; but pure and untainted enjoyment is not the lot of mortals in this life. I mourn'd over her fate with tears of real sorrow, and my father express'd his repentence for his usage of her.

Perfectly easy now in my situation at home once again, my thoughts became fix'd to their old object, and my *Tommy*'s absence and my ignorance of his fortune drew incessant tears from my eyes. The arguments of Mr. *Gordon*, more than any thing, supported my spirits, he represented your strange fortune, the miracles that had, almost, been performed in your favour, and told me he did not doubt but God would restore you to us. But ah! my dear *Tommy*, year after year rolling away, and no tidings of you, reduced my soul to the very brink of despair, and my body almost to the grave. Oh! heavens! in this situation, how good you was to me and my afflicted mother! — Letters arrived from you in *Virginia*, accompanied by this dear watch, which has been my constant companion ever since, tokens of remembrance to your other friends, all displaying that good, that grateful breast, and letters of your strange and blessed reverse of fortune.

Oh! the tumultuous joy my soul then experienced — in short, I had not strength to support the glad tidings, but fainted in my father and mother's arms; and when I recover'd — I survey'd your constancy and perseverance, in your love to me, with a gratitude that is inexpressible, and that still increased my affection, if possible, to the object of my fear and my care. My father was charm'd with your disposition and temper; for, if you remember, you ask'd after his welfare kindly, in your letter to my mother, and said, he hoped he should live to prove deserving your forgiveness; but providence, perhaps, alas! to punish his former obdurateness,[1] permitted him not to live to this joyful day; for soon after he fell ill of the spotted fever,[2] which carried him off in less than a week.

He, by his will, left 8000 *l.* to me, and the rest of his fortune, which my mother has since turn'd into cash, being 5000 *l.* more, to her for life, and then to me and my heirs, and desired to be remembered with his last breath to you. Indeed he had latterly behaved so kindly, so much like a parent, that we lamented his death with unfeigned tears. And now, expecting your return every day with impatience, I began to grow distracted almost with your delay, when Mr. *Ferguson* was so good to take a tour to *Virginia*, on purpose to get tidings of you; and here again, we were informed, you was unfortunately a prisoner to the *French*, and was likely to be sent to *Europe*. Thus my full-blown hopes again

---

1 Hardheartedness, stubbornness.
2 Most likely typhus, a fever attended by spotting of the skin.

were blasted, and since that my mother and I have dragg'd on a wretched being, always divided betwixt beguiling hope and cruel fear. But at last God has given you to my eyes, and you are safely returned to possess that place in my arms that was always destin'd for you.

CHAPTER XVIII

Here the charming maid ceased her affecting narration, and Mr. *Anderson* folding her in his arms, told her he now hoped to recompence all her sufferings, and never more to be out of her sight. He lamented the death of her father, and said, if he had lived he should have thought himself still more happy, and over and over, bestow'd the warmest encomiums[1] upon the behavior of *Squanto*, *Martha*, and her two deliverers, wishing they had liv'd till his arrival, and saying he should not have thought half his fortune a sufficient recompence for their goodness to his darling *Fanny*. In short, thro' the whole story of her injurious treatment, he was now work'd up to passion, anon[2] melted into tears, and again lifting up his hands and eyes in admiration and thanksgiving.

When they returned into the house, he once more embraced his dear friends, and flinging his arms round Mrs. *Barlow*'s neck, said, my dear madam! I have two mothers now; but you was my first, and shall ever have my warmest affection. He then propos'd, that, in a day or two, they should take a tour to the ship, telling them he had brought some things as a testimony of his gratitude and respect, and others from his parents, as presents to them — which he hop'd would prove agreeable. He presented *Fanny* with the ring from his father, and the rich box from his mother, which she received with her usual grace, her eyes sparkling upon her lover, and her bosom heaving with acknowledgment, and they were admired by the whole company.

The next day he earnestly besought his dear Mrs. *Barlow* to spend the rest of her days with him and her daughter in *England*, to which she answered, that she needed no intreaty to that, but was ready to depart when they did, for life would be life no where without them, and she had disposed of all her affairs in *Maryland* in order to settle where they thought proper. Her grateful son returned her a thousand acknowledgements for her condescen-

---

1 Praises.
2 Soon thereafter.

sion, and promised to consult her ease in all he did. He then endeavour'd to persuade Mr. *Ferguson*, his spouse and Mr. *Gordon* to come to the same resolve, promising they should be sharers of all his fortune; but as they were now quite wedded to the country and climate, they did not choose to remove to *Europe*; and therefore, he first made Mr. and Mrs. *Ferguson* a present of 1000 *l.* and 500 *l.* to Mr. *Gordon*, promising that on all occasions, at the least warning, they should command any sum he was master of. They would have declined such unexampled favours, but he would not hear the least mention of it. For honest *Duncan Murray*, he bought a pretty plantation, and gave him 100 *l.* to stock it and settle on it, and made magnificent returns to major *McDougal* and his spouse for their goodness to his *Fanny*.

In a few days they visited the captain, on shipboard, when Mr. *Anderson* presented to Mr. *Gordon* and Mr. *Ferguson* the library he had purchased for them, as a joint possession between them, which cost him near 150 *l.* at which Mr. *Gordon* said, Well, Sir, this indeed is some small amends for the loss we are going to sustain of your society, and that of these two ladies. The ladies were all three pleased with the rich silks, sent by Mrs. *Anderson*, which were of the finest fabrick and the newest patterns, and it was a work of some days to convey all these things up to *Senepuxon*.

At length the expected day arrived, which was to unite the hands of the most faithful pair, that ever enter'd the bands of *Hymen*.[1] They never looked more beautifully than that day, and Mr. *Gordon* performed the ceremony with an edifying solemnity. A superb entertainment, at which all the neighbouring planters assisted, with music and dancing, according to the genius of the country, succeeded; and the rapturous night made them still dearer to each other, than ever.

> *Here love lights up his golden lamp,*
> *Reigns here and revels!*[2]

Three weeks longer were spent in all the delights of love and friendship at *Senepuxon*, when our lovers began to think of

---

1 A common poetic description of marriage.
2 A very loose quotation of *Paradise Lost*, IV.763–65.

departing for *Europe*, and, having taken a mournful, affectionate farewell of Mr. *Gordon*, and Mr. and Mrs. *Ferguson*, who saw them to the ship, Mr. *Anderson* and his lady and Mrs. *Barlow* embarked, and sail'd up *James* river, from whence they repair'd to *Williamsburgh*, where they were nobly entertained by Mr. *McKensie*, with whom Mr. *Anderson* settled his own affairs and his father's. Here he received letters of thanks and fine presents from the governors of *Canada* and *Moville*, in return for those he sent from *France* — and heard, to his great satisfaction, that all Capt. *Matthewson*'s servants, to whom he had been so generous, prosper'd in their affairs.

Their voyage to *England* was speedy and prosperous, and Mr. *Anderson* landed at *Portsmouth*, with a cargo, his lovely wife and dearest mother, superior, in his mind, to all the gold and diamonds of the *Indies*. From thence, after shewing them every thing remarkable in the journey, they went to *London*, in a coach and six,[1] where, upon advice from him, his father and mother were arrived at Mr. *Perkins*'s to receive them, and with grateful affection embrac'd their daughter-in-law and her mother, who soon became their inseparable companions, and extremely fond of their new cousins.

After they had seen every thing curious in *London*, all their goods were arrived from the ship, and Mr. *Anderson* had made the captain a valuable present for his care and kindness, they set out with a grand retinue[2] for their seat in *Yorkshire*, to enjoy that rest and felicity their worth and goodness had so much merited. He did not fail to inform the marquisses *D'Aville* and *Du Cayle*, and their ladies with the fortunate turns of his affairs, and ever afterwards frequently corresponded with those worthy friends, and Mr. *Gordon* and Mr. and Mrs. *Ferguson*, and in the usual time they were blessed with a beautiful boy, the exact image of his father.

Old Mr. *Anderson* and his lady, and Mrs. *Barlow*, lived to a good old age, bless'd in receiving the dutiful attendance, and viewing the supreme felicity of their children, and a numerous race of grandchildren, who inherit all the perfections of their father and mother. Mr. *Anderson* and his lovely *Fanny* are still

---

1 A coach drawn by six horses was a standard emblem of wealth. Compare Carter's offer of a coach drawn by "Negroes instead of horses" on p. 159.

2 A large group of servants.

living, and, tho' now in the decline of life, experience, that love founded on good sense and virtue can never know decay, and that providence ever showers down blessings on truth and constancy.

> *Oh! never let a virtuous mind despair;*
> *For heaven makes virtue its peculiar care.*[1]

THE END.

---

1   Adapted from the concluding lines of Colley Cibber's play *She Wou'd and She Wou'd Not* (1702), which read: "O never let a virtuous mind despair, / For constant hearts are Love's peculiar care."

Appendix A: Kimber's Other Writings on North America and Slavery

[In September 1742, the 22-year-old Edward Kimber set sail from Gravesend, England, for America. During the eighteen months he would spend in the American colonies—much of it spent in the militia of James Oglethorpe, the British governor of Georgia—Kimber had a series of experiences that would inform not only *Mr. Anderson* but dozens of his poems, essays, and travel narratives as well. Most of these pieces eventually appeared in the *London Magazine*, the well-known English monthly edited by Kimber's father, Isaac. The excerpts from Kimber's American writings included below provide useful points of reference for his later treatment of Native Americans, slavery, and plantation culture in *Mr. Anderson*.]

1. From Edward Kimber, *A Relation, or Journal, of a Late Expedition to the Gates of St. Augustine, on Florida: Conducted by the Hon. General James Oglethorpe, with a Detachment of his Regiment, &c. from Georgia* (London: T. Astley, 1744), pp. 15–17

[One of the highlights of Kimber's adventures in North America was his participation in James Oglethorpe's raid on the Spanish colony of St. Augustine, Florida. In this pamphlet, addressed to his father back home in England, Kimber gives a day-by-day account of Oglethorpe's expedition. Along the way, he occasionally pauses to comment on New World curiosities, such as the Native Americans described in the passage that follows.]

Friday, March 11 [1743].... At four o'Clock, the *Cowhati Indians*,[1] who went to *Augustine*, after so long Expectations, and divers Conjectures about their long Stay, return'd; bringing with them five Scalps, one Hand, which was cut off with the Glove on, several Arms, Clothes, and two or three Spades; which they had the Boldness to bring away, after having attack'd a Boat with upwards of forty Men in it, under the very Walls of the Castle, killing about twenty of them, and over-setting the rest; who also

---

1 The Coweta tribe, part of the Creek Confederacy and allies of the English.

had met with Death, but for the continu'd Fire of their great Guns. It seems, that they were Pioneers, and were going, under an Officer, to dig Clay for the King's Works. We heard them long before they came in Sight, by the melancholy Notes of their warlike Death-houp. For the *Spaniards* having kill'd one of their People, they, as usual with them in that Case, gave no Quarter, and therefore brought his Excellency[1] no Prisoner; which was what he earnestly desir'd. To give you a lively Idea of what occurs here, of these Sons of the Earth, I premise some Description of their Figure, Manners, and Method of making War. As to their Figure, 'tis generally of the largest Size, well proportion'd, and robust, as you can imagine Persons nurs'd up in manly Exercises can be. Their Colour is a swarthy, copper Hue, their Hair generally black, and shaven, or pluck'd off by the Roots, all round their Foreheads and Temples. They paint their Faces and Bodies, with Black, Red, or other Colours, in a truly diabolic Manner; or, to speak more rationally, much like the former uncultivated Inhabitants of *Britain*, whom *Tacitus* mentions.[2] Their Dress is a Skin or Blanket, tied, or loosely cast, over their Shoulders; a Shirt which they never wash, and which is consequently greasy and black to the last Degree; a Flap, before and behind, to cover their Privities, of red or blue Bays,[3] hanging by a Girdle of the same; Boots about their Legs, of Bays also; and what they call Morgissons,[4] or Pumps of Deer or Buffalo Skin, upon their Feet. Their Arms, and Ammunition, a common Trading-Gun; a Pouch with Shot and Powder; a *Tomohawk*, or Diminutive of a Hatchet, by their Side; a Scalping-Knife, Pistol, &c. But, however, you'll see their Dress, by those the General has carry'd to *England*.[5] As to their Manners, tho' they are fraught with the greatest Cunning in Life, you observe little in their common Behaviour, above the brute Creation. In their Expeditions they hunt for their Provision, and, when boiled or barbecu'd, tear it to Pieces promiscuously with their Fists, and devour it with a remarkable Greedi-

---

1 James Oglethorpe (1696–1785), the founder and governor of colonial Georgia.
2 The Roman historian Gaius Cornelius Tacitus (55–117 CE) wrote of the early inhabitants of Britain in *Agricola* (98 CE).
3 Coarse, woolen fabric.
4 Moccasins.
5 In a 1734 return trip from Georgia to London, Oglethorpe was accompanied by several Creek Indians, whose appearance caused a considerable stir in the city.

ness. Their Drink is *Weé-tuxeé*, or Water, on these Occasions; but, at other Times, any Thing weaker than Wine or Brandy, is nauseous to them; and they'll express their great Abhorrence by spitting it out, and seeming to spew at it: All which is owing to the Loss of their native Virtues, since the *Europeans* have enter'd into all Measures for trading with them; for, view them without Prejudice, you will perceive some Remains of an ancient Roughness and Simplicity, common to all the first Inhabitants of the Earth; even to our own dear Ancestors, who, I believe, were much upon a Level with these *Indian* hunting Warriors, whom his Excellency has so tam'd, since his being in *America*, and made so subservient to the Benefit of the *English* Nation.

2. Edward Kimber, "Fidenia: Or, the Explanation" *London Magazine* 13 (March 1744): 147–48

[A footnote included in the original *London Magazine* version of this poem explains that Fidenia was: "A very beautiful Negro Girl, aged 16, from *James* River in *Guinea*, who, by every superior Accomplishment, seems far beyond any of her Kind. She learnt the *English* Tongue in three Months Time, and in four, read the *Spectators* and *Tatlers* with inimitable Grace. She has endear'd herself to a grateful Master by her Fidelity and Affection, tho' he has been much censur'd for his Regard to her." In her primitive charms, the young woman here described resembles several earlier "noble savages" in English literature, including Imoinda from Behn's *Oroonoko* and Yarico from Steele's "*Spectator* No. 11" (see Appendix B.2 below). There is a stark contrast, however, between this footnote's tone and that of Kimber's poem. Whereas the note is largely detached, focusing on Fidenia's intellect, the poem revolves around her sexual allure and the bewitching exoticism of other women the speaker encounters in the colonies. In part, the sexual desire on display here is conventional, as Kimber's speaker belongs to a long tradition of amorous pastoral swains struggling to keep their passions in check. Even with this explanation, however, it remains rather striking that so amorous a poem should have proceeded from the same author as the utterly chaste *Mr. Anderson*.]

Tune, Love's Goddess in a Myrtle Grove, &c.[1]

1.

YE fair, whose worth I so esteem,
  Who sport on *Britain's* vivid plains,
Still may your smiles upon me gleam,
  For still your lover wears your chains.
Think not, tho' longer I endure   5
  This tedious absence from your eyes,
That time, or distance, e'er can cure
  Those passions that from you take rise.

2.

Tho' sweet *Fidenia*, born of kings,
  From *Afric's* shores, attracts my sight;   10
What tho' her praise, your *Strephon*[2] sings,
  And eager grasps the new delight?
What tho' her soft and jetty[3] hue
  Gives yet unfelt, untasted joy?
Remembrance speaks such charms in you,   15
  As all her blandishments destroy.

3.

Tho' *Amblerena*[4] spread her snare,
  And caught me in the am'rous vein;
Her vicious[5] soul, her gloating air,
  The thrilling ecstacies restrain.   20
Unhappy females, loosely bold,
  Where southern climates raise desire,
Your faint attractions ne'er will hold,
  Where reason sprinkles but the fire.

---

1 A popular early-eighteenth-century Scottish ballad, the words to which
  were written by the celebrated Edinburgh poet Allan Ramsay
  (1686–1758).
2 Kimber adopted this conventional name for the swain in pastoral poetry
  as a pseudonym for much of his amorous verse.
3 Jet black.
4 From this and the next paragraph, it remains unclear whether Amblerena is a Native American or, like Fidenia, an African slave. In either
  case, Kimber represents her as another example of the exotic tempta-
  tions Englishmen face in the colonies.
5 In this context, either savage or mischievous.

4.

Rather let me, where *Gambia*[1] flows,   25
 With black *Fidenia* spend my days,
Than tempt those arms,[2] where lust all glows,
 And mingle with the curs'd embrace.
See! with what majesty she walks!
 What modesty adorns her mien!   30
How simply innocent she talks,
 Inchanting slave! my *Indian* queen![3]

5.

E'er my exalted, matchless friend
 Had sav'd me from the enrag'd deep,[4]
With what sad cries, thou wail'dst my end,   35
 And how my faithful slave did weep!
How shouts broke forth, with joy replete,
 When sav'd, they cast me on the shore!
With rapture, how you hugg'd my feet,
 And all thy gods, how didst implore!   40

6.

For this, I'll grateful, thee convey,
 Where ev'ry precept shall combine,
To chace the savage quite away,
 And all thy motions to refine.
And ev'ry maid, and ev'ry swain,   45
 Shall melt at thy uncommon tale,
With admiration, tell thy name,
 And me, thy happy master, hail!

7.

Nor you, ye fair ones, will condemn
 A grateful mind, for acts like these;   50

---

1 One of the major rivers of West Africa.
2 I.e., the arms of Amblerena.
3 While this phrase possibly describes Amblerena, it seems more likely
 from the context that Fidenia is the speaker's "Indian queen." If so, the
 speaker is apparently implying that, despite her African heritage, Fidenia
 has taken on the "Indian" spirit of America.
4 [Kimber's note] He was in Danger of drowning in the great Bay of
 C[hesapeake]; and 'tis impossible to express the tender Concern she
 show'd, in her Way, on that Occasion.

Nor such a tenderness arraign,
  Where sense, and wit, and prudence please.
Thou, my *Maria*, shalt embrace
  Fidenia, with a glad surprise.
Hortensia[1] too, her beauties trace,   55
  And own the lustre of her eyes.

3. From Edward Kimber, "Itinerant Observations in America," *London Magazine*, 1745–46

[Soon after returning to England, Kimber wrote a series of essays on his American adventures for the *London Magazine*. In the passages excerpted below, he recounts his harrowing passage from New York to Maryland, revealing in the process how little value he placed on the lives of black slaves. On board ship, he was generally oblivious to the slaves' sufferings—unless, that is, they caused him inconvenience, whereupon he lapsed into classic stereotypes of the lazy tropical African. The worst part of the slaves' horrible shipboard deaths for Kimber seems to have been the smell of their corpses. Later in his essays, he shows greater compassion, professing abhorrence for slavery; in the end, however, his principal argument for treating "negroes" well is that this would increase productivity (as well as reproduction) among the slaves. Also of interest here is Kimber's depiction of Maryland's white planters. While most of the colonists described here come off well, the elite planters do not; in the midst of an idyllic reverie about Maryland, Kimber shifts abruptly to describing the vast wealth and unchecked power of the great planters. He does not denounce them here, but the seeds of the Carters and Mr. Barlow of *Mr. Anderson* are sown.]

Some Account of a VOYAGE *from* New-York
to Sene-puxon *in* Maryland[2]

We had no Reason to complain of our Master, indeed; but of an Illness that confined him to his Cabin the whole Voyage, (which was many Days longer than we expected or desired) and which

---

1 In "The Vindication: An Heroic Epistle," one of Kimber's earlier *London Magazine* poems (published February 1744), he had sung praises to the beauty of several maidens, including a Maria and a Hortensia.

2 Sinepuxent, on Maryland's eastern shore, is also the site of the Barlow estate in *Mr. Anderson*.

rendered the only able Seaman we found amongst us of no Service. The Vessel was our greatest Grievance we soon found, being prodigiously foul, rotten, and leaky; and a Pack of stupid Planters, the Crew, who never had been 10 Leagues from Land since they were born, increased that Misfortune. Unknowing all this, we went on board as gaily as we would have done into a Packet-Boat, and found the Master in Bed, which Inconvenience we readily put up with, as the Voyage was so short and safe, and as he informed us, his Mate was a very able Mariner. Our Complement then was, 6 Hands belonging to the Sloop,[1] 3 Passengers, and 7 Negro Slaves....

[During a delay before sailing from New York,] two of our Negroes had lost the Use of their Hands and Feet by the Frost (which was excessively severe) notwithstanding they were warmly clad, and had the free Use of that necessary Liquor (on these Occasions) Rum, in what Quantity they pleas'd. Our Regret at the Disadvantages we had fallen upon, and which our Time and Occasions would not permit us to remedy, could be equalled by nothing but the Displeasure we felt at leaving that delightful Country....

[As the leaky ship was tempest-tossed,] we now began to think seriously of the Danger we were involv'd in, and the Death that seem'd inevitable. We had no Carpenter, nor one Person that understood Sea Affairs by Profession, of the whole Crew left, and in short every Thing was fallen into our Hands; we were but two, and the Negroes were all unable to move, the Frost having so affected their Limbs, as to call for present Amputation; two of them being mortified to the Knees and Shoulders: And here, I must observe, that in general, they are the most awkward, ungain[2] Wretches, in cold Weather, that can be met with, and if not stirr'd up, will sit whole Days shivering in a Corner without moving Hand or Foot: They seem to be form'd only for the sultry Climate they were born in, and those they are principally apply'd to the Use of; tho' when inur'd to a cold one long, they bear it tolerably well....

Bread, Water, and Rum, were all we had left; these were our Provisions for the Sick, these our only Sustenance....We forebore to see after the Negroes [below deck], but nail'd down the Hatches, and left them to the Mercy of Providence.[3]

---

1 A relatively small, one-masted sailing vessel.
2 Surly.
3 Excerpt from *London Magazine* 15 (Mar. 1746): 125–27.

★ ★ ★ ★

[Upon safely landing in Maryland,] we now examin'd our Cabin Associates, and found only the inanimate Remains of three of them. The others had some Signs of Life, and were convey'd on Shore by the Planters who visited us, and were their Neighbours. A thousand Times they lifted their Eyes up with Astonishment at our forlorn Condition. Our Negroes were our next Concern, and here only two were found alive, and such a Stench of Putrefaction in the Hold, as made it necessary to have Recourse to the usual Preservatives from infectious Smells.[1]

★ ★ ★ ★

We pursu'd our little Voyage, of about 14 Miles, thro' the several Creeks that convey you to *Golden Quarter*....On every Side, you might discern the Settlements of the Planters, with their industrious Clearings, surrounded by the native Woods of the Country; whilst the distant Curlings of the aspiring Smoak, wantoning in the Breeze, direct your Eyes to the happy Places of their Residence, where they, generally bless'd with Innocence and Chearfulness, a compliant Confort,[2] and a numerous Race at their Boards, enjoy a Life much to be envy'd by Courts and Cities....

Mush[3] and Milk, or Molasses, *Homine*,[4] Wild Fowl, and Fish, are their principal Diet, whilst the Water presented to you, by one of the bare-footed Family, in a copious Calabash,[5] with an innocent Strain of good Breeding and Heartiness, the Cake baking upon the Hearth, and the prodigious Cleanliness of every Thing around you, must needs put you in mind of the Golden Age, the Times of antient Frugality and Purity. All over the Colony, an universal Hospitality reigns; full Tables and open Doors, the kind Salute, the generous Detention, speak somewhat like the old roast-Beef Ages of our Fore-fathers,[6] and would almost persuade one to think their Shades were wasted into these Regions, to enjoy, with greater Extent, the Reward of their Virtues. Prodigious Numbers of Planters are immensely rich, and I think one

---

1 Excerpt from *London Magazine* 15 (May 1746): 248.
2 An archaic form of "comfort."
3 [Kimber's note] Made of *Indian* Corn, or Rice, pounded.
4 [Kimber's note] *Indian* Meal, pounded or ground with the Husks, and fry'd. *Great Homine* has Meat or Fowl in it.
5 [Kimber's note] The Shell of a Fruit so called. Some of them hold two Quarts.
6 An allusion to Henry Fielding's patriotic anthem of 1731 "The Roast Beef of Old England."

of them, at this Time, numbers upon his Lands near 1000 Wretches, that tremble with submissive Awe at his Nod, besides white Servants: Their Pastures bless'd with increasing Flocks, whilst their Yards and Closes boast Hundreds of tame Poultry, of every Kind, and their Husbandry is rewarded with Crops equal to all their Ambition or Desires....

Wherever you travel in *Maryland* (as also in *Virginia* and *Carolina*) your Ears are constantly astonished at the Number of *Colonels*, *Majors*, and *Captains*, that you hear mentioned: In short, the whole Country seems at first to you a Retreat of Heroes; but alas! to behold the Musters of their Militia, would induce a Man to nauseate a Sash, and hold a Sword, for ever, in Derision. Diversity of Weapons and Dresses, Unsizeableness of the Men, and Want of the least Grain of Discipline in their Officers or them [are the norm]....

The Negroes [in Maryland] live as easily as in any other Part of *America*, and at set Times have a pretty deal of Liberty in their Quarters,[1] as they are called. The Argument, of the Reasonableness and Legality, according to Nature, of the Slave-Trade, has been so well handled on the Negative Side of the Question, that there remains little for an Author to say on that Head; and that Captives taken in War, are the Property of the Captor, as to Life and Person, as was the Custom amongst the *Spartans*; who, like the *Americans*, perpetuated a Race of Slaves, by marrying them to one another, I think; has been fully disprov'd: But allowing some Justice in, or, at least, a great deal of Necessity for, making Slaves of this sable Part of the Species; surely, I think, Christianity, Gratitude, or, at least, good Policy, is concern'd in using them well, and in abridging them, instead of giving them Encouragement, of several brutal and scandalous Customs, that are too much practis'd: Such is the giving them a Number of Wives, or, in short, setting them up for Stallions to a whole Neighbourhood; when it has been prov'd, I think, unexceptionably, that Polygamy rather destroys than multiplies the Species....

As to [the planters'] general Usage of [their slaves], 'tis mon-

---

1 [Kimber's note] A Negro Quarter, is a Number of Huts or Hovels, built at some Distance from the Mansion-House; where the Negroes reside with their Wives and Families, and cultivate, at vacant Times, the little Spots allow'd them. They are, indeed, true Pictures of Slavery, which begets Indolence and Nastiness.

strous and shocking. To be sure, a *new Negro*,[1] if he must be broke, either from Obstinacy, or, which I am more apt to suppose, from Greatness of Soul, will require more hard Discipline than a young Spaniel: You would really be surpriz'd at their Perseverance; let an hundred Men shew him how to hoe, or drive a Wheelbarrow, he'll still take the one by the Bottom, and the other by the Wheel; and they often die before they can be conquer'd. They are, no Doubt, very great Thieves, but this may flow from their unhappy, indigent Circumstances, and not from a natural Bent; and when they have robb'd, you may lash them Hours before they will confess the Fact; however, were they not to look upon every white Man as their Tormenter; were a slight Fault to be pardon'd now and then; were their Masters, and those adamantine-hearted[2] *Overseers*, to exercise a little more Persuasion, Complacency, Tenderness and Humanity towards them, it might, perhaps, improve their Tempers to a greater Degree of Tractability. Such Masters, and such Overseers, *Maryland* may with Justice boast; and Mr. *Bull*,[3] the late Lieutenant-Governor of *Carolina*, is an Instance, amongst many of the same, in that Province: But, on the contrary, I remember an Instance of a late Sea Officer, then resident in a neighbouring Colony, that for a mere Peccadillo,[4] order'd his Slave to be ty'd up, and for an whole Hour diverted himself with the Wretch's Groans; struck at the mournful Sound, with a Friend, I hasted to the Noise, where the Brute was beginning a new Scene of Barbarity, and belabour'd the Creature so long with a large Cane, his Overseer being tir'd with the Cowskin,[5] that he remain'd without Sense and Motion.

---

1   [Kimber's note] A Negro just purchased from the *Guinea-man*. 'Tis really shocking to be present at a Mart of this Sort; where the Buyers handle them as the Butchers do Beasts in *Smithfield*, to see if they are Proof in Cod, Flank, and Shoulders. And the Women, who have Plantations, I have seen mighty busy in examining the Limbs, Size, and Abilities of their intended Purchases. I do not speak this of *Maryland*; for I never saw a Lady at the Market there, but have elsewhere in *America*.
2   Proverbially, adamant is the hardest of stones.
3   William Bull (1710–91) served as lieutenant-governor of South Carolina from 1737 until 1743.
4   A slight indiscretion.
5   [Kimber's note] A Cowskin is so called, from being a large Thong from the Hide of that Animal, twisted into the Shape of a Swish-Horse-Whip, and as hard as a Bull's Pizzle [penis]. The common Method is to tie them up by the Hands to the Branch of a Tree, so that their Toes can

Happily he recover'd, but, alas! remain'd a Spectacle of Horror to his Death; his Master deceas'd soon after, and, perhaps, may meet him, *where the Wicked cease from troubling, and the Weary be at rest*:[1] Where, as our immortal *Pope* sings,

No fiends torment, no christians thirst for gold.[2]

Another, upon the same Spot, when a Girl had been lash'd till she confess'd a Robbery, in mere Wantonness continu'd the Persecution, repeating every now and then these christianlike, and sensible Expressions in the Ragings of his Fury, "*G-d d-mn you, when you go to Hell, I wish G-d would d-mn me, that I might follow you with the Cowskin there.*"

Slavery, thou worst and greatest of Evils! sometimes thou appearest to my affrighted Imagination, sweating in the Mines of *Potosi*,[3] and wiping the hard-bound Tears from thy exhausted eyes; sometimes I view thy sable Livery under the Torture of the Whip, inflicted by the Hands, the remorseless Hands of an *American* Planter: At other Times, I view thee in the Semblance of a Wretch trod upon by ermin'd[4] or turban'd Tyrants, and with poignant, heart-breaking Sighs, dragging after thee a toilsome Length of Chain, or bearing *African* Burdens. Anon[5] I am somewhat comforted, to see thee attempt to smile under the *Grand Monarque*; but, on the other Side of the *Alpes*, thou again resum'st thy Tears, and what, and how great are thy *Iberian* Miseries![6] In *Britain*, and *Britain* only, thy Name is not heard; thou hast assum'd a new Form, and the heaviest Labours are lightsome under those mild Skies![7]

★ ★ ★ ★

---

hardly touch the Ground; but in the *West-Indies*, they are so habituated to ill Usage, and their Spirits so sunk, that the Overseer need only bid them cast up their Arms over their Heads, which the poor Creatures readily do, and then the Torturer taking a Run to him, lashes him; and this Discipline is repeated sometimes forty Times: Hardly a Negro but bears the Marks of Punishment in large Scars on his Back and Sides.

1 Job 3:17.
2 Alexander Pope, *An Essay on Man*, I.108 (1733).
3 The Spanish silver mines, located in present-day Bolivia.
4 Robes of ermine were traditionally worn by noblemen or magistrates.
5 Soon.
6 An allusion to the widespread slavery within the Spanish and Portuguese empires.
7 Excerpt from *London Magazine* 15 (July 1746): 321–26.

York-Town [in Virginia], Capital of the County of that Name, is situated on a rising Ground, gently descending every Way into a Valley, and tho' but straggingly built, yet makes no inconsiderable figure. You perceive a great Air of Opulence amongst the Inhabitants, who have some of them built themselves Houses, equal in Magnificence to many of our superb ones at *St. James's*[1]....Almost every considerable Man keeps an Equipage, tho' they have no Concern about the different Colours of their Coach Horses, driving frequently black, white, and chestnut, in the same Harness....There are some very pretty Garden Spots in the Town; and the Avenues leading to *Williamsburgh, Norfolk,* &c. are prodigiously agreeable. The Roads are, as I said before, some of the best I ever saw, and infinitely superior to most in *England.* The Country surrounding is thickly overspread with Plantations, and the Planters live, in a Manner, equal to Men of the best Fortune.[2]

4. From Edward Kimber, "Itinerant Observations in America," *London Magazine* 15 (July 1746): 326–27

[Although Kimber drew upon many sources when writing *Mr. Anderson*, the plot is largely rooted in the following tale, which Kimber heard while in Maryland and later recorded in his *London Magazine* essay for July 1746. In comparing this passage against *Mr. Anderson*, it is interesting to note how Kimber reworked the story for his novel. Most notably, he made Tom Anderson's degradation (and consequently his heroic inner nature) greater by altering the length of the boy's servitude and the character of the planter who bought him.]

Above 60 Years ago, Capt. ——, Master of ———, walking thro' *Lincoln's-Inn-Fields,* beheld a very pretty Child, about six Years of Age, bewailing himself for the Loss of his Father, whom he had some how or other stray'd from: He sooth'd the Child, persuaded him to dry his Tears, and told him he had Orders from his Father, who was just set out for the Country, to bring him to him. The innocent Victim, without Thought of Harm, follow'd his Deliverer, as he thought him, who carry'd him in the Stage Coach to *Bristol,* and there immediately put him on board his Vessel, which sail'd a Fortnight after for this Part of the

---

1   The fashionable London district.
2   Excerpt from *London Magazine* 15 (Dec. 1746): 622–23.

World. Still fed up with Hopes of seeing his Father, and that he was going but a small Trip by Water, where he was, and indulg'd by the Captain in all he desir'd, the Time slipt away, till the Brute made appear, by the vilest Actions, his accurs'd Design: The Lad suffer'd much, but his Innocence render'd him incapable to judge of the Propriety of such Actions, and he was acquiescent. When he arriv'd at the End of his Voyage, being very ill, he sold him to a Planter for 14 Years,[1] for 12 Guineas. The Planter, a Man of great Humanity, taking a Fancy to the Child, heard his simple Tale, and perceiv'd the Villany, but not till the Vessel had sail'd. He enquir'd his Name, and just so much he could tell him, and sent over to advertise him in the publick Papers; but before this Design could be compleated, near two Years elaps'd, from his first being kidnapp'd, when, probably, his Father and Mother were both dead, and, perhaps, the Cause of their Death, this Accident. In short, his Master lik'd the Youth more and more, who was sober and diligent, and marry'd him to an only Daughter, leaving him at his Decease his whole Substance. Thirty Years elaps'd, and tho' under great Pain for his Ignorance of his Parents, yet happy in his Family and Affairs, he liv'd with great Content; when a Ship with Convicts coming in, he went to purchase some Servants, and the Idea of his barbarous Captain was so impress'd in his Mind, that he knew him at first Sight, and bought him eagerly; it appearing, afterwards, a notorious Crime had brought him into those Circumstances, and entirely ruin'd him. As soon as he brought him home, he carry'd him into a private Room, and lock'd himself in with him; but what Words could express the Wretch's Confusion and Astonishment, when he understood whose Hands he had fallen into! for he had no Notion before of the Gentleman's being the same, that, when a Lad, he had us'd so vilely. Struck with Remorse, and the Fear of Punishment, he fell on his Knees and begg'd Forgiveness. 'Twas in vain, he was interrogated about his Master's Parents; he knew as little of them as himself; the Master inrag'd, order'd him to be lock'd into an upper Room, resolving to keep him to the hard Service he deserv'd the Remainder of his Life; but the next Morning he was

---

1 Children's indentures typically ran much longer than the usual four-year term—most often they served at least until reaching adulthood. The normal term convicts served when transported to the colonies was 14 years. While this child was no convict, then, the term laid out in this story was much more realistic than Kimber having little Tommy sold for life in *Mr. Anderson*. Obviously, Kimber sacrificed plausibility for dramatic effect in the novel.

found stabb'd to the Heart, with a Knife that had been uncautiously left in the Room; and so despairingly finish'd a wretched Life. The Gentleman is now near 70, and very hearty and well.

5. From Edward Kimber, *The Life and Adventures of Joe Thompson* (London: John Hinton and W. Frederick, 1750) vol. 2, pp. 123–25

[Kimber's first and most popular novel, *Joe Thompson*, shares much in common with *Mr. Anderson*, taking readers through a series of hair-raising adventures in Britain, on the high seas, and throughout the colonies. Near the middle of the tale, the title character reunites with an old friend, William Prim, who tells of his years as a castaway on an isle off the coast of Africa and how he had been rescued by an American slave-trading vessel. Prim's representation of the ship's captain, the benevolent, refined Virginia planter Mr. Nelson, contrasts markedly with the portrait Kimber would later draw of the tyrannical Barlow in *Mr. Anderson*. One noteworthy similarity, however, is that both characters boast a charming daughter named Fanny, whose hand is widely coveted by planters' sons throughout the surrounding counties. The passage that follows picks up at the moment when Nelson rescues Prim.]

The Captain's Name was *Nelson*, and that of his Ship, the *Charming Susanna*. I found he was very rich, and a considerable Planter, in *Virginia*; that the Vessel was his own; that he had carried a Lading of his own Tobacco to *London*, from whence he took in a proper Cargo, to trade on the Coast of *Africa* for Slaves....There were 150 Negroes on Board, he having lost near 80 in these Seas by Sickness.

When Mr. *Nelson* had heard my Story, which he animadverted[1] upon with great Sweetness, and found that I was not a Seaman, but bred up a Trader, he gave me Charge of his Books, and made me also his Steward, as well as his Clerk, having lost his former Steward in the Voyage; and never was Man's Condition so altered for the better, for he was a mild, sociable, humane Creature, had little of the rough Seaman, but a vast deal of the Gentleman, about him; and had, I soon found, studied, and read, the best Authors. In short, I loved him, and served him so readily

---

1 Pondered.

and affectionately, that I perceived I gained much upon his Mind; and you'd be surprised to think how dearly he valued me in so short a Time; but now he never would eat or drink without me; I became his constant Companion; and, by the Civilities I was thereby enabled to confer on my Shipmates, gained the Esteem of the whole Ship's Crew. I found my Captain had in *Virginia* a Wife, and one Daughter, of whom he was often talking with great Tenderness; and he promised me, if I'd settle with him there, he would give me an handsome Salary, to look after his Affairs; which Proposal I readily closed with; and indeed one main Inducement was, the Character he gave Miss *Fanny*, of whom I became perfectly enamoured, and already conceived Hopes of possessing her, and making my Fortune.

Appendix B: British Attitudes Toward Colonial America

[As discussed in the Introduction to this volume (pp. 18–26), during the late seventeenth and early eighteenth centuries, British accounts of America increasingly tended to exaggerate the negative aspects of the colonial experience. While, on the whole, *Mr. Anderson* offers a balanced perspective on America, several of its passages are reminiscent of traditional accounts of colonial coarseness, hardship, and cultural backwardness. Following is a sampling of some of the most revealing and influential pieces in this large body of literature.]

1. From Ebenezer Cook, *The Sot-weed Factor* (London: B. Bragg, 1708)

[Born and raised in London, Ebenezer Cook (1667–1733) moved to colonial Maryland sometime in the 1690s, where he practiced law, purchased a plantation, and set up as a "sot-weed factor" (or tobacco merchant). During a visit back to England in 1708, he arranged to have the London publisher Benjamin Bragg print his satirical poem *The Sot-weed Factor*. On one level, Cook's poem offers a biting indictment of life in the American colonies. At the same time, though, some readers have felt that with his jaded narrator Cook satirizes Old World prejudices toward the New, implying that Britons predisposed to find backwardness and degeneracy in colonial America will inevitably find just that, whether it exists in reality or not. In reading these excerpts from the poem, note how the plot resembles that of *Mr. Anderson*, where the hero is forced to America but ultimately escapes and makes his way back to England. Unlike Tom Anderson, however, the narrator of Cook's poem is not in any way redeemed in colonial America, which in his final line he deems a land where "no Man's faithful, nor a Woman Chast[e]."]

Condemn'd by Fate to way-ward Curse,   1
Of Friends unkind, and empty Purse;
Plagues worse than fill'd *Pandora's* Box,
I took my leave of *Albion's* Rocks:[1]

---

1 Albion is a traditional poetic name for England.

With heavy Heart, concerned that I 5
Was forc'd my Native Soil to fly,
And the *Old World* must bid good-buy.
But Heav'n ordain'd it should be so,
And to repine is vain we know:
Freighted with Fools, from *Plymouth* sound,[1] 10
To *Mary-Land* our Ship was bound[.]

[After a miserable voyage, they arrive at Piscataway, on the Maryland shore.]

I put myself and Goods a-shore:
Where soon repair'd a numerous Crew,
In Shirts and Drawers of *Scotch-cloth*[2] Blue 25
With neither Stockings, Hat, nor Shooe.
These *Sot-weed*[3] Planters Crowd the Shoar,
In Hue as tawny as a Moor:
Figures so strange, no God design'd,
To be a part of Humane kind: 30
But wanton Nature, void of Rest,
Moulded the brittle Clay in Jest,
At last a Fancy very odd
Took me, this was the Land of *Nod*;[4]
Planted at first, when Vagrant *Cain*, 35
His Brother had unjustly slain:
Then conscious of the Crime he'd done,
From Vengeance dire, he hither run;
And in a Hut supinely dwelt,
The first in *Furs* and *Sot-weed* dealt. 40
And ever since his Time, the Place,
Has harbour'd a detested Race;
Who when they cou'd not live at Home,
For Refuge to these Worlds did roam;
In hopes by Flight they might prevent, 45
The Devil and his fell intent;

---

1 A major port in southwest England.
2 [Cook's note] The Planters generally wear *Blue Linnen*.
3 Tobacco, so called in Cook's day because of its inebriating qualities (a
   drunkard was also called a "sot").
4 In the Biblical tale, as punishment for murdering his brother Abel, Cain
   is cast into exile, where his first home is "the land of Nod, on the east of
   Eden" (Genesis 4:16).

Obtain from Tripple Tree[1] reprive,
And Heav'n and Hell alike deceive:
But e're their Manners I display,
I think it fit I open lay   50
My Entertainment by the way;
That Strangers well may be aware on,
What homely Diet they must fare on.
To touch that Shoar, where no good Sense is found,
But Conversation's lost, and Maners drown'd.   55

[In his travels through Maryland, the narrator meets up with a
rough-edged planter, who offers him uninviting fare and potent
home-brewed rum. Thoroughly inebriated after a night of drinking, the narrator stumbles toward his sleeping quarters.]

I scarce cou'd find my way to Bed;
Where I was instantly convey'd
By one who pass'd for Chamber-Maid;
Tho' by her loose and sluttish Dress,
She rather seem'd a *Bedlam-Bess*;[2]   150
Curious to know from whence she came,
I prest her to declare her Name.
She Blushing, seem'd to hide her Eyes,
And thus in Civil Terms replies;
In better Times, e'er to this Land,   155
I was unhappily Trapann'd,[3]
Perchance as well I did appear,
As any Lord or Lady here,
Not then a Slave for twice two Year.[4]
My Cloaths were fashionably new,   160
Nor were my Shifts of Linnen Blue;
But things are changed, now at the Hoe,
I daily work, and Bare-foot go,
In weeding Corn or feeding Swine,
I spend my melancholy Time.   165

---

1 "A gallows (in reference to its three parts)" (*OED*).
2 A madwoman. "Bedlam," or the Hospital of St. Mary of Bethlehem, was
   Britain's most famous insane asylum.
3 Lured.
4 [Cook's note] 'Tis the Custom for Servants to be obliged for four Years
   to very servile Work; after which time they have their Freedom.

Kidnap'd and Fool'd, I hither fled,
To shun a hated Nuptial Bed.[1]
And to my cost already find,
Worse Plagues than those I left behind.

[Assailed by barnyard fowl and other farm animals while trying
to sleep in the house, the narrator hopes to find respite in nature.]

I to the Orchard did repair,
To Breathe the cool and open Air;
Expecting there the rising Day,
Extended on a Bank I lay;
But Fortune here, that saucy Whore,   210
Disturb'd me worse and plagu'd me more,
Than she had done the night before.
Hoarse croaking Frogs[2] did 'bout me ring,
Such Peals the Dead to Life wou'd bring,
A Noise might move their Wooden King.[3]   215
I stuff'd my ears with Cotten white,
For fear of being deaf out-right,
And curst the melancholy Night;
But soon my Vows I did recant,
And Hearing as a Blessing grant;   220
When a confounded Rattle-Snake,
With hissing made my Heart to ake:
Not knowing how to fly the Foe,
Or whether in the Dark to go;
By strange good Luck, I took a Tree,   225
Prepar'd by Fate to set me free;
Where riding on a Limb astride,
Night and the Branches did me hide,
And I the Devil and Snake defy'd.
Not yet from Plagues exempted quite,   230
The curst Muskitoes did me bite;

---

1 [Cook's note] These are the general Excuses made by *English* Women,
   which are sold, or sell themselves to *Mary-Land.*
2 [Cook's note] Frogs are called *Virginia* Bells and make, (both in that
   Country and *Mary-Land*) during the Night, a very hoarse ungrateful
   Noise.
3 In Aesop's fable of "The Frogs Desiring a King," Jove grants a group of
   frogs' wish for a ruler by dropping a giant log into their swamp and
   declaring it their king.

Till rising Morn' and blushing Day,
Drove both my Fears and Ills away;
And from Night's Errors set me free.

[With the planter's son as his guide, the narrator sets forth on his
journey through Maryland. After observing an Indian hunting
party, the narrator and his guide fall into a debate over how the
Indians first came to America, with one theory being that the
devil himself had put them there. This discussion ended, they go
on to the nearest town, where the narrator hopes to observe the
customary proceedings of an American courtroom.]

Scarce had we finish'd serious Story,   375
But I espy'd the Town before me,
And roaring Planters on the ground,
Drinking of Healths in Circle round:
Dismounting Steed with friendly Guide,
Our Horses to a Tree we ty'd,   380
And forwards pass'd among the Rout,
To chuse convenient *Quarters* out:
But being none were to be found,
We sat like others on the ground
Carousing Punch in open Air   385
Till Cryer did the Court declare;
The planting Rabble being met,
Their Drunken Worships likewise set;
Cryer proclaims that Noise shou'd cease,
And streight the Lawyers broke the Peace: 390
Wrangling for Plantiff and Defendant,
I thought they ne'er wou'd make an end on't:
With nonsense, stuff and false quotations,
With brazen Lyes and Allegations;
And in the splitting of the Cause,   395
They used such Motions with their Paws,
As shew'd their Zeal was strongly bent,
In Blows to end the Argument.
A reverend Judge, who to the shame
Of all the Bench, cou'd write his Name;[1]   400
At Petty-fogger[2] took offence,

---

1 [Cook's note] In the County-Court of *Mary-Land*, very few of the Justices of the Peace can write or read.
2 An underhanded or conniving lawyer.

And wonder'd at his Impudence.
My Neighbour *Dash* with scorn replies,
And in the Face of Justice flies;
The Bench in fury streight divide,   405
And Scribble's take or Judge's side;
The Jury, Lawyers and their Clyents,
Contending fight like earth-born Gyants:
But Sheriff wily lay perdue,[1]
Hoping Indictments wou'd ensue,   410
And when ————————————————
A Hat or Wig fell in the way,
He seiz'd them for the *Queen* as stray:
The court adjourn'd in usual manner
In Battle Blood and fractious Clamour;   415
I thought it proper to provide,
A Lodging for myself and Guide,
So to our Inn we march'd away,
Which at a little distance lay;
Where all things were in such Confusion,   420
I thought the World at its conclusion;
A Herd of Planters on the ground,
O'er-whelm'd with Punch, dead drunk we found;
Others were fighting and contending,
Some burnt their Cloaths to save the mending.   425
A few whose Heads by frequent use,
Could better bare the potent Juice,
Gravely debated State Affairs.
Whilst I most nimbly trip'd up Stairs;
Leaving my Friend discoursing oddly,   430
And mixing things Prophane and Godly:
Just then beginning to be Drunk,
As from the Company I slunk,
To every Room and Nook I crept,
In hopes I might have somewhere slept;   435
But all the bedding was possest
By one or other drunken Guest:
But after looking long about,
I found an antient Corn-loft out,
Glad that I might in quiet sleep,   440
And there my bones unfractur'd keep.
I lay'd me down secure from Fray,

---

1 To lie in waiting.

And soundly snoar'd till break of Day;
When waking fresh I sat upright,
And found my Shooes were vanish'd quite;   445
Hat, Wig, and Stockings, all were fled
From this extended *Indian* Bed;
Vext at the Loss of Goods and Chattel,
I swore I'd give the Rascal battle,
Who had abus'd me in this sort,   450
And Merchant Stranger made his Sport.
I furiously descended Ladder;
No Hare in *March* was ever madder;
In vain I search'd for my Apparel,
And did with Oast[1] and Servants quarrel;   455
For one whose Mind did much aspire
To Mischief,[2] threw them in the Fire;
Equip't with neither Hat nor Shooe,
I did my coming hither rue,
And doubtful thought what I should do: 460
Then looking round, I saw my Friend
Lie naked on a Tables end;
A Sight so dismal to behold,
One wou'd have judg'd him dead and cold;
When wringing of his bloody Nose,   465
By fighting got we may suppose;
I found him not so fast asleep,
Might give his Friends a cause to weep:
Rise *Oronooko*,[3] rise said I,
And from this Hell and Bedlam fly.   470

[After months of miserable illness, which worked as "seasoning,"
and having been cheated in business even by a Quaker—"a Pious
Conscientious Rogue"—the narrator goes to the capital to seek
redress for his losses.]

---

1 Host.
2 [Cook's note] 'Tis the Custom of the Planters, to throw their own, or
   any other Person's Hat, Wig, Shooes or Stockings in the Fire.
3 Cook's note here reads, "Planters are usually call'd by the Name of
   Oronooko, from their Planting *Oronooko-Tobacco*." This is also likely an
   allusion to the title character of Aphra Behn's 1688 tale.

Up to *Annapolis*[1] I went,   665
A City Situate on a Plain,
Where scarce a House will keep out Rain;
The Buildings fram'd with Cyprus rare,
Resembles much our *Southwark* Fair:[2]
But Stranger here will scarcely meet   670
With Market-place, Exchange, or Street;
And if the Truth I may report,
'Tis not so large as *Tottenham Court*.[3]
St. Mary's once was in repute,
Now here the Judges try the Suit[4]   675
And Lawyers twice a year dispute.
As oft the Bench most gravely meet,
Some to get Drunk, and some to eat
A swinging share of Country Treat.
But as for Justice right or wrong,   680
Not one amongst the numerous throng,
Knows what they mean, or has the Heart,
To give his Verdict on a Stranger's part:
Now Court being call'd by beat of Drum,
The Judges left their Punch and Rum,   685
When Pettifogger Doctor draws,
His Paper forth, and opens Cause:
And least I shou'd the better get,
Brib'd *Quack* supprest his Knavish Wit.
So Maid upon the downy Field,   690
Pretends a Force, and Fights to yield:
The Byast Court without delay,
Adjudg'd my Debt in Country Pay;
In Pipe staves, Corn, or Flesh of Boar,[5]
Rare Cargo for the *English* Shoar: 695

---

1 [Cook's note] The chief [or capital] of *Mary-Land* containing about
   twenty-four *Houses*.
2 A fair held each September in Southwark, the London neighborhood
   south of the Thames renowned during this era for its poverty and
   crime.
3 A relatively small district in London's west end.
4 That is, St. Mary's City was once the capital of the colony. In 1694
   Protestants succeeded in moving the colonial seat from St. Mary's, a
   Catholic stronghold, to Annapolis (originally named Providence).
5 [Cook's note] There is a Law in this Country, the Plantiff may pay his
   Debt in Country pay, which consists in the produce of the Plantation.

Raging with Grief, full speed I ran
To joyn the Fleet at *Kicketan*;[1]
Embarqu'd and waiting for a Wind,
I left this dreadful Curse behind.
May Canniballs transported o'er the Sea   700
Prey on these Slaves, as they have done on me;
May never Merchant's trading Sails explore
This Cruel, this inhospitable Shoar;
But left abandon'd by the World to starve,
May they sustain the Fate they well deserve;   705
May they turn Savage, or as *Indians* Wild,
From Trade, Converse and Happiness exil'd;
Recreant to Heaven, may they adore the Sun,
And into Pagan Superstitions run
For Vengeance ripe —————————   710
May Wrath Divine then lay those Regions wast
Where no Man's Faithful,[2] nor a Woman Chast.

2. From Richard Steele, "The History of Inkle and Yarico," "*Spectator* No. 11" (13 March 1711)

[This story of a love affair between an Englishman and an Indian woman captured the imagination of eighteenth-century Europeans, launching all manner of creative works both in Britain and on the Continent. These even included a popular opera written by George Colman and staged in London and elsewhere beginning in 1787. As such it is an important encapsulation of eighteenth-century Europeans' attitudes toward the New World, Native Americans, and slavery. The version excerpted here was written by Richard Steele (1672–1729) as purportedly told him by a young woman who was eager to vindicate the female sex from charges that they were uniquely disloyal in romance. It was published in the 13 March 1711 number of the *Spectator*, the popular and highly influential periodical written jointly by Steele and Joseph Addison. Steele's approach toward his subject is noteworthy, both for its subordination of moral debates over slavery to presumably larger ones about male romantic inconstancy and for its somewhat stereotypical depiction of the Native American woman as a "noble savage."]

---

1 [Cook's note] The homeward bound Fleet meets here.
2 [Cook's note] The Author does not intend by this any of the *English* Gentlemen resident there.

Mr. *Thomas Inkle*, of *London*, aged twenty Years, embarked in the *Downs*[1] on the good Ship called the *Achilles*, bound for the *West-Indies*, on the 16th of *June*, 1647, in order to improve his Fortune by Trade and Merchandize. Our Adventurer was the third Son of an eminent Citizen, who had taken particular Care to instill into his Mind an early Love of Gain, by making him a perfect Master of Numbers, and consequently giving him a quick View of Loss and Advantage, and preventing the natural Impulses of his Passions, by Prepossession towards his Interests. With a Mind thus turned, young *Inkle* had a Person every way agreeable, a ruddy Vigour in his Countenance, Strength in his Limbs, with Ringlets of fair Hair loosely flowing on his Shoulders. It happened, in the Course of the Voyage, that the *Achilles*, in some distress, put into a Creek on the Main of *America*, in Search of Provisions: The Youth, who is the Hero of my Story, among others went ashore on this Occasion. From their first Landing they were observed by a Party of *Indians*, who hid themselves in the Woods for that Purpose. The *English* unadvisedly marched a great distance from the Shore into the Country, and were intercepted by the Natives, who slew the greatest Number of them. Our Adventurer escaped among others, by flying into a Forest. Upon his coming into a remote and pathless Part of the Wood, he threw himself, tired and breathless, on a little Hillock, when an *Indian* Maid rushed from a Thicket behind him: After the first Surprize, they appeared mutually agreeable to each other. If the *European* was highly Charmed with the Limbs, Features, and wild-Graces of the Naked *American*; the *American* was no less taken with the Dress, Complexion and Shape of an *European*, covered from Head to Foot. The *Indian* grew immediately enamoured of him, and consequently sollicitous for his Preservation: She therefore conveyed him to a Cave, where she gave him a delicious Repast of Fruits, and led him to a Stream to slake his Thirst. In the midst of these good Offices, she would sometimes play with his Hair, and delight in the Opposition of its Colour, to that of her Fingers: Then open his Bosom, then laugh at him for covering it. She was, it seems, a Person of Distinction, for she every Day came to him in a different Dress, of the most beautiful Shells, Bugles and Bredes.[2] She likewise brought him a great many Spoils, which her other Lovers

---

1 A common rendezvous point for ships off the southeastern coast of England.
2 "Bugles" here are tube-shaped glass beads; "bredes" is a variant spelling of "braids."

had presented to her; so that his Cave was richly adorned with all the spotted Skins of Beasts, and most Party-coloured Feathers of Fowls, which that World afforded. To make his Confinement more tolerable, she would carry him in the Dusk of the Evening, or by the favour of Moon-light, to unfrequented Groves and Solitudes, and shew him where to lye down in Safety, and sleep amidst the Falls of Waters, and Melody of Nightingales. Her Part was to watch and hold him awake in her Arms, for fear of her Country-men, and wake him on Occasions to consult his Safety. In this manner did the Lovers pass away their Time, till they had learned a Language of their own, in which the Voyager communicated to his Mistress, how happy he should be to have her in his Country, where she should be cloathed in such Silks as his Wastecoat was made of, and be carried in Houses drawn by Horses, without being exposed to Wind or Weather. All this he promised her the Enjoyment of, without such Fears and Alarms as they were there tormented with. In this tender Correspondence these Lovers lived for several Months, when *Yarico*, instructed by her Lover, discovered a Vessel on the Coast to which she made Signals; and in the Night, with the utmost Joy and Satisfaction, accompanied him to a Ship's-Crew of his Country-Men, bound for *Barbadoes*. When a Vessel from the Main arrives in that Island, it seems the Planters come down to the Shoar, where there is an immediate Market of the *Indians* and other Slaves, as with us of Horses and Oxen.

To be short, Mr. *Thomas Inkle*, now coming into *English* Territories, began seriously to reflect upon his loss of Time, and to weigh with himself how many Days Interest of his Mony he had lost during his Stay with *Yarico*. This Thought made the Young Man very pensive, and careful what Account he should be able to give his Friends of his Voyage. Upon which Considerations, the prudent and frugal young Man sold *Yarico* to a *Barbadian* Merchant; notwithstanding that the poor Girl, to incline him to commiserate her Condition, told him that she was with Child by him: But he only made use of that Information, to rise in his Demands upon the Purchaser.

3. From Daniel Defoe, *Moll Flanders* (London: W. Chetwood and T. Edlin, 1722)

[Published three years after his wildly successful *Robinson Crusoe*, Defoe's *Moll Flanders* purports to be the autobiography of an Englishwoman who, as the title page informs us, "was Born in Newgate [Prison], and during a Life of continu'd Variety for

Threescore Years, besides her Childhood, was Twelve Year a *Whore*, five times a *Wife* (whereof once to her own Brother), Twelve Year a *Thief*, Eight Year a Transported *Felon* in *Virginia*, at last grew *Rich*, liv'd *Honest*, and died a *Penitent*." During Moll's first residency in Virginia, she is reunited with her mother, who had been transported there and whom she had not seen since childhood. After a return to England, Moll is transported back to Virginia and in the end reverses her moral constitution and worldly prospects. Upon achieving this success, she finally returns to England. In the passages that follow, Defoe (1660–1731) depicts the American colonies receiving only the down and out and criminal classes of the English population. While transported felons sometimes improve their fortunes and clear their names in the New World, they cannot "enjoy" their wealth and status until they return to the civilized world of Europe.]

[From the Preface, which rehearses the lessons to be learned from the adventures that follow:]

[Moll's] application to a sober Life, and industrious Management at last in *Virginia*, with her Transported Spouse, is a Story fruitful of Instruction, to all the unfortunate Creatures who are oblig'd to seek their Re-establishment abroad; whether by the Misery of Transportation, or other Disaster; letting them know, that Diligence and Application have their due Encouragement, even in the remotest Parts of the World[.]

★   ★   ★   ★

[Upon settling for the first time in Virginia, Moll meets up with her long-lost mother, who teaches her about the types of people to be found in the colonies.]

[My mother] often told me how the greatest part of the Inhabitants of that Colony came thither in very indifferent Circumstances from *England*; that, generally speaking, they were of two sorts, either (1.) such as were brought over by Masters of Ships to be sold as Servants, *such we call them*, my Dear, *says she*, but they are more properly call'd *Slaves*. Or, (2.) Such as are Transported from *Newgate* and other Prisons, after having been found guilty of Felony and other Crimes punishable, with Death.

When they come here, *says she*, we make no difference, the Planters buy them, and they work together in the Field till their time is out; when 'tis expir'd, *said she*, they have Encouragement given them to Plant for themselves....

Hence Child, *says she*, many a *Newgate* Bird becomes a great Man, and we have, *continued she*, several Justices of the Peace, Officers of the Train Bands,[1] and Magistrates of the Towns they live in, that have been burnt in the Hand.

★　★　★　★

[Having returned to England, Moll tries in vain to convince a lover to join her in a voyage to Virginia.]

I then gave him a full and distinct account of the nature of Planting, how with carrying over but two or three Hundred Pounds value in *English* Goods, with some Servants and Tools, a Man of Application would presently lay a Foundation for a Family, and in a very few Years be certain to raise an Estate.

I let him into the nature of the Product of the Earth, how the Ground was Cur'd and Prepared, and what the usual encrease of it was; and demonstrated to him, that in a very few Years, with such a beginning, we should be as certain of being Rich, as we were now certain of being Poor....

I added, that after seven Years, if we liv'd, we might be in a Posture to leave our Plantation in good Hands, and come over again and receive the Income of it, and live here and enjoy it; and I gave him Examples of some that had done so, and liv'd now in very good Circumstances in *London*.

★　★　★　★

[Near the end of the tale, Moll is imprisoned in an English jail, where one of her fellow prisoners turns out to be a long-lost husband, who has been reduced from a gentleman into a highway robber. Here he contemplates the relative horrors of being transported to America and being sent to the gallows.]

He hop'd he should be clear'd; that he had had some intimation, that if he would submit to Transport himself, he might be admitted to it without a Tryal, but that he could not think of it with any Temper, and thought he could much easier submit to be Hang'd.

I blam'd him for that, and told him I blam'd him on two Accounts; first because, if he was Transported, there might be an Hundred ways for him that was a Gentleman, and a bold enter-

---

1 Companies of trained citizen-soldiers.

prizing Man to find his way back again, and perhaps some Ways and Means to come back before he went. He smil'd at that Part, and said he should like the last the best of the two, for he had a kind of Horror upon his Mind at his being sent over to the Plantations as *Romans* sent condemn'd Slaves to Work in the Mines; that he thought the Passage into another State, let it be what it would, much more tolerable at the Gallows, and that this was the general Notion of all the Gentlemen, who were driven by the Exigence of their Fortunes to take the Road;[1] that at the Place of Execution there was at least an End of all the Miseries of the present State, and as for what was to follow, a Man was in his Opinion, as likely to Repent sincerely in the last Fortnight of his Life under the Pressures and Agonies of a Jayl, and the condemn'd Hole,[2] as he would ever be in the Woods and Wildernesses of *America*; that Servitude and hard Labour were things Gentlemen could never stoop to, that it was but the way to force them to be their own Executioners afterwards, which was much worse, and that therefore he could not have any Patience when he did but think of being Transported.

---

1 I.e., to become highway robbers.
2 The forerunner of the modern-day death row.

Appendix C: Slavery and Servitude

[*Mr. Anderson*'s theme of slavery in the colonies paralleled a growing British literature on the subject in the eighteenth century. Naturally, this literature explored the themes of slavery almost entirely as it related to Britons: white servitude in the colonies, white slavery in North Africa, and the place of black slavery in the Empire. Some of these themes—especially the bondage of unfortunate fellow Britons in America and Barbary—had been of interest and concern to British readers for over a century by the time Kimber engaged them.]

1. From James Revel, *The Poor Unhappy Transported Felon's Sorrowful Account of His Fourteen Years Transportation at Virginia in America* (ca. 1660–80)

[One of the earliest and most compelling literary accounts of forced labor in the American colonies is James Revel's verse tale *The Poor Unhappy Transported Felon*. Although internal clues suggest this poem was written in the late seventeenth century, the earliest known published editions of it did not appear until a century later, when several London publishers printed chapbook versions of the tale. (The copy-text used here is an undated chapbook "Printed and Sold in Stonecutter Street, Fleet-Market," London, between 1760 and 1780.) In part because of the long delay between composition and publication, some scholars have questioned whether it is better treated as historical fiction than as the authentic autobiography it claims to be. In either case, Revel's poem remains a useful comparison of the life of the African slave and the transported felon. Sentenced to fourteen years' labor in Virginia for thieving, the English narrator emphasizes that his experiences from first to final sale were not much different from those of the black slaves at this early date in the colony's history. The excerpt below picks up at the point when Revel and his fellow convicts set sail for America.]

From Part II

In a few days we left the river quite.
And in short time of land we lost the sight,   70
The captain and the sailors us'd us well,

But kept us under lest we should rebel.
   We were in number much about threescore,
A wicked lousy crew as e'er went o'er,
Oaths and tobacco with us plenty were,   75
Most did smoak, but all did curse and swear.
   Five of our number in the passage dy'd,
Who were cast into the ocean wide,
And after sailing seven weeks or more,
We at Virginia all were put on shore.   80
   Then to refresh us we were all well clean'd,
That to our buyers we might the better seem,
The things were given that to each belong,
And they that had clean linen put it on.
   Our faces shav'd, comb'd our wigs and hair,   85
That we in decent order might appear,
Against the planters did come down to view,
How well they lik'd this fresh transported crew.
   The women from us separated stood,
As well as we by them to be thus view'd,   90
And in short time some men up to us came,
Some ask'd our trade, and others ask'd our name.
   Some view'd our limbs turning us around,
Examining like horses if we were sound,
What trade my lad, said one to me,   95
A tin man, sir. That will not do for me.
   Some felt our hands, others our legs and feet,
And made us walk to see if we were compleat,
Some view'd our teeth to see if they were good,
And fit to chew our hard and homely food. [...]   100

Part III

Down to the harbour I was took again,
On board a ship loaded with chains,
Which I was forced to wear both night and day,
For fear I from the sloop should run away.   120
   My master was a man but of ill fame,
Who first of all a transport thither came,
In Raphannock country[1] he did dwell,

---

1   Rappahannock County no longer exists, having been divided into
    Richmond and Essex Counties in 1692.

In Raphannock river known full well.

When the ship was laden and some sent, 125
An hundred miles we up the river went,
The weather cold and very hard my fair,
My lodging on the deck both hard and bare.

At last to my new master's house I came,
To the town of Wicowoco[1] call'd by name, 130
Here my European cloaths were took from me,
Which never after I could ever see.

A canvas shirt and trowsers me they gave,
A hop sack frock in which I was a slave,
No shoes or stockings had I for to wear, 135
Nor hat nor cap, my head and feet were bare.

Thus dress'd into the field I next did go,
Among tobacco plants all day to hoe,
At day break in the morn our work begun,
And lasted till the setting of the sun. 140

My fellow slaves were just five transports more,
With eighteen negroes which is twenty four,
Besides four transport women in the house,
To wait upon his daughter and his spouse.

We and the negroes both alike did fare, 145
Of work and food we had an equal share.
And in a piece of ground called our own,
The food we eat first by ourselves is sown.

No other time to us they will allow,
But on a Sunday we the same must do. 150
Six days we slave for our master's good,
The seventh is to produce our homely food.

And when we a hard day's work have done,
Away unto the mill we must be gone.
'Till twelve or one o'clock a grinding corn, 155
And must be up by day light in the morn.

And if you get in debt with any one,
It must be paid before from thence you come,
In publick places they'll put up your name,
As every one their just demands may claim. 160

But if we offer for to run away,
For every hour we must serve a day,
For every day a week, they're so severe,

---

1 A misspelling of Wicomico, a seventeenth-century village in
   Northumberland County on Virginia's eastern coast.

Every week a month, for every month a year.
    But if they murder, rob or steal while there,   165
They're straitway hang'd the laws are so severe,
For by the rigour of that very law,
They are kept under and do stand in awe.

Part IV

    At last it pleased God I sick did fall,
But I no favour could receive at all.   170
For I was forc'd to work while I could stand,
Or hold the hoe within my feeble hand.
    Much hardship then I did endure,
No dog was ever nursed so before,
More pity then the negroe slaves bestow'd   175
Than my inhuman brutal master show'd.
    Oft on my knees the Lord I did implore,
To let me see my native land once more,
For through his grace my life I would amend,
And be a comfort to my dearest friends.   180
    Helpless and sick and left alone,
I by myself did use to make my moan,
And think upon my former wicked ways
That had brought me to this wretched case.
    The Lord who saw my grief and smart,   185
And my complaint, he knew my contrite heart,
His gracious mercy did to me afford,
My health again was unto me restor'd.
    It pleas'd the Lord to grant to me such grace,
That tho' I was in such a barbarous place,   190
I serv'd the Lord with fervency and zeal,
By which I did much inward comfort feel.
    Now twelve years had passed thus away,
And but two more by law I had to stay,
When death did my cruel master call.   195
But that was no relief to me at all,
    The widow would not the plantation hold,
So we and that were to be sold,
A Lawyer who at James town did dwell,
Came for to see and lik'd it very well.   200
    He bought the negroes who for life are slaves,
But no transported felons would he have,
So we were put like sheep into the fold,
Unto the best bidder to be sold.

2. From John Locke, "Of Slavery," *Two Treatises of Government* (London: Awnsham Churchill, 1690), Book II, Chapter 4

[As evidenced in Chapter III of *Mr. Anderson*, Kimber consciously reflected on the English philosopher John Locke's (1632–1704) theories of liberty and slavery when drafting his novel. Particularly in Locke's *Two Treatises of Government*, Kimber would have found ample philosophical precedent for shuddering over white slavery while having no significant moral scruples over the enslaving of "conquered" Africans. However strong his rhetoric of personal liberty, Locke himself was deeply invested in the slave-trading Royal Africa Company and quite likely helped draft "The Fundamental Constitutions of Carolina," a document which granted Carolina planters absolute authority over their slaves.]

22. The natural Liberty of Man is to be free from any Superiour Power on Earth, and not to be under the Will or Legislative Authority of Man, but to have only the Law of Nature for his Rule. The Liberty of Man, in Society, is to be under no other Legislative Power, but that established, by consent, in the Commonwealth; nor under the Dominion of any Will, or Restraint of any Law, but what that Legislative shall enact, according to the Trust put in it. Freedom then is not what Sir *R. F.*[1] tells us, *O. A.* 55. *A Liberty for every one to do what he lists, to live as he pleases, and not to be tyed by any Laws:*[2] but Freedom of Men, under Government, is, to have a standing Rule to live by, common to every one of that Society, and made by the Legislative Power erected in it. A Liberty to follow my own Will in all things, where that Rule prescribes not; not to be subject to the inconstant, uncertain, unknown, Arbitrary Will of another Man. As Freedom of Nature is to be under no other restraint but the Law of Nature.

23. This Freedom from Absolute, Arbitrary Power, is so necessary to, and closely joyned with a man's Preservation, that he cannot part with it, but by what forfeits his Preservation and Life

---

1 Sir Robert Filmer (c. 1588–1653), the seventeenth-century political writer against whose theories of absolute monarchy Locke directed his treatises.
2 As Locke's shorthand citation suggests, this quotation comes from p. 55 of Filmer's *Observations upon Aristotle's Politiques Touching Forms of Government* (originally published in 1652).

together. For a Man, not having the Power of his own Life, cannot, by Compact, or his own Consent, enslave himself to any one, nor put himself under the Absolute, Arbitrary Power of another, to take away his Life, when he pleases. No body can give more Power than he has himself; and he that cannot take away his own Life, cannot give another Power over it. Indeed having, by his fault, forfeited his own Life, by some Act that deserves Death; he, to whom he has forfeited it, may (when he has him in his Power) delay to take it, and make use of him to his own service; and he does him no injury by it. For, when-ever he finds the hardship of his Slavery out-weigh the value of his Life, 'tis in his Power, by resisting the Will of his Master, to draw on himself the Death he desires.

24. This is the perfect condition of Slavery, which is nothing else, but the State of War continued, between a lawful Conquerour, and a Captive. For, if once Compact enter between them, and make an agreement for a limited Power on the one side, and Obedience, on the other; the State of War and Slavery ceases, as long as the Compact endures. For, as has been said, no Man can, by agreement, pass over to another that which he hath not in himself, a Power over his own Life.

I confess, we find among the *Jews*, as well as other Nations, that Men did sell themselves; but, 'tis plain, this was only to Drudgery, not to Slavery. For, it is evident, the Person sold was not under an Absolute, Arbitrary, Despotical Power. For the Master could not have Power to kill him, at any time, whom, at a certain time, he was obliged to let go free out of his service: And the Master of such a Servant was so far from having an Arbitrary Power over his Life, that he could not, at pleasure, so much as maim him, but the Loss of an Eye, or Tooth, set him free, *Exod.* XXI.[1]

3. Mary Barber, "On Seeing the Captives, Lately Redeem'd from Barbary by His Majesty," *Poems on Several Occasions* (London: C. Rivington, 1734), pp. 271–74

[In reading Kimber's account of a white boy being abducted into slavery, many eighteenth-century readers would have recalled recurring news reports of Europeans being captured and taken

---

1 The biblical laws of slavery practiced by the ancient Israelites are set forth in Exodus 21.

into bondage by pirates while sailing off the Barbary Coast of North Africa. Rather remarkably, among those who were most appalled by the often sensationalized tales of white Christians being enslaved by "godless" Africans were many who had never been in the least bit troubled by the transatlantic slave trade. Typical of European outrage over Barbary Coast slavery is Mary Barber's poetic commemoration of King George II's ransoming of a group of Britons from their African captors. While Barber forcefully decries slavery, it is never fully clear whether her indignation extends beyond the immediate context of the enslaving of English travelers along the Barbary Coast.]

A Sight like this, who can unmov'd survey?
Impartial Muse, can'st thou with-hold thy Lay?
See the freed Captives hail their native Shore,
And tread the Land of LIBERTY once more:
See, as they pass, the crouding People press,   5
Joy in their Joy, and their Deliv'rer bless.

  Now, SLAVERY! no more thy rigid Hand
Shall drag the Trader to thy fatal Strand:
No more in Iron Bonds the Wretched groan;
Secur'd, BRITANNIA, by thy Guardian Throne.   10

  Say, mighty PRINCE! can Empire boast a Bliss,
Amidst its radiant Pomp, that equals this?
To see the Captives, by thy Pow'r set free,
Their Supplications raise to Heav'n for Thee!

  The god-like Bounty scatters Blessings round,   15
As flowing Urns enrich the distant Ground:
No more shall Woes the fainting Heart destroy;
The *House of Mourning* now is turn'd to *Joy*:
See Arms in Grief long folded up, extend,
To clasp a Husband, Brother, Kinsman, Friend: 20
See hoary Parents, tott'ring o'er the Grave,
A Son long-wail'd, to prop their Age, receive:
And, Have we liv'd to see thy Face? they cry;
O! 'tis enough——We now in Peace shall die:
O bless'd be Heav'n! and bless'd, while Life remains,   25
Shall be the Hand, that has unbound thy Chains!

  FORBEAR, my Muse; know Art attempts in vain,
What Nature pictures to the Breast humane.

To WAGER[1] turn; for WAGER raise thy Voice;
To feed the Hungry, long has been his Choice,   30
And make the Heart, born down by Care, rejoice.

Say, ye Luxurious, who indulge your Taste,
And, by one Riot,[2] might a Thousand feast;
Do you not blush to see his Care to feed
The Captives by your Monarch's Bounty freed?   35

The bitter Cup of Slavery is past;
But pining Penury approaches fast.

And shall the ROYAL RACE[3] alone bestow?
Shall not Compassion from the *Subject* flow?
Shall not each free-born *Briton*'s Bosom melt,   40
To make the Joys of Liberty more felt?
So, *Albion*,[4] be it ever giv'n to thee,
To break the Bonds, and set the Pris'ners free.

4. From James Annesley, *Memoirs of an Unfortunate Young Nobleman, Return'd from a Thirteen Years Slavery in America, Where he had been Sent by the Wicked Contrivances of his Cruel Uncle* (London: J. Freeman, 1743), pp. 55–56, 60–64

[Although the principal source for *Mr. Anderson* appears to have been a local legend Kimber heard while traveling through America (see Appendix A4), he certainly was also tapping into a long tradition of tales of Britons being either press-ganged into the navy or kidnapped into a life of servitude in the colonies. Perhaps the most sensational of these accounts during Kimber's lifetime was that of James Annesley (1715–60), the claimant to the estates and title of Lord Anglesey, who at the age of twelve

---

1 [Barber's note] Sir Charles Wager, who entertain'd the Captives at their coming to London, Nov. 11, 1734.
2 A noisy, extravagant feast.
3 [Barber's note] When the Captives attended his Majesty at St. James's in their slavish Habits, to return Thanks for their Deliverance, his Majesty was graciously pleas'd to order 100 Guineas to be distributed among them; and their Royal Highnesses the Duke and the Princesses gave above 50 more.
4 A traditional poetic name for Great Britain.

was secretly sold into servitude by a nefarious uncle who plotted to clear the path of succession for himself. Eventually Annesley escaped from the American plantation to which he had been sold, joined the British navy, and rather fortuitously met up with sailors who recognized him from his childhood. Soon thereafter he returned to his native Ireland, and in 1743 he sued his uncle to reclaim his inheritance. Hoping to capitalize on the publicity surrounding the case—and undoubtedly also aiming to win popular sympathy for his claims—Annesley penned a lightly fictionalized version of his travails, the *Memoirs of an Unfortunate Young Nobleman*. Not surprisingly, the tale proved an instant success, appearing both as a full-length novel and in at least two condensed, pamphlet-length Irish editions. In the end, legal technicalities left Annesley's case still unsettled at his death in 1760. But he has gained some measure of posthumous revenge against his uncle in the world of literature, where his story has inspired numerous novels, including Tobias Smollett's *Peregrine Pickle* (1751), Walter Scott's *Guy Mannering* (1815), William Godwin's *Cloudesley* (1830), and Charles Reade's *The Wandering Heir* (1872). To this list, we might in all likelihood add Kimber's *Mr. Anderson*. Kimber certainly would have known of the Annesley case, both through popular reports and through accounts of the trial in the *London Magazine*. Some of the general similarities between the plot of Kimber's novel and Annesley's *Memoirs* are on display in the excerpt that follows. Note particularly how emphatic the narrator is in using the word "slave" to describe James's condition and how this slavery compares with the white slavery in the Muslim world (here termed "*Turkish*" slavery) decried by Mary Barber. Furthermore, adding the picture of Drumon here to the likes of Barlow and the Carters in *Mr. Anderson* gives a good sense of the composite image of the American planter in this sort of literature.]

The first Step this inhumane Uncle took, was to agree with the Master of a Ship bound for *Pensilvania*, for a certain Sum of Money to transport the Chevalier *James*[1] thither, and then he was to make what Advantage he could of him, by disposing him in the Plantations to who bid most. The Story he invented to bring the Master of the Vessel into this Project was, That the Boy being the

---

1   The novelistic equivalent of James Annesley. "Chevalier" is a generic chivalric title for a nobleman rather than an actual rank.

natural[1] Son of a Person of Condition, and not meriting the Pro-tection of his Father on account of a Propensity to vile Actions, it was thought proper to send him where he might have less Opportunity of following his Inclinations. Whether this gain'd any real Credit with the Person to whom 'twas told, cannot be said, but it served him as an Excuse for entering into a Bargain he was sure to be a Gainer by....

Not many days after this, the Baron *de Altamont*[2] was taken ill and died; he was too suddenly snatched away to settle his Affairs, or make any Declaration concerning his Son, as it is probable he would, had he thought himself so near his End. As he had lived for a great while extremely private, his Death made no Noise, and would scarce have been mentioned but for the Debts he left unpaid. The Chevalier *Richard*[3] immediately took upon him the Title of Baron *de Altamont*, and with it the Estate appertaining, the late Possessor being able to dispose of it only for his own Life.

The young Chevalier, now real Baron, was kept too close a Prisoner to hear any thing of this Change in his Family, and the Ship being ready to sail in a short time, he was conveyed privately on board, knowing no other than that he was going somewhere for Education; and as he had been told that nothing should be wanting to repair the Time he had already lost, he run over in his Mind all the Sciences he remember'd to have heard the Names of, and computed how long the Study of each would take him up. In this manner did he amuse himself till they got out to Sea, but then a sudden Storm arising, less agreeable Ideas took the Place of those I have been mentioning.

★ ★ ★ ★

[Once at sea, young James realizes he has been tricked and is not being taken to a boarding school (as he had been told), but to America, where he will be sold into servitude.]

But I shall have no Learning and shall be a Slave, said the Chevalier. Yes, yes, replied the dissembling Captain, you will have Opportunities enough to learn any thing—nor is there any thing so terrible in the Name of Slave as you imagine—'tis only another Name for an Apprentice—you will only be bound for a certain Time, as many Noblemen's Sons in England and Ireland are; and when your Time is expired you will be your own Master....

1 Illegitimate.
2 James's father.
3 The villainous uncle.

These delusive Hopes, added to good Eating and Drinking, and civil Behaviour, recovered the Rose in our young Voyager's Complexion, and on their landing he seemed to have lost nothing by the Fatigues he had endured; so easy is it to repair the Decays of Youth, while Age in vain endeavours to retrieve the Plumpness in the once-fallen Cheek.—It was now the Captain's Business to dispose of his Property to the best Advantage he could for himself, which he did without any Regard to the Promises he had made when he was under Apprehensions of losing him. The Person he sold him to was a rich Planter in *New-Castle* County,[1] who after paying the Money agreed on between them, took home the young Chevalier, and immediately entered him among the Number of his Slaves....

A new World now opened itself to the View of the Chevalier *James*, in which every thing he saw was strange to him: The Habits and odd Manners of the *Indian* Men and Women, the various Birds and four-footed Animals, so different from those of *Europe*, would have afforded an agreeable Amusement to his attentive Mind for a considerable Time, had he been permitted to indulge it; but *Drumon*, so his Master was called, soon found him other Employment.—He had slept but one Night in the House of Bondage, when he was called up at Day-break and sent to work in the Field with his Fellow-Slaves.

The Labour that fell to his Share and several others that Day, was cutting of Timber to make Pipe-Staves,[2] which Commodity is a considerable Branch of the Traffick of that County: this was a Work our noble Slave was so little skill'd in, and was indeed so much beyond his Strength, that he had many Stripes[3] for his Awkwardness before he had any Meat. This first Day gave him a Sample of what he was to expect, but as he hoped from the deceitful Promises the Captain had made him that it would not be of any long Continuance, he set himself with all his might to do the best he could to gain the Favour of a Person in whose Power he soon found he was as absolutely as an Ox or an Ass, or any other Property he had made purchase of; but there are a sort of People in the World that are not to be obliged, and the greater your Endeavours for that End, the less will be your Effect. *Drumon* was one of these, and among the Number of Wretches

---

1 The northernmost county in Delaware.
2 Boards used for making casks.
3 Lash-marks.

under his Command, there was not one who could do any thing to please him—He seemed to take a savage Pleasure in adding to the Misery of their Condition by continual ill Usage, and to do every thing in his Power to degenerate them from the human Species, and render them on a Level with the mute Creation.

Nothing is indeed more strange than that any who have ever known a better State, can support with Life the Hardships of an *American* Slavery, which is infinitely more terrible than that of a *Turkish* one, frightful as it is represented; for besides the incessant Toil they undergo, the Nature of their Labour is such, that they are obliged to be continually exposed to the Air, which is unwholsom enough, the Heats and Colds, which the different Seasons of the Year bring on in these Parts, being far greater than any we know in *Europe*. Then, after being allowed no Shelter from either of these Extremes, all the Refreshment afforded them is Poue, or a sort of Bread made with *India* Corn, heavy on the Stomach, and insipid to the Palate, with a Draught of Water, or at best mingled with a little ginger and Molosses; they feast with a Dish of *Homine* or *Mush*, both which are made of the same Kind of Corn is set before them, moistened with the Fat of Bacon or Hog's Lard. This is the Manner in which the Slaves or Servants to the *West-India* Planters in general live; but some Masters there are that appear more human than *Drumon*, and soften in some measure the Severity of those poor Creatures' Fate by gentle Words, whereas that cruel Monster, as I said before, took a delight in heightning their Calamities. Nor Age, nor Sex, nor the Accidents which occasioned their being in his Power, could move him to the least Compassion, but on the contrary, those received the worst Treatment from him that were intitled to the best.

5. From Malachy Postlethwayt, *The African Trade, the Great Support of the British Plantation Trade in America* (London: J. Robinson, 1745), pp. 6, 14–15

[A decade before Kimber published *Mr. Anderson*, the British political economist Malachy Postlethwayt (c. 1707–67) began penning a series of pamphlets emphasizing the crucial importance of slavery to Britain's economic well-being. These treatises, which were apparently subsidized by the Royal Africa Company, a leading slave-trading corporation, are best remembered for Postlethwayt's blunt suggestion, made in a 1746 tract entitled *The National and Private Advantages of the African Trade Considered*, that "The *Negroe-Trade*, and the natural Consequences resulting from it, may be justly esteemed an inexhaustible Fund of Wealth and Naval Power to this Nation." The passages included below, which appeared a year prior to this statement, express similar sentiments. Here Postlethwayt warns against French incursions on the slave trade and suggests that protecting the traffic of slaves from Africa to the American colonies is essential if Britons hope to preserve the way of life to which they have become accustomed. As such, this pamphlet provides an important counter-image to most of the representations of American planters found elsewhere in this edition. Without commenting on their morality, he emphasizes their vital economic role. This sense that slavery and the slave trade were necessary to the wealth and power of the empire was part of what kept the scattered objections to slavery in this period from cohering into any organized anti-slavery movement.]

But is it not notorious[1] to the whole World, that the Business of *Planting* in our *British Colonies*, as well as in the *French*, is carried on by the Labour of *Negroes*, imported thither from *Africa*? Are we not indebted to those valuable People, the *Africans*, for our *Sugars*, *Tobaccoes*, *Rice*, *Rum*, and all other *Plantation Produce*? And the greater the Number of *Negroes* imported into our *Colonies*, from *Africa*, will not the Exportation of *British* Manufactures among the *Africans* be in Proportion; they being paid for in such Commodities only? The more likewise our Plantations abound in *Negroes*, will not more Land become cultivated, and both *better* and greater *Variety* of *Plantation Commodities* be produced? As those Trades are subservient to the Well Being and Prosperity of each other; so the more either flourishes or declines, the other must be necessarily affected; and the general Trade and Navigation of their *Mother Country*, will be proportionably benefited or injured.

★ ★ ★ ★

But if the whole *Negroe Trade* be thrown into the Hands of our Rivals, and our Colonies are to depend on the Labour of the *White Men* to supply their Place, they will either soon be undone, or shake off their Dependency on the Crown of *England*. For

---

1 As becomes clear below, no negative connotations are intended in this usage of "notorious."

White Men cannot be obtained near so cheap, or the Labour of a sufficient Number be had for the Expence of their Maintenance only, as we have of the *Africans*. Has not long Experience also shewn that *White* Men are not constitutionally qualified to sustain the Toil of Planting in the Climates of our *Island Colonies* like the Blacks?

Were it possible however, for *White Men* to answer the End of *Negroes* in Planting, must we not drain our own Country of *Husbandmen, Mechanicks,* and *Manufacturers* too? ...

Doctor Davenant[1] tells us, that in the Time of King CHARLES II[2] our *Merchants*, interested in the *American Trade*, made a Representation to that King, setting forth, that by a just Medium, they made it appear, that the Labour of an hundred *Negroes* was, at that Time of Day, 1600 *l. per Annum* profit to this Nation, deducting therefrom the Amount of Value of what we consume in Plantation Produce. It was then estimated there were no more than 100,000 *Negroes* in *America*; but the most experienced Judges now do not rate them less than 300,000: So that if we reckon them of no more Worth to *Great Britain* now than at that Time, and estimate the Value of our Home Consumption of Plantation Commodities at the highest Rate, the annual Gain of the Nation by *Negroe Labour* will fall little short of Three Millions *per Annum*:[3] And it is to be hoped we shall not sacrifice such an Annuity rather than give all just and reasonable Encouragement for the due Support of our *African Company*, which has been the FOUNDATION of such Profit to these Kingdoms!

---

1 Charles Davenant (1656–1714), one of the leading British political economists of his era.

2 Charles II reigned from the Restoration of the monarchy in 1660 until his death in 1685.

3 Roughly £390,000,000 (or $780,000,000) in 2007 currency. As discussed in the Note on Eighteenth-Century Money (pp. 41–42), however, even this large sum is misleadingly low to a modern audience, for it would not be nearly the same share of GNP as it was in 1745.

Appendix D:
Novels in the Mid-Eighteenth Century

[Judged by today's standards of literary taste, *Mr. Anderson* might seem to some overly emotional and moralistic. But, at its publication in 1754, Kimber's novel subscribed quite closely to prevailing norms for characterization, plot development, didacticism, and sentimentality. The excerpts that follow provide a glimpse into the theory and practice of novel writing in the mid-eighteenth century.]

1. From Lord Chesterfield, *Letters Written by the Late Right Honourable Philip Dormer Stanhope, Earl of Chesterfield, to His Son, Philip Stanhope, Esq.* (written ca. 1740, published in 1774 by J. Dodsley [London])

[While Lord Chesterfield (1694–1773) is most frequently remembered in literary history for his half-hearted patronage of Samuel Johnson's dictionary, during his lifetime he was widely admired for his wit, taste, and good breeding. Chesterfield's principal literary achievement is the collection of advice-imparting letters he wrote to his illegitimate son, Philip Stanhope, beginning in 1737. (The letters were not published, however, until 1774, a year after Chesterfield's death.) The following letter, likely penned in late 1740, when Chesterfield's son was just 18, offers a concise comparison of the popular historical romances of the seventeenth century and the new breed of fiction known as novels. In the process, Chesterfield wittily summarizes many of the basic conventions Kimber would follow in *Mr. Anderson*.]

Letter LII[1]

My Dear Child,

You are now reading the Historical Novel of Don Carlos, written by the Abbé of St. Real.[2] The foundation of it is true; the Abbé has only embellished a little, in order to give it the turn of

---

1 Chesterfield originally wrote this letter in French. The translation that follows comes from the first (1774) edition of Chesterfield's letters.
2 The French author César Vichard de Saint-Réal's *Don Carlos* appeared in 1672.

a Novel; and it is prettily written. *A propos*; I am in doubt whether you know what a Novel is: it is a little gallant history, which must contain a great deal of love, and not exceed one or two small volumes. The subject must be a love affair; the lovers are to meet with many difficulties and obstacles, to oppose the accomplishment of their wishes, but at last overcome them all; and the conclusion or catastrophe must leave them happy. A Novel is a kind of abbreviation of a Romance; for a Romance generally consists of twelve volumes, all filled with insipid love nonsense, and most incredible adventures. The subject of a Romance is sometimes a story entirely fictitious, that is to say, quite invented; at other times a true story, but generally so changed and altered, that one cannot know it. For example, in Grand Cyrus, Clelia, and Cleopatra, three celebrated Romances,[1] there is some true history; but so blended with falsities, and silly love adventures, that they confuse and corrupt the mind, instead of forming and instructing it. The greatest Heroes of antiquity are there represented in woods and forests, whining insipid love-tales to their inhuman fair one; who answers them in the same style. In short, the reading of Romances is a most frivolous occupation, and time merely thrown away. The old Romances, written two or three hundred years ago, such as Amadis of Gaul, Orlando the Furious,[2] and others, were stuft with enchantments, magicians, giants, and such sort of impossibilities; whereas the more modern Romances keep within the bounds of possibility, but not of probability. For I would just as soon believe, that the great Brutus, who expelled the Tarquins from Rome,[3] was shut up by some magician in an enchanted castle, as imagine that he was making silly verses for the beautiful Clelia, as he is represented in the Romance of that name.

---

1   The first two tales in this list, *Artamène, ou Le Grand Cyrus* (1649–53) and *Clélie* (1661) are by Madeleine de Scudéry, seventeenth-century France's most famous writer of historical romances. The third, *Cléopâtre* (1646–57), is by Scudéry's contemporary Gautier de Costes, sieur de La Calprenède.

2   The courtly romance *Amadis de Gaula* likely originated as an oral tale (in Portuguese) in the late thirteenth or early fourteenth century but was first transcribed by Garci Ordóñez de Montalvo (in Spanish) in 1508. Ludovico Ariosto's *Orlando Furioso* (1516) is widely considered the great literary epic of the Italian Renaissance.

3   Lucius Junius Brutus, the founder of modern Rome, ended the Tarquin dynasty in 509 BCE.

2. From Samuel Johnson, "*Rambler* No. 4," 31 March 1750[1]

[Samuel Johnson's (1709–84) fourth installment of his twice-weekly periodical the *Rambler* is widely considered the first major critical essay on the fledgling novel genre. The immediate occasion for Johnson's essay was the recent publication of Tobias Smollett's *Roderick Random* (1748) and Henry Fielding's *Tom Jones* (1749), two novels which Johnson deemed morally suspect. After beginning with a useful delineation of the differences between the historical romance and the "comedy of romance" (or the novel), Johnson devotes most of "*Rambler* No. 4" to expounding on the detrimental social and spiritual effects of those novels which ask readers to sympathize with less-than-virtuous characters. Johnson's dictums on "black-and-white" character development would have an immense impact on writers over the next century, one of the earliest of whom was Edward Kimber, who just four years after "*Rambler* No. 4" put its core principles into practice in *Mr. Anderson*.]

Simul et jucunda et idonea dicere Vitae. HORACE.[2]

The works of fiction, with which the present generation seems more particularly delighted, are such as exhibit life in its true state, diversified only by the accidents that daily happen in the world, and influenced by those passions and qualities which are really to be found in conversing with mankind.

This kind of writing may be termed not improperly the comedy of romance, and is to be conducted nearly by the rules of comic poetry. Its province is to bring about natural events by easy means, and to keep up curiosity without the help of wonder: it is therefore precluded from the machines and expedients of the heroic romance, and can neither employ giants to snatch away a lady from the nuptial rites, nor knights to bring her back from captivity; it can neither bewilder its personages in desarts, nor lodge them in imaginary castles.

---

1 The copy-text used below comes from the first collected edition of Johnson's *Rambler* essays (London: J. Payne and J. Bouquet, 1752).
2 Johnson quotes the concluding phrase of a famous dictum from Horace's *Art of Poetry* (line 334), which, in its entirety, reads, "Poets wish to delight and instruct the reader, or to say what is both pleasing and useful for life."

I remember a remark made by Scaliger upon Pontanus,[1] that all his writings are filled with the same images; and that if you take from him his lillies and his roses, his satyrs and his dryads,[2] he will have nothing left that can be called poetry. In like manner, almost all the fictions of the last age will vanish, if you deprive them of a hermit and a wood, a battle and a shipwreck.

Why this wild strain of imagination found reception so long, in polite and learned ages, it is not easy to conceive; but we cannot wonder that, while readers could be procured, the authors were willing to continue it: for when a man had by practice gained some fluency of language, he had no further care than to retire to his closet, let loose his invention, and heat his mind with incredibilities; and a book was produced without fear of criticism, without the toil of study, without knowledge of nature, or acquaintance with life.

The task of our present writers is very different; it requires, together with that learning which is to be gained from books, that experience which can never be attained by solitary diligence, but must arise from general converse, and accurate observation of the living world. Their performances have, as Horace expresses it, *plus oneris quantum veniae minus,* little indulgence, and therefore more difficulty.[3] They are engaged in portraits of which every one knows the original, and can therefore detect any deviation from exactness of resemblance. Other writings are safe, except from the malice of learning, but these are in danger from every common reader; as the slipper ill executed was censured by a shoemaker who happened to stop in his way at the Venus of Apelles.[4]

But the danger of not being approved as just copiers of human manners, is not the most important apprehension that an author of this sort ought to have before him. These books are written chiefly to the young, the ignorant, and the idle, to whom they

---

1 Julius Caesar Scaliger (1484–1558), a leading scholar of the Italian Renaissance, attacked the works of the Italian poet Giovanni Pontano (1426–1503).

2 In classical mythology, dryads are tree-nymphs and satyrs are half-human, half-beast creatures who haunt forests and mountainsides.

3 Horace, *Epistles,* II.i.170.

4 According to an anecdote famously recorded by Pliny the Elder (23–79 CE), the renowned Greek painter Apelles of Kos (fl. 4th century BCE) reconsidered the way he drew feet after his painting of Venus was critiqued by a common shoemaker.

serve as lectures of conduct, and introductions into life. They are the entertainment of minds unfurnished with ideas, and therefore easily susceptible of impressions; not fixed by principles, and therefore easily following the current of fancy; not informed by experience, and consequently open to every false suggestion and partial account.

That the highest degree of reverence should be paid to youth, and that nothing indecent or unseemly should be suffered to approach their eyes or ears; are precepts extorted by sense and virtue from an ancient writer, by no means eminent for chastity of thought.[1] The same kind, tho' not the same degree of caution, is required in every thing which is laid before them, to secure them from unjust prejudices, perverse opinions, and incongruous combinations of images.

In the romances formerly written, every transaction and sentiment was so remote from all that passes among men, that the reader was in very little danger of making any application to himself; the virtues and crimes were equally beyond his sphere of activity; and he amused himself with heroes and with traitors, deliverers and persecutors, as with beings of another species, whose actions were regulated upon motives of their own, and who had neither faults nor excellencies in common with himself.

But when an adventurer is levelled with the rest of the world, and acts in such scenes of the universal drama, as may be the lot of any other man; young spectators fix their eyes upon him with closer attention, and hope by observing his behaviour and success to regulate their own practices, when they shall be engaged in the like part.

For this reason these familiar histories may perhaps be made of greater use than the solemnities of professed morality, and convey the knowledge of vice and virtue with more efficacy than axioms and definitions. But if the power of example is so great, as to take possession of the memory by a kind of violence, and produce effects almost without the intervention of the will, care ought to be taken that, when the choice is unrestrained, the best examples only should be exhibited; and that which is likely to operate so strongly, should not be mischievous or uncertain in its effects.

The chief advantage which these fictions have over real life is, that their authors are at liberty, tho' not to invent, yet to select

---

1 An allusion to the opening lines of Juvenal's fourteenth satire. Juvenal's writings are notoriously racy.

objects, and to cull from the mass of mankind, those individuals upon which the attention ought most to be employ'd; as a diamond, though it cannot be made, may be polished by art, and placed in such a situation, as to display that lustre which before was buried among common stones.

It is justly considered as the greatest excellency of art, to imitate nature; but it is necessary to distinguish those parts of nature, which are most proper for imitation: greater care is still required in representing life, which is so often discoloured by passion, or deformed by wickedness. If the world be promiscuously[1] described, I cannot see of what use it can be to read the account; or why it may not be as safe to turn the eye immediately upon mankind, as upon a mirror which shows all that presents itself without discrimination.

It is therefore not a sufficient vindication of a character, that it is drawn as it appears, for many characters ought never to be drawn; nor of a narrative, that the train of events is agreeable to observation and experience, for that observation which is called knowledge of the world, will be found much more frequently to make men cunning than good. The purpose of these writings is surely not only to show mankind, but to provide that they may be seen hereafter with less hazard; to teach the means of avoiding the snares which are laid by Treachery for Innocence, without infusing any wish for that superiority with which the betrayer flatters his vanity; to give the power of counteracting fraud, without the temptation to practise it; to initiate the youth by mock encounters in the art of necessary defense; and to increase prudence without impairing virtue.

Many writers, for the sake of following nature, so mingle good and bad qualities in their principal personages, that they are both equally conspicuous; and as we accompany them through their adventures with delight, and are led by degrees to interest ourselves in their favour, we lose the abhorrence of their faults, because they do not hinder our pleasure, or, perhaps, regard them with some kindness for being united with so much merit.

There have been men indeed splendidly wicked, whose endowments threw a brightness on their crimes, and whom scarce any villainy made perfectly detestable, because they never could be wholly divested of their excellencies; but such have been in all ages the great corruptors of the world, and their resem-

---

1 Indiscriminately.

blance ought no more to be preserved, than the art of murdering without pain.

Some have advanced, without due attention to the consequences of this notion, that certain virtues have their correspondent faults, and therefore that to exhibit either apart is to deviate from probability. Thus men are observed by Swift to be grateful in the same degree as they are resentful.[1] This principle, with others of the same kind, supposes man to act from a brute impulse, and pursue a certain degree of inclination, without any choice of the object; for, otherwise, though it should be allowed that gratitude and resentment arise from the same constitution of the passions, it follows not that they will be equally indulged when reason is consulted; yet unless that consequence be admitted, this sagacious maxim becomes an empty sound, without any relation to practice or to life.

Nor is it evident, that even the first motions to these effects are always in the same proportion. For pride, which produces quickness of resentment, will obstruct gratitude, by unwillingness to admit that inferiority which obligation implies; and it is surely very unlikely, that he who cannot think he receives a favour will acknowledge or repay it.

It is of the utmost importance to mankind, that positions of this tendency should be laid open and confuted; for while men consider good and evil as springing from the same root, they will spare the one for the sake of the other, and in judging, if not of others at least of themselves, will be apt to estimate their virtues by their vices. To this fatal error all those will contribute, who confound the colours of right and wrong, and instead of helping to settle their boundaries, mix them with so much art, that no common mind is able to disunite them.

In narratives where historical veracity has no place, I cannot discover why there should not be exhibited the most perfect idea of virtue; of virtue not angelical, nor above probability, for what we cannot credit we shall never imitate, but of the highest and purest kind that humanity can reach, which, exercised in such trials as the various revolutions of things shall bring upon it, may, by conquering some calamities, and enduring others, teach us what we may hope, and what we can perform. Vice, for vice is necessary to be shewn, should always disgust; nor should the graces of gaiety, or the dignity of courage, be so united with it, as

---

1   Alexander Pope, not Jonathan Swift, is the actual source of this quotation.

to reconcile it to the mind. Wherever it appears, it should raise hatred by the malignity of its practices, and contempt by the meanness of its stratagems; for while it is supported by either parts or spirit, it will be seldom heartily abhorred. The Roman tyrant was content to be hated, if he was but feared; and there are thousands of the readers of romances willing to be thought wicked, if they may be allowed to be wits. It is therefore to be steadily inculcated, that virtue is the highest proof of understanding, and the only solid basis of greatness; and that vice is the natural consequence of narrow thoughts, that it begins in mistake, and ends in ignominy.

3. From Samuel Richardson, *The History of Sir Charles Grandison* (London: S. Richardson, 1753–54)

[Among British novelists of the mid-eighteenth century, none was more widely read or admired than Samuel Richardson (1689–1761). After publishing two wildly successful tales of damsels in distress in the 1740s (*Pamela* and *Clarissa*), in the early 1750s he set out on a new project in which he would portray the ideal modern gentleman. The result was *Sir Charles Grandison* (1753–54), an epic-length tale of a young Englishman who blends manly courage and strength with the more traditionally female qualities of strict piety and deep moral feeling. Not surprisingly, the novel became an instant classic—fifty years later it would still rank among Jane Austen's favorite novels—and helped create the "cult of sensibility" that would dominate British fiction in the latter half of the eighteenth century. Interestingly, *Sir Charles Grandison* was published almost simultaneously with Kimber's *Mr. Anderson*, with the former appearing in three installments between November 1753 and March 1754 and the latter appearing in January 1754.[1] Whether Kimber had the opportunity to read Richardson's first installment while drafting *Mr. Anderson* is unknown, but it is noteworthy that both tales feature early examples of the character type that would later be dubbed the "man of feeling." The first excerpt below, from the fifth volume of *Sir Charles Grandison*, captures the extreme sentiment frequently on display in Richardson's tale, showing the hero

---

1 Precise dating for the publication of *Mr. Anderson* comes from the January 1754 issue of the *London Magazine*, where Kimber's novel is listed among the month's new releases.

to be much like Kimber's Tom in his susceptibility to tears, out-bursts of passion, and fainting fits. The second excerpt comes from Richardson's "Concluding Note" to the novel, in which he justifies the extreme goodness of his hero and offers a moralistic theory of fiction reminiscent of his friend Samuel Johnson's "*Rambler* No. 4."]

Letter XXIV.[1]

Sir CHARLES GRANDISON, *To Dr.* BARTLETT.[2]

Bologna, Sat. Evening.

I sit down, now, my dear and reverend friend, to write to you par-ticulars which will surprise you! Clementina[3] is the noblest woman on earth! What at last — But I find I must have a quieter heart, and fingers too, before I can proceed.

❖ ❖[4]

I think I am a little less agitated than I was. The above few lines shall go;[5] for they will express to you the emotions of my mind, when I attempted to write an account of what had then so newly passed....

[Grandison proceeds to recount how he arrived at Clementina's home, intent on proposing marriage.]

When I entered the room, the young Lady[6] was sitting in a pensive mood, at her toilette; her hand supporting her head. A fine glow overspread her cheeks, as soon as she saw me: She arose, and, courtesying[7] low, advanced a few steps towards me; but trembled, and looked now down, now aside, and now con-sciously glancing towards me.

---

1 Like Richardson's earlier novels, *Sir Charles Grandison* is in epistolary form, unfolding its plot through a series of letters.
2 A venerable old clergyman with whom Grandison frequently corre-sponds.
3 A beautiful young Italian noblewoman with whom Grandison has fallen in love while tutoring her in English.
4 These marks indicate a pause while Grandison gathers his emotions.
5 Shall remain in the posted letter.
6 Clementina.
7 Curtsying.

I approached her, and, with profound respect, took her hand with both mine, and pressed it with my lips. I address not myself now to Lady Clementina as my pupil: I have leave given me to look upon her in a nearer light; and she will have the goodness to pardon the freedom of this address.

Ah, Chevalier! said she, turning her face from me, but not withdrawing her hand — And hesitating, as if not knowing how to speak her mind, sighed, and was silent.

I led her to her chair. She sat down, still trembling. God be praised, said I, bowing my face on both her hands, as I held them in mine, for the amended health of the Lady[1] so dear to all who have the happiness of knowing her! May her recovery, and that of our dear Jeronymo,[2] be perfected!

Happy man! said she, happy in the power given you to oblige as you have done! But how, how shall I — O, Sir! you know not the conflict that has rent my heart in pieces, ever since — I forget when. — O Chevalier! I have not power — She stopt, wept, and remained silent.

It is in your power, madam, to make happy the man to whom you own obligations which are already overpaid.

I took my seat by her, at her silent motion to a chair.

Speak on, Sir: My Soul is labouring with great purposes. Tell me, tell me, all you have to say to me. My heart is too big for its prison, putting her hand to it: It wants room, methinks; yet utterance is denied me — Speak, and let me be silent....

[At this point, Grandison proposes to Clementina; but when he reiterates his unwillingness to convert to her Catholic faith, she tearfully hands him a letter and retreats to her closet. The letter expresses deep feelings for Grandison but even deeper convictions that she cannot marry a "heretic." Her only recourse, she explains, is to flee to a convent and take a nun's vows. Grandison's stunned reaction to this letter follows.]

Never was man more astonished, perplexed, confounded. For a few moments, I forgot that the angel was in her closet, expecting the issue of my contemplations; and walking out of her dressing-room, I threw myself on a soffa, in the next room, not

---

1 Clementina had just recovered from a severe illness.
2 Clementina's brother, whom Grandison had rescued from would-be assassins.

heeding Camilla,[1] who sat in the window. My mind tortured; how greatly tortured! Yet filled with admiration of the angelic qualities of Clementina, I tried to look again into the paper; but the contents were all in my mind, and filled it.

She rang. Camilla hastened to her. I started as she passed me. I arose; yet trembled: And for a moment sat down to re-assure my feet. But Camilla, coming to me, roused me out of the stupidity that had seized me. Never was I so little present to myself, as on this occasion — A woman so superior to all her own Sex, and to all that I had read of, of ours. — O Sir, said Camilla, my Lady dreads your anger. She dreads to see you: Yet hopes it — Hasten, hasten, and save her from fainting — O how she loves you! How she fears your displeasure! — Hers indeed is *true* Love!

She said this as she conducted me in, as I now recollect; for then all my faculties were too much engaged, to attend to her.

I hastened in. The admirable Lady met me half-way, and throwing herself at my feet — Forgive me, forgive the creature, who must be miserable, if you are offended with her.

I would have raised her but she would not be raised, she said, till I had forgiven her.

I kneeled to her, as she kneeled; and clasping her in my arms, Forgive you, madam! Inimitable woman! More than woman! — Can you forgive me for having presumed, or for still presuming, to hope such an angel mine!

She was ready to faint; and cast her arms about me to support herself. Camilla held to her her salts:[2] — I myself, for the first time, was sensible of benefit from them, as my cheek was joined to hers, and bathed with her tears.

★ ★ ★ ★

A Concluding Note by the Editor

The Editor of the foregoing collection has the more readily undertaken to publish it, because he thinks Human Nature has often, of late, been shewn in a light too degrading; and he hopes from this Series of Letters it will be seen, that characters may be good without being unnatural. Sir Charles Grandison himself is

---

1 Clementina's governess.
2 Smelling salts used to revive those who have fainted.

sensible of imperfections, and, as the reader will remember, accuses himself more than once of tendencies to pride and passion; which it required his utmost caution and vigilance to rein-in....

Notwithstanding this, it has been observed by some, that, in general, he approaches too near the faultless character which critics censure as above nature: Yet it ought to be observed too, that he performs no one action which it is not in the power of any man in his situation to perform; and that he checks and restrains himself in no one instance in which it is not the duty of a prudent and good man *to* restrain himself....

It has been said in behalf of many modern fictitious pieces, in which authors have given success (and *happiness*, as it is called) to their heroes of vicious, if not of profligate, characters, that they have exhibited Human Nature as it *is*. Its corruption may, indeed, be exhibited in the faulty character; but need pictures of this be held out in books? Is not vice crowned with success, triumphant, and rewarded, and perhaps set off with wit and spirit, a dangerous representation? And is it not made even *more* dangerous by the hasty reformation introduced, in contradiction to all probability, for the sake of patching up what is called a happy ending?

The God of Nature intended not Human Nature for a vile and contemptible thing: And many are the instances, in every age, of those whom He enables, amidst all the frailties of mortality, to do it honour. Still the *best* performances of human creatures will be imperfect; but such as they are, it is surely both delightful and instructive to dwell sometimes on this bright side of things; To shew, by a series of facts in common life, what a degree of excellence may be attained and preserved amidst all the infection of fashionable vice and folly.

Select Bibliography

Sources on Kimber and His Works

Rev. of *Mr. Anderson*. *Monthly Review* (London) 10 (Feb. 1754): 147.

Black, Frank Gees. "Edward Kimber: Anonymous Novelist of the Mid-Eighteenth Century." *Harvard Studies and Notes in Philology and Literature* 17 (1935): 27–42.

Boulukos, George. *The Grateful Slave: The Emergence of Race in Eighteenth-Century British and American Culture*. Cambridge: Cambridge UP, 2008.

Ebersole, Gary L. *Captured by Texts: Puritan to Postmodern Images of Indian Captivity*. Charlottesville and London: UP of Virginia, 1995.

Hayes, Kevin J., ed. Introduction. *Itinerant Observations in America*. By Edward Kimber. Newark: U of Delaware P, 1998.

Herrle, Jeffrey. "Edward Kimber." *Oxford Dictionary of National Biography*. Vol. 31. Oxford: Oxford UP, 2004. 585–86.

Homestead, Melissa J. "The Beginnings of the American Novel." *The Oxford Handbook of Early American Literature*. Ed. Kevin J. Hayes. Oxford: Oxford UP, 2008. 527–46.

Kimber, Edward. "Memoirs of the Life and Writings of the Reverend Mr. Isaac Kimber." *Sermons on the Most Interesting Religious, Moral, and Practical Subjects. By the Late Reverend and Learned Mr. Isaac Kimber*. London: C. and J. Ackers, 1756.

Kimber, Sidney A. "The 'Relation of a Late Expedition to St. Augustine,' With Biographical and Bibliographical Notes on Isaac and Edward Kimber." *Papers of the Bibliographical Society of America* 28 (1934): 81–96.

Mercer, M.J., and Alexander Gordon. "Isaac Kimber." *Oxford Dictionary of National Biography*. Vol. 31. Oxford: Oxford UP, 2004. 585.

Milne, W. Gordon. "A Glimpse of Colonial America as Seen in an English Novel of 1754." *Maryland Historical Magazine* 42 (1947): 239–52.

Snader, Joe. *Caught Between Worlds: British Captivity Narratives in Fact and Fiction*. Lexington: UP of Kentucky, 2000.

Tepaske, John Jay, ed. *A Relation, or Journal, Of a Late Expedition to the Gates of St. Augustine, on Florida: Conducted by the Hon. General James Oglethorpe, with a Detachment of his Regiment, &c. from Georgia*. Gainesville: U of Florida P, 1976.

General Primary and Secondary Sources

The Adventures of a Kidnapped Orphan. London, 1747.

Amussen, Susan Dwyer. *Caribbean Exchanges: Slavery and the Trans-*

formation of English Society, 1640–1700. Chapel Hill: U of North Carolina P, 2007.

Anderson, Fred. *Crucible of War: The Seven Years' War and the Fate of Empire in British North America, 1754–1766.* New York: Vintage, 2000.

Bailyn, Bernard. *Voyagers to the West: A Passage in the Peopling of America on the Eve of the Revolution.* New York: Alfred A. Knopf, 1986.

Baldick, Robert. *The Duel: A History of Duelling.* New York: Clarkson N. Potter, 1965.

Basker, James G., ed. *Amazing Grace: An Anthology of Poems About Slavery, 1660–1810.* New Haven and London: Yale UP, 2002.

Beasley, Jerry C. *Novels of the 1740s.* Athens: U of Georgia P, 1982.

Behn, Aphra. *Oroonoko, The Rover and Other Works.* Ed. Janet Todd. New York: Penguin, 1992.

Berlin, Ira. *Many Thousands Gone: The First Two Centuries of Slavery in North America.* Cambridge, MA: The Belknap Press of Harvard UP, 1998.

Blackburn, Robin. *The Making of New World Slavery: From the Baroque to the Modern, 1492–1800.* London and New York: Verso, 1997.

Block, Sharon. *Rape and Sexual Power in Early America.* Chapel Hill: U of North Carolina P for the Omohundro Institute of Early American History and Culture, 2006.

Breen, T.H. *Tobacco Culture: The Mentality of the Great Tidewater Planters on the Eve of Revolution.* 2nd ed. 1975; Princeton and Oxford: Princeton UP, 2001.

Brown, Christopher Leslie. *Moral Capital: Foundations of British Abolitionism.* Chapel Hill: U of North Carolina P for the Omohundro Institute of Early American History and Culture, 2006.

Brown, Raymond. *The English Baptists of the Eighteenth Century.* London: Baptist Historical Society, 1986.

Carroll, Paul. *Baroque Woodwind Instruments: A Guide to their History, Repertoire and Basic Technique.* Aldershot, UK: Ashgate, 1999.

"A Catalogue of Books: In the Library of 'Councillor' Robert Carter, at Nomini Hall, Westmoreland County, Virginia." *William and Mary College Quarterly Historical Magazine* 11 (July 1902): 21–28.

Colley, Linda. *Britons: Forging the Nation 1707–1837.* New Haven: Yale UP, 1992.

Conway, Stephen. "From Fellow-Nationals to Foreigners: British Perceptions of the Americans, circa 1739-1783." *William and Mary Quarterly*, 3rd Ser., 59.1 (Jan. 2002): 65–100.

Davie, Donald. *Essays in Dissent: Church, Chapel, and the Unitarian Conspiracy.* Manchester, UK: Carcanet, 1995.

Davis, David Brion. *The Problem of Slavery in Western Culture.* Ithaca, NY: Cornell UP, 1966.

——. *The Problem of Slavery in the Age of Revolution, 1770–1823.* Ithaca, NY: Cornell UP, 1974.

Davis, Robert C. *Christian Slaves, Muslim Masters: White Slavery in the Mediterranean, Barbary Coast and Italy, 1500–1800.* New York: Palgrave Macmillan, 2003.

Defoe, Daniel. *The History and Remarkable Life of the Truly Honourable Colonel Jack.* 1722; London: The Folio Society, 1967.

——. *Moll Flanders.* London: W. Chetwood and T. Edlin, 1722.

Ellis, Markman. *The Politics of Sensibility: Race, Gender and Commerce in the Sentimental Novel.* Cambridge: Cambridge UP, 1996.

Ellison, Julie. "There and Back: Transatlantic Novels and Anglo-American Careers." *The Past as Prologue: Essays to Celebrate the Twenty-fifth Anniversary of ASECS.* Ed. Carla H. Hay and Syndy M. Conger. New York: AMS, 1995. 303–24.

Ferguson, Moira. *Subject to Others: British Women Writers and Colonial Slavery, 1670–1834.* New York: Routledge, 1992.

Genovese, Eugene D. *From Rebellion to Revolution: Afro-American Slave Revolts in the Making of the New World.* New York: Vintage, 1981.

Gillingham, Harrold E. *French Orders and Decorations.* New York: American Numismatic Society, 1922.

Hammond, Brean, and Shaun Regan. *Making the Novel: Fiction and Society in Britain, 1660–1789.* New York: Palgrave, 2006.

Jones, Howard Mumford. *O Strange New World; American Culture: The Formative Years.* New York: Viking, 1964.

Joyce, William L., *et al.,* eds. *Printing and Society in Early America.* Worcester, MA: American Antiquarian Society, 1983.

Main, Jackson T. "The One Hundred." *William and Mary Quarterly* 3rd ser., vol. 11, no. 3 (July 1954): 354–84.

Matar, Nabil. *Britain and Barbary, 1589–1689.* Gainesville: UP of Florida, 2005.

McCusker, John J. *Money and Exchange in Europe and America, 1600–1775.* Chapel Hill: U of North Carolina P, 1978.

McGann, Jerome. *The Poetics of Sensibility: A Revolution in Literary Style.* Oxford: Clarendon, 1996.

Moraley, William. *The Infortunate: The Voyage and Adventures of William Moraley, an Indentured Servant.* Ed. Susan E. Klepp and Billy G. Smith. 1743; University Park: Penn State UP, 1992.

Moretti, Franco. *Atlas of the European Novel, 1800–1900.* London and New York: Verso, 1998.

Morgan, Kenneth. *Bristol and the Atlantic Trade in the Eighteenth Century.* Cambridge and New York: Cambridge UP, 1993.

Parent, Anthony S., Jr. *Foul Means: The Formation of a Slave Society in Virginia, 1660–1740.* Chapel Hill and London: U of North Carolina P for the Omohundro Institute of Early American History and Culture, 2003.

Price, Richard, ed. *Maroon Societies: Rebel Slave Communities in the Americas*. Baltimore and London: The Johns Hopkins UP, 1979.

Pritchard, James. *In Search of Empire: The French in the Americas, 1670–1730*. Cambridge: Cambridge UP, 2004.

Pulsipher, Jenny Hale. "*The Widow Ranter* and Royalist Culture in Colonial Virginia." *Early American Literature* 39 (2004): 41–66.

Richetti, John. *The English Novel in History, 1700–1780*. London: Routledge, 1999.

Richetti, John, ed. *The Cambridge Companion to the Eighteenth-Century Novel*. Cambridge: Cambridge UP, 1996.

——. *The Cambridge History of English Literature, 1660–1780*. Cambridge: Cambridge UP, 2005.

Rozbicki, Michal J. *The Complete Colonial Gentleman: Cultural Legitimacy in Plantation America*. Charlottesville and London: UP of Virginia, 1998.

Shreve, Forrest, *et al*. *The Plant Life of Maryland*. Baltimore: The Johns Hopkins P, 1910.

Smith, Abbot Emerson. *Colonists in Bondage: White Servitude and Convict Labor in America, 1607–1776*. New York: W.W. Norton, 1947.

Stevens, Laura M. *The Poor Indians: British Missionaries, Native Americans, and Colonial Sensibility*. Philadelphia: U of Pennsylvania P, 2004.

Sullivan, Alvin. "*The London Magazine*." *British Literary Magazines*. Vol. 1: The Augustan Age and the Age of Johnson, 1698–1788. Ed. Alvin Sullivan. Westport, CT: Greenwood, 1983.

Swaminathan, Srividhya. "Developing the West Indian Proslavery Position after the Somerset Decision." *Slavery and Abolition* 24 (Dec. 2003): 40–60.

Taylor, Richard C. "James Harrison, *The Novelist's Magazine*, and the Early Canonizing of the English Novel." *Studies in English Literature* 33 (1993): 629–43.

Todd, Janet. *Sensibility: An Introduction*. London: Methuen, 1986.

Underwood, A.C. *A History of the English Baptists*. London: Kingsgate Press, 1947.

The Vain Prodigal Life and Tragical Penitential Death of Thomas Hellier. London: Sam Crouch, 1680.

Wahrman, Dror. "The English Problem of Identity in the American Revolution." *American Historical Review* 106 (Oct. 2001): 1236-62.

Warner, William B. *Licensing Entertainment: The Elevation of Novel Reading in Britain, 1684–1750*. Berkeley: U of California P, 1998.

Williams, Ioan, ed. *Novel and Romance 1700–1800: A Documentary Record*. New York: Barnes and Noble, 1970.